The Banff Springs Hotel. Silver City. Mugs & Jugs. Theater Faux. UWO. Nat Bailey's Expo86. SFU. The Armouries. Albert Street Diner. IUB. The Church. Bentleys. Strange Angels. Earls. Call the Office. Mel's.

This book is dedicated to the many people with whom I experienced the very best of times in the very best of places - in and out of the kitchen. You know who you are. We slept extraordinarily little, but it was worth it. They were times like no other.

My thanks to Chef Alex Begbie at Say Cheese and Stratford Chef School under whom I first apprenticed – and Chef Joan 'Lady Bechamel' Brennan at Strange Angels, whose Conceptual Ravioli inspired me to cook - regardless of the consequences.

Prologue

Nice, France, December 5

Nice, the fifth day of December, and it's 25 degrees beneath the palm trees lining the clogged Promenade des Anglais. The artery threads its way through the city, past the tourists, the busy market square, and the coffee bar littered beach. We run up the embankment to the street and weave through the snarled traffic back to the hotel hand in hand. We reach her room on the 5th floor of the Meridien Hotel and fall onto the still unmade bed now warm from the sun shining through the open French windows. There is a thudding desire welling up within me. Am I being too reticent?

We almost drag each other back from the beach, through the snarled traffic to our hotel room and, the engorgement in my loins threatening to burst, we tumble onto the still unmade bed, I pull her to me and ... "I want you ..."

She grabs my arm, then my hair, pulling me up to her face, raising a strict finger in front of my nose. "You're going to miss your flight …" Her laugh is throaty, full of irony and expectation. "... so, hold onto that thought. We'll see each other next week. Now call a taxi …"

My plane is ninety minutes late. 'Unforeseen technical difficulties', 'apologies for any inconvenience' and 'would passengers Choi, Brady and Parvez please make their way to the departure gate' echo through the departure lounge in English, French, Russian, and Penguinese …

'Technical difficulties'. What exactly does that mean? A loose wing hurriedly riveted back into place? A baggage handler strike? Co-pilot stuck in traffic? We are not given any details.

"Hydraulic fluid cable." Wearing a rumpled suit and a day-old growth of black stubble, the guy sitting next to me eats duty free crostini from the box and accompanies his verdict with a spray of crumbs. "It'll be the hydraulic fluid cable." He offers me the box. I decline with a weak smile and a wave of my hand. He shakes the box, peers inside, grunts, stands up and wanders over to the crowded espresso bar.

Sixty minutes later, difficulties resolved, we are herded onto the plane. It takes off incredibly badly. After the shuffling and the curses, the tense smiles of the crew and the admonitions to please store all luggage beneath the seat or in the overhead compartment, the plane takes to the air with a sudden, sickening, lurch. Like a kite, it rises a thousand meters then banks sharply back towards the stained tarmac of Aéroport Nice's runway. Then all hell breaks loose. I nod knowingly to myself thinking, 'hydraulic fluid cable' – then I panic.

Oxygen masks release from above our heads and many of the passengers cross themselves. The woman seated next to me begins wailing hysterically, making the emergency announcement difficult to understand - though, if we're going to crash, I doubt whether my seat being returned to an upright position or not will really matter. A man tries to open the emergency door across the aisle but is fought off by the couple sitting next to it.

I think about the roughness of her tongue, the spread of her hips beneath my hands, the warm dustiness of her hair, her fingers on my cheeks smelling like caramel but her lips tasting of the garlic mayonnaise toasts she had just eaten at the kiosk beside the parking lot. Our last kiss. The plane shudders and levels out. A flight attendant runs down the aisle in her stockinged feet and we are told to do something indiscernible in a calm yet garbled voice which rattles out from the intercom. I desperately want to tell her how much I love her.

And I just had.

Four months earlier … the University Club, August 17

Dennis is sweating profusely. All the trees around the outdoor pool were removed long ago, leaving little opportunity for shade, but saving the need for skimming leaves from the water. He pulls irritably at his XXL t-shirt – the largest the sports department had but sadly one size too small for his girth. When Dennis was much younger, he worked as varsity swim coach, and it is for reasons of seniority that the university still employs him. Dennis now manages the main pool facility, and most often takes the morning shift.

He walks over to the shower stalls, glistening wet in the hot August sunshine, and tests the taps by turning them on and off. The pool is empty and still. The regular *chutchutchut* from the playing field sprinkler system can be heard in the distance. Dennis walks to the end of the pool, glancing over the pristine surface as he goes, and leans back against the railing which makes up the foot of the diving platforms. He watches the first arrival come out the doors and through the disinfectant foot bath before walking along the rubber topped concrete to the edge of the pool.

Dr. Beatrice Wells, lecturer in Microbiology, enjoys the ten minutes of emptiness the pool offers. When she is not swimming, Beatrice lectures in General Microbiology, Virology, and Immunology to the Freshman classes - the great unwashed of the university hierarchy. She is always the first one in the pool mornings, and relishes having the pool to herself if only for a moment. Beatrice is a large woman, not fat, though there is noticeable thickening about her stomach and hips as she bends down to test the water with her fingers. She is big boned, large breasted and has broad hips. She looks about the pool critically as she splashes her fingers in the water.

Dennis unconsciously sucks in his stomach as her gaze passes over him. Beatrice appears to be judging the bacterial content of the water. Dennis is strongly aware of both her beauty and, being a young Professor, her intelligence. Beatrice has high cheek bones, pale blue eyes, a dazzling smile. At 27, she is the university's youngest tenured Professor. Having a PhD in Microbiology and an almost certain knowledge of things he does not understand, makes Dennis even more uneasy.

He feels uneasy about anything he does not understand. He does not wish to have the presence of harmful microbes discovered in the pool on his watch - even though the pool is immaculately cared for using the prescribed doses of regulated chemicals. Worse, he would not want Beatrice to attribute an unclean pool to himself, personally – to be marked as inefficient and possibly incompetent - by her. Dennis feels threatened by Beatrice's youth and beauty but mostly by the fact that she has absolutely no interest in him. Dennis feels threatened by most women for this reason.

Beatrice stands up again, purposefully kicks off the blue flip flops from her large feet, and stretches her arms up over her head, standing on tiptoes. This act is observed by Dennis, who clenches in his stomach even tighter as though he were preparing himself to be punched. He feels rather more than 'a bat's squeak of sensuality' as he watches her stretching. He has read this phrase in a book and likes the sound of it.

He observes Beatrice in appreciative and fine detail knowing that the view of her underarms, the calloused heels of her feet, the unslung heaviness of her breasts beneath the thin material of her swimsuit, the faintly visible stretch marks on the backs of her broad thighs and the area of slightly paler skin at the edge of her swimsuit between her legs attesting to a recent bikini waxing are very private and very personal. They are hidden during the day beneath her clothing and revealed to others on only rare occasions.

Dennis is not alone in his frightened admiration of Beatrice – as much as he would deny it; she is not without admirers of both sexes. She dives in, breaking the glassy blue-white surface of the pool without a splash, and swims the length of the pool beneath the surface. Dennis does not wait for Beatrice to resurface - his attention has been diverted by the unexpected appearance of three frat boys, horse playing in the foot pool by the doors. Their legs are red and mottled from last night's annual Greek Council leg waxing charity event. Dennis raises himself from his position against the railing, blows his whistle once, and points a large, cigarette stained finger at them.

My attention is diverted from the view afforded by the University Club's floor to ceiling second floor windows which overlook the pool and the university gardens - by the urgent smell of burnt sugar. I quickly pull the pan from the flame and begin to separate the apple crepe from the pan with a spatula - over-caramelised sugar sticking to the bottom. “Fuck.”

“I like mine well done. I’ll take that crepe if you don’t mind Jess?”
I look up and raise an eyebrow. “Hi Wendy – are you sure?” I lift the crepe out of the sticky goo and place it in the middle of the plate she holds in her rough, unmanicured fingers.

Wendy Pirk is Vice President for Executive Education. I am very fond of Wendy and we sometimes have coffee together. Of all the Vice Presidents she runs the smallest group of departments. From my observations over the last months of catered meetings, I find her one of the very few of the university Vice Presidents I would not sack.

“Yes, thank you.” I gesture towards the bowls of cinnamon sugar and butter, but she shakes her head. “No, this is perfect. See you later.” She turns and returns to her seat. The club’s single conference table runs the length of the club’s second floor dining room and can comfortably seat the university’s twenty-four Vice Presidents.

“… it would be nice to have a calendar on the website.” “We have a calendar.” “I can’t find it. Does anyone else have trouble finding it?” “It’s on every page. It appears over 3000 times on our website.” “It should be a calendar where I can find just those events I want. I can filter the events.” “You can do that already.” The monthly Vice President’s brunch is not going well for Wallace Brice, Vice President for Sales

& Marketing. This is not his fault, nor is there anything he could do to counter the animosity that rages against him from the other vice Presidents. The interoffice wars raged long before his arrival at the university. It is his inheritance. No one likes the communications departments, and no one would be able to tell you why. The world is full of myriad innate prejudices. Wallace's best strategy to overcome the assault on his departments is to team up with Wendy who is herself often under fire from the other, larger departments. For some reason he does not realise this and treats her with the same defensive gestures he uses to fend off the others.

Wallace gets up, walks over to the screen on the wall where an oversized version of the university website is beamed, and points to the calendar icon on the right-hand side which is obvious even at the distance I stand from it. Some lean forward in their chairs and remove their glasses to view the screen, to add credence to the complaint. "I never saw that before."

Wallace looks back at the group askance. "Top right-hand column, 30% of the page in width, responsive, automatically rotating with new dates, linking to the main calendar, visible on every page, events sortable for any institution by day, week, or month --- sort of hard to miss."

University President, Prof. em. Dr. Dr-Ing. E.h. Dr. h.c. mult. Samuel van Middelberg, grunts, unfolds his hands on which he has been resting his chin, gets up out of his chair and walks slowly but purposely to the screen. He points to the calendar and turns to face the

group. “This is exactly the sort of calendar I’d like to have.”
“Well … that’s good. We have it …” Wallace smiles weakly and walks over to the buffet, looking over his shoulder once as he goes, as if he were afraid, he’d perhaps imagined the calendar on the website. He has a pained expression on his face and is trembling slightly as he takes a plate. In contrast to Wendy, his hands are long and smooth and appear to have been recently manicured. His tailored Hugo Boss suit is in stark contrast to Wendy’s rumpled blue off the rack pant suit.

“Good Morning. I’d like a crepe please.” I smile at him and place an extra portion of apple on the crepe, fold it gently over and place a spoonful of caramel butter on top. Any time I encounter Wallace, I find him friendly and pleasant. I think many see his polite friendliness as a sign of weakness and perhaps insecurity which exacerbates their aggression.
“There you are. Enjoy.”
“Thank you.” He smiles, again painfully, and takes his seat. He then returns to collect a fork and a knife, smiling at me again. However, Wallace is unable to begin eating his crepe. In his short absence his adversaries have regrouped and are again on the offensive. The defeated silence in his short absence from the table has been replaced by a new battle cry.

“In the directory listings, it would be good to have the ability to change my phone number when I’m not here – like on holidays. I could click and another number would appear.” Eager nods all around. “yes yes yes …” Wallace looks around in confusion, like a man who finds himself suddenly drowning, and holding his knife and fork raised in one hand like a call for help. "What? So, you mean instead of transferring your telephone, or activating the answering service you'd want to edit your directory entry on the website!?"

"Colleagues …", a new voice enters the fray - cultured, smooth, and dangerous. "I think it would be productive to use this as a starting point for further discussions at a later date on how the website can be improved." Wallace noticeably grips his cutlery even tighter and bites his bottom lip. "*Im-proved?* It was just re-launched three months ago. We spent two years in discussion with the web committee and have invested a quarter of a million dollars in the project. You want to make changes *now*?" His disbelief is accompanied by speckles of saliva as he gesticulates with his cutlery in a wide arc to his right.

Sitting to his right and slightly behind him, Mary Leeson, Wallace's sultry personal assistant moves with experienced subtlety out of the path of the silverware. She straightens her skirt and purses her lips, brushing her long black hair from her cheek and wishing she were already aboard the chartered flight to South Africa which she booked with her mother, last month. She looks at her watch and calculates how many more minutes until lunch and the first of three cigarettes she allows herself each day.

Across the table from her, Dr. Fiorella Accardo's condescending smile surveys the table. She clicks her long, painted fingernails together like a hungry insect and looks around the table for support – which is immediately signaled by a respectful silence and bowed heads. Of the Vice Presidents, Fiorella is the most feared and disliked, though this never coalesces itself into any public attack on her department or her policies.

When the Provost died of a heart attack in his hotel room while attending a conference in Brussels last year, Fiorella, then his assistant, was first on the scene in his hotel room. There were many rumours. While the machinations of university politics run at lightning speed, the actual workings of its departments run disproportionately slower. It has been four years since Fiorella was left to temporarily take over the Provost's office while the university went through the motions of seeking a replacement. She rises from her seat and passes her assistant a thick stack of papers she has been signing during the meeting. "Wallace, no one is questioning the project *per se*. In everything there is always room for improvement."

As Wallace turns to speak with Mary, who begins scribbling furiously in the hardcover notebook which rarely leaves her side, Fiorella pushes her chair back from the table and walks up to the buffet. She brushes down an imaginary crease in her grey silk Prada skirt - all eyes in the room track her long legs as she moves. She smiles at me with an emotionless and well-practiced curve of her mouth. Her cheeks dimple. "I'd like a crepe with no apple please."

Fiorella is always impeccably dressed, but I believe she wears too much lipstick. Her long red hair, often worn loose, is today pulled into a tight bun displaying her ears which appear too small for her head. She turns to look back at the group. Her face, while mostly beautiful when viewed directly, is not flattered when seen in profile. Today she is wearing two exceptionally large and heavy rings on her long fingers which are probably extremely dangerous at close quarters.

She stands with her arms crossed, watching the crepe pan in my hand. "Is it ready now? It seems ready." I look at her and plate the crepe, restraining the desire to smack the hot pan onto the back of her outstretched hand. "Thank you." She takes some cutlery and returns to her seat.

It's not yet ten in the morning and despite the air conditioning the air feels thick and wet. It's going to be a scorcher. One of the advantages of working in a kitchen is that it's always hot, so there is little differential summer or winter. I turn off the burner and walk into the open kitchen, looking back to see if anyone else is going to now want a crepe. They all appear very absorbed in their renewed attack on Wallace. He has pushed his uneaten breakfast sadly to the side and is gesturing to an enlargement of the university magazine which has replaced the website on the screen. Poor Wallace.

I open the glass fronted refrigerator, take out a can of Starbucks iced cappuccino and empty it in a few gulps. I place the empty can on the counter just as Peyton comes in from the dining room where she has been discretely serving coffee and removing soiled plates. Peyton is a graduate student who also works as the club's head waitress. She is both efficient and popular with the members. She is not my favourite amongst the club's staff, but the I don't appreciate having two groups of staff to deal with anyway. Like Dennis, I probably also feel threatened by Peyton's intelligence, youth, and beauty.

Peyton is tall and blonde, well-tanned and with the slightly upturned nose, blue eyes and shapely curves which, despite her PhD research in cognitive systems, might lead one to the assumption that when not waitressing, she was either a model, or a fitness instructor. As there is always some truth at the core of most stereotypes, Peyton does drive a 4x4, have a boyfriend named Randy who plays for the university football team and does own a pedigree chocolate brown Labrador called Tobler. I haven't checked, but I wouldn't be surprised to find she had a profitable influencer Instagram account.

"Do they need anything else?"
"I don't think so. I've refilled the coffee thermoses and put out the muffins and fruit."
"Okay. I'm going to be in the office for a few minutes. Could you clean up when the meeting is over? I need to get back to the restaurant."
"Of course, Jessie. No problem."
"Thanks." I go into the small office wishing Peyton had refused to clean up, but she is always very friendly and considerate. I find this makes me dislike her even more than her perfect legs, her tan, her 4x4, Randy, her dog, or her probably fictitious side career as a fashion and lifestyle influencer. I sit in front of my laptop where I spend fifteen minutes updating the many posts,

tweets, likes, and pushes that make up the online face of my business.

I go over the calendar which displays each day of the month on both the left and the right – one for club events and one for the restaurant. There is nothing happening today I need worry about. I notice that it's Professor Grell's birthday. I send off a short email to his account from the club staff, and then am diverted by the sudden need to empty and rearrange all the little compartments in the desk drawer which hold staples, rubber bands, stamps and odd coins.

I go back into the kitchen and toast a bagel. I offer Peyton one which she declines in favour of a blueberry yoghurt. I eat three dried apricots while waiting for the bagel and ask Peyton politely about her dog. "The heat's got him down."

I nod sagely while spreading the toasted bagel thick with goat cheese. Then, chewing the bagel, I go outside via the malfunctioning emergency door which opens onto the swimming pool's lawn without emitting an alarm. I lean against the wall and watch the growing crowd of students splashing about in the cool water. I feel pensive.

The University Club is in a wing of the university's oldest building, the McClarksen Campus Center - so named for the generous contribution about a hundred years ago by one of the university's first Alumni of the then princely sum of $125 000. Originally McClarksen Hall, it was renamed in the 1970's, like many university buildings across the nation, to fit the vibrant, new, business-oriented face of the modern university.

Shortly after the arrival on campus of the first consultants in the 90's, the university was advised to outsource its peripherals. The catering contract was the first to go, quickly followed by the grounds, security, maintenance, housing, library, and finally even IT. Why, university administration was advised, should they carry the burden of cumbersome pay rolled staff and equipment maintenance when it was much cheaper to outsource that to someone else. Let another company pay the overhead on lawnmowers, banquet tables, server maintenance, bedding, and employee contributions.

The University Club, in its heyday, was the haunt of faculty, visiting lecturers, guest lecturers, and the odd privileged research fellow. Staff were infrequent visitors and nervous crowds of gauche freshmen still have the club passed off during their o-week tours as "the place where profs lounge about on leather sofas and to which we're barred access". I attended an exhibition of chocolate sculptures here once with Alex last year. Some British artist. Warren Laine … something … pretty disturbing pieces I recall.

While the leather sofas were extremely comfortable, at that time, even though they had a kitchen, the gastronomic offerings were limited and uninspired. We took over the catering last August, and of course things have significantly improved since then.[1] The club is neither as fancy as the Oxford Cambridge nor is it as old as Harvard's, but it has heart.

"… I happen to be one of those people who still believe that a university is more than a place to get a degree so you can get a job. When I went to university we were involved – skipping classes to protest the latest outrage - marching, signing petitions – venting our youthful ideals - that sort of thing -. There were no subsidies – I had to work to pay my tuition and once missed a year when I didn't have enough saved. I also worked on the student newspaper for a few dollars a week as the production coordinator, putting out a paper long before we had the internet, laptops, CDs, bank machines, mobile phones, email, or even chat rooms. We used to go to the library and wait tedious evenings for the return of books, drop into the student union to shoot pool, drink pitchers of beer standing about on soggy carpets, and chat up the co-eds behind the bar. We'd even smoke in public places! Ooh very dangerous it was!"

The sound of Dr. Donald Bleary's voice draws me back into the club. "University was a rite of passage – a lifestyle. Now, I very much fear, it has become yet another commodity – students have outsourced their social life to TikTok and WhatsApp, while faculty opt for e-lectures and digital libraries in an ever more 'create your own' world. Your average student these days doesn't have the social skills necessary to formulate a complete sentence when passing you in the main quad. Not to speak of their horrendous writing skills …"

Another voice answers, "Progress waits for no man, Donald."

"Or woman, for that matter."

I come in through the door as both men chuckle.

"… Hello Jessie! … It's the dictatorship of the proletariat in the guise of the new technology. I won't accept it." Bleary is in animated conversation with the recently retired VP of Student Affairs, Dr. John Zontag.

"Yes … yes, I entirely agree with you, Donald. I recall my own student days with fondness. And it was only in my eldest's final year that we replaced his typewriter with a PC. Between you and me I find it ludicrous that you have to stand outside the student bar if you want to smoke now."

"Dr. Bleary," I shake his outstretched hand and then extend my hand to the other man, "Dr. Zontag, I don't think we've met."

Bleary turns to him, "John, this is Jessie Watkins." The latter nods to me and shakes my hand. "- given the club a second life. We even get in the local papers now thanks to Jessie's food." I smile and nod. "Jessie, how are the *vvvvips* doing? I wanted to have coffee with Dr. Zontag before lunch - and I wanted to talk with you about the Alumni dinner." He accentuates the abbreviated *VIPs* as if he were making the noise of a motorboat and smiles at the pleasure it gives him.

"You can sit in the back near the window without disturbing them. Peyton's here but I was about to drive back to the restaurant for lunch." Peyton steps into the hall on cue and both men stand noticeably straighter. Inwardly I roll my eyes and then attempt to regain Bleary's attention.
"Dr. Bleary? It's Professor Grell's birthday today."

“Oh, yes, thank you Jessie. Are we doing anything for him?”
“There’s nothing in the book. I sent him an email from the club staff.”
“Hmm. Okay, thank you. I hope the Secretary sent him a card. Wait a minute.” Bleary puts his hand to his face. “Oh no. He’s dead.”
“Excuse me?”
“I remember now. He died. Last week.” There is a pause.
I look at him in amazement. “The club Secretary is dead?!”
“No, no, Dr. Grell.”
“Oh.” I look at the floor and then up at him again. “We should update the membership database.”
“Yes, yes, I’ll get Robert to take care of it. How embarrassing.”

Bleary is, since his retirement last year and in an honorary capacity, the university Alumni liaison and, more importantly, President of the University Club. Even with rising unemployment in many universities you can often still get a job after retirement. As a Professor, Bleary is the embodiment of the stereotype. He is tall and gangly, and jerky in his movements. His grey hair covers the back of his head, rises to the crown, and then shoots off in all directions as if he were standing in front of a fan. His teeth are large and somewhat yellow, and his face always appears red with exertion. Bleary dresses each day in a cord jacket, faded jeans, brogues, a shirt, and thick sweater vest with a knit tie.

Zontag in contrast is rather stout and moves with a measured consideration to his movements. He wears a beard – and a small diamond stud earring - his suit is well cut; he is well groomed, and he seems very conscious of his appearance.

"Dr. Bleary, I have the catering proposal in the office. Can you look it over and we'll talk after lunch?"
"Of course, Jessie. We'll talk later." Both men seem interested only in Peyton.
"Peyton, don't we still have some fresh muffins - for the gentlemen?" Peyton smiles and turns, and the men follow her into the club.

Marlies, Jessie's restaurant, later that morning

I nurse a Starbucks tall blonde sitting in the tail end of traffic on the way back into the city. While Starbuck's have a great concept, I do prefer the coffee at Dunkin Donuts, but that's over on the other side of town. In addition to being the worst consumer whore, I do like participating in the fascination of tribal brand identification. However, let's face it, if you're crap at basketball, then a Nike logo on your shirt isn't going to help - but we still buy Nike gear.

I live in the south of the city, the university is in the north and Marlies, our restaurant, is downtown - right in the middle. I have a case of 1986 Los Vascos Cabernet Sauvignon in the back of my car which I need to drop off at Marlies – wine I not only found *but* an entire case of it if you can believe that.

Like most small cities, ours has a respectable chic big city wannabe attitude, so small, boutique restaurants like ours do well. There's the university, the regional wine festival every September and the food festival every July – all well attended, supported and attracting exactly the prima donnas you would expect of such an unholy trinity. The city has everything I need, and there's an even bigger city with even more chic an hour to the north. Their wine festival isn't half as good as ours and to be honest neither is their university and I'd rather be a big fish in a small pond than shark bait in an ocean any time.

The city is positively littered with traffic lights and I manage to catch every red one of them before I finally make it to the restaurant.[2] I drive past and turn in behind to park in the back alley. My ageing TR6 long past due for inspection, audibly shudders and farts to a standstill. I get out and carry the case of wine from the trunk to the back door - almost having to wrench it from its rusted hinges. I open the mailbox and catch sight of the latest issue of Chocolatier lying invitingly at the bottom. I love this magazine but in general find food magazines these days to be extremely pretentious.

At a time when we should be getting back to basics some people are still doing these ridiculous Bunraku conceived chocolate pieces with their hidden wires held out of the shot by glue-spraying assistants so that the work glistens as it towers over the plate defying all laws of gravity – and making it impossible to reproduce as millions of amateur chefs have discovered to their dismay. I stand there rifling through the magazine wishing I could play with chocolate instead of facing the menagerie waiting for me at lunch. I open the centerfold. Mmm … white chocolate lavender truffles sitting on a bed of dry ice. Food porn: you just cannot beat it.

"Hey!" The kitchen, in full swing with lunch prep, is loud and busy. Barb looks up and smiles as I enter. She appears almost circular in her whites. Barb is both quite round and quite short. She has shoulder length blond hair which she wears pulled back to reveal her round face. Her cheeks are most often bright red. She has pale green eyes. Barb reminds me a lot of Mrs. Santa. She's a great partner – her optimism counters my cynicism.

"Hey you. How's the club? Bring us back a glass of white wine when you come - and I could also use a scotch. Did we get our delivery today?" Barb breaks chocolate from a 2-kilo block and tosses it into a metal bowl as she fires questions at me.

"Delivery's in the back. Club was fine. Dr. Grell passed away and I saw Dr. Bleary." I stop and think about when the last time a delivery got here on time. "I thought we were doing the chocolate cakes without scotch this time?"
Barb halts her attack on the chocolate and looks at me over the rims of her glasses. "He didn't die in the club, did he?"
"No, thank God. Look, I left Bleary our proposal for the Alumni dinner – he's going to call us after lunch."

I walk through into the dining room and put the case of wine behind the bar. I take down the bottle of Oban, open the wine cooler and select a bottle of Spanish Chardonnay – Castano Maccabeo 2007 – and pour two glasses. I call across to Judith. "Morgen!" She turns and smiles, "Hi Jess", making final adjustments to the table settings. Judith is tall and long and appears to flow rather than walk when she moves. Barb and I met her in Berlin our last year of culinary school. Last year she turned up on our doorstep, out of the blue, and she's been running the front of house for us ever since.

Judith is the most interesting person you could ever want to meet. I don´t mean those women that merely appear out of place with their fourteenth century names, porcelain like skin and books on white witchcraft. I mean a woman whose very existence defies causality violation, the uncertainty principle and what you can't understand unless you majored in business physics or four vector algebra. She is … *enigmatic.*

“Like a glass?” She gives me a nervous grin and unlocks the front door to the restaurant. “Nein. I don’t know - I’ve sort of gone off wine lately.”
How can you go off wine? “How can you go off wine?” I pour myself a glass and take a big mouthful of the cool, grassy, stuff. I make a lot of horrible noises in my mouth before swallowing.
Judith screws up her nose, “You need to ask?”
“What? This from my Front of House Manager? This from the best waitress on the continent? I am releasing the hidden nuances of the wine lain dormant in the bottle.”

I put the wine bottle back in the cooler, pick up the glasses and the bottle of Oban and move in the direction of the kitchen.
“Wine is the new snobbery, haven’t you heard?” Judith responds as she carries wine glasses to a table.
“I thought it was chocolate.” I counter. “Well, just don’t convert our customers – wine has a 300% profit margin.”

Back in the kitchen Barb isn’t to be seen, so I walk around to the office. She’s on the phone and signals to me with a wave of her hand to wait. “... I understand Dr. Bleary, but when I talk about cutting back, I mean fat, not bone marrow – we can reduce our offer by 5% but nothing close to what you’re asking. … I don’t know where you should find the money Professor, honestly … how about the English department's budget?" Barb smiles and sticks out her tongue at me - I majored in English Lit.

She hangs up and tosses me the catering offer. "We have a problem."
I put the bottle of scotch and her glass of wine on the desk. "Was that Bleary?" I told him to call after lunch. I guess he's already eaten …
"So, the Alumni homecoming dinner in October? Well it turns out, if you peruse the offer, that the total there was understood by him to be per table not per person. We would in effect be catering not for $34 a head as we had assumed but for $34 a table. And …" Barb quickly clicks on the calculator beside her and laughs "… assuming we have any costs at all, means we would oddly enough be paying the university for the pleasure of catering this extravaganza." She finishes with a smile.

I look at her. "Is he mad?!" I pick up the offer. "It even says 'per person' here … Do they think we're idiots?" Barb takes the glass of wine, drinks, and holds it up to the light. "Mmmm, nice – what does Judith think of the new wine?" She takes some licorice from the package on the table and tosses them in her mouth.

"Judith has 'gone off wine'."
"How can you go off wine?" Barb looks at me askance.
"How can you eat licorice with Chardonnay?" I raise my eyebrows and smirk, "GM shares still traded after they declared bankruptcy, Judith's going off wine – anything's possible ... so, what did Bleary say?"

"Well at $34 a head he almost went into hysterics. But after he had calmed down, he mentioned contributing to the good of the campus community."
"Balls! Community? My fingers are half their length from contributing to the campus community."
A crash comes from behind us in the kitchen followed shortly by a plaintive 'sorry'. I stick my head out the doorway.

Donnie, our new apprentice, is fumbling on the floor with a broken glass bowl of egg yolks. "Be careful – don't cut yourself … and use a metal bowl next time okay? … the glass ones are for catering".
He grins a nervous apology over his shoulder as he goes, "Okay Chef."

I watch him almost collide with Judith as she comes in from the dining room, and then look at the pool of eggs on the floor. Cleaning up eggs from a tile floor is a real pain. I don't have the feeling Donnie is going to make it as a chef. Something about the silly grin.
I turn back to Barb and the catering offer as she speaks through another mouthful of licorice, "We'll need to cut back on … ummum … something, but even then, we're not going to … umnum … come within their budget. The dinner would be great … numnum … advertising for us though."

I smile at her with great affection. "You should take up smoking again. For the amount we'd lose, we could take out a half page ad in Food & Wine for a year. We'd need a logging mill to cut back the amount he's asking. I'll call him after lunch."

Barb gets up taking the bottle of scotch from the desk as she leaves. "Then I will leave you to the lunch crowd while I explore the subtle intricacies of this lovely single malt and the Valrhona chocolate."

By the time lunch peaks we've got a four table wait and a sudden cloudburst which means the garden is out of service and people don't wait for lunch, so we lost two of those. Three tables of Japanese university delegates arrived after their campus tour tempted by our tempura sushi which, ever since we did it on a local television cooking show last year, we're famous for – even the baby asparagus is fresh - it's a really delicious item.

The freaky August weather meant the sun was shining again two minutes before their arrival and with a quick wipe of the tables we sat them in the garden. After lunch I'm chatting with the boys in the dish pit and getting the kitchen cleaned up when Kate calls. Kate Morris is the manager of Costers, and since our move onto campus, our nemesis. She's a bit of a bossy cow, and a hard ass, but also a pretty good chef. Overseeing 10 000 covers three meals a day has got to turn anyone into a dictator - if you run a successful kitchen then you're going to have to bring the whip out - and I've always been a sucker for big, smart, bossy women. She's been trying to convince me for months to come in with her on an abandoned truck stop a few kilometers down the highway. A slush fund courtesy of a waitress in the X position is extremely tempting.[3]

"Hello Jessie. Did I wake you?"

"Haha – we just did a packed house for lunch thanks - how are you Kate? Happy Birthday by the way!" I take some licorice from the open packet on the desk … you cow … "How are the teeming masses?"
She responds breezily, "Oh it's the usual feeding frenzy here. You remembered my birthday; how sweet, thank you. Look, the reason I'm calling - are you thinking of catering the Alumni dinner in October?"
How do they know about that already? I bet Bleary asked her for a quote as well. "Probably, hopefully, why?"
"I just thought, you know, it would be a lot easier if perhaps we did it."

I throw one of the darts sitting on the desk across the office to land in the dartboard on the opposite wall. Taped to the board is a photo of Jamie Oliver. "Thanks Kate, but I think we'll be fine. Why don't you make a counteroffer – the best chef wins?"
"I sent in my offer already – I hope it wasn't much lower than yours? – but now I'm wondering if I did the right thing telling you." She sighs audibly. "1000 guests, 5 courses, sit down dinner - I don't know how you imagine you'll be able to do so many covers from the club kitchen, Jessie. Makes even me think twice … hey, do you want to come over for coffee?"
Can you actually hear someone smiling in evil glee? "Sure Kate. About three, okay?" She murmurs something and hangs up.

Judith walks into the office munching a cheese scone. Crumbs fall from her mouth. She's followed by one of our service staff who's berating the fact that the MA on Shakespeare his girlfriend just completed wasn't a real

MA. Judith stops chewing and turns her face as I reach out to wipe a smear of lipstick from her cheek.

"I thought there was something there … what a mess I am."
"Ha. Lipstick face. Where are you off to?"
"To get flowers for dinner. I'm taking Sammy here with me." Sammy is from Georgia. He speaks with a thick accent that together with his swarthy good looks and permanent 5 o'clock shadow make him a real hit with our female guests. He adores Judith and works unpaid overtime on her shift.
"Sure. Can you see if they have any rosemary plants? Ours in the back seems to be dying suddenly. I hope we don't have cats jumping over the fence spraying everywhere again."

Barb comes into the office with two small cups of chocolate mousse. "Try this." She gives Judith and I each a spoon and a cup.
"Is there peanut butter in it?" I ask.
"There is *not*." Barb icily answers.
I smile and take a spoonful of the dessert. "You should try it. I love peanut butter." The dessert is amazing.
"Mmmm … oh that's brilliant Barb. You'll be serving it, what do you think?" I pass a spoon to Sammy. He looks at Judith, then dips the spoon into the mousse and tastes it.
"Mmm yes, nice ... a bit too much …. the herb is too much for my taste?"
"Nice? Nice?!" Barb waves her hand in front of his face. "Basil. The herb is basil." We laugh and Barb leaves the office with a flourish of her apron.

"Don't listen to him Barb, it's superb!" Judith calls out after her.

Judith applies fresh lipstick and pulls her shoulder length burgundy coloured hair back into a ponytail - her 'professional no time for a hair wash look'. She keeps it down when she's serving. This is against the health code but goes over well with our male guests. The bag hanging on her shoulder is big and flashy, covered in old airline baggage stubs. "We're off. Back in 30 minutes."

"Don't forget the rosemary!" I call as she and Sammy leave out the back door. The hinges cry out in loud protest as it opens and closes. We must get that door replaced.

I dial Bleary's office. After five rings I'm about to hang up when a faraway sounding voice quickly splutters out
"Robmurphyuniversityservicesadministrativesupporthowmayihelpyou?"
After a few seconds I timidly counter the verbal assault with "Ermm … Rob? This is Jessie Watkins."
"Hi Jessie."
"So, you're okay. Good. Is Dr. Bleary in his office?"
"Oh, sure – just one moment. What do you mean, I'm okay?"
"Sorry, private joke."
"Oh." There is a pause.

"Hello Jessie!"

"Dr. Bleary, hello. I understand you called and talked with Barb earlier? Sorry, but we just finished lunch service."
"No, no worries Jessie."
"What can I do for you Professor?"
"Well, the problem is the Alumni banquet."
"Yes, I think there's been a misunderstanding about the price per head?"
"Hmm, yes … Jessie, your cost estimate is far too high. I can get an entire catering company working on this event for the price you're asking. I could even ask our campus food services to do the dinner."
"Professor, we are an entire catering company, and as you know our food and wines are much better than Costers. Plus, we're talking about 1000 people."
"Well … a bigger company then, with, with tents and a band …"
A band? When did he ever want a band …and what will he do with tents in Alumni Hall?

"Oh, I have no doubt about that, Professor, however, we've been working for you the last few years and, I'm sure you'd agree with me, you are beyond the trivial showmanship of your colleagues. Elegant dinner banquets, whereas not precluding bands and tents, simply work better without. Your Alumni are coming so that you can stroke them with your wit, charm and my incredible menu, not to be irritated by theatrics."
"Yes, but I have to look at the bottom line. These prices are way out of line."
Like his budget doesn't need to be spent by the end of the fiscal year anyway. Use it or lose it as they say.
"Dr. Bleary, what about the service costs. Can we use the university student job pool? That would save

almost 20%. If you'd really like some music, why don't I talk with the jazz club? They do a good set - very subtle, very adult – we had them the other night at the club." Their singer, Svetlana - when she sings it's like being covered in warm honey. "You could apply to the campus activities office for student activity funding which would pay for the cost of the band." After a year as resident associates in our dorm, Barb's and my knowledge of university accounting runs deep.

Bleary is audibly excited, "Yes … Yes, I've seen them, yes, she's very good. This is a great idea. Subtle, elegant but still a bit of life at the party. Okay, please give them a call, I'll sort out the pay with student activities – you're right – their budget is bottomless … did you know that only last week a group of students received funding to go to a soccer game with their exchange counterparts claiming 'cultural benefits'? I don't know what my colleagues are smoking half of the time …"
I laugh - "I feel your pain Professor. I'll email you a new estimate and then you can get back to me."

Jesus - as if there wasn't enough competition in town. However, I included 5 percent for entertainment in the proposal. There are two things I have learnt over the years. Always charge more than you want because you will always have to negotiate down. And the only way to sell an idea, or a price, is to make the client think they arrived at it. Tents and bands. It will be gypsy caravans of microwaved chili and performing poodles next. I check my stocks online to see that those I sold yesterday have risen and those I bought have fallen. I don't believe it. Ack! Even the AMD shares I sold last month have somehow risen 100% … What?! "Arrrrrrr ….!"

My scream raises no eyebrows in the kitchen. One of the dishwashers walks up, and with downturned eyes gently shuts the office door, then returns to the dish pit.

Costers University Food Services, University Campus, that afternoon

Kate was on the phone scant seconds after Jessie first parked the Marlies catering van behind the McClarksen Campus Center. She was anything but pleased with another caterer on campus. Kate has had designs on the university club facilities since her arrival at the university. She is more than pissed about this development but is not a woman who gives up easily. It's been only a year – anything might yet happen. It just required a catalyst. Kate believes in three key competencies – never saying no, doing the job no matter what, and being there when your competitor screws up.

Kate takes a mouthful of cold coffee from the cup on her desk and flips through the stack of mail in front of her. Half of the envelopes she sorts out to one side then slides them together into the garbage basket before one catches her eye. She reaches into the bin, removes the buff coloured envelope, opens and scans it. Excitedly Kate picks up the phone and dials the Provost's office. "*Al* – ice …", she hiccups, "Sorry. Is Fiorella in?" Kate sounds jumpy - like she's desperate for a pee. She tries to control her voice - control is particularly important to her.
"Kate, hi – sorry, she's not back from her meeting. Can I have her call you?"
Kate takes a cigarette from the pack in her top drawer, lights it and inhales deeply. How can a meeting go on so long? "Would you please?" Calm has again entered her voice. She feels back in the driver's seat. She

thankfully exhales a long plume of smoke from her lips.
"Of course, Kate. I don't expect her again today though. Her calendar is blocked for the rest of the afternoon. She's out on private business."

Kate can feel her teeth grating against each other. She presses her mouth tightly closed and then opens it again wide before resuming. Kate knows Fiorella well - they began work at the university at the same time and quickly became particularly good friends.
"Sure – Have a nice day." Kate replaces the phone on the desk, gets up and walks to the large office window which overlooks the concrete beach food court and the campus green.

Kate hesitates to call Fiorella's cellphone - she knows she will be at her lover's apartment this afternoon. Kate envies her that. At the same time, her own appreciation of Fiorella leaves her a bit angry at the thought of her having a lover. Well, if she doesn't get Bleary to see sense about who caters the alumni dinner, she is very sure she can count on Fiorella's assistance. She looks at the letter in her hand – an invitation to the Alumni dinner. The guest of honor will be the university's largest benefactor – the same benefactor Kate knows (through Fiorella) is thinking of pulling out next year. What if something went wrong at the dinner? What an embarrassment for the caterer – no, a *disaster* - if the dinner were not perfect – if something were to *happen*. It might be another nail in the coffin.

On reflection, Kate thinks that on reflection it might be better to let Jessie cater the dinner after all. She looks back from the window and around her office, smiling broadly.

On the walls hang a PhD diploma, various framed awards, certifications, and family pictures. Kate looks at the largest photo, of her three kids, taken with her partner during a recent sailing trip, and loses half her smile.[4] She frowns - her mouth has a horrible taste – the metallic aroma that signals to the world that she's menstruating. Kate stretches and returns to her desk, opens the top drawer, and extracts a stick of spearmint gum. She unwraps it and places it into her mouth as Jeannie, her kitchen supervisor, knocks and enters the office.

Jeannie is the same age as Kate. The women have been working together since Jeannie began at Costers six years ago. "Is the dishwasher working again?" Jeannie makes a face as Kate walks towards her.
"Still working on it. It won't be ready until this evening."
Kate holds onto Jeannie's shoulder for a moment before walking to her desk. "It's almost three." Kate sighs again and inhales deeply, feeling the need for air.
"Jessie's coming over." Jeannie sits in the chair facing Kate's desk. She drinks again from her cup of cold coffee.

Jeannie smiles. "I'll get some coffee organised. I guess you wouldn't like to have dinner tonight?"
Kate purses her lips. "My partner is away on a business trip. I'll be at home with the kids – they're making me a cake the darlings. Another night." Kate clicks through the calendar on her desktop. "Thursday night."

Jeannie breathes in and expels her breath loudly. Then she smiles and stands up. “Ok.” Kate smiles back at her. “I’ll put the coffee service on the patio.”
“Thank you. I don’t know what I’d do without you sometimes Jeannie.” Jeannie grips the back of the chair, looks at Kate for a moment, smiles, and leaves the office. The two women have become incredibly good friends over the years and often have dinner together. Last year, on Jeannie’s suggestion, they began having dinner together at Jeannie’s flat instead of going to a restaurant.

Thirty minutes later Jessie enters the back door of the production kitchen and offices of Costers Food Services - officially University Food Services as written on the sides of all their campus vehicles. The offices are strongly air conditioned and are very cold compared with the warmth of the Indian summer outside. Jessie and Jeannie pass on the stairs and exchange a brief smile and a hello. Jessie walks along the hallway to the single open door, looks in and knocks. Kate comes out from behind her desk. This is the first time Jessie has been to Kate’s office. Jessie, for some time, has been caught between conflicting feelings of both desire and wariness for Kate. She leans in and kisses Jessie on both cheeks then steps back smiling. Kate feels completely in control.

“Jessie!”
“Hi Kate. Happy Birthday! I brought something for you.” Jessie smiles, hands Kate a still cold bottle of champagne brought from the club and takes in Kate’s office.

“Jessie, thank you. Sweet. I could do with a drink – lunch was hell. Our dishwasher broke down. We had to bring all our backup hardware from storage to cover us over lunch – it had to be sanitised - what a pain.” Kate takes the champagne and guides Jessie out the door of the office and down the hall. She shows Jessie out onto a small patio adjacent to the office. There is a small table and chair set with coffee and tea. A large china plate is filled with various petit fours. “I thought you might like something to go with your coffee. Just wait here a moment and I’ll get us some glasses.”

Kate leaves Jessie to admire the petit fours. With a critical eye Jessie notes the fine condensation on the chocolate coverings denoting either frozen and thawed, or fresh and refrigerated. Jessie tends towards frozen and thawed. Kate returns with two champagne glasses, an ashtray, and the open bottle of champagne.

“They’re fresh – well, fresh from last night’s opening party at the … some conference or another - we cater so many. Anyway – a toast to birthdays – “she passes Jessie a glass half full of champagne and raises hers. “– may they be few!”

“To you Kate …” Jessie drinks and takes one of the cigarettes Kate offers. “Was that a PhD diploma hanging in your office? That’s not very common in our business. Impressive.” They sit down. Kate nods and crosses one leg over the other. The sandal she wears dangles from her foot and Jessie’s attention is drawn to Kate’s bare feet and calves visible below the hem of her skirt. She notices Jessie’s gaze and smirks knowingly. Kate lights her cigarette, reaches over to light Jessie's and squints against the smoke. She shakes out the match, and drinks from her glass. Then she laughs – a high, tinkling, but dangerous sounding laugh.

"Life is short Jessie – and I want a lot out of it. I didn't do anything with the doctorate, but perhaps it helped me get this job – I don't know." Kate passes Jessie the sweets, her smirk growing and creating a dimple in her cheeks. "The students prefer junk food and the chefs have university degrees. The world isn't what it used to be." Jessie nods and raises their glass, "Cheers", and drinks. Thirty minutes of small talk later Jessie leaves. Kate returns to her office and dials the number to Dr. Bleary's office.

Jessie's House, that evening

Country country house, country country country, country country house. From my living room I can see an old farmhouse which was turned into a restaurant and then finally abandoned. Behind that the fields go on forever. Our subdivision sits on the edge of some prime parkland. The developers have however put up the first billboards and skeletal wood frames heralding the next subdivision. Development. Improvement. The words sort of have an ironic ring to them though, you know? You expect something better and you usually get something a lot worse.

Last night the wind was so strong coming across the fields, now mostly stripped of trees, that most of the housing frames collapsed and now lay on the muddy ground. Sitting in an older and more wisely built house of bricks I feel like one of the three little pigs.

We don't open Monday or Tuesday nights for dinner. Our lunch crowd is always good, but we never did get much action on these nights, so we stay closed. If there's a special event, we'll open but otherwise not. No one goes out for dinner early in the week. Unless they work in the business - like me. Do you really want to cook for someone who does it for a living? I go out the open front door, light a cigarette and look back across the sun-drenched living room at the moving boxes, then back out the door across the fields. I really don't want to pack. I'm a procrastinator - if it can be done tomorrow then you won't find me doing it anytime today.

I walk up and down the creaking stairs that go between the main floor and the top floor which I use as an office. I stare out the front door again. When I return my gaze to the living room the moving boxes are still there. I walk past them, past the bedroom and into the kitchen, switch on the oven and prepare a batch of chopped walnut biscotti, wrapped in white chocolate and lavender- anything to get out of the job at hand. After baking and while the cookies are drying in the oven, I carry the stack of old magazines I've collected at the foot of the stairs down to the recycling bins at the end of the street. I greet my neighbour on the way. I rummage through the dozen back issues of Wine Spectator he's just chucked out and take two of the better issues. Then I walk back home, go down into the basement, and begin the laundry.

If Alex came back right now, she'd think I'm doing the sheets as some sort of symbolic act of parting; but they haven't been washed in two weeks. Hell, I'll do all the laundry … there must be like eight loads here … perhaps not. I go back upstairs, pour a shot of good Belarussian vodka – all good vodka comes from Belarus - from the bottle in the freezer and call Alex's cell number. Which is no longer in service. That was fast.

I walk into the kitchen, kicking one of the defenseless and still empty moving boxes as I pass. I take the vodka bottle, a family box of chips, a handful of still warm biscotti - sadly not yet wrapped in white chocolate and lavender - and head upstairs. Everything is precariously balanced on top of my laptop along with a sheaf of catering plans. It's three pm. Alex is en route to New York, some eighteen-hour drive, beginning her new life without me. I've got two weeks to move the twenty minute drive to my new place – loads of time to pack, type up a few menus, some catering offers, do the account books from last month, go to the gym once – maybe – and I don't know, maybe put my hand in the trash compactor at this rate of emotional instability. It will probably be much longer than two weeks before I ever see Alex again.

It was Alex's dream to live in New York. When she landed a one-year contract to write for a magazine there, she jumped at it. I was curious enough to go along for regular visits, but my restaurant and my life is here. We never thought about what the distance might do to our relationship, but I'm not really a big city person. I must admit that the timing of our breakup couldn't have been better.[5]

Alex moved out a week ago, but I can still feel her hand against my cheek. Yesterday she gave into my pleadings and came over for dinner so she could pick up the rest of her things. Actually, she gave into Judith and Barb's pleadings because I hadn't shown my face in the restaurant since Alex left and business was beginning to go to hell. I made her favourite dishes - roast pumpkin and smoked ham lasagna and Caesar salad with garlic-yoghurt dressing, bruschetta, and Padano cheese. The wine – a Marques de Riscal 2008 Rueda - was excellent.

After dinner we slept together. When I woke, she had left without a word or a note, which is bad, but to be honest, while we're being all honest and open with each other, I guess her plans didn't include me.

Jessie's house, August 18

I awake with a start, covered in sweat after a long haul through the horror chamber of my dreams. I look over at the alarm clock and groan. I took the day off today too. I invariably awake far earlier than necessary. My dreams - I must start taking something against these dreams of mine. Real time is down time compared to my dreams. What goes on in my head - is it just me? Does everyone have a carnival waiting off stage that roars into life as soon as they drop off to sleep? I fall back onto the pillow exhausted and turn on my side. My left hand is lying atop the empty ice cube tray. The vodka bottle lying next to it is not empty which is a good sign. I get up and go into the bathroom. After a cold shower I search the medicine cabinet, but Alex has taken not only all the face creams with her but also the aspirin. I still feel weird that Alex and I slept together. It's as though the entire point of our relationship had just been sex.

I had hoped we could begin again and so I asked and begged and pleaded with her to tell me that this wouldn't just be sex, right? As we were pulling at each other's clothes and I'm falling into the bed with this sexy, brilliant woman I still wanted reassurance. I wanted guarantees. But because couples can't really communicate with each other when sober and even less so after double vodkas, a bottle of wine and too many sad little pheromones in the air what she meant was "It isn't just sex because I will always love you, but it's still over." while what I meant was "I don't want to sleep with you unless we are going to make another go of it." I go into the kitchen, drop a bagel into the toaster and fill a glass with orange juice. I don't have any time for self-pity - it's the middle of August and classes begin in two weeks.

Being a university town, the local populace is going to swell by another forty thousand people in search of enlightenment, pizza, drunken freshies, or simply a job after graduation. I must seriously begin moving if I have any hope of finding a parking space again before next summer. Most of my possessions have been long since sold or discarded in my varied and regular moves but being a chef, I do own enough cookbooks and kitchen paraphernalia to choke a horse - and they won't move well without the help of a forklift. I carry the bagel – sesame seed with goat cheese and blackcurrant marmalade and the juice to the table, flip on my laptop and check my messages. Nothing from Lori – luckily – I don't think I could handle that right now. Nothing from Alex either but that comes as no great surprise. Bank statement, phone bill, Russian brides, better orgasms, and a few mails from complete strangers pleading with me to allow them to deposit millions of dollars into my bank account.

I rest the cold glass of juice against my forehead. I'm not going to get any packing done and desperately need some Tylenol. I grab the car keys just as my phone rings. I rush for it thinking it might be Alex. "Hey, Jessie? Angie! Hi!"
"Oh, Hi Ange, how's it going?" My sister and I have been living in the same city since we left home. We moved clear across the country and landed in the same city.

"Jessie, I have to go out of town on business – can you look after Nicki for me for a few days?" "Sure, where you off to?"
"Thailand …"
"What!? I'm lucky to take the train on business. What sort of company has enough money to fly their people to Thailand for a chat?" If I look at my stocks, it sure can't be one that's publicly traded.
"Don't whine. Nicki can help you pack."

My sister was a dyed in the wool home care Mum until her partner and she divorced, sending her back into the workforce. After less than a year back with her old consulting company and suddenly she's an outspoken lobbyist for outsourced interstate daycare. Nicki is here so often half of his stuff is in the closet. Sometimes I've grabbed a pair of his sneakers by mistake and wondered what the hell was happening to my feet when they wouldn't go in. "Okay sis, sure, when are you leaving?"
The doorbell bell rings. "Now."

Before I get to the door it opens and Angie and Nicki tumble through it - Nicki dragging his scout bag, which could do with a new wheel and zipper, behind him.
"Hey - were you just standing outside?!" I give Nicki a hug and then my sister, who, as usual, has a phone stuck in her ear and too much lipstick on her lips.
"Hi," Angie offers me her cheek and smiles, "Nicki isn't eating his vegetables like he does with you. How do you make him eat them? … no, I need those reports emailed to me now …" She snarls through her mobile at some unfortunate in her office.

"Well, I don't give him a choice for one thing. He always eats his vegetables with me. He even sometimes cooks his vegetables when he's here *and* cleans up after himself."

Nicki is rummaging through the kitchen cupboards in search of breakfast. "Do you want a coffee?"
Angie has closed her phone and is looking at herself in the hall mirror. She can't hear me as she is lost in contemplation. "Hmm? What?"
"Coffee?"
"… No. No, sorry I have to get to the airport."
"Hey!" comes a plaintive cry from the kitchen, "You're out of Frosties!"
"I'm always out of Frosties – I don't buy them!" I call back, "The Weetabix is on top of the fridge". I think my sister is a bit slack and he takes advantage of it. Hell, the kid wasn't born yesterday.

"Listen, Ange, did you talk with Nicki about Mum yet?" The subject makes her nervous, which it would of course - it makes me nervous. It makes everyone in our family nervous. Mum has breast cancer. Nicki is her only grandchild and we've thought a lot about what to tell him. I think he has enough on his plate being an eleven-year-old without having to deal with anything like terminal illness. Angie and I flew out a little while ago with Nicki and Alex while Mum was first in remission and he had a great time. My mother was wearing a wig. He'd never seen anything as funny as someone who could remove their hair.

If I ignore the subject someone else will talk to Nicki. I find I'm incapable of doing so, and its really Angie's job anyway. Let it be someone else's fault that he loses his innocence. When I lost mine, I couldn't sleep for nights afterwards and still have weird dreams. I was informed about my mortality as matter of factly as being reminded about my homework. *"Hey kid, let's get cleaned up and get ready for bed now okay? Oh, and don't forget, you're going to die one day and cease to exist forever so after you finish your homework brush your teeth well."* Yeah, great. There are some things better not knowing about. Telling your children about sex, drugs and how to cheat on their taxes is one thing because it can go either way, so any advice is going to help. But death will get you every time.

Angie turns to me, "Look, I'm still thinking. I will though…" Then there's a long pause as she gazes into space, then at her watch. "I've gotta go…" She pecks me on the cheek and looks at herself in the mirror one last time. "Bye Nicki! Be good!"
"Jaaa …" comes the answer from Nicki's cereal filled mouth in the dining room.
"Bye sis. Bring us back something okay? Maybe one of those huge Toblerone bars from duty-free."
I hug her exactly as she decides to spray herself with d'Imperfiction and get a blast of the perfume right in my face. "Sorry! It's all business, Jess, no time for shopping – you have no idea!"
"Argh – that tasted good – Thanks!" I wipe my hand over my face and grimace. "You've outfitted yourself on four continents Ange. So, you've heard of duty-free right?" I call as she makes her way to her car. She smiles and waves as she backs out the driveway and heads off down the street with a honk from her new red Audi Quattro. I stare forlornly at my rusting thirty-

year-old green TR6. The love of my life. It starts when it wants to and the repair bills kill me, but like all my bad habits, I just can't get rid of it.

Nicki, or should I say Nuri, his alter ego, is digging his way through cereal and juice while rocking on his chair. I can hear the wood beginning to give when I come through from the front. Nuri is a mystical, medieval Japanese ninja apprentice while Nicki is an 11-year-old embryo teen ready to boil over from too much sugar, computer games and allowance. Nicki reads too many Manga and is a bit obsessed with martial arts, but I guess it could be worse - it could be gangsta rap and crack. "Please don't rock on the chair, it'll break and then I'll have to buy another one."
"Was it expensive?" he asks while slopping orange juice into a glass.
I grab the sponge from the sink and wipe up the splattered juice on the counter. "Yes. The entire set cost a grand and I don't have another grand to replace it with."
Nicki looks thoughtful as he lifts the glass of juice from the table. "How much were the glasses?" "Ha. The glasses are from the restaurant, but I'd like to have them around a bit longer."

Ignoring my advice to eat a healthy cereal, Nicki's picking out the raisins from what he has instead chosen, while I lean against the wall eating a yoghurt – peach and granola with some honey on top. I wonder how much fiber I should eat today on account of the clubhouse with country fries I ate for lunch yesterday. The clubhouse came within 5 minutes which was a big improvement on the 40 minutes it had taken the time before. At least they had toasted the bread. I've been looking for a good clubhouse for a few years now. I was once served a clubhouse untoasted with what seemed like an entire turkey breast in between the bread slices with enough sauce to float a whale. I sent it back. I was told 'this is the way we make our clubs here'. Great - then write on the card 'Conceptual Clubhouse' instead of 'Clubhouse the Great American Favourite'.

The silent raisin sorting process is broken by Nicki's indignant cry, "Hey what's that? This isn't a raisin it's a nut – have you been mixing the cereals? Wait … is there *granola* in here!?"
"Why? Granola kills now? I must have missed the warning." My father would have said 'thank your lucky stars they're raisins and not shrapnel' and made me eat the lot. I don't understand his aversion to raisins, Nicki not my father. He eats grapes. When I was a kid the biggest selling cereal on the shelves was with 'two big scoops'. Don't all kids love raisins?

As we're washing the breakfast things Nicki asks, "Where's Alex?"
I dry the glasses and put them away in the cupboard beside the sink. "Mmmm … she had to go to New York for a few days." I lie. He's noticed that the TV is gone.
"She left you, didn't she? I knew it."
"How did you know this? But, yeh – I did something stupid and now she's gone." I hang up the dish towel and rummage on top of the fridge for a cigarette.
"You already broke up once. Why don't you see Marta? She's cool."

"Whoa, little guy. Marta and I are good friends. Alex and I were together for years"
"Well, I like Marta a lot more. I rarely saw Alex, and when I did, she was always busy. She was too *grown up* ..."

He's right there, I noticed this myself. While grown up isn't bad, it just isn't a state I've reached yet.
"You aren't allowed to smoke inside when I'm here, remember?"
I put the cigarette back and grab a biscotti – the walnut ones that never got even close to being wrapped in white chocolate and lavender - from the jar. I adopt a philosophical pose. "Look. There are different types of people." I gesture with the biscotti, crumbs flying about in front of me. "I don't know. I was really crazy about Alex and I still am. I know it doesn't make any sense to you, it doesn't make any sense to me most of the time, but that's the way it is. Shit happens."

"When I grow up, I'm not going to be a heartbreaker like you." Nicki sadly shakes his head.
"What do you mean?"
"You just go from girl to girl; and you don't even have good ideas about girls. First Lori and now Alex. Why don't you move in with Marta? She likes you."
I grab another biscotti. "You weren't even born when Lori and I were together – how do you know about Lori?"
"Mum told me. Look, you're always talking about saving money - you would save even more money! And you wouldn't have to move – Marta could move in here!"
I raise my eyebrows, "How would I save money?"

"If you aren't together with someone you spend money going out for dinner. And gifts! You have to spend more on presents."
Now I really must wonder what he's been watching on television. "How do you figure this? I hate to break it to you, but I didn't spend that much on presents for Alex."
"You know what I mean."
"Ahhh… well there are one or two loopholes in your theory Dr. Ruth, but I think I know what you mean. I didn't really spend so much on Alex. For Lori yes but … we were together when I did. Look, when you and Sarah went to the movies last time, who paid?"
"I did."
"And for the popcorn?"
"Yes."
"Well what's the difference? You aren't saving much money when you go out with Sarah are you?"
"That's different. True love knows no price."

Coughing, I almost lose the remainder of my coffee – regular instant with sugar and milk - down my front. "How come it's 'love is blind' when we're talking about you but it's 'you're stupid' when we're talking about me. You're only 11!"
"Some things you know, okay?"
I put my cup into the sink and fill it with water. "Ok - we're late and we need to go. We'll talk more about this scintillating topic tonight." Where have my car keys gotten to?
"But I haven't watched any TV yet."
"As you noticed I no longer have a TV."
"Then I could play a game on your laptop."

I find the car keys. Where are my glasses …? "Look, you didn't get here until 30 minutes ago and your couch session just made you late for day camp."
"Ok. I just have to find my game boy…"

We're headed for the car when we run into Marta and her daughter Anna coming out from next door. Like most of the town, she works at the university. Specifically, she works for Fiorella in the Provost's office. She previously worked in the diplomatic corps and seems to know a lot about weapons, systems administration, and wine. Swims like a fish. Makes a wicked salad. The French eh? She has very small hands and feet but huge eyes behind overly long lashes. She cuts her hair short which gives her face a very odd appearance. To be honest, she looks a lot like a fish.

"What a nice dress you have on today Anna. Really pretty."
The five-year-old – blonde and blue eyed compared with Marta's dark features - looks at me suspiciously and replies; "I also have on pretty shoes you know."
"Why, yes you do!" I reply as Nicki smirks behind me, tosses his knapsack into the car, gets in the car, and shuts the door. Marta and I kiss on both cheeks - very European. She looks bothered. "Morning! **smack** How are you? You seem off colour this morning."
"Jessie, 'allo, **smack** Off colour? My makeup?"
I laugh. "Hahaha no, not your makeup, you look lovely today. Off colour – not your usual chipper self."
She looks at me "… chips? You look at me and you think of chips?"
"Never mind. Is everything all right?"

“Oh, I have meetings all day today and no time to work.” she pauses and then “I have no time to work today because of all the meetings I have?”

She looks at Jessie and wrinkles her nose. Marta often rephrases her sentences. She speaks with a hesitant urgency which Jessie finds charming. “On top of everything, last week we received notice that our largest donor is thinking of pulling out next year - it’s causing a lot of fallout – very hush hush okay? Our business plan is not the best … there must be changes to administrative structures … you can imagine.”
“Wow, really? Maybe it’ll put some fire under some asses. The university isn’t the most efficient of places. You’ve got like a thousand staff up there – it wouldn’t work that way in a restaurant.” She laughs. “We need the staff – who would come to our meetings? Who would I send my memos to?”
“Ha ha! Supper tonight with the kids?”
“Oui, simple yet elegant. Don’t be late.”

I get in the car and wave, turn the key in the ignition, beg and scold the darling into starting and … it starts! “Couldn’t we have pizza tonight?” Nicki asks over the blare of the radio and the staccato roar of the engine. I turn down the volume on the radio, “No, let’s make something good. We’ll have pizza tomorrow.”
“Oh man … Anna likes pizza too… you know, you should really move in with Marta.”
“So, we’d eat pizza every night? I happen to know Marta hates pizza. As you recall Alex was no great lover of pizza either.”
“I bet Alex left because of that.”
“Pizza?”

"No, because Marta is always flirting with you."
"She flirts with me? When?"
Nicki shakes his head and looks out the window. "Oh boy are you dumb…"
"Hey chief, Alex left for a lot of reasons – but I really doubt Marta was one of them. That I know of ..."
"She's always liked you. And now Alex has gone."
I drive through the streets with this unfinished sentence dangling in front of me like a carrot. I drop Nicki off at the day camp on the way into town. "See you later- have a good time!" I call as Nicki gets out of the car.
"Sure, thanks!" He smiles, waves, and loses himself in the swarming crowd of kids at the bus stop.

I swing by the drugstore for Tylenol and toilet paper. Then I visit the Dunkin Donuts drive thru. One Boston cream, one maple glaze with chopped peanuts, two yoghurt-berry, and two glazed with jam filling. A half dozen is always cheaper than four. I order a regular low-fat cappuccino - now *that's* good coffee - then I drive over to my new place to take some measurements.

Marlies Restaurant, that afternoon

With Alex planning to move to New York and me mostly sleeping in the restaurant we had already cancelled the lease on the house for the end of the month. The place was too big for just one person. Now it all seems like too much hassle and I wish I'd just kept the place. I've rented a little single-story bungalow not far from the river and about 15 minutes' walk from the restaurant. I thought some exercise might do me good. Don't worry - when the snow hits, the mercury drops and the car won't start, this 15-minute walk will feel more like an hour anyway.

My landlady, Mrs. Baxter, is talkative but otherwise harmless. She conveniently but questionably lives in the house next door. Today she is having a birthday luncheon in her backyard. She has set everything out beneath three large party umbrellas which I can watch from a respectable distance from the kitchen window while I'm finishing off the doughnuts. As I was signing the lease, Mrs. Baxter told me her daughter was visiting from Spain for the summer (that would be her in the white summer dress carrying out the cheese tray …) and that her boyfriend (that would be him in overly tight shorts and a large beer belly in an orange button down polo shirt …) collects antique gramophones. From what I recall and … her daughter? Speechless. Magical. Let's not go there. Now about that guy with the gramophones …

At the restaurant there is the usual blip of random chaos. In the middle of lunch Sammy walks out, knocking over a tray of glasses in his rage. Because

Judith won't go out with him after work. I mean, how does this even happen!? "He is a little … how can I say it? He is a bit of a pet, ja. He's high strung – overly passionate. But a good waiter – he'll come back." Judith explains to me afterwards, chain smoking filter-free Chesterfields. She blows cigarette smoke out the side of her mouth and picks tobacco flakes from her tongue as she fidgets.
"He doesn't need to come back, Judith." I take a drag from her cigarette and undo my apron, hanging it on a hook behind the bar. "I'm serious – and you should be careful – he seems a little too intense. No shit." Judith raises her eyebrows as I pass the cigarette back to her. "Please. We have other wait staff but only one of you."

I go into the office. We have 753 emails – most of them from the same people. Spamming has become a question of volume – talk loudly and often. We never used to have this many emails but now we have a new provider and a new server which is unfortunately called Uranus. Really. "Where do we put the mails? On Uranus. How's Uranus looking today?" Why couldn't it be called Saturn or Jupiter or the Moons of Venus? I erase all the spams and the rest I scroll through as quickly as possible as Barb comes into the kitchen from the front with John. We don't buy much in the way of dry goods but when we do, they come from John. He's been in the business since before microwaves and has the unique ability to find even the rarest tripled milled organic rice flour or rudely shaped takeout containers. "… no, no …. no … maybe … yes …. NO … no, nonononono … Hey! Most of these emails are 'no', why did you leave them all for me to answer? Hey, John, how's it going?"

Barb walks into the office and drops a stack of mail on the desk. John nods and smiles big and toothy as he follows her in. "I've already forgotten the password for the server. And I don't want to touch Uranus." Big laugh all around.

"Haaaaaa Ha Ha … the password is written down in the account book, here. There is nothing wrong my bottom thank you very much. Sammy's gone. I told Judith. Cut him a check for the days he's worked and have it ready in case he comes in. Deduct the price of the glasses."

Barb nods, "Done."

"So, John – what do you have in the way of wasabi cheese and sweet balsamic vinegars? We have a new dessert creation."

John undoes his bag and pulls out his laptop, raising his eyebrows. "Where I come from dessert is a slice of pie and if you're lucky a scoop of Safeway ice cream." He begins searching his files, "What you kids do down here is some sort of witchcraft."

Barb pulls out our ordering notes and recipes, "Well, let's see if you can get us some more of those free wine samples from last month or I'll turn you into a frog." Barb, it should be noted for the record, is a witch; or to cater to the politically correct, 'Wiccan'. Her mother is a witch as well - but not her elder sister; so, it's not something that necessarily runs in the family. There aren't as many witches about as there once were or maybe there are, and they just aren't saying. In certain overzealous times in our history just being a beautiful woman who happened not to die of the plague would almost certainly have sent you to the stake as a witch.

Maybe today they're just a little more careful outing themselves.

"Okay. Let's talk chocolate." The Strand Hotels' annual chocolate festival. Each year we never even rate an honorable mention, but this year I want to get noticed. I lean back in the chair and expand on my grand plan. "I envision a sort of Lego world diorama of chocolate. Rotating. Big. Quagswagging Big. It must be gigantic. A towering cruelty of multi-layered chocolate in answer to the need for repetition in representing the unrepresentable … I want to put the Strand away with this one!"

Barb and John look at me. "Quagswagging??"
I smile. "We'll need a few days to move in supplies - sleeping bags, three hundred kilos of Valrhona chocolate, barbed wire ..." John stops typing the order on his laptop and Barb just stares at me. Then she flips closed her notebook.

"And you are going to transport it to the hotel how?" John pipes up – "You could fly it down on your broomstick" and starts laughing to himself until he looks like he'll rupture something.
Barb takes off her glasses and reaches out with her pencil which she begins to wave in front of John's face in ever quickening circles "Jessie, why don't we just do a nice chocolate cheese mousse in the shape of John?"
"Okay Okay! I know when I've outlived my welcome. Here's your copy of the order – though I can't guarantee the jellied rose petals this week. Call me later about the chocolate."

John removes two packets of curry flavoured jelly tots from his sample bag. "Here, try these – they're new."
"Thanks John. Talk with you later."
We get up and John makes his way out the back door.
"I'm going to finish some things up here before I go." Barb says as she sits down in front of the computer.
"I have to get home and pack, or this move of mine is never going to happen."
"Did you see this?" Barb sorts through the mail on the desk, pulls out an opened and official looking buff coloured envelope and passes it to me.
"Not yet. What is it?" "It's from the tax office. It says we didn't submit a return for the restaurant last year."
"What?! Impossible. My own taxes are up to date. Unlikely those of the restaurant aren't. Doesn't the accountant submit it? We do all the paperwork together each spring."
"I called them and left a message." I look over the letter requesting the missing tax declaration. "It says here they'll conduct an audit if we don't submit. Great."
Barb looks at me. "But everything is above board, right? We don't have anything I don't know about?"
I laugh. "Barb this is a restaurant. Haha! Fish comes in the back door and we pay cash – the odd catering for cash – the usual. Nothing major though. We don't have anything to worry about." I place the letter back in the envelope and attach it to the memo board above the desk with a large magnet. "Weird we didn't get any reminders though. I gotta go." I drop my chef jacket into the clothing bin, grab my keys, kiss Barb on the cheek, and leave by the back door. It closes again slowly, in rusty complaint, as I walk into the sunlit alley.

Marta's house, later that day

At four o'clock I'm sitting across the street to the bus stop waiting for the return of the camp bus. The passenger door opens and in springs Nicki. "Hey!"
He plops his knapsack down and smiles. "Hey back – where was the bus? – where have you been?"
"We came back early. Some kid broke his arm on the skateboard ramp this afternoon. They decided to bring everyone back instead of coming in with only him. We were at McDonalds across the street, and I saw you drive up." He takes some of the curry jelly tots from the pack on the dashboard. "Hey! Yuck! What are these?" he spits them back into his hand. "Joke jelly tots?"
I laugh and pass him a napkin from the glove compartment. "Jelly tots for grownups."

We drive by the market to grab some things for dinner on the way. I think we'll do some fish tonight with a little potato salad. How come I can never find the horseradish… purple potatoes? … arugula … "Nicki, put the Captain Crunch back, it'll make you sick …I don't care that they taste great. Flavour is not a good tradeoff for lousy nutritional value. Believe me … no, not even with a toy thrown in" … olive oil …. fish. Fish fish fish. "What sort of fish do you want? Fish sticks aren't a fish, they're a shape" … white fish? Cod, cod…. No cod … "What? No, they don't have any John Dory - where do you think we are, Maine?" Where did he hear about John Dory? …
Nicki comes up to me with a package of Corn Flakes and tosses it in the basket. "I read that when they began making fish sticks, they got like only 300 pieces out of

a block of fish, but today they have these laser thin blades and can get 400 pieces!"
"Really? So how come the price of fish sticks didn't go down?" … White fish, white fish … what about some flounder? "Here's a cool fish, the one that's flat with the two eyes on top of their heads … Yeah? okay then flounder. No, the eyes are gone… Go grab some cookies for later but not the stupid ones..." We have, through many years of practice, an understanding as to which cookies are acceptable and which not. We get to the check out and unload the cart. $80?! For a bit of dinner? Well, yeah, for four people, that's not bad. I guess … Fish sticks would have been cheaper.

Marta is looking out her front window when Jessie and Nicki drive down the street and turn into her driveway. She opens the door, happy to see Jessie. She goes out to help carry the groceries. Nicki is quite right - she does like Jessie a great deal and is not terribly upset that Alex left. She has been alone since separating from her partner and not met anyone who excites her quite like Jessie. They exchange a kiss on the cheek and fumble with the grocery bags. Nicki races through the open door and with Anna makes for the Play Station. Marta and Jessie go into the kitchen, open a bottle of wine, and catch up on the day while prepping dinner. "… and then my boss? What a bitch, I swear she's been reading my emails!" The potato Marta is slicing becomes more and more erratic in width, so Jessie gently slows her hand. "My boss is reading my emails - I swear! Ah, pardon … there were unread emails in my folder when I went out for lunch, and when I came back, they were open. No one else has access to my office but her. Stupid bitch."

She tosses the potato into a large bowl, then splashes in the oil, vinegar, apple, and onion slices while Jessie breads the fish.
"Are you sure it was her?" Jessie takes a sip of wine – a very cold Niagara Gewürztraminer – "perhaps you forgot you read them."
Marta chops the parsley and cold boiled eggs for the remoulade sauce, "Alors!" She points the knife into the air and shakes it, "I know it is her - she is having this affair, just flaunting it – and at the same time – she is worried everyone knows. She believes I'm telling people because I saw her yesterday afternoon with her tongue down his throat. In her office, as I came back from lunch, in broad daylight! Disgusting. The woman is married with children and she's carrying on like a teenager – it is her ego … she has her lover wrapped so tightly around her finger he doesn't … shit without her okay … she is a … a … I cannot say this word ... merde!" She brings the knife down quickly and hard against the chopping block as she attacks the shallots.

"She's having an affair?" Jessie recalls Fiorella in the club during the Vice President's brunch and wonders at the man brave enough to sleep with her. "Wow. Probably midlife crisis." Jessie stops cutting and looks at Marta. "Fiorella's a real princess … Peyton tells me undergrads call her 'her majesty'. Is she having an affair with someone younger?"
Marta shakes her head, "No, about the same age, I think. Midlife crisis! Yes!" she shakes the knife in Jessie's direction. "Do you know, she was ridiculing this poor Professor just yesterday, because he is a man and has bought a sports car. That this is typical for a man in midlife crisis she says – but do you know? She

has one herself! She is a … a hypocrite. Alors! I despise this woman. She is such a … not a princess, no … an ... an … Empress! Yes, with her airs and … always posing and smiling to get what she wants from people … and it works!" She raises the knife as Jessie backs off. "Oh ... I am sorry Jessie." She lowers the knife, and puts her hand on Jessie's arm, smiling.
"Hey, no problem. Perhaps you should get the plates, let me do the rest of the chopping." Jessie counters, as she places the knife on the cutting board, now notched with deep grooves.

Marta insists on making her condiments fresh – which endears her to Jessie. Can you get remoulade sauce in a jar? Heaven forbid. Anyway. No this is not food snobbery; do you have any idea what must go into ready-made sauces so that they're able to sit on a shelf for 24 months? And exactly how long does it take to blend a bit of boiled egg, onion, mustard, pickle, yoghurt, and oil into a paste? Good. Don't come over all high and mighty with me, I might just save your life. No, I mean this isn't rocket science and if you don't have any pickle then what the hell, use capers or some sour apple. What I'm saying here is just relax. Enjoy your food. Just keep it simple, do it yourself and enjoy. Food. Is. Easy.

Later, over dinner, Marta sits back feeling content. She wouldn't mind being together with Jessie and Nicki on a more regular and perhaps live-in basis. "Where were you so long anyway; I had expected you sooner?"
"We were trying to find the right fish, then I couldn't find the wine I wanted." Jessie takes a mouthful of wine and swirls it about.

Marta smiles and shakes her head. "Fish sticks would have been fine …"

"Seeeee?! I told you!" Nicki is stuffing fish into his mouth. Marta takes a drink and looks at Jessie over her wine glass. Her eyes are very big and spaced wide apart from her nose – really a lot like a fish … it's weird at first but, she has been told, sort of sexy after you get over the initial shock. Jessie appears to blush then looks away, taking a fork of Nick's potato salad.

"Eat your potato salad."

"I don't like the green stuff."

"Yes, you do, it's arugula and you eat it every time you eat my pesto."

He beams at Jessie, "This isn't pesto, it's potato salad."

"Do you want dessert?"

Marta drains her wine glass and refills it. She smiles at the exchange.

"No."

"Well, eat the potato salad anyway. There are a lot of starving people who would kill for some potato salad."

"You can send them mine." Nicki responds, which earns a scowl from Jessie.

Anna pipes up in her bright little way. "I'll eat it!"

"Thank you, Princess." Marta is immensely proud of Anna. She's a very sweet kid and she knows Jessie adores her. Not for the first time Marta wonders if she and Jessie could raise a child together.

"Can we get down?" this from Nicki.

"You have to ask the hostess when there is one at the table - women, then older men. Same as when you're serving remember?"

Nicki knows this but always asks. "Yeah, Grandpa hates that when he's here … 'older men'…" he guffaws.

"Mama, can we get down, pleeeeease?" this from Anna. Marta scoops the remains of Anna's fish onto her fork and puts it into her mouth.
"Oui but wash your hands before you do anything else. Toute suite!"

Jessie begins to clear up the dishes from the table and Marta asks the question she's been wanting to all evening. "I saw Alex moving her things out the other day. I know she was going to New York, but this, this looked different somehow - n'est ce pas?"
"Mrrrm – I don't want to talk about it. I was a bit of an idiot and … Alex left me – I really hurt her." Jessie continues clearing up the dishes. "Let's not talk about it okay?"
"D'accord, as you wish Jessie." She gets up and takes the remaining glasses. "Mais … you will tell me if you would like to talk, okay?"
"Hey, thanks, and I appreciate your concern." Jessie gives Marta a gentle squeeze as they pass in the kitchen. Some place deep inside of her makes a sudden, involuntary jump.
Marta smiles and tosses the dish towel at Jessie, "You should. Alors! You will dry."

The sound of my mobile calls me out of the kitchen. I walk through the living room where Nicki and Anna sit lost in their virtual Play Station world. "Yep?"
"Hi, it's Barb. Someone threw a brick through the front window. The dining room's a mess." "Oh shit. Did you call the police?"
"Of course. Jessie, I think it was Sammy. The brick's painted on one side 'you' and the other 'bitch'." I relay this to Marta who is standing there watching the

kids. She covers her face with a hand and shakes her head.

"Barb, give the police Sammy's address and number, tell them about what happened at lunch. I'll be over as soon as I can. You know, it could have been Janet from the dry cleaners. We still haven't paid their bill from the jackets they ruined last month." I chuckle.
Barb's laughing. "You think so? I'll put the cops onto her then okay? See you soon."
"Oh, Barb – take some photographs of the window for the insurance. Is Judith still there?" "Yes."
"Okay. See you in a few minutes." I close my phone.
"Jess, I'm sorry."
"Yeah. One of our staff, I think. I need to go to the restaurant. Can Nicki stay here for an hour or so?"
"Of course."
I kiss Marta on the cheek, put my jacket on and open the front door. "Thanks Marta. Nicki, I'll be back in a bit. Be good."

Marlies, that evening

I start the car and swing into traffic, lighting a cigarette as I go. As I drive down the street past Marlies I see a police cruiser parked in front and Barb on the street taking photos of the damage from the outside. The front window is completely gone. One brick? We obviously have very weak glass. One of the drapes is gently blowing in and out with the breeze. I honk and Barb waves as I turn into the alley. I go in the back door, walk past the dish pit and into the dining room. Barb comes in through the front door and places the camera on the bar. The police cruiser drives away, as an emergency glass repair truck pulls up in front.

Judith is standing at the bar. "I called the glass repair guys. Does our insurance cover loss of income you think?" I go behind the bar, place three glasses full of ice on the counter and open a bottle of scotch – Dalwhinnie – from which I pour a generous amount into each glass, then slide one in front of each of the girls. "I'd be surprised if our insurance covers anything to be honest. Let's wait and see. I'll call them after we get the cost estimate for the window." I lift my glass, "Here's to young male hormones - may they always find a better outlet."

Judith smiles weakly and Barb empties her glass in one. "Here's the brick, by the way." She walks over to the hostess desk and returns with a large red brick painted with white letters on each side. I slide it over to Judith. "This belongs to you I believe."
Judith stares at it without a word. "Did the police say anything?"

"I gave them Sammy's number and address, but it's pure speculation that he threw the brick. There were no witnesses." I shake my head.
"I can't believe no one from the other stores or a single passerby saw someone throw a brick through the front window."
"We're on a corner – if you heard something and looked up, he could have already been around the corner and in the back alley."

I turn to Judith. I inhale deeply and look at her, "You're not *fucking* Sammy, are you?"
She laughs, but doesn't look at me, "Scheiß! Of course not Jessie."
I nod and look at her. "He's a good-looking guy. I might not say no ..." I wink and blow out a long trail of smoke from my lips.
Barb looks at us both and pours herself another drink. "Nice. The police said they'll go by and see what Sammy has to say. He's scheduled to work dinner tomorrow anyway."
I finish my drink and pour another round. "Somehow I doubt he'll be coming in."
The window repair guy is measuring the window and calls over, "We're going to need to seal this for tonight. We don't have the glass in stock. It will be here in the morning ok? Sorry."
I raise my glass as Barb walks over to him and goes over the details.

Marlies, August 19

Lucky for us our storefront has pseudo standard sized windows - the glass was delivered in the morning, as promised, and replaced before lunch. Just our cool logo is missing from the window. It feels weird. Naked. From last night's tragedy only the faint aroma of silicone caulking remains. I jump back surprised at the loud, plastic ringing sound of the fire alarm that breaks out from the hood above me as the heat from the flames in the sauté pan in my hand almost take off my eyebrows. That's like the third time this month, I think - stupid, defective hood system. I turn off the gas and calm the anxious faces that look up from dicing, pureeing, mixing, and weighing about the kitchen. "False alarm again guys". Barb comes in from the dining room with Judith and the service staff in tow like a mother hen. "False alarm again." They about face and march away, except for Barb.

"We have to get this thing fixed." She climbs up into the hood above the burners and looks at the receptors. "It'll be a real fire that doesn't set these stupid things off one day." She climbs back down, her round face red with exertion.
"You should get to the gym girlfriend." I look at her worriedly and set the burners back on to finish sautéing the apples.
"I thought you liked big girls. What are we doing about the Alumni dinner? Did you wow Bleary with your great ideas?" she asks as she fishes out bits of apple from the bubbling sugar and pushes herself against me.
"Watch your fingers – crazy – I love big girls – it's your heart I'm worried about. Listen. Kate called, and

she thinks we should bow out and let her cater it." I finish off the apples and put the pans to the side to cool.
Barb's licking apple from her fingers. "No way. What a cow – I'd do it at a loss just so she doesn't get it."
"Well let's wait and see what Dr. Bleary says when he calls back – I think we'll get the job. It won't be an easy catering. We haven't completely thought about how we're going to pull this off." I taste some of the apples and add a dash of nutmeg.
"The Alumni wouldn't bring us much new business if we cut them a deal anyway. If it were Exec Ed., then I'd be more willing to lose a bit now for new business later. You know?"
Barb nods her head in agreement, "Well, you always say yes to whatever crazy requests we get and think about how we'll pull it off. Hey, what are we doing about dinner tonight? There's the Black Crowes concert in town – maybe we'll get some late action."
I smile, walk over to the cooling pans on the stove top, scrape the remaining caramelised sugar into a bowl and carry them over to the dish pit where the dishwasher eagerly takes them from me.

"Thanks Charlie – everything okay here?"
"Oh yes fine – thanks."
"What do you think of our new air conditioning system we tried out in the dining room – pretty slick eh?"
He laughs and nods his head picking up a stack of trays far too heavy for him.
"Here let me take that."
"Yeah, great idea Jessie. Now we put up a sign and we can have takeout service." He laughs, spittle coming out of his mouth.

I set down the trays on the shelf behind him. "Good idea Charlie!" I laugh. Charlie is seventy if he's a day. A small, thin man with an earring and a lot of tattoos on both arms, I inherited him from the previous owner. One of the best workers I've ever met. If he's not washing dishes, he's whipping butter or peeling carrots. Just ask. If you don't ask, of course, then he's usually sitting out the back on this rickety old lawn chair we have by the door smoking a cigarette and reading the newspaper.

I walk back to Barb, "I doubt we're really the sort of place for Black Crowe fans, but you know, call me if you need anything tonight even if it's late. I'm going to head out after the main dinner rush is over; I've got Nicki and I don't want to leave him alone."
Barb follows me into the walk-in, and I start to pass her some mise en place for dinner. "We've always pulled off the wildest of caterings, and I don't like saying no. Nothings impossible – remember catering the wedding in the middle of that field? … just the dinner on campus will require a bit more … imagination than usual."

I smile weakly. Barb looks at me and raises an eyebrow. We both walk back into the kitchen and place produce onto the prep tables. "Sure." Barb says half convinced. "Angie ever think of hiring a tutor and having Nicki tag along with her? The woman's never in town."
I laugh, "I'm trying to convince her to give me some of her air miles actually …"

Jessie's house, later that afternoon

Barb is taking tomorrow evening off to give cooking demos at the market. I'm working a double tomorrow so after the dinner rush I take the rest of the night off to watch Nicki. Still, I have this uneasy feeling - this little voice telling me I should be in the restaurant tonight. I get this little voice a lot. I'm sure you do too. It's the little voice that says don't buy the sweater because it will be on sale next week, or don't buy gas today because tomorrow it will be cheaper or I bet you forgot to turn off the iron when you went out. This little voice drives me crazy, but it is always, *always*, right. I have this theory, however, that it is always right because you do what it says thereby creating a self-fulfilling prophecy; so, I try to rebel in little ways and not always listen. I am a figure of destiny, carving my own future out of the rugged wasteland free of little voices. Right.

When I get home, Nicki has already ordered himself a pizza for dinner, the open box with a slice left over for me still stands on the kitchen counter. After inhaling and tasting the thirty dinner covers from a few hours earlier all I wanted was a big vodka martini shaken with lots of ice. I log on to check the latest stock prices in New York … then I log off and sit down with Nicki to watch 'Lost in Translation' for the hundredth time, still hoping to find a clue that Bob and Charlotte get together on their return stateside. Funnily enough, each time we watch the movie we both feel as though we've found more evidence to justify that fact. The first time I watched the movie I was left sort of numb. I'm a big romantic but I need closure. I go into the kitchen, open

the fridge, and begin rummaging through it for the can of cola I know was there.
"Hey Nicki! Did you drink the last cola?!"
"Nurrrr……" comes from the bathroom. So where did it go?

As I contemplate the disappearing cola the telephone rings and I reach over. "Yeah, Hello?"
"Jess, it's me, Barb." she sounds breathless and there's a lot of noise in the background.
"What's up? Sounds crazy." I'm getting that feeling again, deep in my stomach, the little voice ... mocking me …
"Crazy isn't the word. Get down here! You have no idea who just came in." And with that the line goes dead.
I stand motionless in front of the open fridge. Shit. shitshitshitshit … I run down the hall. "Nick?! I have to go to the restaurant!" I grab my shoes and rummage through all the crap in the drawer for my car keys. Nicki comes out of the bathroom with a toothbrush protruding from his mouth.
"*Huh?*"
"Never mind, will you be okay? I have to go to the restaurant. Do you want me to ask Marta to come over? Will you be okay!?" I'm hopping up and down trying to get my shoes on.
"Yar. OK." He turns and goes back into the bathroom.
"I'll be back in a bit. If the phone rings answer it okay? It might be me and important. Oh, and close the fridge for me!"
"*Yar.*" And with that I'm out the door and running for the car. Which won't start.

Marlies, that evening

What is with my life lately? Is there to be no peace? Who came in? Sammy and his gang? Paul Bocuse? Keanu Reeves? Why didn't I bring my phone with me? I cut through the park past the theater, my lungs complaining bitterly at the now added strain of running up a hill. Everything in town is more than centrally located around the park and ideally having a house right in the middle of it and not two kilometers away would be great. Now would have been a great time to have a house in the middle of the park.

I see a bus coming. I usually manage to retain my dignity in the pursuit of a bus. The pursuit is everything, because as the bus pulls into the stop and a dozen people run like crazed devil rodents to catch it before it departs, I saunter. I cast a knowing glance about the seats and take in the panting, sweating commuters who have just done the 1500 meters in thirty seconds in order to arrive at the bus stop before anyone else but for what reason I have never been able to fathom. I must conclude that, as the bus is going to travel the same speed as it always does, the business of 'the run' is an indication that these people are 'busy' and therefore 'important'. Much too important to walk like the rest of us.

This time, however, I throw in the towel of my dignity and plow my way through the half-closed bus doors and flop onto the plastic seat nearest the door. My chest heaving, eyes watering, gasping for breath I'm respectfully ignored by the rest of the passengers.

Except for the one I'm sitting on. "Hi. Would you like some chips?"

I get up and apologise. "Sorry, sorry, but I didn't see you there. I've spilt all your chips. Oh God." Her lap is covered in broken chips. Her eyes behind her glasses are green and oval. She has thick black hair and a beautiful crooked smile that begins at her chin, takes in her mouth, and finishes at her nose.

"That's okay, I shouldn't eat them anyway. My ass ... the food on campus … it's pure poison."

I laugh. "Ah, so you are a student. Kate would love to hear that. You should cook for yourself. The food's always better." I hold out my hand, "Jessie."

She looks at me, wipes her hand on her jeans and passes it to me. "Lidia. Who's Kate?"

"Private joke. Where are you from?" I look out the window to see where I need to get off.

"Campus."

"No, I mean, your accent – are you an exchange student? Where are you from?"

She nods, "Yes. Latvia. I am from Latvia."

"Lidia from Latvia? No kidding? Your parents have a great sense of humour."

"My real name is Lauma, which I really don't like, and my parents are both without humour, so no joke was intended."

"… Ah …" I look out the window and see the restaurant in the near distance. "I have to get off here. Sorry – was just a joke. I'm sorry about the chips too. See the restaurant there, Marlies? Come in any time and I'll cook you lunch to make up for the chips, okay?" I point to the pale, round, sign of the restaurant

illuminated in the distance. The bus stops and I jump out, looking back at her.
As the bus pulls from the curb Lidia opens the window and yells out, "I don't eat a lot, but I will come if you make me a soup!" Then she shuts the window and waves as the bus drives away.

I should have called. I'm always in a panic. Always worrying. Always thinking the worst of a situation. A band. The opening act for the Black Crows. Uncommon Ground, a local band made good and now very well-known, is in the restaurant after their concert and drinking our most expensive wines. Oh, did I mention it's Barb's favourite band? I mean, I really love them and it was great they came in after the concert, signed their names on the wall beside the tables where they ate and rang up a huge bill what with their fans clambering about and then the press will be good for business but I mean, I don't know.

I thought it would have been a food critic or some famous chef, the university's CEO, and his family, or even perhaps some long dead celebrity. Had I known, I would have calmly called a taxi or called Rodd to come by and pick me up. Rodd's a good friend of mine, and his own garage band, 'Down with the Transistor', is a real hit with the undergrad crowd - even though they originally formed the band simply to get into clubs and drink beer for free. Come to think of it, Rodd will kill me when he finds out Uncommon Ground were here, and I didn't call him. Anyway. We took some pics and enjoyed a few drinks together. I thanked the lead singer for sharing their music with us, or something equally corny. I mean, I wanted to say I liked their stuff and they were good, real, good - but I didn't want to come across all idolatrous. It's a hard place in which to find a happy medium.

I wanted to call Marta to look in on Nicki but now it's almost midnight and the last of the wine bottles have been cleared away. I pick up one of the empties. Wow, they bought one of the 1996 Hattricks. $210 a bottle. At least they had better have bought it … and who scrawled '*We love Judith*' in red marker on the back wall?! … "Judith?!"

An hour later Barb and I are lounging on the sofa in the front entrance of the restaurant after the last of our staff have gone home. "I can't believe I cooked for them. They ate *my* food." Barb slurs. She's glassy eyed and barely coherent after far too much scotch.
"Well, if it's any consolation it was *my* food they ate as I had to cover for you when I got here. In your feverish state you suddenly could no longer hold a sauté pan." I light a cigarette and look at her, shaking my head. "I can't believe you! A bunch of skinny musicians in old jeans and leather jackets and it's moist panty time. Honestly. You don't see Judith carrying on like that do you?"

I look around the restaurant. "Where is Judith anyway? Barb knocks back the rest of her drink and undoes her apron, tossing it onto the pile of dirty laundry in the corner. "She left with the backup singer." She gets up unsteadily and tries putting on her jacket.
I help her find the arms. "What? Really?" I follow Barb to the front door and turn off the lights. I whistle for a taxi from the stand down the block. I hold onto

her with one hand, so she doesn't fall down the steps and lock the restaurant door with the other as the taxi pulls up to the sidewalk.
"Yup."

I open the door and Barb falls into the backseat of the cab. I get in beside her and give the driver her address. "Barb?" I rest my head against hers as the cab drives down the street.
"Yeh ...?"
She's falling asleep. "Barb …? I'm going to have to help her inside, she won't make it alone. Oh God, why wasn't I a farmer or a teacher or something and safely in bed?
"ummm?"
Oh, she's coming back again. "Barb, the backup singer was a woman." I look down at her, but she's fallen asleep with a big smile on her face.

Wholesale Food Market, August 20

It's far too damn early in the morning. Why can't I place my order on the telephone like a normal person? I put on my jacket and, as the car won't start, walk the 15 minutes to the market to clear my head. Except for it being a bit early, it's an exceptionally beautiful morning. I take brisk strides down the hill and over the stone bridge. (This is all part of the 'athlete' image developed in many of my daydreams) The rising sun burns off the mist which swirls about the dew laden grass. It is reflected in apricot hues on the grey blue water of the river below. A group of brown ducks glide silently across the still surface. A young family picnics out of the back of a station wagon on the far bank. The husband, in sweater and chinos, pours his wife a steaming cup of coffee as she waves to her son fishing from the bank. At 6:00 in the morning? - it must be coffee withdrawal hallucination… It's 6:20 when I get to the market only to discover Barb already there and going through the produce stands. I didn't really need that extra sleep - not when I could have been walking the streets while hallucinating the Nescafe family into existence...

"What are you doing here Jess?" I look over what she's piled on our cart and give her a hug.
"I didn't think you'd make it, you were having such a good time last night, I thought I'd come down just in case. Why are we buying kiwis?"
Barb adds a crate of small, purple potatoes onto our growing collection. Why did she get a box of kiwis?
"Sleep is for the customers." I'm sorting through the

produce she has chosen. A few of the items I remove from the wagon.
“I thought it would make a change from pears in the kiwi tart …” She looks at me with hooded eyes. Barb returns the items I have removed from the cart and continues down the aisle.
“Why are we doing kiwi tart? I hate kiwi tart.” I wave to a couple of the vendors in greeting. “Because you were being such a generous spirit that when the Faculty Council asked for kiwi tart for their luncheon tomorrow you said we’d do it.”
“Ahhh… those kiwi tarts.” I begin moving towards the cheese stands. “You shouldn’t leave me alone with these people Barb, before you know it, we’ll be doing Quail with little paper hats stuck on their legs and turned vegetables. It’s the tip of the wedge I tell you… Hey, you know we switched today right? You have lunch and I dinner?”
“Mmhmm ... yeh, no problem.” She’s looking over a beautiful display of edible flowers, then turns to me. “Jessie, what happened between you and Alex? Are you still together? You didn’t tell me anything.”
“Oh look, coffee. You want a coffee?” I look around in the direction of the coffee shop.

“Jess … okay, you don’t want to talk about it, fine, sure, grab me a coffee and I’ll meet you back … somewhere here …” She wanders off down the aisle pulling the wagon behind her. The market isn’t the most charming place to be at 6:30 in the morning but the coffee shop is almost open and there’s the off chance that the Strand’s chef might come by and then I can catch up on the gossip. I really could do with a coffee and a bun. Do I have a cigarette or not? I’m supposed to be giving it up and am doing a good job so far, down to a few a day instead of a few packs a day. Filthy habit- will stop soon. David Wilcox is the Strand's executive chef and a bit of a legend in town – he once fired an entire shift of waiters just because one of them dropped a flat of clean silverware on the kitchen floor. Hotel Chefs are hard. European Chefs are hard as nails. David's Scottish which means he probably eats nails with his morning oats. Oh God here he comes now …

"Morning David."
"Mormm" he answers from beneath his small, greying moustache, his eyes squinting at me. "Coffee shop's not open yet." - like it's my fault? I hope he doesn't see this as a sign of weakness. "How're things for the big Jacobs wedding this afternoon? It's the talk of the town." Arrg! Wrong thing to say - I stole their pastry chef last month. He's looking at me now. In this nasty way. The coffee shop's metal curtain raises up loudly and I quickly order a coffee and orange-nut bran muffin from the girl inside.

"Sa yer dinna kenn?" he barks, shaking the small change (nails?) in his pocket, "Gorn and got meesen Eyetalian. Furst class sooker man." He buys a coffee and a packet of John Players, then tears off the plastic wrapper with his teeth. I'm amazed at just how hot coffee in these stupid plastic cups can be. I don't understand why it should be so hot you can't drink it. Where's the sense in that?

"Why does everyone think the Italians to be such good pastry chefs?" I respond, adding sugar and cream to the melting plastic cup of brown water on the ledge in front of me, “I’ve always liked the French better, especially for chocolate.” Not a very smart thing to say. Brain to mouth: close!

David draws deep on his cigarette and tips half of the boiling coffee down his throat without flinching. “Yeh shit kip yer gob shat und yer ass n oars open Jassie.” He pokes me with his finger, the smoldering cigarette burning dangerously near. “Perheps weel suprass yeh!” I jump at the reference to keeping my ass open. Surely that’s slanderous. Wait. Did he just call me a shit? With that he gives me a nasty grin, which I take to mean “If you were in my kitchen I’d cut you up into little bits and feed you through the shredder” and moves off down the aisles.

I buy another cup of coffee and go in search of Barb. To my surprise I see her and David in very close proximity and conversation near the pineapple display at the far end of the fruit section. And she’s *laughing*. Or is she flirting? I wait a few moments until he leaves before joining her. “You know David?”

Barb jumps, flustered, her round cheeks colouring. Oh ho – what’s this? “Of course, I know David – who doesn't? Finally, my coffee – what took you? Did you grind the beans?” She takes a sip and instantly burns her tongue. “Fuck! What *is* this?” Now it’s my turn to jump, not having heard Barb utter more than two explicatives in all the years I’ve known her. We both stand there, sort of tongue tied for long minutes. I get the feeling I’ve trodden in something … “Come on Jessie,” Barb tosses the cup of smoldering coffee into the nearest waste basket, “Let’s get this stuff to the checkout.” With that she walks away, waving me on with wild gestures of her hand to follow…

Jessie's house, later that morning

I'm back home after the market run, looking into the remaining coffee in my cup. "Yuck." I stare out the window as the clouds begin to move in with the promise of a thundershower. In the background the radio is promising wind, clear skies and a mild 20 Celsius – I guess just not here. I go into the kitchen and rinse the coffee cup out, pour a glass of juice, take a cigarette from the packet of Bangkok duty free Dunhill Angie left me an hour ago when she picked up Nicki, and place the carton back on top of the fridge. I put the cigarette back again after finding my lighter empty and no more matches.

I stare at the bagels on the counter which I picked up on the way home – two raisin, one sesame, one whole wheat onion. Something has been tugging at the back of my mind all morning, and it wasn't Judith's lesbian adventures of last night – though this did occupy most of my thoughts before falling asleep … and what's up with Barb and David? She's not thinking of going to the Strand, is she? She couldn't … The banking can wait until tomorrow, the ordering is done, Nicki is safely back home … I'm clearing my mind; I'm clearing my mind. Damn. Whatever it is will have to dig its own way out. The doorbell rings, so I walk down the hallway and open the door to two large, hairy-knuckled men behind whom in the driveway rests a small moving container. Shit. That's what it was. Moving day.

Three hours later most of my possessions have been stored in the moving container. I'm sitting on the front porch as the rain begins to fall. I love these summer thunder showers – ten minutes of intense rainfall and then the sun comes out again. Afterwards everything is green, lush, full. Makeup for the eyes. Around the corner comes the staccato sounds of a green city recycling truck which beeps and flashes as it slowly makes its way around the little paths of suburbia.

Getting up, I drink the last of my beer – Duckstein from the north of Germany - and go inside. From the window I notice that my driveway is the only one with no little blue recycling box sitting at the end. I appropriated my blue box almost immediately to store tools in. In its place at the end of the driveway forlornly sits a stack of yellowed newspapers topped with a single empty condensed milk can with the label torn off. I look over to the end of Marta's driveway – blue box filled with what appear to be washed yoghurt containers, ironed newspapers and polished, flattened tin cans.[6]

The University Club, that afternoon

Thursday is the busiest night of the week and not the best day for Jessie to be away from the restaurant but there's a last-minute Faculty Council luncheon followed by a dinner party for a visiting group of Alumni rowers hosted by Dr. Bleary. After lunch Kate knocks on the open door of the club dining room and calls into the kitchen where Jessie is putting a batch of Crème brûlée into the oven. "Jessie! Hi - do you mind if I come in?"[7] She walks the length of the dining room, tightening her leg muscles and moving purposely slower as she advances. Her hair is loose, down to her shoulders, and her sunglasses are perched on her head. She's wearing a simple white blouse and black skirt combination with backless heels that slap against the soles of her feet as she walks along the hardwood floor. Jessie waves and comes out of the kitchen.

Kate and Jessie kiss each other on the cheek, hands placed gently on each other's hips as they greet – a gesture that has become a pattern over the last months. "Kate, Hi." Jessie looks her up and down appreciatively, "Why all dressed up? Where are the whites?"

Kate smiles and keeps a hold of Jessie's arm longer than necessary, with the excuse of balancing herself as she bends her leg at the knee to adjust one of her shoes. Jessie's gaze is on her leg, and as Kate looks up at Jessie's face, she easily reads Jessie's thoughts. Jessie suddenly feels naked and exposed. Kate is very much aware of Jessie's desire for her, and how hard Jessie is fighting that desire. She smiles and straightens up with a dimpled smirk on her face, “I had a meeting with my boss today – they come in once a month to see how things are going. They’re not going so well.” She moves over to one of the chairs and sits down, “Do you mind if I’m open with you Jessie?”

Jessie unconsciously changes to a less casual stance. “I don’t know Kate, can you? It might just be me, but I don’t really get the feeling that I can trust you.”
Kate raises an eyebrow and smiles again. “Why? Is it the truck stop? Or something else?” Jessie tenses measurably and Kate laughs. “Oh Jessie, don’t be so sensitive. I found someone else who was interested in the truck stop, and between you and me, you lost out on a great opportunity.”

Kate opens a package of cigarettes and looks at Jessie who passes her an ashtray from a stack on the table by the wall. She lights the cigarette purposefully, slowly shakes out the match, inhales deeply. “You see, Jessie, there isn’t much money to be made serving students each day – I had hoped to be able to take over the club kitchen myself, before you came along.” She waves her hand before Jessie can speak. “So, I have my costs to cover which is fine, but I’d like to make a profit, a real profit, something that would make my boss take notice and get me the hell out of here and onto better things.” She exhales smoke out across the table in Jessie’s direction. “I told you, life is short and now, as turning a good profit isn’t easily going to happen with student meal plans, I have nowhere to expand and you, Dearest, are a bit of a thorn in my side. If, as I said, I can talk honestly and openly with you?” She smiles again and gets up, walks over to Jessie, and crosses her arms in front of her.

"Jessie – there are a lot of ways I can help you, and in return you could help me." Jessie stands straighter and backs up a fraction of a step. "Dearest, don't think of this as an assault – think of it as a great business opportunity." She walks back to the table, stubs out her cigarette and turns back to Jessie. "Can you do that for me Jessie? Can we talk about some of the opportunities there are for us here? We could be great together!" Jessie looks at her, between desire and disdain, silent for some time. "Ok. Sure Kate. Why not? Let's get together and talk."

Kate smiles deeply and turns to walk away. "Thank you, Jessie. I'd very much like to work together. I'd like to get out of this cafeteria, and you'd like to get in deeper. You're the only caterer in town who's allowed on campus. I can help you take full advantage of that."

Kate walks the length of the dining room and turns back to face Jessie. "Have a nice afternoon Jessie. Don't forget to take the cremes out of the oven." Then she is gone. Jessie rushes into the kitchen, opens the oven doors and removes the Crème brûlée which are overcooked and completely ruined. "Fuck! Kate, you bitch…" The sound of Kate's high heels against the wood of the stairs as she descends to the first-floor echoes back and then it is gone.

Jessie's house, that evening

After dinner at the club, an easy service, I grab a taxi to the restaurant and an hour later Judith drops me off at my new place. The moving container is sitting in the driveway waiting for me - the half dozen small boxes of my 'must haves' awaiting me in the kitchen where I left them on my way to the restaurant this afternoon. Groceries, toiletries, a change of clothes - should be enough until I get around to unpacking.
"You okay Jessie? You've been odd tonight." She turns off the ignition and turns to me.
I want to tell her about Kate, but I don't. All I've been thinking about since this afternoon is Kate. "I think something's going on between Barb and David from the Strand, my car is dead, I wonder how Alex is doing, when Sammy might next strike - and I'm also wondering how the taxes from the last three years didn't go through. Other than that, everything's fine."

I wind down the window and light a cigarette, blowing the smoke outside.
"Barb and David?! Are you serious?" Judith grabs onto my arm, positively animated.
"I don't know – it's some feeling I have. I saw them at the market – then she was all flustered when I came up after he left. I don't know …"
"You want some wine?" Judith holds up a bottle from the restaurant – Jacobs Creek 1997 Sauvignon Blanc - with condensation still dripping down its sides.
"I think I need something stronger. Let's take a rain check okay?" I lean over and kiss her cheek. "Gut. Then I will drink this myself – I need to develop this

Barb scenario further." She turns the key in the ignition and her car springs easily into life.
"Sure, thanks for the ride – just don't let on I said anything okay?" I get out and shut the door. She waves and drives away.

I open the back door, toss my keys onto the counter, open the freezer, and take out the half empty bottle of Smirnoff and a glass. What a night. What happened to dining room etiquette? Why are people so insistent on putting out their cigarettes on their dessert plates? When did we forget about cutlery placement during meals? If you put your cutlery together it means you are finished. If you place them in a V shape on the plate it means you are still eating. If you don't have any cutlery at the end of your meal you are probably eating at McDonalds. Simple. As a child I understood cutlery placement. People have forgotten and it causes my blood pressure to rise just seeing a plate with cutlery together in front of a guest; I go to remove it and am immediately spat upon with a curt ′I′m not *finished* yet!′ Well, how the hell am I supposed to know that? My job is to hover silently, invisibly attend to you 'en table' - not pop up with a boisterous *"A′rai Chuck? Hat enuff denn?! Good an yer!"* My God, I need cues! Thank Christ I only have to come out from the kitchen at will.

I grab my mobile phone from the counter and switch it on. I have twelve missed calls - ten from my mother, one from Marta and one from Kate. I dial my mother's number assuming she'll still be up as her last call was three minutes ago. She answers easily on the first ring.
"Hi Mum! How are you doing?"

“Fine, why didn’t you answer your phone? When are you coming out to see me?” She always starts the conversations with these lines, and of course she has every right too.
“Sorry. I was moving today, and I forgot to take my phone with me when I went to the restaurant. How are you?”
Silence. “I’ll be out soon Mum. I must get the restaurant and the club straightened away and then I’ll come out for a few days. We were just out there. (relatively – we were out three months ago) You have Lea and Rachel there for you if you need anything. You’ll be fine.”

My younger brothers and their wives both still live within spitting distance from our mother. My younger sister and myself, on the other hand, fled as soon as we were old enough for a credit card. We natter on for about ten minutes before she wants to go lay down.
“How’s Alex? Is she coming out with you again?”
“Alex moved to New York – I don’t think she’ll be able to get away.” I truthfully lie.
“Just come out okay? And give my grandson a big hug for me when you next see him.”
“Alright Mum, take care of yourself okay? You’re going to be just fine, give me one of the girls please. I'll be out there very soon. Love you.”
Rachel comes onto the phone and I can hear the murmur of conversation between her and my mother in the background. “Hi Jessie.”
“Hi Rachel, how’s everything?”
“Up and down. Today she’s having a good day.”

"Anything I can do?" I ask hopefully. "She just wants everyone around her now. When are you and Angie coming out?" She asks accusingly.
"I know, we should get out more and for longer – but it's difficult. We don't feel good about it, just so you know."
There is a short pause before she answers, "Jessie, it's not for anyone else but her. It won't cure her, but she'll feel better. Please try."
"I will. Give everyone my love." And with that we say goodbye.

Ever wondered how long you would have to stay on the telephone while your Mum blabbered on about people you don't know and recipes for dishes you don't like? Well anytime you wonder about this don't. Just be happy that she's calling. My Mum used to do this all the time too and it really got on my tits, but as time goes by... well, especially now, you can't feel anything bad about her.

I begin to dial Kate's number as my phone rings. "Hi Jessie. How was dinner?"
I laugh, "HI Kate. I managed to remake the cremes you ruined if that's what you mean."
"You should concentrate less on my legs. Listen, I'm finished here – what about a drink?"
"A drink? Sure, umm, you want to come over to the restaurant?"
"I have a better idea – why don't I come by for you in ten minutes? Can I meet you at the club?" "I'm already home. Why don't I meet you downtown?"
"Okay. You know Moo's, by the river? 10 minutes?"
"Sure." I answer, but she's already hung up.

Moo's Bar, later that evening

Jessie calls a taxi and ten minutes later is standing in front of the restaurant as Kate arrives in her red BMW convertible. Moo's is a chic little patio bar by the river Jessie doesn't often frequent but where Kate and Geneviève often have drinks together. They get a table right by the water as another couple leave, and sink into the deep, soft chairs next to each other. Kate motions to a waitress, orders a Granville Island lager and turns to Jessie.

"Same for me. Are you hungry Kate?" She shakes her head while Jessie looks over the Appies they have on offer. "No, I'm fine then, just the drink." The waitress leaves, and Jessie leans back looking at Kate. Jessie points to her car. "What do you drive your kids around in? You can't get many kids in that."

She laughs, "We have a minivan as well, my partner drives it."

"Aha. So, what's up?"

Kate smiles, then laughs again. She wonders if she's laughing too much to cover her nervousness. Except for plotting the downfall of her competitor, propositioning them, and cheating on her partner, what does she have to be nervous about? "Wow, you're just all business Jessie."

"Sorry, but I'm not much for chitchat tonight. I've still got a lot of work to do."

Their beers arrive and they knock their bottles together. Kate takes a long sip. "You don't like me very much, do you Jessie? Why is that?"

Jessie drinks half of bottle then looks at Kate "… I guess it's your reputation. There's something about you I find scary. In fact, some of my wait staff at the club even call you 'the scary lady' …"
"Hahaha! I'm just very no-nonsense Jessie." She takes another sip of her beer and stares at Jessie. "As I said, maybe it's not me, but something else which has you scared."

Jessie looks at Kate. "Why do you think that?"
Kate laughs, "Okay, I'll cut to the chase Jessie. I'd like to use the University Club for some of my functions. I'd pay you a percentage if you rent me the space. That's the first thing. The second thing," Kate counts on her fingers, "is I've got a lot of new equipment and supplies coming. I don't have room to store it all. I'd like to store them with you in the club basement. Of course, again, I'd pay you."
"Aha. Okay, well, I'd need to check this with the club but … sure, why not."

Kate leans across the table closer to Jessie and softens her voice, "Jessie, you know, I think you'd like me a lot more if we just ..."
Jessie's hand stops as Kate's fingers reach out. "… *fucked* … see … I know you want me … and I'd like you … so …" They look at each other, Jessie speechless except for a croaked "Yeh." Kate smiles and leans back in her chair.
Jessie looks frantically about. "Kate, you're married – you have kids – you're … yes … yes I've thought about ..." Jessie tries to look at Kate but cannot.
Kate leans forward and takes Jessie's chin in her hands. "Shut up Jessie." Kate pulls Jessie to her as she

leans further over the table, brushes her tongue slowly and gently over Jessie's lips, and leans back. "Mmmm - that wasn't so hard was it? Let's stop playing games."

Kate smiles, releases Jessie, finishes her drink and stands up. "You said you had work to do." She fishes out her car keys and drops a twenty-dollar bill on the table for the drinks. "Let's go." As they walk to the parking lot Kate dangles the bait again. "You can dwell on how much you want me a few more days. It'll be better … but I have to warn you Darling - I'm *very* pleasure oriented." She looks back and smiles at Jessie who is standing still at the edge of the parking lot. "Christ." Jessie blushes and laughs and walks quickly to catch up. "Thanks for the drink Kate …"

Kate takes Jessie's arm in her hand and pulls Jessie quickly and firmly to her. Their mouths meet forcibly, and suddenly all the desire of the last weeks bubbles up and it becomes awfully hard for Jessie to breathe. Kate can feel Jessie's passion and holds onto the kiss for as long as she can. They break apart after some minutes and Jessie gasps.
Kate smiles, laughs, "You've been thinking about this for some time, haven't you?"
Jessie is breathing hard. "I want you ..."
"I want you too Dearest. Think about what we talked about earlier. I'm going to help you, you're going to help me, we're going to be *really* good together Jessie." Kate puts her fingers to Jessie's lips, then removes her hand, gets into her car, and starts it. "Think about me tonight." She puts the car into gear, honks, and drives away.

Kate smiles contentedly - that went over much easier than she had imagined. She did not have an alternative plan should Jessie have spurned her advances - however she knows better than to leave Jessie dangling for long - just long enough. A few weeks. 'I'll order the hardware tomorrow and see what workshops I can pass along to Jessie. Nothing too big. Just enough to bait the trap.' she thinks to herself. She drives onto the on-ramp of the highway and quickly picks up speed.

The wind in her hair is a welcome relief from the thick, hot evening. She coasts along at high speed with her left hand gripped loosely on the steering wheel. Kate brings her right hand across from the stick shift and squeezes it tightly between her thighs. The moment with Jessie has excited her but she is thinking not of Jessie, but of Fiorella. Kate is thinking specifically about a night last month when the two families vacationed together in the north of France. Their partners had taken the children, drawn by the amusements of a Fair in the neighbouring town, while she and Fiorella had remained at the house they were sharing and consumed a serious amount of local red wine. Kate thinks of Fiorella's abruptness and her forcefulness, her outer coolness of character - traits which irked her early in their friendship but which she has come to appreciate.

Kate sighs, and looks into her rear-view mirror before signaling. "Ti desidera." she murmurs out loud. Kate replaces her hand on the stick, gears down, and takes the next off-ramp. She turns beneath the highway and returns quickly back in the direction in which she came. Before Kate reaches home her phone rings. Kate looks at the display and smiles – Fiorella. She lifts the phone to her ear, “Ciao Bella! Che c'è di nuovo?”

***

Marlies, September 12

You leave the house at 5 in the morning, so you won't hit any traffic jams on the way back through Italy, but you needn't have bothered because you hit them anyway. A long hot cruel 40-kilometer traffic jam just before Bologna because some semi has decided to kick it and rests now in a ditch at the side of the road. A truck stop. A rest stop. The truck was tired and just decided to heave it over to the side but tripped. So now you all must have a look and the line crawls slowly but resolutely towards the big city. This is Bologna. It certainly is ... You go for the holy water fount as soon as you enter the darkness of the cathedral. People, they dip their fingers in like they'll burn themselves. Who are these Vampires anyway? It's not perfume for God's sake. You'd think they're anointing themselves with myrrh the way they graze the end of their finger along the surface.

You are much more generous, much more confident of your status with Him, you practically have your whole hand in the font and generously splash yourself with repentance. For some reason there are a few coins lying there at the bottom of the fount. Can you still buy plenary indulgences? Is it so casual now? "Bob, grabbing a few indulgences for Beatrice and me, can I get you one? Betty? Indulgences? Well I'll toss in a couple of bucks anyway..." The cathedral is the place to go if you want to pay 8 bucks for gelati or 15 for a slice of chocolate cheesecake with cream. You can pay 18 dollars, but this is served with silver cutlery and a cloth napkin. This is in the restaurant. At the edge of the cathedral.

There is something about the prices at the foot of God. God has high overhead. High property prices. There is something about the ticket prices near the stage that defy imagination. What price the wages of sin? You know, in comparison, it's a damn fire sale, the price of sin. They're damn near giving it away. Ever check out the price of a muffin near the train stations of this world? Near the all-night electronic stores and cheap watch and postcard boutiques, the sex stores, and streets full of stagnant water even during the summer? Near all that sin? This is dirty, messy, complicated. It is bedlam. A muffin will cost you but a dollar from a McDonalds or a Burger King there and the foot of God, even though he is omnipresent, seems far out of sight. You don't even know which way to look. Sin is far cheaper, far more accessible, without hassle and without pride. You don't feel so nervous or cheated when you sit in the cheap seats, when you're sinning at a chocolate vending machine. You know you are paying for what you get. You can't sin this way at home. It's too streamlined, too global, too packaged. But you always feel you could have done better somehow.

In the front rows, at the dessert palaces of the righteous you always marvel at the buying power of the cake, the ice cream, the silly portion of whipped cream or the poorly turned out latte. Shit, you think, I could have done this tart for a dollar and still had it looking edible. And this latte? Hell, the kids could do that up better and the milk would have still been warm. For this mousse au chocolat, you could have bought a day's groceries at home you know?

You think you've been cheated somehow. Like after working this hard, paying so much and giving up other pleasures you would have been rewarded with a desert that brings tears to your eyes; a cake that you wouldn't want to eat because it radiated perfection and joy. But you are mostly disappointed. And feel somehow guilty. The wages of sin? Forget the wages of sin; the wages of piety are taxed to the teeth. You get to sit in the front row but damn it's expensive...

It's a beautiful Sunday morning. Barb and I are sitting outside in the restaurant's garden preparing ourselves mentally for the onslaught of brunch.[8] Barb is arranged with her head leant back to catch the morning sun and her hands folded sedately in her lap. I look up at her from the travel section of the Sunday paper and reach for my coffee – double espresso and a pitcher of warm milk - drink, and then take another doughnut. "You should read this article. Powerful stuff. Katrin Lawson. I read her blog - she uses words like blunt instruments." I stammer out between mouthfuls, fold up the paper and toss it on the table.
Barb stirs. "Isn't she in Food & Wine this month?"
"Yep." I pick up the cup Barb has before her, grimace at the aroma of cinnamon apple chai, and put it back. "Christ ... how can you drink this stuff?"
Without opening her eyes, she replies, "How can you eat three maple glazed doughnuts?" I lick my fingers, "Ummm, because they taste great? While, your tea smells like furniture polish?" Barb sits up and looks at me with a smirk on her face. "I needn't remind you that doughnut glaze actually consists of ingredients found in furniture polish, okay? Because this you already know right?" 15-love Barb.

"Hi! Can I get a soup here?" We both look up. From the brightness of the garden I can just make out, through the patio doors, the student from the bus ride – the chip incident – I had almost forgotten. She is walking through the restaurant looking at things, lifting things up, raising herself up to look at things on higher shelves, moving things, peeking, and poking as she glides across the floor like a dancer. She moves with a proud elegance, and, without her gum chewing bangle draped expression of youth she could be beautiful.
Barb begins to get up, "I'm sorry but we're …" just as Meredith, our brunch hostess, comes in from the front, "Hey Jessie? The young lady said she knew you?"
I get up and raise my hand, "No problem. Yes, this is … Lidia? Lidia! Yes, Barb and Meredith, this is Lidia."
Barb gets up and shakes her hand, "Hi, I'm Barb.", while Meredith retreats to the dining room raising her eyebrow at me.
"Hi." She drops her bag from her shoulder and smiles. "You said you would make me a soup." She comes up to us and explains to Barb, "See I was told I should come here because the food is so good and so here I am." She's looking around, holding her arms crossed in front of her. "Is it okay? Are you open? I don't have to dress special, do I?"
Barb looks at her over her glasses and then to me and smiles. "Soup?" I smile sheepishly as Barb begins clearing up the papers and coffee cups.
"Lidia is a student; from Latvia." I pipe up.
Barb raises an eyebrow. "Why don't I go into the back and see what sort of soup we have from dinner. Do you like chicken, or pumpkin?"

“Cheeecken? I looove chicken soup! I don’t know pumpkin soup.”

Barb smiles and walks to the back. “I didn’t think students got up this early.” I motion her to a chair. She sits down and looks around the garden, fumbling through her bag, producing cigarettes and a lighter. I go over to the sideboard near the garden doors and bring back an ashtray.
“We don’t. I haven’t been to bed yet. Can I smoke here?” I nod. She lights the cigarette, offers me one.
I shake my head. “Thanks, but never before lunch.”
“This is a great place, much better than the places on campus.”
“Actually, we have a place on campus as well, in the University Club; but we’re currently only open for special events.”
She exhales a long stream of smoke through her half open lips and turns to the ashtray. “Really? I think I know where the club is. Never been there though.”
“You should, if you get the chance.” She nods. “I used to live on campus. Barb and I both went to the university and were resident associates.”
“Really?! Which house?”
“Spoke Maitland. For two years. We were roomies.”
“I live in Mercer Hall.” She draws on her cigarette, lets out a cloud of smoke, and stubs it out. “Did you like it?”
“Not especially.” Barb appears carrying a large bowl of soup and a basket of warm rolls on a tray, places them on the table with a spoon and napkin, and smiles at me on her way back to the kitchen. “Thanks Barb.” I get up and ask, “Lidia, would you like some wine, or something to drink?”

"Wine?! Sure – thanks. So how come you have a restaurant? Didn't you finish your degree?"
I go behind the bar, take out an open bottle of wine – an Okanagan sauvignon blanc - and return with two glasses.
"We both did, but there aren't many real jobs for humanities majors so we both went to chef's school. We usually don't serve wine before lunch," I say as I pour some of the cold, golden liquid into each glass and recork the bottle, "but I'll make an exception."
She's eating the soup with a passion. "That's okay, I usually don't drink wine before lunch either. It goes right to my head and I get drunk after half a glass. This is great soup! Do you use real chickens?"
"Of course, we use real chickens." I laugh, take one of the rolls and dip it into the soup. "Do you mind?" She shakes her head and continues eating as I taste the soup-soaked bread. The soup is quite good. I must remember to find out which of our growing brigade made it. The music has just been turned on in the dining room, and the speakers in the garden come to life to the strains of Tom Waits.

I'm leaning against the wall watching her eat. "It's not true, what you said about your ass." She looks up from her soup and stares at me. "You mentioned that you hated your ass – that night – on the bus. I was watching you as you came in. You move like a dancer. If you don't mind my saying so." I contemplate her as she laughs in disbelief.
"Agh! My ass is horrible. Let's not talk about it. And I was a dancer, yes. You are trained as a dancer to walk as though you had a broom up your ass." She laughs deeply displaying her teeth, raising fine black

eyebrows, her eyes lighting up as if flicked on by a switch.

I'm going straight to the top, straight to where the air is fresh and clean ... If you know me, you know what I mean ... I can't let Mr. Sorrow pull me down … She laughs and continues eating, dropping her napkin onto the floor … "sorry, sorry, please, disregard me …" she leans over and picks it up "… were you always happy being a waiter …?"
"Sorry? … A chef you mean?"
"But you like serving people." I nod in agreement as she eats more of the soup and points to one of the photos, of two young girls exchanging a delicate kiss, which hang just inside the entrance to the garden. "That picture, what would you say is the punctum?" I look over and shake my head. "The pelvic bone of the brunette --- there is the suggestion of her pubic bone also but the kiss ... if the kiss weren't the subject but, well …"

I'm gonna take you New York. ... I'm drinking Manhattans … She places the spoon in the now empty soup bowl. "Give me your hand ..." she takes my hand and traces the furrows of the skin with her long, narrow fingers … "You will die shortly after you are 70 in an accident … hmm ... perhaps there will be some lingering, but I think not much." She looks at me for a long moment. "Thank you, but I have to go." She gets up, deposits the bowl on the sideboard, picks up her bag, plucks her chewing gum from where it has dried onto the top of the table where she placed it and pops it back into her mouth. Then she spins gently through the dining room, waving to me as she goes. I get up and follow her out the door, leaning against the window and watching her go.

"Don't go there."
"Huh?" I turn around to find Barb at my shoulder following my gaze. "She's ... what, nineteen? … Just don't go there."
I turn to her, "Hmm?" Lidia disappears around the corner of the street as I exhale and return the cigarette I plucked from Meredith's fingers. Then, I notice the first guests standing in front of our door peering at us.
"She's amazing. Alas I prefer older, and plumper, specimens." There is a long pause. "Great soup by the way." I return the cigarette to Meredith, clap my hands, turn, and follow Barb into the kitchen.

Farrell's Ice Cream Parlour, September 13

Nicki, Marta, Anna, and I are sitting at the kid's favourite ice cream parlour - Farrell's – the late summer sunshine reflecting off our sunglasses. We sit on the crowded patio with perhaps twenty others, similarly accessorized, so we look like a gaggle of celebrities at St. Moritz. Nicki and Anna are digging into their banana splits while Marta and I split a hot fudge brownie parfait. I put down my spoon and look at Nicki. "So where did your Mum go this time Nicki?"

Marta appeared in the restaurant after lunch with Nicki and Anna in tow. Angie had come by her place after not being able to reach me – well, I was working the middle of a lunch rush, wasn't I? Nicki is spearing the last of the banana as Anna attempts to lick up the last of the chocolate sauce. "I don't know."

"You don't know? Did she say?" I signal to the waiter for the check. I look at him then at Marta, who is wiping her mouth with a napkin.

"Your sister is on her way to … Chicago … for a meeting."

Incredible. "I love Chicago. Why didn't she take me? I could have carried her laptop." Nicki laughs and Anna opens her mouth to laugh loudly, sticking her tongue out at him.

"Jessie, how is your mother? Nicki tells me she is not well."

"Hmmm. No, she isn't. I have to get out and see her soon." I pay the check and we get up. The metal chairs squeak across the wood of the patio as we push them back.

"If Angie is not here, I can look after Nicki. But perhaps you should take him with you." Marta looks at me.
"Yes, he should probably come – but Angie will have to organise that. I don't know – you're always asking me the most difficult questions Marta."
"That is because you never voluntarily want to talk about these things. You are silent, and I would like you to talk about them. Alex, your Mum, work – anything - you can talk with me."
"I know. Thank you -." I squeeze her hand as the kids scramble past us towards the street corner on our way through the park to the car. I eventually managed to get the car towed to the garage, fixed, and back on the road. I'm sure the mechanic felt sorry for me as I stood there nervously waiting like a girl for the results of a pregnancy test. He tweaked and fiddled and ordered a few new parts in, met with his partners - their backs to me in consultation with many a furtive backward glance, and then slapped me with a bill I could almost afford if I didn't buy gas for the next five months. He gave the car ten thousand miles or twelve months – whichever came first.

As we reach the other side of the street, we meet Rodd, sporting his heavy faggot goatee and standing in front of a Pizza Stop waiting for his order. Rodd and I know each other from way back when I started cooking and he was bartending at the student bar. In addition to his band, he's still at the university where he intelligently took a position after graduation as some sort of IT officer and is now sitting on a salary grade 18 job for life. What a bastard eh? Like few others will he call me at three in the morning wondering what I'm doing while describing in detail the bag of Cheezies he´s eating.

“Don’t you say a thing about Alex, Nicki please.” I instruct him. I look to Marta who raises her hands in a defensive gesture.
“Jes-say! And little Nick, heeeey!” Rodd bounds over to us with a slice in his hand. “Little Buddy, how ya doing!? What’s up?” Nicki and Rodd are in the middle of performing some sort of elaborate tribal handshake. He sees Marta and Anna and bows slightly, smiles, and offers his hand. “Hel-lo.”
“Rodd, this is Marta and Anna. This is my friend Rodd,” I introduce them.
“Rodd, Hi.” Marta turns to me – “Jessie, I must go the other way, I have to get some things for Anna’s school project. We will see you later? You are bringing Nicki to my place for the evening?” I nod and thank her; we kiss each other on the cheeks as Rodd looks on.
“Sweet … Erm, where’s Alex?” he asks appreciatively following Marta with his eyes as she walks away - “Who’s that?”
“She’s my neighbour Rodd. Alex is in New York. Remember she was going to New York? That’s where she is. New York. Why do you ask?”
He raises his eyebrow and exchanges a shrug of the shoulders with Nicki, “Okay, I believe you – look, there’s this great band I know playing at the student bar this week. The drummer coats himself in cooking oil and the lead singer tosses individually wrapped Kraft singles into the crowd between songs!”
I light a cigarette. “We’ll have to check that out. When are you coming by the restaurant? – you really should let me feed you properly.”

Rodd has a meatball pizza slice in his hand from which Nicki is taking a huge bite. "Man, I have been meaning to come by. I want to bring Tara for dinner, you know?"
"Anytime. You have carte blanche. Bring her and let me spoil you two." I take Nicki in tow before he devours the complete slice. "I think after the ice cream, pizza is a bad idea, Sport." Rodd bows as we retreat. "You're good people!"

We walk to the car as Nicki pipes up "Rodd is so cool."
"Yes, and if you eat your vegetables, do all your homework and get at least B`s in math you too can be so cool."
"Rodd told me that Einstein got a D in math and ate meatball subs for dinner!"
"Yeah, well Einstein didn't have any kids – so we don't know if that was genetically a good thing or not, do we?"
"Jessie, do you need some more cigarettes? I could get you some here, look, in the machine … wait, these aren't cigarettes … what are they?'"
Oh great. "They're condoms."
"What are condoms?"
"They're a sort of rubber material that goes over a penis, when you have sex to help prevent a woman becoming pregnant or either of you getting a sexual disease; but let's not get into that right now."
Nicki's doubled over, hysterically laughing. "Oh Weird! Hahahaha! Why do they sell them on the street?"
"Sometimes you need one in a hurry and you haven't any at home. It happens."

"Do they have different sizes? Here it says XXL."
"I guess they do, but most men use a normal size condom." They probably only sell them in XXL boxes for men's egos come to think of it. Nicki takes a thoughtful pause.

"Does my Mum use condoms?"
"Well, obviously not always, otherwise you wouldn't be here." Nicki is again silent for a few seconds.
"Jessie, what do you find hot in a girl?"
"Whoa, I don't know – hard to say exactly – where's all this coming from? It's relative – I mean, I like different things in different people. Tough question. Alex is smart, and funny. Lori was gorgeous – in a standard sort of way – she was a head turner. Though I've been with some who you wouldn't notice on the street, but I've found beautiful for other reasons. Though that's all just physical." I light a cigarette and lean against the car, Nicki kicking the tires and looking up at me. "I guess the most important thing for me is their laugh, and their smile. Mouths. I like big mouths – big teeth. Big feet. Big in general … I guess that's what I find hot."
Nicki is almost wetting himself. "Hahahahaha! You like big feet? Big teeth?! Oh, you are so weird Jessie!"
"Yeah, yeah, that's me, Weird Jessie …"
"I saw a picture of you and Lori at Mum's. How old were you when you were with her?"
"Oh … it was about ten years ago I guess. Why?"
"Yeah, then I guess when you were younger you had better taste."
"Huh?" I flick my cigarette away and look at him.

"Well when you're young you know what's pretty and when you get older your taste obviously goes down the toilet. Hahahaha!"

"Thanks Nick." I clip him about the ear as he moves away laughing. "Tell me again about the girl in your class you like so much? Jordan is it? What do you find so pretty in her?"

"Oh, she's the most beautiful girl in the whole school! Her hair is blonde on one side and then brown on the other. I can't concentrate when I see her."

"You're failing math because you have a crush on a twelve-year-old girl who dyes her hair two different colours? I think we should talk about the direction your taste is headed before you trash mine okay?"

Marlies, later that afternoon

I drop Nicki off at the house and then head back to the restaurant after making him promise to get his homework done before any Play Station when he goes over to Marta's. I get to the restaurant, make myself a coffee – double espresso with milk warmed not steamed and two sugars – and go into the office. The first thing I do is send Alex an email. Her number is still out of service and I don't have a new one; I guess I could track her down at the magazine's office but – an email is easier. 'Alex – I hope you're well in the big city. I'm sorry – let's talk.' I look at the screen for a while, delete everything except for 'I'm sorry' click send, then write an email to Angie. 'Please call or email me. I need to go see my Mum. Would you also come?'

I see there's an email from Kate as well – 'Jessie, let's have drinks tomorrow. Interesting ideas coming into my head.' I look at that for some time – 'interesting ideas'? A bit kinky perhaps but okay – I answer her 'Looking forward to it. Give me a call. Could use some help transporting fifty kilo chocolate sculpture to hotel week after next. Do you have larger van than us?' I send this and smile, wondering how that will sit with her. I shut down the email program and tweet about the chocolate festival. Then I call my Mum, whose number is busy. There is a gentle 'ping' from the computer, and I look up to see my mail to Alex has been returned 'mailbox full'. Louder than normal voices come from the kitchen, so I jump up and walk to the dish pit where Judith and Sammy are having a small, but loud, discussion.

"Hey hey – what's up you two?" Sammy glares at me, throws down the apron he has bundled in his hand and puts his hands on his hips. "What are you doing here anyway? It's Monday."
"I came in to check the schedule because I saw Judith in the window. She's changed the schedule and I've already made plans – now she expects me to change them – I can't."
I look at Judith and raise my eyebrow. "It's fine Jessie – I'll work it out."
"OK," I raise my hands and go into the walk-in cooler to collect some ingredients. Through the door, still open a crack, I can hear them.
"Why have you changed the schedule? Now we don't have any of the shifts together that we had. I'd like to be working with you; what is wrong Judith?"
"Sammy, we always work together – now I'm giving Alissa the chance to work some shifts with me. I don't see what the problem is. We'll work out your holiday arrangements, don't worry about it."

"You don't like me anymore. For some reason you were very friendly and now suddenly you are not."
"Sammy, you're being silly. Of course, I like you. I think you're being a little over dramatic." There is a long moment of silence and then the sound of footsteps and the backdoor opening. I take the containers of salad and fruit from the shelf and walk into the kitchen, kicking the walk-in door closed behind me. Judith is standing there adjusting the schedule hanging on the wall near the office. "Everything okay?" she looks back at me and nods, then turns back to the schedule. Was her lipstick smeared?

"Judith, I don't want to tell you your job – they're your crew – but in the end Barb and I pay their salaries. So, if there's a problem with Sammy let's distance ourselves from it sooner than later. Okay?"
"Ok Jessie. Ja - I'll take care of it."
"So, what are you doing here anyway?"
"I could ask you the same question."
"Trying out some new recipes, and you?"
"I wanted to hang this month's pictures in the dining room and was... restless I guess."
"Oh." I reply. "You like a glass of wine?"
"Sure, I'll grab something and bring it in."
"Okay." She goes out into the dining room. I watch her go, and then open the boxes, remove spinach, romaine lettuce, and young beet leaves, and begin washing them all gently in the cold water which slowly fills the sink.

Judith and I are still in the restaurant many hours later - working through the previous week's receipts and enjoying another bottle of wine – Henry of Pelham Chardonnay. Judith hums with a pencil in her teeth as she types in numbers on the keyboard of the laptop. I light a cigarette and toss the lighter on top of the stack of papers in front of us looking at her. "How did it go with Sammy?"
She takes the pencil out of her mouth. "Fine. I've given him the week off and asked him to come back in a better mood."
"Has anyone lately told you how sexy you are?"
She looks at me laughing. "Not today, no Jess. Are you drunk?"
"No, I am not drunk. I am 'sufficiently suffoncified' … hahaha …. no, you are, not like mainstream sexy but in

a very individual way. It's your brains, I think. You're so damn smart, witty, I don't know, it makes you sexy."
"Wow, what a compliment. My body and my face escape your notice but my brain? How do you fantasize about a brain? This charm of yours, does it work on Alex as well or do you save this up for me special?" She takes a long draw on her beer and looks at me.
"Oh, sorry – I forgot about you guys." I smile at her and pour myself another drink.
"Don't worry about it. I should call her again …" I am silent. Pensive. "I like intelligence in a woman – intelligence and practical skills - they're sexy, Judith." I finish my wine. "You know about reincarnation and everything?" Judith groans loudly, rolls her eyes and shakes her head, putting down her glass and taking a cigarette from my pack. "How far along do you consider a Front of House Manager to be in the Big Picture?" I'm rifling through her paperwork hoping to find something interesting.
"You are drunk. Should I drive you home?"
I shake my head. "No, this is a real question, I'm not drunk, really. I'm interested." I take a spoonful of the chocolate mousse in front of me and sit back, watching her.

"Front of House Manager *is* the Nirvana my soul has sought after my successive rebirths all these centuries." She puts the cigarette to her lips and lights it. "It is the Seat of Perfection…" she blows out a long cloud of smoke, "… And if you're looking for the credit card slips you forged and included in the till they've already been disposed of. You owe me $235 but I'll take $200 and call it even. Or is this why you're chatting me up?"

"What? No *NO*, Will you take a cheque?"
"A cheque?" she laughs, "A moment ago you were telling me how intelligent I was. You know at this rate you'll never attain Nirvana."
"I'd settle for attaining my pension qualification actually ...." A message lights up my mobile – from Marta– 'Kids have eaten, Nicki is ok. Come over soon?'
"Marta's really nice." Judith is looking at me.
"Yes, yes, she's brilliant," I counter, folding my mobile closed and replacing it on the table. "Jessie, it's okay that you like her – she's wonderful, and you're such good friends – you are adults," she stubs out her cigarette. "There's nothing wrong with any of the feelings you have for her, or that she might have for you."
I smile weakly at her and kiss her on the cheek, "Okay, and you keep Sammy in line – I don't want any problems okay?" Judith looks up at me and smiles, crooking her little finger at me. "Men, young men, need to be kept on a short leash."
I laugh, "Aha. Just long enough for them to choke themselves if they pull too hard eh?" She laughs, and I pick up the menu plans and my empty glass and walk unsteadily into the kitchen.

Jessie's house, that evening

An hour later I'm at home, Nicki is watching TV, and I'm lying on the sofa reading when … *BLEAHAGGG*!! My book and half empty glass fly from my stomach where they had rested and land with a wet crackle on the floor. And ... I've fallen asleep.
"You okay?" Nicki moves out of the way of the broken glass.
"Yeah, fine, I fell asleep." I look at the clock, swear, fall off the sofa onto the floor, swear again and trudge into the kitchen for a cloth. The phone rings, and my Mum is on the other end. "Mum? What time is it?" I look at the clock – she's three hours ahead – "It's almost midnight Mum – why aren't you asleep?"
"I can't sleep – and I'll have more than enough sleep soon. How are you? Did you talk with Angie about coming out?" her voice sounds very far away, and very small.
"Angie is in … Chicago Mum. Nicki is with me again. I tried to reach her – we'll organise something as soon as she's back. I'm sorry Mum – it's just so busy here with the restaurant and now the club ..." [9]
"Neither of you had a second thought leaving home. Why don't you like it here? Didn't I make it nice for you?"
Oh good. More guilt. "Mum, you made a great home, and you're a great Mum – Angie and I just are not the same as the boys – they'll die right there where they were born – but Angie and I, we can't – we need to move about – I don't know. It's us, not you. Don't think that."

"Jessie, I'm going to die here too – it's a long way from where I was born – but I'm not going anywhere else. I want to see you again… Good night Jessie."
"Mum … I love you. Good night – get some sleep." I hang up the phone, go into the kitchen, and then I start to cry.

Marta's house, September 14

Over breakfast I have a coffee in one hand and a screwdriver in the other as I try to install Marta's new telephone. Her answering machine broke ($50), so she bought an entire new cordless telephone system ($300). First thing in the door and she says she's nervous about whether she might be returning it or not if she didn't like it so I should be very careful whatever I do. I´m only just opening the box and a little bit of the corner starts to tear and the kids point this out and she loses it, like ".... Arg! That's it - now I can't return it because there's a tear in the box."

Well, we are working on setting this thing up, and we´re nearing the end - hanging the cordless stand on the wall. I´m trying to figure out how the clips fit into the stand to stop the phone from falling to the floor - we've already tried seeing if it just suspends itself against the wall by the force of its own will which it did not - and I'm being really careful because I don't want to snap off the little plastic pieces – but it's almost half past eight and we all have to leave. Well, then she's just so casual "Jessie, just push them in, it doesn't matter ..." Oh so now it's ok. A few minutes ago it´s 'be careful and not tear the box and squirm about on the rug like I've spilt wine over the new sofa' but now it's 'Oh just jam those clips on, doesn't matter that they'll break into five pieces and I can't return it …' I just don't get it.

The University Club, later that afternoon

I spin by the club after lunch to drop off some catering brochures I've picked up from the printers before getting Nicki from the lab tour field trip he's on at one of the university's animal labs. "It's where the vegetarians study." He explained to us in the morning. "You mean veterinarians?" I asked him. "Because I don't think you'll find many vegetarians there today." Then I drive him to the rec center where there's a drop-in karate practice he wants to get in on. I use the hour sitting there to plan the menus for the coming week. There's way too much to do - tonight there's a small dinner of the Admission Committee, and we only have another month until the chocolate festival. Nicki karate chops one of the other kids and a scuffle breaks out. Now there are twenty-five little kids karate chopping each other while the sensei tries to get their attention. Ooooh! A very small girl with a ponytail has just karate chopped the sensei in the knee. Ow! Bet that hurt! Oh, now she's down. Annnnd now the kids are all dogpiling onto the poor woman. This is better than television.

"Nicki!" I stand up and wave him over. "Just wait here until this is over big guy."

"*Oohhh whhhyyyy*!? This is so cool!"

"Yeah, well I don't think you want to be the last one standing when your sensei regains consciousness." A few parents, spoilsports the lot, wade in and help restore order as the sensei is led to the first aid room and all the kids are herded into the changing room. I thought karate practice would be boring.

Marta is waiting at the door of the club when we return, and I hand over Nicki to her with a hug.
"You're great for doing this – Angie should be bringing you back the duty free."
"You will make me dinner this week - and we'll be even." She digs through her bag and pulls out a small collection of mail. "Did you not redirect your mail Jessie?" She hands me the envelopes, takes my arm, and kisses me on the cheek. "Have a good night and I will see you later, okay?"
"Thank you, Marta." She and Nicki walk across the concrete beach and I flip through the stack of envelopes and flyers. One is in a telltale buff coloured government envelope, and the other is postmarked New York, in Alex's handwriting with no return address. I tear it open and read the brief text written on the back of a postcard of the city skyline:

Jessie - New York is amazing. I'm glad I came. I would like to be able to say that I miss you – but I still feel really hurt. I feel deceived and ... I need trust. I don't feel I can trust you Jessie. I'm sorry. I hope your Mum's okay. Give her my love please. Alex.

I put the postcard in with the rest of the mail, stuff it into my bag and go into the club. I turn on the lights, the stereo, sit down at the bar and flip open my laptop. There are no emails of any great importance, so I check my stocks – which are still falling – and then … then a new email arrives from … Kate. Could I do her a favour and give a 'first aid in the kitchen' talk to a group of new students? Why me? Doesn't she have tons of staff? Ah … Russian exchange students. Ha! Something I can do that Kate can't – I can speak a little

Russian. Of course, Kate can speak German but ... I see on Katrin's blog that she's speaking at the 'Foodbuzz' bloggers conference … hmm ... oh, in Nice … in France. It would be really nice to go. I haven't been to a major food show in years. I think Marta is from Nice actually … hmmm. I sigh, close the laptop, and stretch, go up the stairs and notice the lights to the kitchen are on. I peer in and see the doors to the dining room are ajar and the lights on there as well. I cross the kitchen and peer into the dining room.

Kate is standing against one of the tables smoking a cigarette and smiling at me. She exhales, removes a piece of tobacco from her lips. "I thought you'd never get here. Hope you don't mind my letting myself in but, well, membership has its privileges." She smiles and presses the cigarette into the ashtray, looking at me as she speaks. "You still thinking about me?"
"Kate, I've got …" She crosses the distance between us quickly. "Off!" she calls, and the dining room lights shut off with a resounding click. Bleary never told me they did that.[10]

Marta's house, that evening

Later that evening I drive to Marta's to pick up Nicki. I park in the driveway, sitting for some time in the car thinking about what just happened. I can't recall a moment of dinner prep. Kate was gone as quickly as she came. I don't remember if I even locked the club. After some minutes, Marta opens the front door and looks out. She comes outside in her pajamas and leans down into the open passenger window. "Jessie, what are you doing outside? Are you okay?" I look at her, still somewhat numb. "Jessie? What is it?"

I come back to myself slowly and look at her, smile, "Nothing. I'm okay. Just something at work got me thinking. How was Nicki?" I get out of the car and follow her into the house.

Once inside she turns and looks at me questioningly. "He's fine. How are you?" She looks at my face, long and hard. "You don't look very well. OK, let's have a drink." She walks down the hallway and into the kitchen, leading me by the hand behind her.

"How was Nicki?" I ask again when we get to the kitchen.

She opens the fridge, removes a cocktail shaker, fills it with ice and makes us a martini – two parts vodka, one-part vermouth – and hands me one. "He was fine. He's a good kid."

"To friendship between nations." I toast. Marta laughs. We knock our glasses against each other and drink. "But I really think Nicki needs a mother who is around him more often."

"Mmm," I nod my head in agreement, downing my drink in one and refilling my glass from the frosted metal container on the counter. "It's a problem." I down a second martini empty quickly and put my glass back on the counter. "I need to get back home, Marta. Thanks for watching him. You're amazing." I smile at her and run my hand down her forearm as she leans against the counter. I rummage in my pocket for my keys and kiss her cheek goodbye.

"Jessie, you can't drive now, you …" she places her half empty glass on the counter next to mine and takes my arm in hers, and we both say nothing for a small second. I gently run my fingers down her cheek, her throat, and then we pull each other close and kiss, very gently and for an exceptionally long moment.

"I booked three tickets to Nice in December. There's a food show there … you're ... from, Nice right?"
Marta looks at me for a long time with her huge eyes."
"Oui. You booked a trip. For us. To Nice."
"Yes. You, me, and Anna." We kiss again.
"D'accord. We will go." She kisses me and takes my hand.

We move into her small and cluttered bedroom and she swipes the clothes that are laying on her bed onto the floor with her arm, pulls her pajamas over her head and tosses them onto a chair in the corner where they land atop other things while I quickly undress, watching her, and then we fall into the large, overstuffed bed that smells like a field of wildflowers, naked against each other, moving and touching everywhere we have wanted and needed to touch for a very long while.[11] I didn't see this coming, but to tell you the truth I'm really fucking glad it did.

Marta's house, September 15

Marta is still asleep, her small shape twisted in the comforter. Arms and legs and tiny feet and hands against my length and coarseness. I feel like an elephant compared to her. Her lips are the palest of red and she has a warm spicy smell to her. I roll over and look out the window. I blink twice, vision clearing. Damn rain's back again; literally pouring down a wall of rain. Powerful stuff. The last time I ever saw this much rain I was living in the Canadian Rockies. I go into the kitchen, marveling at the sight outside the kitchen window, fill the espresso machine and toss some pumpkin seeds to Anna's hamster, which is pressing itself against the bars of its cage by the window in excitement at the new face in the house.

I reach up for the toaster which sits above the refrigerator, emptying the contents of the crumb tray as it flips open over my head as I lower it down. Great beginning to the day. I drop a bagel into the toaster – sundried tomato - and turn on the espresso machine, looking out the window. Yesterday it hadn't even been damp outside. Barb must have done a Tarot card reading unsupervised again. I go into the bathroom and turn on the shower. What if one of those cards she was reading had come up sideways? We could have woken up under eight feet of water .... I look in the mirror. I wonder if it's okay when your tongue is a sort of orange colour? I feel a hand on my shoulder turn around and look down to face Marta. We fold into each other's arms and kiss. She smiles at me. "I smell coffee and toast? You know your way around my kitchen so well?"

I kiss her cheek and brush away a few strands of her hair and smile. “I’ve cooked in your kitchen before. It’s not a magic trick.”
I hold onto her very tightly and feel all the remaining stress in my stomach and my shoulders disappear.
“I will bring you a coffee, go have a shower, Anna and Nicki will be up soon.” She goes into the kitchen and returns in a few moments with two cups of coffee, shutting the bathroom door behind her. “Jessie,” she looks up at me, “Last night was beautiful – I’ve wanted this for so long – you and I – it was so good … but …” She bites her lip and drinks from a cup, then cringes as she tastes the sugar – “Bleah – this is yours.” I laugh. “Jessie – I don’t want you to feel anything, anything must change – I,” she puts her fingers against my mouth as I begin to speak. “No - no listen to me please Jessie. We are such good friends – this, this last night was magic – but I don’t want either of us to get our expectations up. Do you understand? I don’t … I don’t know where this is going to go. Maybe nowhere – I don’t know.” She pushes herself against me.
“You - … I feel the same. Last night was so … it was … it felt so right and so good. And I want … “she puts her fingers again to my lips and hushes me, shaking her head.
“Mmm … it was good.” She smiles at me and we look a long time into each other's eyes. Then sounds of Anna come from the other end of the hallway, followed by Nicki’s voice from the other side of the door. Oh my God I’d forgotten Nicki was here.
“Get showered, I will stall the children.” Marta opens the door, hustles the kids out of the doorway and orders them to the guest bathroom in the basement - “Allez!

School will not wait for you! There is breakfast still to be eaten …"

Nicki and Anna are eating their breakfast when I walk into the dining room, my hair still damp from the shower. Marta brings me another cup of coffee and a bagel, and then refills the juice glasses of the two dumbstruck children. "Jessie had rather a lot to drink last night and so slept here with us. Lucky for you, Nicki, "she ruffles his hair as he tries to get away, "because now you get a ride to school rather than having to take the bus."
"Is Jessie drunk Mama?" pipes up Anna from behind a box of Cheerios.

I almost choke on my toast, as Nicki starts laughing, and Marta joins in. "No, no of course Jessie isn't drunk. I said that Jessie had had a lot to drink last night, Mama also. Adults do this sometimes when they have a lot on their minds, or are very happy, or, well for a lot of reasons. Eat your cereal. You'll be late for school."

We get the kids ready and I offer to take Anna with me and drop her off on the way. "Did you say thanks to Marta for last night Nicki?" He stops midway out the door and turns to hug her, and then exits for the car. Marta kisses Anna goodbye. "Be a good girl for Jessie and I'll see you after school." Anna runs off to the car where she and Nicki immediately begin a fight over who sits in front.

I turn to Marta, "I …" she puts her fingers to my lips.

“Say nothing. I know what you want to say. I told you, it’s good. I care about you very much Jessie. Don’t think anything more about last night. It was simply the right thing at the right time, n'est ce pas?”

“Yes.” I wait a moment, looking at her, and then I turn to the car, in which Nicki and Anna are now trying to rock back and forth by jumping up and down together on the back seat.

Marlies, that morning

After I drop the kids off at school, I drive over to the restaurant. No one is there yet, which is the way I usually like it – being there first. I go into the office and call my Dad. After the first ring he picks up. "Dad – happy birthday! Happy six five!"

"Jess – Hey, this is a surprise – thanks for calling the old man!" My Dad lives alone, and my parents have been divorced almost as long as I can remember. Dad's a big gardening buff, and a very down to earth sort of guy - He once ripped out the entire covering on the inside of the cab of his truck instead of repairing the tear in the fabric; tied a bootlace to the broken windshield wiper in order to manually work it from inside instead of fixing it; cut a hole in the door panel to gain access to the locking mechanism in order to manually work that when that broke; and once attached vice grips to the knob of the window lever when that came off; you could open the window - but never fast enough to use an automatic parking ticket dispenser.

"How are you Dad? Have you talked to Mum lately?" "She already called me this morning - a great gal – it's too bad how this sickness has gotten her." There is a bit of a pause before my Dad rallies, "You know my pension card came today? And a gift certificate for a free senior's portion liver and mashed potatoes at Denny's." He sounds like a kid after visiting Santa at the mall, "I think I'm going to just love this whole pension thing. How are you doing Jessie – and Nicki? How's Nicki?"

"Fine – all is well. Busy – busy, but everything is good. Nicki's doing great – he's staying with me while Angie is away on business."
"She does that often? Leave him with you while she's away?"
"Angie? No …" I lie.
"Good, good … Well, it was great to hear from you kid – you take care now and give Nicki and Angie a hug for me when you see them.
I put down the phone at the same time I hear the back door close. Strangely enough I didn't hear the grinding screech of its' rusted hinges as it opened though. I peer my head out of the office and see Sammy coming towards me. He stops, sort of nervously nods and says Hi, and continues in the direction of the dining room.
"Hi Sammy." I call out as he passes by. He's here a bit early I wonder. I get up and check the schedule beside the door. He isn't even scheduled to work today. The back door opens again, and Barb fumbles her way through with her bag, red faced and out of breath. I walk the length of the kitchen. "Hey stranger!" I take the bag from her. "Did you jog here?"
She nods - "Almost, yeah." She's a bit out of breath.
"Did Sammy come in here just now?"
"Yeah, he just went into the dining room, why?"
"I called out to him to hold the door, but he just ignored me."
"Weird kid. We should probably get rid of him – this whole thing with Judith is getting way too uncomfortable."
"'The whole Judith thing'?"
I laugh – "Hahaha! That's what Judith said when I told her about you and David - 'The Barb thing.'"
"Me and David?" she looks at me in disbelief –

"What? Like I don't know about you and David?" She puts her hands on her hips and closes her eyes tightly shut. "Okay Jess. You tell me about Alex, what you were doing with Kate last night, the woman with the little girl I see you with pretty regularly, the student who came by the restaurant and – and," she continues pointing a finger at me, " 'the Judith thing' – and I'll tell you about David."
I take a deep breath – "Okay, I think we need a coffee." I slip my arm into hers and we walk into the dining room, pushing through the doors at the same moment that Sammy pushes against them coming the other way. "Oh, Hey! Sorry about that." He grins and smiles.
"Hi, Sammy. You don't work today, what were you doing in the dining room?"
"Oh, I worked last night. I left my wallet in the drawer." He produces a well warn, brown leather wallet. "Sorry, I hope it was okay that I came and got it – I didn't want to bother you."
Barb looks at him, then at me, and continues into the dining room as I hold open the door for her. "Sure Sammy, no problem. Just maybe say something next time?"
He grins again, and raises his hand, "Sure, thanks Jessie. See you tomorrow." Then he walks the length of the kitchen and leaves out the back door.
The smell of coffee fills the dining room as Barb makes us two large lattes – the milk foaming and hiding her behind a wall of steam.
"I don't trust him - we should have searched him." Barb calls over the sound of the steam.
"Hmmm … probably right." I look around the dining room and the bar. "Stereo's still here."

Barb turns off the machine. "Seriously. Let's get rid of him okay? Talk to Judith, Jess."
"I already did. I will again," I raise my hands in defense as Barb glares at me with her lips pressed firmly against each other. She carries the two coffees to the couch in the entrance and sits down. I grab the jar of biscotti – white chocolate chunk with dried cranberries - from atop the bar and join her.
I take a long drink of my latte. "Mmmm – beautiful Barb – thanks!" Barb smiles over the rim of her cup. "Ok – tell me everything."

Thirty minutes later Barb still has her mouth open. When she shuts it, it is long enough for her to blink and then she says, "You slut Jessie!" which she follows with a laugh and a shake of her head. "Umm … what is with you and Kate? How does this sort of thing happen? We hate Kate, remember?"
"It wasn't planned – it was something that had sort of been building up. Look, I'm sorry – my hormones got the better of me – but look at you and David!"
Barb sits up straight and looks at me indignantly. "David isn't married Jessie, and he doesn't have kids."
"Okay, let's forget all that. Let's say I'm a bad person – I didn't throw myself at either Kate or Marta. I really like Marta – and Kate, you forget, grabbed me."
"Jessie don't let this screw with the business okay?"
"Barb, I could say the same. David is as much competition as Kate is."
Barb screws up her eyes. "Okay, Okay, Okay … Let's agree to disagree. Point one. We have to get Sammy out of here. Point two – business first before David OR Kate. Point three – what is point three?"

I shrug my shoulders. "Lunch? We should get ready for lunch?"
Barb is holding onto her third finger. "Possibly – possibly it's lunch. I'm getting hungry. NO!" she grabs her finger shaking her hand at me. "The student – the one with the soup."
"Lidia? I'm not getting involved with a student. I like listening to her. I like her energy. Ok, let's make a pact." I put down my coffee and raise my right hand, taking hold of Barb's and lifting it into the air. "We do solemnly swear- repeat after me – We do solemnly swear, that neither of us will let anyone or anything come between us and making a shit load of money", Barb lets out a laugh, "a shit load of money with this restaurant, and that neither will bad-mouth anyone the other is sleeping with."
She nods and smiles. "I do."

We grab our cups and move into the kitchen. As we head through the door Barb pipes up – "What do we tell Judith anyway?" we put the cups into the dishrack as we pass by.
"She knows about you and David already, but I don't think we need to bother her with Kate okay?" I grin as she looks back at me, shaking her head in disbelief.

Marlies, that afternoon

Lunch is pretty tame – there are twenty-five covers and with the exception of the bald couple from the insurance company down the street who regularly order the roasted veggie focaccia with sweet potato fries and always complain there's not enough salt on them, most everyone else orders our arugula salad with grilled scampi and Cajun catfish topped with sweet dill mustard and Crème fraiche, served with ciabatta and roasted garlic. The garlic is slowly roasted and still warm, so you can spread it over the bread like butter. Delicious. Barb and I alternate catching up on the office work and getting the walk-ins cleaned out after the initial rush – and then share a glass of wine – Italian Primitivo - with Judith when she arrives later that afternoon. We're trying out a new dessert in the evening – white chocolate goat's cheese parfait with mango and papaya salsa – so we're playing around with it a bit after the wine, which has totally ruined our mouths for much more than steak if you must know. We call over Sarah and Dennis from their prep work and Alissa and Teresa from the dining room to have them try the parfait – then we add a bit of red pepper which we've caramelised in honey and everyone is nodding their heads, so we've got a winner for dinner, as they say.

"Did either of you see my wallet when you were here earlier?" Judith asks later that afternoon. "I left it here last night, fairly sure it was in the bar in the drawer. Barb and I look at each other. "Was it sort of brown? Worn?"
"Yeah, that's it – did you find it?"

"Son of a …" I smack my hand on the counter.
"Sammy was here earlier, he said he'd forgotten his wallet last night and showed me one, then left."
"Oh no - same wallet?" Judith asks, looking at Barb and I.
"Oh, yeah, I bet it was your wallet. What's he doing with your wallet?"
"Home address?" Judith looks at me.
"So, it's official. He's stalking you now. What a day – first Jessie's sleeping with Kate and now this. I'm calling the police." Barb puts down her wine glass.
Judith turns to me in shock, "You're sleeping with Kate?! When did this start? I thought we hated her. She's our competition? What are you thinking?"
I stare daggers at Barb, "Hey!" I raise my hand in defense and lie. "I am NOT sleeping with Kate ... on a regular basis … it was once."
Barb drains her glass. "You'll be shagging like squirrels within the week …" and lets her sentence trail off.
"Have you slept with David yet?" I cross my arms and stare at Barb who sheepishly returns my gaze. "Ack! You have?!" Barb and I stare each other down, drawing closer and closer.

Judith drains her glass, looking at us in disbelief. "I'm calling Sammy – I need a diversion …"
Barb sticks out her tongue at me as I turn to Judith. "Judith, we were thinking it's probably better if we let Sammy go – it's getting a bit weird with him, and I don't want any more trouble for you or for the rest of the staff." I return Barb's salute.

“You should call and cancel your cards Judith.” Barb is bouncing from foot to foot, deliberating. “We should call the police.”
We follow Judith into the office. She opens the telephone book, finds Sammy’s number, and dials it. We look at each other, waiting for him to pick up. After a while she puts down the phone and says, “No answer.”
“When is he on next?” I ask, moving to the schedule on the wall. “Tomorrow night. So, do we wait until he comes in or what? Judith, your call.”
“Okay, we wait until he comes in and then I’ll talk with him.” Judith replies.
“I want this dealt with though.” We spend a few seconds looking at each other, then Barb moves off to the kitchen, Judith to the dining room, and I sit down in front of the computer. “Barb?” I call out into the kitchen, “You know we really have to update our website. It’s completely out of date, and boring.” Barb comes up behind me and looks over my shoulder. “Looks okay to me.” She’s wiping her hands on her apron and then points to the screen. “Except here, that’s not our correct phone number …”

Sarah, our new apprentice, comes up to the doorway and motions Barb away … and then the phone rings.
“Hi.” Kate’s voice is on the other end and my stomach tightens slightly.
“Hi.” A longish pause and then, “When can I see you again?”
Kate laughs. “We have some things to talk about Jess – can you meet me at the club before dinner?”
I look up at the clock. “I can meet you for a few minutes – why?”

"I have a delivery of equipment arriving. I wanted to store it with you remember?"
"Today? How long is this going to take?"
"I thought you wanted to see me. Where are your priorities Jessie?" Kate purrs into the receiver.
"Priority is the restaurant Kate … but I'd like to see you. As much as this is something, I don't want to admit to you, actually."
She laughs again, "Jessie, you're too sensitive. Just like my partner. Get in your car and drive over to the club, let me get this delivery stored downstairs and you'll be back at the restaurant in an hour."
I look at the clock again and then out into the kitchen which is slowly prepping for dinner. "Okay Kate, I'll be at the club in ten minutes. See you then." I hang up, grab my car keys, and go over to Barb.
"I have to run over to the club - we have a delivery."
She looks at me – "What? There's nothing coming that I know of."
I take a handful of gooseberries from a bowl on the counter. "I don't know – the security guys called and said there's a truck on its way to the club with a delivery. So, I'll go by and see what's up. Back soon."
Barb continues slicing and I turn to leave. "Don't be long – we have the catering for tomorrow to get ready."
I raise my hand back to her in acknowledgement and leave out the back door.

The University Club, later that afternoon

Forty-five minutes later ten full pallets have been stored beneath the University Club and Kate and I are pressed against the cool brick wall of the basement, our lips finding each other's, our fingers intertwined. Along the walls play patterns of light from the small windows running at ground level above us, interspersed with shadows cast by passersby on the path running the length of the building. It's damp and cool and the stillness is broken only by the sound of our breathing and the rub of my jacket against the brick as Kate pushes me up against it. We break apart and stare at each other. I look her directly in the eyes. "I really missed you."
"Oh really? Last night when I drove away, you looked like a frightened deer caught in the headlights. This is a different side of you."

I press my lips against hers again and kiss her. We break apart. "I want you Kate. I want you so much." She laughs and gently pushes me away, straightening her jacket and pants. "Tomorrow you should come over to my place. My partner is away for the night. When the kids are asleep you and I could have a glass of wine together."

I move towards her, but she stops me with her hands. "Dearest – you need to get back to your restaurant and I need to get back to mine." She takes my face between her hands and kisses me firmly. "Tomorrow. But get enough sleep tonight; I need you full of energy." She raises her eyebrow and smiles at me.

“Oh, I doubt that. With what’s running through my mind …”

“Dearest, if this is too much for you, then we can always just have coffee – I’m not without a lot of other admirers.” Kate looks at me, pulls her car keys out of her pocket and stands impatiently. “If not, then ...” She kisses me on the cheek, laughs, and I follow her up the stairs to the main floor of the building. When we get to the top she stops and turns to me. “Last night I dreamt of you.” She pauses and jangles her keys, looking at her shoes. “I have no idea why ...” She raises her eyes to seek mine, waits, pushes the heavy metal door open, and we enter with a jolt, the maelstrom of sunlight, noise, and activity of the main campus concourse.

Marta's house, that evening

That evening after prepping the next day's catering and doing a few measly covers for dinner, Marta and I are sitting on her sofa while the kids are in Anna's room playing something noisy on the Play Station. We have the sound on the TV down very low, watching a rerun of Mad Men. I lift my wine glass and take a mouthful as she leans against me. "Jessie? If there is nothing else between us, this is so very good." She turns to me and runs her fingers across my cheek.

"Do you want anything more or less than this?" I ask.
"We both wanted last night, for some time now. I think it was an exorcism of a sort." She sits up and takes a sip from my wine glass. "I think it is something that had to happen but will not happen again. Do you think this as well?"
I nod. "I wanted to make love with you tonight - but I think we're not destined for that." I kiss her on the cheek. "I have the feeling it will ruin our friendship over a long time."
Marta nods. "Oui. This is what I'm thinking Jessie." She kisses me back. "I am very, very fond of you – but not in love with you. We released a lot of demons last night, not angels." She smiles, and then Nicki and Anna come out of the bedroom to the kitchen in a noisy rush in search of snacks.

Jessie's house, September 16

Nicki, Angie, and I perform our regular dance in front of her car as he bundles his bag into the trunk and there is a trade of duty free in exchange for Nicki's school reports. "He isn't doing very well in math Ange – you should get him a tutor." I pass her Nicki's latest math test.
"Do you have any idea what a tutor costs Jess?" She lights a Dunhill with a gold lighter – also Dunhill – and offers me the pack.
I shake my head, "Thanks, but I'm trying to cut back. Lately I can't taste my own cooking." I point to her lighter. "I bet the lighter would pay for a few tutorials."
"Ha Ha. You know what I mean. Is he studying at your place or just playing computer?"
"Sort of fifty-fifty." I admit. "Anyway, the problem won't go away, he'll just get deeper into a hole and it will be more difficult to get him out once he's there. Listen, we should plan a trip to see Mum real soon. How are you looking in a couple of weeks? Just after the Alumni dinner I could get away for a few days. Second week of October, how does that look for you?"
Angie pulls out a new Samsung phone from her bag and is searching through the calendar. "At the moment that works for me. I have to go away the first week of October to Paris and then it's clear."
"Paris. Your life is hard sis …" I shake my head and laugh.
"Well - someone has to live it." She kisses me on the cheek, crushes out her cigarette and walks around the car to the driver's door. I walk over to the passenger side and lean down to Nicki who has the window open and the radio blaring. Angie gets in the car and turns

down the volume. "Hey Nicki, study hard and I'll see you in a few weeks. We're going to fly out to see your Grandmother second week of October."

He nods, "Sure." He seems just *pumped* with enthusiasm.

I wave goodbye as they drive away, and then walk back to the house as my mobile rings.

I stop on the doorstep, look at the number, and answer. "Hi, Barb."

"Hi, it's me. When are you coming in? Can you bring some gold leaf on your way?"

"Sure, no problem. Why do we need gold leaf?"

There's a pause. "I'm wrapping the chairs in it, Jessie – because you didn't get it yesterday and it would look great on the cakes you're delivering today? And the tuiles? What's wrong with you lately?"

"Oh right!" I can't remember a thing anymore. "Why don't we just grate some gold from your heart Barb?" I've just remembered there were gold leaf cigarettes at one time; so, my memory mustn't be that bad.

"If you don't bring me a Tim Horton's coffee and morning glory muffin with you then it'll be your fingers we grate instead of my heart." Barb threatens laughingly.

"Got'cha. One Timmie's coffee and muffin on its way." I end the call and go inside to get my stuff.

Capital City, later that morning

Judith and I are driving up the road two hours to the capital to cater an office opening - a simple 3C catering - cakes and champagne, with a few canapes to start. Their real estate broker also has an office here in town, just happens to be a regular and loves our chocolate and goat cheese parfait. No, it isn't disgusting, it's brilliant. Besides, it's all the rage in Japan and they're lactose intolerant. One day I'm reading the Wall Street Journal and, I couldn't believe it, after spending ten years working with chocolate and cheese combinations, here's some French chef with chocolate shops in Japan talking about "discovering chocolate and cheese". The French eh?

I drop off the coffee and muffin for Barb, leaving her to take care of what will probably be a slow lunch at the restaurant. When I walk into the kitchen, I see Judith's wearing a skirt, so I'm at first unsure it's her; Judith not being partial to anything other than clingy biker clothing. We load all the food into the van and, as a Briteway truck enters the back alley, drive away before they can block us in – and almost run over Sammy crossing the road from the cafe across the street. I slam on the brakes; he looks at us in a sort of shocked way and runs back in the direction he came. Judith rolls down the window and yells out, "Sammy! Hey!" to no avail as he loses himself down the alley between the cafe and the bookstore.
I turn to her, "We really have to get rid of this kid as soon as he comes in tonight Judith."
She looks out the window and answers, "Ja. Yes, you're right."

Usually an office catering for 150 means a catering for 100 and as we usually drive back from these events with enough food to fill the garbage bin I now regularly prep-down. So, it came as no surprise really when about 200 people show up for the reception. After the cakes – white chocolate lavender cream with spun sugar and dark chocolate basil-infused ganache with gold leaf, champagne – Veuve Clicquot of course and canapes - puff pastry with lobster bisque mousse and savoury grilled eggplant with pepper mini charlottes - are laid out, Judith disappears for a smoke. I'm left alone with my amazing interpersonal skills to create an aura of calm and wellbeing in the eyes of the organiser – Britta - a tall, somewhat insecure, woman with a strong Czech accent and long blonde hair secured in a tight bun. She was being a complete cow to myself and the company employees while a fawning sycophant to the company executives – her laughter would carry across the reception area at regular intervals, giving me to recall the sound of rusty barbed wire being scraped across glass. That done I ferret Judith out from the women's toilet where she's smoking and send her in the van to the cafe, we passed down the street to purchase chocolate cakes and a few more bottles of champagne. I mean, it can go either way.

Once, we catered a reception for the varsity football club and were expecting a few hundred people and I think maybe 40 showed up. I recall this event specifically as it was then that one of the coaches mistook the butter for a pale cheese and sliced off an overly large chunk, slapped it onto his bread and then almost threw up in surprise as he scoffed it down.

Greedy bugger. Then there was the art show where we delivered wine and water for 200 and about 35 showed up so we got to carry it all back again and then that open house one summer for 30 people and an extra 100 showed up. Thank God for handling costs. I figure in the additional people on the bill and the organiser books us again next time. ... it has always been one of my endearing talents that the hotter and crazier it gets on the outside the calmer and better organised I become on the inside. I'm a lot like a human antiperspirant.

Lunch in the city, that afternoon

Being in the big city makes me kind of crazy, and during a work week it makes me vibrate like a kid on sugar- there's simply too many people and too much energy. After the catering we walk down to the harbour front and find a little restaurant on the river to relax before the drive home. We're into our wine, happily spearing each other's salads – slices of roasted duck breast, pear and endive for Judith and a spicy Caesar salad with extra lardons for me - when Darlene and Ted, and their little girl, old friends from town who moved to the city last year, suddenly throw themselves and their toddler into our booth. Darlene used to work for student activities at the university until she became pregnant. While she was away on maternity leave, Ted magically appeared on the payroll for a year as Manager of Intellectual Properties. Anyway, nepotism is not a word to banter about lightly but when you look through the university's staff directory, you have the urge to play Happy Families.

"Hey, what are you guys doing in town?" Darlene orders a white wine – St. Michelle Cape Riesling, and Ted a beer – Russian Baltika #3.
I reach over and stroke the hand of the little girl and get a big toothy smile in return. "Catering today in town. How's it going?" The drinks arrive and our plates are cleared. The waitress asks if we'd like coffee and we shake our heads no.
Darlene takes a big sip of her wine. "Have you seen the new coffee commercials? Active businesswomen all strung out on caffeine, taking over the world."

"I like the one with the doctor cum aerobics instructor who still has time to have a lover in the evening, live in a beautiful apartment overlooking the city, all the while singing about her active life.
It´s not as frightening, however, as the woman who fairly hugs the cup to her breast while singing about 'her' coffee. Her 'best' coffee. Like she has a plantation or something? "Judith replies.
"HaHaHa! Yeah like when you go over to this woman´s house, are you getting the best? Or are you getting the stuff the servants grind with their feet?" This from Ted which turns us to a fit of laughter accompanied by the gleeful banging on the table of the cutlery by their little girl, Peg.

I remove a fork from the toddler's sticky grasp before she does any damage, "You guys should come see us some time – come for brunch on a Sunday. We never get to see you anymore." I say, calling for the check. "Sorry but we have to get back to the restaurant." Darlene and Ted nod, feeding apple chunks to Peg in between which the toddler sucks and then removes from her mouth with drooly fingers and places on the table. "We'll be in town next month; Darlene has a reading at 'The Office' – maybe we could stay overnight with you."
I pay the check and turn to Darlene, shaking my head. "No can do. I moved. I have a little place now and no more guest room. Guest couch at most." "Did you publish the book, the one about the waitress?" she nods. "Hey that's great! I want a signed copy. What's it called?"
"'Not Now, Judith'."

She laughs and I look over to Judith. "Oh, you're kidding me! Why did you call it that?" Judith asks. "Remember every time we'd be in the restaurant and you'd pester me with dessert because I was on one diet or another – I always said, 'Not Now, Judith' - it sort of stuck with me."
Judith smiles – "If I had known I'd have come up with something more memorable."
Darlene smiles, "No, it's a perfect title - Jessie, what about Alex?"
"Alex moved to New York. She got a job there."
"Wow, great for her! What about you guys, still together then?"
"Ermm … no. Alex and I have parted ways at this juncture in time. Long story."
"Oh, I'm so sorry Jessie." She turns to Ted, "We know someone who would really like you!"
I take her arm in my hand gently, "Oh, no no no! I think I've got enough on my plate now."
Judith picks up her bag and smiles at Darlene, "Jessie's plate is running over at the moment." and raises two fingers.
We all move to the door. "That's too bad Jess, my girlfriend is completely hot – and her family have a winery."
I kiss Darlene and Ted on the cheek and wave bye to Peg - "Yes, thanks, I needed to know this Darlene."
She laughs and kisses me back. "Let me know if you change your mind!"
I smile crookedly and we walk back up the street to the van, waving goodbye to them as they turn the corner.
My mobile rings and I look at the time. "It's after 3, Barb must be wondering where we are."
"Hey you, what's up? We're just on our way back."

"No worries – everything was ready for dinner, but it doesn't matter now."
"What do you mean 'was ready for dinner'?" I stop walking and take hold of Judith's arm to stop her.
"Well, I don't think we'll be serving dinner tonight."
"Power is out along the entire block. There's a fire at Hansom's, it's almost gutted, and all the power lines are down."
"Really? That sucks. Hansom's was a nice store. We'll be back in a few hours. Call the staff and … wait – we need to do something about the prep. How about staff dinner meeting?"
"Sounds good. I'll make the calls."

The University Club, that evening

Our staff are a good bunch, and all have turned up – even those without shifts - except for Sammy, who doesn't appear for his. "Tonight, as a sign of our generous natures, we're giving you the night off and treating you to dinner."
"Done deal", says Neil, "Who's serving?"
"Self-service" replies Judith and tosses Charlotte an apron, while Barb takes Neil's arm. "And you can help me cook, okay?"
In the end there's half a dozen staff for dinner and we decide to pack everything up the drive over to the club and cook there, none of the crew apart from Alissa, ever having seen the University Club yet. Dinner with foodies is a bit different than normal dinners. There's much more 'hands on'. We do some lamb in garlic and rosemary which we toss onto the grill with some fresh gnocchi in swiss chard pesto afterwards and turn some butternut squash, eggplant, and yellow tomatoes into gazpacho. We've got the wait staff are making Caesar salad at the table, and then we do a dessert – peach and white chocolate muffins with a caramel ice cream. Judith has this thing for ice cream, so we do a tarragon sorbet for in between the lamb and the dessert – which isn't an ice you've probably ever tried so if you haven't don't pretend! Go make it! And, I must tell everyone that pesto can be made yourself and never need be bought and it costs you nothing anyway. Maybe I'm out of touch but people are always sort of surprised, 'oh you make your own pesto?' This is tantamount to 'oh you make your own mashed potatoes?' Umm … is there any other way?

Dishes are washed, staff come and go with wine between the bar downstairs and our table upstairs; there's a lot of casual banter and drinks passed back and forth and after many hours the club is quiet and empty save for Judith, Barb and myself. We go downstairs, put on some jazz, and then all drop into a sofa. No, really, the sofas are that big … huge, soft, deep, black leather furniture – along with designer office chairs, were a major hit when university budgets were still wide open.

"Let's go downstairs and see what Kate's stored in the basement.", suggests Barb. Judith and I nod, and we walk down the stairs into the dampness of the basement; now exceptionally spooky as the small windows along the top of the walls are dark and the lightbulbs a low wattage. I open the door to the club storage, and we enter the big, still mostly empty, room. The ten pallets of boxes are still there. "What is all this stuff?" Barb asks as we walk past the stacks of cartons.

"Kitchen equipment for Costers I assume. Kate's basement is full."

Barb removes one of the packing slips. "Hey, don't rip anything." She looks up at me and undoes the envelope containing the packing slip. She unfolds the paper and scans it. "This box isn't kitchen equipment. They're chairs."

"Chairs for the cafeterias? Close enough." I reply.

"That's a lot of chairs – there are … like a thousand chairs here." says Barb.

"That's a lot of chairs." says Judith.

"Not if you think there must already be close to five thousand cafeteria chairs on campus already. Must be replacing the old ones." I say.

“Hmm. I guess. Chairs. I was expecting fryers or something, you know?” says Barb.
“Me too actually.” I muse.
Barb pulls out the penknife she carries about with her and gently undoes the top flap of a carton. Inside are disassembled wooden IKEA chairs with metal legs wrapped in plastic. “Definitely chairs.” Says Judith as we peer inside.
The ringing of my mobile breaks the silence in the cellar, echoes off the walls and makes us all jump in surprise. “Hello?” The reception is bad. “Hi Rachel. Uh huh, oh. Okay. Okay thanks. I’ll call you back. Thanks. Give her my love.” I close the phone. “My Mum’s doing worse.”
Barb takes my arm and hugs me. “I’m sorry Jess.”
I light a cigarette as we move out of the cellar, close the door, and walk up to the club. “I wish I had all the time I need. Alumni dinner, chocolate festival, school just back … I could use another twelve hours to the day.”

Jessie's house, later that evening

At home that night, and I call Angie. "Hi Ange, you in bed?"
"No, I'm working on some reports for the office. Did Rachel call you?"
"Yep. We need to go out and see Mum. When can you?"
"Never. You know I'm as busy as you are Jess – and what about Nicki? We hadn't planned to go out until his school holidays."
"I know. I know. I could ask Marta – she'd take care of him. We need to go."
"Mum's probably just going through another bad spell. She'll get through it and we can see her in two weeks like we planned."
"What if she doesn't get any better?"
"Oh Jess, how the hell do I know?! I hate this. I hate that she's sick, and I hate that I *can't* do anything about it."
"I know Ange. I feel the same. I can't save her; I don't want to deal with it either. I feel guilty whichever way I think about it. I'm just not cut out to be sitting there with her like the others are."
She laughs. "I know – we move too fast for them."
"It's because we're scared."
"Probably … Look, I'll call you tomorrow. I need to check things at the office. You check your own schedule. We'll come up with something. I've got to get back to work."
"Me too." Eyeing the slowly emptying wine bottle on the counter beside me.
I hang up and then realise with a sickening lurch that I was supposed to meet Kate tonight. I look at the clock.

A few minutes after ten. I dial Kate's mobile which rings and rings. I hang up and go into the kitchen for some more ice. My mobile rings and I walk back into the living room. "Hello?"

"Where are you Darling? It's after ten. I thought you'd changed your mind."

"I've had a bitch of a day Kate, sorry. I'm not really at my best this evening."

"I've just put the kids to bed. You could come over right now."

"I don't think that would be a good idea. I've had a bit too much to drink and I'm not feeling up to anything now."

"Why don't we forget the whole then? I don't want to stress you."

"I'm not interested in forgetting you Kate I'd like to devote my attention to you – and I can't do that right now."

There is a long silence. "My partner is away for most of the week. Come for dinner tomorrow."

"Tomorrow night would be perfect. Are you cooking, or am I?"

Kate laughs, "You are of course."

Marlies, September 17

We should order some Beaujolais Nouveau for the Alumni dinner … Still no email from Alex. I can't believe some of the things I do. Junk, junk, junk, whoa - a mail from Dr. Bleary. … Hey! We got the deposit on the Alumni dinner! This is great. I ring Barb who answers the phone with a groggy voice. "Hey, you, were you still in bed?"

"Not really, we were just getting up. What's up Jess?" I hear another, recognisable, voice in the background.
"We? you aren't alone … is that … David?"
Barb sighs. "Yes, Jessie, it's David. Did you want to talk with him?"
"No! No, that's okay. I just wanted to tell you that I got an email from Bleary. He paid the deposit on the Alumni dinner!"
"Great! Finally - then let's look over some menus after lunch tomorrow okay?"
"Sure. Okay, then, have fun"
"Already had it Jess - but thanks" Barb laughs.

I hang up. It must be so weird sleeping with David. I can't imagine it somehow.
The phone rings and I pick it up. "Barb?"
"Sorry, no this is Inspector Peters. Is this Jessie Watkins?"
"Yes, speaking."
"Good morning. I'm calling regarding the vandalism you had at the restaurant."
"Oh. That was a month ago ... I'd almost forgotten about it."

"Yes, well, we went to the residence of your employee, Samil Micheal Mcerik? If that is how you pronounce his name?"
"Might be. I only know him as Sammy."
"Fine. We were unable to find him at home, and his neighbour informed us he'd moved out."
"Oh really? Well, he never showed up for his shift at work last night."
"Well, we are unable to establish a connection with Mr. Mcerik and the incident at this time. The file will be kept open for the next eight weeks. If you have any new information you should come by and speak with an officer."
"Okay, thank you. Oh, what about the insurance company? We still need something from you for my insurance claim."
"Of course. I'll mail you a copy of the report. If you would like to note the case number?"
I reach over for a pen – which isn't there. "Sure, ummm just need to find a pen." Why are pens never where you need them? I go into the kitchen and take one from the cutlery drawer. Always useful to have a pen or two there for when you need to make notes in a recipe. "Okay, got one."
"The report number is 3758992-D8849. Got that?"
I repeat the number back to him. "Thanks Inspector. If we hear anything about Sammy, I'll be in contact. Goodbye."
"Goodbye." I hang up and wonder where Sammy's gotten to. I call Judith. "Hi. How's it going?"
"Mmmm Jess, I was asleep. What time is it? Ach Gott, it's only eight Jessie!"

"Sorry. Listen, the police called, and they couldn't find Sammy. He's sort of vanished. You should be careful. He's out there somewhere."
"Mmmm Okay, Thanks Jess." Then she hangs up. I look at my watch; I've arranged to meet Rodd for coffee this morning.[12]

Coming back to the restaurant I'm almost run over by Pete, the old guy who does the market deliveries, in the back alley. Friendly wave, friendly wave back; like he isn't almost completely blind anyway. Great guy though. Pete was a chef when he was younger, spent a lot of time in Asia apparently, then moved back here when he retired and went to work at the market. When it comes to food, he really knows his kiwis from his kumquats so you can pretty much trust you get what you ordered.

Pete has some amazing stories about what it was like cooking in the 1960s when everyone only wanted French Cuisine and you spent like five years apprenticing on the steam table turning potatoes and mushrooms while mobsters were unloading crates of Lucky Strike and pant suits in the cold rooms. Hard times. Glad they're over. I've done my fair share of turned vegetables though my contact with the mob has been limited. I know this may come as somewhat of a shock, but I must tell you that while they may look nice, they taste the same as unturned ones. Vegetables not mobsters. I like honest food but for my taste it can climb a few inches over the plate. Mashed potatoes? Great. Mashed potatoes with paper thin potato slices slowly roasted in the oven until golden brown with

sprigs of thyme nestled in between and then placed on top? Greater. Turned potatoes? Mash 'em I say.
"Hey Jessie, how's tricks?" Pete gets down from the cab of the truck and shakes my hand before putting on his gloves.
"Great Pete, thanks." I unlock the door leading to our delivery elevator and open the doors, securing them to the wall. The delivery elevator is one of the coolest things about Marlies. A complete relic, accessible from both inside and outside, great for deliveries in the rain. We just can't put too much weight on it because if it ever broke, we would need to get a brand new one to replace it. "They don't make 'em like this anymore." whistles Pete as he wheels over the first stack of crates of produce.
"Nope. Sure, don't Pete. Just hope it doesn't break halfway down one day."
"Naaa – Jessie, look at me - I'll be 77 this year. 77! I'll bet the elevator isn't that old."
"Probably not Pete. Okay, so I'll check everything and leave you to it." I take the delivery list from him and double check it. Everything that's supposed to be there is, and of course there a few things extra I'm sure Barb ordered afterwards. Yep. Three crates of gooseberries and a sack of Hokkaido pumpkin. Sounds interesting. "Just let me check this with Barb while you're unloading okay?"
Pete nods and disappears into the back of the truck. I open the back door and go into the kitchen. I say hi to the crew and go in search of Barb. I find her in the dining room supervising the installation of the new front window. I take hold of her from behind and kiss her cheek. "Hey you."

"Hi. Did the delivery get here?" She looks at the list in my hand.
"Yes. What are we using the gooseberries and pumpkin for?"
"Gooseberry and pumpkin compote. I want to sell it in our grab and go section. There was an article in this morning's paper. I think people will buy it. Let's see."
"Sounds good, delicious in fact. Why don't we do a spicy version as well. Like a chutney?"
"Sure. Yeah, a sweet and a savoury." Barb beams at me. "Is this the Jessie I used to know and love?"
"Ha ha. I'll always be chasing Barb. Cut me some slack. I'm not as homespun as you. You're the sensible one and I'm the wild one. That's how we work so well together." I pinch her cheek. "Oh, and the police finally called. Seems Sammy has skipped town. At least he moved out. Has he called here?" Barb shakes her head. "I called Judith and told her to be careful."
"Hmm. Totally odd. I hope he doesn't come back." She takes the delivery list from my hand and turns to walk into the kitchen. "Get dressed and make some coffee okay? I'll go downstairs and get this stuff sorted out."
"Okay, oh – get someone to grab the pumpkins before they go downstairs. Save us dragging them back up later.
I go behind the bar and make Cappuccinos for Barb and me. I take them into the back, check on the prep, and then go into the office. I close the door and change into my jacket and pants, hanging my stuff on the back of the door. We have a small change area for the staff, but Judith, Barb and I keep our stuff in the office. I take my coffee, leaving Barb's on the desk, and walk over to Chris and Frank to see how they're doing with

lunch prep. As I'm about to try a piece of the mango and papaya tart Frank has just finished, a horrendous crash comes from the back - soon followed by screams and cries. Everyone races to the back door. Pete is peering down the elevator shaft and my heart drops to my stomach. The cries grow louder as I run down to the basement three stairs at a time. At the bottom of the elevator lies Barb, holding onto her right leg which is beneath a pile of toppled crates. The elevator is skewed at an angle. Barb is crying and holding onto her leg.
"Barb – what happened!? What are you doing?"
"What am I doing!? Fuck Jessie, I've broken my leg or something. Oh fuck! Fuck, this hurts!"
I call up the stairs, "Frank, Chris! Come here!" Pete accompanies them downstairs and we pull the crates from Barb's leg and pile them against the wall. "Chris, go get a bag of ice. Frank, can you call an ambulance?" They go back upstairs. Pete looks worriedly on.
"I guess it was too much weight for the elevator. I'm sorry Barb, sorry Jess."
"Hey, Pete, not your fault. We should have had the thing replaced. How did you get underneath everything?"
"It came down suddenly. I moved, slipped and … Owwwwwww Shit! Jess, get me a glass of scotch, would you?"
"No, better not Sweetheart – they'll probably give you something at the hospital. Don't want to give you any alcohol."
"You're so kind."
"I try."
Frank and Chris return. We take the bag of ice and gently raise Barb's leg, resting the foot on half the ice and piling the rest gently over her lower leg.

"Oh Man that hurts worse!"
"It should help. At least there's nothing cut."
"The ambulance says they're on their way."
"Thanks Frank. Would you and Chris do me a favour and see what still needs to be prepped for lunch? Prioritise down the list beginning with the Appies. I'll come up just as soon as Barb is taken care of." They both nod and run back upstairs. "Don't run on the stairs!" I call back to them.

30 minutes later I've got the prep back on track for lunch and Barb safely on her way to hospital. Judith arrived just as the paramedics were carrying Barb up the stairs, which wasn't easy, they are narrow and curving. The stairs, not the paramedics. In the back of my mind swims the terrible thought that I'm now going to very likely be alone for more than the next few weeks. After lunch Judith and I drive over to the hospital to see how Barb is doing. We find her, after three stops at various stations, laying in a bed with her leg propped up and covered in plaster.
"Eight weeks?!" I almost shriek. Barb nods her head, biting her lip. "Oh my God." I sit down on her bed and take her hand, Judith following suit on the other side of the bed. "How are you feeling? You'll have to let us know what we can bring you."
"I feel like shit. I'm sorry Jess. The ankle is shattered and there's something about the tendon. They want to wait until the swelling is down and then the doctor says they'll have to operate. Even after that I'm going to be on crutches for a while. At least I can come in, but I'm going to be a complete gimp for the next couple of months." She squeezes my hand.

"Oh man. The Alumni dinner – and I was going to fly out to see my Mum…" I shake my head and smile weakly. "At least you'll be up and about for Christmas!"

"Can you call David and let him know I'm here? I'll make you a list and give you my keys. You could bring me some pajamas and stuff. And I think I could use some books!"

"You can plan menus for the next half year while you're here." I muse out loud.

The University Club, early that afternoon

I drive over to campus and once through the main gates almost run over a group of freshmen crossing from the coffee shop who still haven't learnt that the roads on campus aren't in fact large sidewalks but in fact roads for cars. Two grad student families coming from the family housing quad on the other side of the roadway however wait patiently before crossing with their bags of shopping and baby buggy. The speed limit on campus is 20 but my car doesn't even idle at that speed, so I always get dirty looks from campus security when I drive by at 30 or 40.

The University Club is quiet and cool when I enter. I water the plants, the collection, the botanic zoo which is housed in the club and has grown over the years. Everyone gets a measured amount. It's somewhat soothing wandering about with my watering can, watering those few life forms that still need my assistance. I am God. Not The God, but A God. I am the rainmaker. Then I wipe the dust off a few of the surfaces the cleaning company has neglected. I'm going through the small stack of mail I picked up on my way through the mail office in the porter's lodge when a gentle knock on the glass beside the door breaks my reverie and I look up to see Lidia. I wave to her and call out Hi which I'm sure she can't hear through the glass door. I get up and walk to the door, opening it for her. "Hey Lidia, how are you?"
She walks in, her hands behind her back and a big smile on her face. "Hi Jessie – thought I'd come by and see the club for myself. There aren't any profs here, are there?"

I laugh, "Of course not – no lunch today. Did you eat already?"
"I grabbed some fruit. The cafeteria was lined out the door today – there was only one cashier on duty – I wasn't going to stand in the lineup."
"How did you get the fruit then?"
She smiles at me. "Ah ha - I don't have anything here to eat I'm afraid – no dinners planned this week – but would you like something to drink? I'm just on my way out, but I'll have something with you if you'd like?"
"Sure, Thanks – do you have a beer?"
"A beer? Yeah, we have beer – a few types on tap – how about a Barking Squirrel? – totally great beer."
She laughs, "Barking Squirrel? Okay." She nods her head and walks over to one of the sofas, tossing her bag onto the glass table in front of it as she sits down. She looks around – "Nice place you have here. I should be a Professor one day."
I bring over two glasses filled with beer and laugh, "Well, there are probably cheaper ways to get entrance than a PhD and a course load to teach – but yeah, it's a nice place. Cheers!" I raise my glass and we knock them gently together.
The first time I met Lidia I had this tiny feeling in the pit of my stomach that we'd met before. Sometimes you meet people and you instantly feel this bond between you. You feel you've known each other before in a past life even or there's just something so … familiar and wonderful about them that you couldn't possibly be meeting them for the very first time. When I get this feeling I immediately go overboard. That's how I feel about Lidia. Which is exactly why all I can

do is make small talk with her. "So, what's up – how're classes?"
"Hmmm – okay, I guess. Nothing special. I can't really study here what I really want, but the university I like costs too much. I'm waiting for a stipend to get in."
"Hm. What do you want to study? I thought we offered pretty much everything. You know the women's college even offers white witchcraft and religious studies?"
"Yeah, well I want to do theater studies - we do them here but the Professor I'm really interested in studying under isn't – he's in the UK. So, I'm sort of on hold."
"I'm sure you'll get in eventually." I light a cigarette and offer her one.
"You're seeing that scary lady who runs the serveries aren't you?"
"The 'scary lady'? Is that what you call her? Funny, so do her staff."
"What would you call her?" she looks at me over the rim of her glass as she drinks.
"I like women who scare me a bit – I don't like having to be in control. How do you know who I'm seeing anyhow?" I take a big drink of my beer to cover my being a bit uncomfortable.
"The campus isn't that big. She's obvious. You're cute. It isn't a secret what goes on here, you know?"
I shake my head. I'm cute? "We both work on campus - isn't there anything more interesting happening here or are we sending out really loud signals?" I laugh. "She's also married, so I wouldn't say we're seeing each other." I blow smoke out of my mouth and look at her. "I'm attracted to her. I like scary women - stronger women ... what about you - are you seeing anyone here?"

"Ah … no one. No one I like." She takes some gum out of her bag and unwraps it.
I put out my cigarette and look at my watch. "I hate to rush us Lidia, but I need to go, I've got a prior arrangement before I get back to the restaurant."
She finishes her beer. "No problem, I've got a class in fifteen minutes." She replaces the beer glass on the table. "Thanks – it was nice having a beer here." She smiles and gets up. I pick up the glasses and take them to the bar and place them in the dishwasher. Lidia is gently spinning about the large open space near the entranceway.
"You like spinning?" I watch her.
"I was a dancer, you have forgotten?" She laughs and then takes my hand gently – "Thanks again – have a nice day Jessie."
"Lidia?"
She stops for a moment - "Hmm?"
I can't say anything remotely misleading to her though. As much as I want to. I smile. "Nothing. I was just wondering why you didn't continue with your dancing."
She waits a moment and tilts her head slightly to one side looking at me. "You wanted to know that?" Then there's another pause, and she sighs a little bit and begins chewing her gum again. "Ok, umm, I didn't like the hours. I'm afraid I'm not very regimented." Then she smiles at me and leaves the club and I hear the main door outside open and then slowly close.
The sound of the door opening again draws my attention, but it isn't Lidia – it's a delivery guy.
"Hi, is this the University Club?"
"Sure is – what can I do for you?"

"I have a delivery here from Costers – Ms. Morris - instructions that boxes should be delivered here, and we should pick something up?" he says as he checks his clipboard.
"First I heard of it. Maybe I should call her first?" I grab my mobile and quickly dial Kate's office number but there is no answer. "Do you have the delivery order?" He passes it to me, and I read it quickly over – sure enough a new delivery and oddly enough a pickup of the chairs. "You're taking the chairs? Aren't they for campus?"
"No idea – I'm just supposed to pick them up and take them back. Guess they are being returned."
"Very odd. Okay, then let's go to the cellar. Where are you parked?" I shut the front door and lock it behind me, leading him to the main door of the building.
"I'm out back."
"Do you have a forklift? There's ten pallets in the storeroom." We walk along the hallway and down the stairs to the basement.
"There's ten pallets coming in as well."
"Really? What are you delivering?"
"Don't know – it says … trays. Five thousand trays."
"You're kidding me. Is she replacing them all?"
I leave him to remove the pallets of chairs and replace them with the pallets of plastic cafeteria trays and return upstairs. I've arranged to meet Marta for a quick coffee and muffin at Starbucks for which I'm now late. Fifteen minutes later I've signed the delivery papers and left the club. As I draw near to Starbucks, I see her sitting under one of the big green umbrellas - she's looking at me in an exasperated way and she doesn't turn her cheek to take my kiss. "Hi – sorry I'm late - what would you like?"

“Cappuccino with low fat milk and double shot please. Bring me a muffin as well?”
“Sure.” Ok, she doesn’t sound so angry – but something has her fired up. I return a few minutes later with two of the same and an ashtray pilfered from the table next to us.
“How’s your Mum Jessie?”
“Well, it seems she went to the doctors because she was having more pains and he sent her for x rays. The cancer has spread everywhere.”
She puts her hand on mine. “I’m sorry Jessie. How is she taking it?”
“Horrible. Everyone’s horrible. Angie and I were going to see her, but Barb broke her leg – she’s okay – but she’ll be away from work for the next six weeks – I’m going to have to close the restaurant if I fly out. I don’t know what to do.”
”This is your mother, you should go.”
“It won’t help if I fly out or not, you know that.”
“No. She will die anyway Jessie. That is not the point. She will be happy you are there. It will do her good.”
”If I fly out now, I think it will send a very panicky message.”
She bites off some of her muffin. “Have you or Angie told Nicki yet?”
”No. No, I don’t think I can tell him. Angie will have to. His school holidays aren’t for a while, so we wanted to wait until then – unless Angie leaves him here.”
“Nicki can stay with me, you know that?” She covers my hand with both of hers and I give her hand a squeeze. “You’re wonderful Marta – I’ll ask Angie.”

Marta is gently swirling her coffee about and looking at me. "Jessie … why didn't you tell me that you were sleeping with Kate?"
Okay so not even the gossip mill on campus can be this fast – nothing happened other than the kiss in her car, though this could have been caught on the campus surveillance cameras and uploaded onto YouTube ... This is not a good development. "Umm, who were you talking with?"
"Kate. I've been talking with Kate." My heart misses a beat and I stop sipping my coffee for a fraction of a second – but long enough for Marta to notice and to stop drinking hers. "She sits on the Food Committee, Jessie. Of course, we talk. She mentioned seeing you – and mentioned this to me specifically because she is of the opinion that we are close. I don't like the fact that she seems to know about us."

I greet two professors I've seen in the club recently and who sit at the table next to ours and lower my voice, "I've never mentioned your name to her. What did she say anyway?"
Marta follows suit and leans closer to me across the table, "She alluded to the fact that she has seen us together with the children in town, but in a roundabout way. I don't know. She made it somehow noticeably clear that she and you were close – as if she were doing me a favour telling me this. That we women should stick together … it was obvious. She's the same as my boss, this type of woman – I don't like her Jessie. God! She is married. And you were in my bed moments ago! What are you thinking of?" She's put down her muffin and taken up her coffee cup. Something to throw.

Never a good sign. "I live and work here too Jessie. I've talked about this before, about my privacy."
"This has nothing to do with you and your ex-partner Marta. I know you have problems with him and that you value your privacy. This is not the same thing. I really care about you and wouldn't do anything to hurt you."
Now she's gripping her coffee cup really hard. "Damn it but you are doing just those things!"
"Look, Marta – she kissed me – I … I'm …"
"You want her – Jessie it's so obvious when I look in your eyes …"

I can't think of a response. I just look away and smile nervously at the two profs who can hear something of our conversation because of the proximity of the tables. Coffee shoots out of the top of her cup as Marta slams it down on the table – and I'm happy at this point that I got takeout cups instead of the porcelain ones. "Go to hell Jessie!" She hisses and gets up quickly leaving her coffee and untouched muffin and begins to walk away. Then she returns, takes up her coffee and muffin, glares at me, and walks away again. I smile and shrug my shoulders at the couple at the adjoining table, who mimic my gesture and then return to their coffees. Great. Why does everything I want, have to be so complicated, so difficult? This must be my way of adapting my environment to my needs.
I drink my coffee and light another cigarette. I wonder what Kate's doing with all these deliveries. Why order all those chairs and then return them? It's really odd. I muse this over while I eavesdrop on the conversation next to me.

“What do you think about that idea of changing the admission claim, Bill? ‘Tomorrow’s Experts Today’” The other two are nodding their heads in agreement. “I like it. Everyone’s offering the ‘leaders of the future’ anyway.”
“Did you see the memo about the number of women in admin positions? Someone’s done a study that shows there are more female staff than men but less female vice Presidents. Seems the women are making all the coffee and not enough of the decisions.”
“What’s wrong with making coffee? We need coffee. I make my own coffee in the morning. Who’s supposed to do all these little things no one wants to do but need to have done?” The other nods his head. “It’s ridiculous. I hate this affirmative action crap. Next my team assistant won’t be mailing out my publication reports. I should be doing this instead of doing my research I suppose just because I’m a man. Hell, Jim, if they want to make more decisions, then God bless ‘em – let me make less of them so I can get some real work done.”

I finish my coffee as the conversation continues, toss the cup into the garbage bin as I walk away and go back to the club. I go into the basement to look over the delivery notice and packing slips again. I open the basement door and look at the ten pallets of slightly smaller boxes. I pull out the delivery notice I put in my back pocket and read it through. Nothing out of the ordinary. I read through the notice of return for the chairs as well. The return address for the chairs is different from the address of the delivery company though. The chairs aren’t going to where the trays came from. This seems a bit odd if they’re being returned. I turn off the light and close the door again. Then I go upstairs to collect my stuff before driving back to the restaurant for dinner prep. I sit down on one of the sofas and dial my Mum's number but there's a busy signal.

Bronwyn's studio, later that day

Bronwyn lives and works right behind the restaurant. He lives in a big house reminiscent of those Edwardian townhouses Peter Sellers lived in in the movie 'Being There'. A townhouse right in the middle of town. 'Right behind the restaurant' is a euphemism for 'eight blocks behind it'. Judith lives ten blocks from the restaurant and so saying Bronwyn lives 'right behind Judith' and 'a mile from the restaurant', would be more appropriate. I don't want to sound rankled about this differentiation, but I once had to find Bronwyn's place on a very cold February night with just these directions. Patrons looking out from our front window were probably wondering why I was circling the premises, first appearing at one window, and then back again, never passing in the opposite direction. I began pondering the possibility that Bronwyn, who *dabbles* in white magic much to Barb's chagrin, had enshrouded her house with some sort of charm, a 'glamour' they used to call it, making it inaccessible save for at certain times of the year when the borders of Faerie and mortal man are at their thinnest - Beltane, Samhain, you know. Maybe you had to walk around the building a certain number of times (clockwise) before the residence became apparent? I didn't know.

I know you traditionally find all the characters to be introduced somewhat nearer the beginning of a story and not like 50,000 words into it but then life is not a book. How many of the people that you now know did you meet on Page 1 of your life? Okay then. Actually life is like a play, and like a play the characters are all screaming for better lighting as they flit in and out of the wings completely unexpected, unless you were generous enough to invest in the program and read the precursor before the curtain went up. Or you're God. I don't buy programs anymore now that I don't collect them. I don't see the point if I'm just going to throw them away with the next recycling run and any way I can probably just as easily grab a quick peek from someone in the row in front who did buy it.

So, let's presume life is a play and you bought the program but didn't open it until the first intermission, marveling at how far away your seats were from the stage - deceiving those little seating plans on the theater websites aren't they? I know it's also not good to break the train of thought of your readers, I mean, you're hanging on the edge of your seat wondering what's going to happen next and suddenly I'm off on a tangent about theater programs - but I'm trying to pace myself, put everything into perspective at this juncture of possible crisis – and for that I really need Bronwyn.

Bronwyn is a Masseuse – properly a Masseur, but she prefers the feminine. She is flippant, harsh, and vain, and yet very appealing for being completely and utterly ravishingly stunningly unbelievably anime-like, androgynous, drop dead gorgeous. Try saying that ten times quickly.

Bronwyn knows it and is honestly up front about it. She doesn't take any bullshit about her looks or her sexuality, which I can completely respect. I thought she was a woman when we first met years ago, but she is actually a He. Bronwyn is a woman in a man's body. Fashionably so. I have never seen her dress anything but beautifully. I'm sure there are many who would never guess she was not a woman. She lives reliably … disinterested, in what you might expect of her. She's the sort of person who sleeps through their alarm clock but will one day wake to their smoke alarm. *Wooooo weeeeeee Woooo weeeeeee Wake uuuuuuuuuppp You're gonna burrrrrrrrn.* It's not that she's a breath of fresh air – she's more like a wind tunnel that blows all the cobwebs out of your head. She takes me out of myself. And then I can begin with a clean slate.

I run up the stairs to her building, in which Bronwyn occupies the top floors, and ring the bell. The door is buzzed open and I slowly climb the three flights of stairs to the top. The smell of incense grows dizzyingly more intense as I reach the landing, and there's Bronwyn leaning on the door jamb smiling at me. "Jess – long time no see." She opens her arms and takes me in them, hugging me. Bronwyn is on the tall side, very slim and long, and very pale. She models on the side, mostly in tattoo magazines, and is a bit of a celebrity on the tattoo show circuit. This is Bronwyn v.2 - the post mall rat post exotic dancer who found a quiet little niche and widened it to his full potential. If I may be so blunt.

"Hey, how are you?" I hug her close, no longer afraid of her charm as I was when we first got to know each other, shielded as I am by my own desperate plight. "Come on in." I enter her studio and, sighing loudly, immediately fall onto the couch. "Make yourself at home." She smirks and goes into the kitchen – "Want something to drink? Beer? Vodka? Champagne?"

"Champagne? Vodka – definitely, vodka, Bronwyn. Thanks." She goes into a small kitchen, I hear ice cubes hitting glasses, and comes back with two glasses generously filled with vodka and ice, her burgundy leather pants squeaking slightly as she walks. I take the glass she offers me, "Thanks, nice outfit."

She spins around. "You like it? I thought it went with my hair." She still sports waist length, wavy, red hair that looks undeniably hot.

"What brings you by? Problems? You only ever come to see me when you're down Jess. Why is that?"

I drink up the vodka and place the cold, empty glass against my forehead. "Because you make me feel better Bronwyn. You are from another place – far removed from my own – it makes me feel so much better to be far away from my own space sometimes." I smile – "Like right now."

She smiles - "You want another vodka?" I nod. "Thanks."

"How about a little nose candy?" She calls from the kitchen where the sound of ice and glasses resound.

"You know I don't do that stuff – neither should you, Kitten."

She returns with my drink, hands it to me and sits down beside me. "You haven't called me Kitten in ages … You have your poison, and I have mine. Cheers." I raise my glass to him. "What's bothering you Jess?"

"Oh, a lot of things. Mum's sick – like really sick this time – Alex left me, I slept with a good friend of mine, I'm in lust with a very dangerous woman – who is married with children no less – and with whom I will probably sleep – oh and Barb just broke her leg or foot or something and will be out of action for the next month or two leaving me holding the restaurant … and Judith is most probably fucking one of our staff. So, well, a lot really."

Bronwyn laughs – "I don't think I have enough vodka for all that… What have you been doing to yourself? Crazy …" She gets up and puts on some music – some jazz – nice jazz... "When do you have to leave?"
I look at my watch – it's 4. "I have to get the restaurant up to speed before dinner, so I have a bit less than two hours. Tonight's like a time I really wish I could call in sick. You get those days? … Is that Nana Mouskouri?"
"All the time girlfriend - that's why I do what I do when I want to – or not. Yep – Nana from the 60's … early recording … nice eh?" She finishes her drink and takes my hand, lifting me up and taking half empty glass. "Come on, into my office – I'm going to give you a massage and you can sleep for an hour afterwards. You'll feel a lot better than if you keep drinking this stuff."

I follow her into the massage room, overlooking the street and fitted out with a long, wide, padded table. We undress without a word. I lay down on my stomach on the massage table as she looks herself up and down in the mirror leaning against the wall. I look over and admire her long, pale form, the fall of her long red hair down her back, and the black and red dragon that fans out from the back of her right leg, up over her buttocks, filling her back, and tapers out over her left shoulder to her chest. A work of art. Then she comes to the table, takes up some oil from the counter, applies a small amount to my back, and begins massaging my shoulders, then my back, and my legs.

I relax and begin to lose track of time until I feel her cool skin against mine, then the full weight of her naked body as she lays down on top of me. Her perfectly manicured fingers grasp mine and she rests his cheek against mine. Then there is only the sound of our rhythmic breathing until later when I feel her get off the table and pad out the room. From the kitchen I hear the tinkling sound of a fresh vodka on ice and hear her long, bare, feet slapping against the floor. Her voice is gentle as she kisses my cheek. "Hey gorgeous, time to go back to work."

Marlies, early that evening

Forty minutes later I'm feeling energized, and grating Hokkaido pumpkin and tossing it with steamed buckwheat and grated zucchini, some finely diced red onions, egg yolk, some quark and a handful of polenta to make the little pancakes that together with a spoonful of black caviar will make our appetizer for the evening. "Everything on the blackboard – keep it fresh, seasonal and interesting." I instruct Frank and Chris as they finish cleaning the monkfish and slicing the fat from the racks of lamb which we have on as main dish specials - both served with new potatoes and grilled beets with plenty of sour cream. "Frank, what did you come up with for dessert tonight?" He looks over to Chris and then back to me. "Okay, Chris, what did you come up with for dessert tonight?" Chris makes her way over to the walk-in fridge and goes inside, returning in a few seconds with a tray of ramekins filled with some sort of mousse covered in plastic. She puts them down on the counter as Frank comes over.

"So, this is a pumpkin pudding and I thought we could make an egg white layer on top and brown it in the salamander – this would also warm the pudding at the same time?"
"Sounds good – but we have pumpkin on the menu already with the Appies."
"Yes, Frank said the same thing – I blended cinnamon and nutmeg into the mousse at the beginning as well as some white chocolate – if you taste it," she spoons some out and passes it to me, "there's nothing remotely pumpkin - like about it really – except the colour

which is more caramel than orange because of the cream? I thought we could focus on it being squash instead of pumpkin and call it white chocolate squdding … or something?"
I laugh, "Squdding? People will think there's octopus in it." I take the spoon and taste the concoction which is delicious. Both Frank and Chris appear nervous and on any other evening I'd 86 the idea of pumpkin followed by pumpkin disguised under some weird name – but after Bronwyn's massage and three vodkas I'm ready to let a lot fly.
"Okay, let's get some ginger root sliced and caramelised to put on top of the meringue – do we have any tuiles left from lunch? Stick a tuile in it for height – tastes great, let's go for it. But don't tell Judith it's Squdding – tell her it's … roasted caramel custard … get people wondering how you roast caramel … good job guys." They both beam and happily go back to work.
Judith comes in from the dining room - "First table just came in. You want anything Jess?"
"Definitely a glass of something chewy – Chardonnay or something. Chris, Frank - you like something before service?" Both looked shocked and can only shake their heads at the thought of my offering them a drink prior to service. "You sure?" I smile – "Okay. Just bring me a bottle and three glasses – maybe they change their mind."

Judith smiles and nods, picks up a rack of wine glasses from the dishwasher as it comes out from the machine in a puff of steam and goes back into the dining room. From the open back door, the sounds of a thunder shower reach me in the kitchen and the smell of the change in atmosphere is like a tonic. I wipe my hands and go stand in front of the back door, pushing it open and catching the first drops of hurried rain as the skies darken and the thunder rumbles. Behind me, at the pass, the first calls from Judith for Appies rings out and I forget all the stress of the day. I feel utterly happy and complete. I turn around and walk back into the kitchen, untying my apron and then retying it around my waist in reverse. "Chris, you're on the line with me, Frank keep the prep going please – we'll switch in an hour. Let's have a good service folks!"

After everyone has gone home, I turn off the lights in the dining room and the kitchen and sit in the office dialing my Mum's number a few more times but each time it's engaged. I try the numbers of both my brothers but get only their answering machines. "Hey guys, it's Jessie, was trying to get hold of Mum but her phone is off the hook or someone's been talking on it all day. Someone give me a call on my mobile okay?" I make my way out the back door and lock it behind me. Then my phone rings and it's my Mum's number on the display. "Hi Mum?"
"Hi Jess, no, this is Megan. How are you?"
"Oh, you know – same old same old. How's Mum doing?"
"Not so good. She's back in hospital and they have her heavily sedated. Ronnie's there with the boys trying to get her released back home as soon as possible."
I can hear her crying softly. Fuck. "Okay, I'd better come out then. I don't know about Angie and Nicki though - it's all short notice and I'm pretty much screwed here as Barb's in hospital herself now. I'll have to do something about the restaurant."

“Okay Jess. I won’t tell her yet. Do what you can.” Megan was always the more forgiving and tolerant of my brother’s wives.
“Thanks Megan – give her my love and say hi to everyone please.”

Megan disconnects and I spend long minutes standing outside the back of the restaurant. There is no denying the fact that I want to be with Kate tonight. It doesn’t feel like the smart thing to do, but I don’t think I’m ever again going to have a rest until I’ve slept with her – got her out of my system - and it’s probably the only thing that will take the bitter taste from my conscience simply by adding yet another layer of rebuke.

Kate's house, later that night

I leave the car behind and walk the distance from the restaurant to the address Kate gave me - a five story brownstone with large bay windows overlooking the park. I look up from across the street and see her in her kitchen. Then she disappears and the light goes out. I cross the street, ring the bell with her name on it and open the main door when it buzzes. I go up the flight of wide wooden stairs to the first floor. Before I can knock, she has the door opened and is standing there holding a glass of wine in one hand and a half eaten a peach held in the other.

"Hi."

"Hi back." She brushes back some loose hair behind her ear, pulls the peach stone from between her lips, so that her pale, pink tongue briefly appears between her fingers, looks at me and begins closing the front door. "You coming in or are you selling something?"

I laugh and enter her apartment. "You're completely beautiful. How often do you hear that?"

"It's often implied." We kiss each other gently but meaningfully on the lips.

"Are the kids asleep yet?" I take off my shoes, follow her down the hallway and look around the main room. Her apartment is amazing. Turn of the century, big ceilings, and doors along the hallway leading to many rooms; but you can forget parking. I used to live in a place like this in Berlin with about six others. Great to live in but you could never park the car. Not that any of us had a car, but once we rented one for the weekend and spent forty minutes driving around trying to park it. The streets though, those wonderful streets in the old part of town, were built long before cars. No cars, no need for parking spaces. I run my eyes over the floor to ceiling bookshelves that begin in the hallway and continue into another room facing the street. "I love all your books. I wish I still had all my books. I collected books for so long and now they are mostly all gone from moving so much. You even have a library for God's sake … "

She doesn't say a word but takes a long drink of her wine, fills and passes a glass to me. We touch glasses with each other, and I drink from the large, cool glass, looking at the bottle on the table - Lailey Sauvignon Blanc – not bad. "The girls were asleep long ago – it's after ten. And it's not a library, it's a fourth bedroom full of books."

She blows out the candles sitting on the large wooden living room table. "Ask me if I'm a tree."

"Are you a tree?"

"No." She smiles, finishes off the wine in her glass, puts the glass down on the table and begins walking out of the room. "Come on Darling, we'll sleep in the library tonight." I finish my wine and follow her.[13]

Laying there against each other much later, dreaming away the last few minutes before that moment when we are again horribly and irreversibly strangers. In my dreams I am Mickey Mouse. The lost girls and the hobbledehoys. The smoke and idle babbling rabble filling my ears and my lungs like the smell of cheese on a hot summer's day, scraping my eyes like a sunbeam in a rain shower. There is a piece of cheese on my nightstand and it tastes like dust. Its perfumed aroma has disappeared. I pick up the piece of cheese and place it in a piece of paper and place this in the drawer next to the air freshener, the toothpicks, the glass of red peppercorns in watery brine, the Cinzano glass, the contraband. I shut the drawer and go back to sleep again.

Kate's house, September 18

When I awake it's almost seven and Kate's beginning to stir. I get up and dressed before the kids wake up. Out of curiosity I open the drawer beside the daybed and look inside, but it is empty. I look over to Kate who leans on her elbow and turns to me, "What are you looking for?"

I laugh, "My lost innocence?"

Her hair is askew across her face, making her nose and her lips appear crooked. She lays her forearms crossed over her face as she lays back again on the pillow and laughs. "I feel so completely horny. Can we do that again?"

"You're insatiable … I must have come four times. Did we get more than an hour's sleep?" I check my hair in the mirror on the back of the door.

"You'll have to do better than that, Dear. I'm very demanding – I told you, very pleasure driven." She pulls herself up onto her elbows. "It matters how many times *I* come Dearest, not you." She sticks out her tongue at me.

I sit down on the daybed beside her. "Mmmm – you smell so good - I've got to go now – and your kids are going to be awake any second. Want me to get you a coffee?" I lean over to kiss her, and she turns her cheek to my lips.

She shakes her head. "It's Saturday, where are you going? I don't drink coffee outside of work. Oh, by the way, the things I have in your basement?"

"Don't you work today? You mean the chairs or the plastic trays?"

"I have staff who work for me on the weekend. You looked in the boxes?"

"The packing slips. Kate, it would have been odd if I hadn't."
"The chairs, yes – the trays came already? Sorry, they weren't due until Monday."
"No problem – what are you doing with all this stuff? The chairs were returned you know. And what about the storage fee? Do you want a bill?"
"Darling don't be tiring. I'll give you your money, but don't send me a bill. Don't ask so many questions. How much do you want?"
"Give me what you think the storage is worth to you. It was a bit odd that the chairs weren't being returned to the delivery company but to another address."
"I'd have thought you'd want to store things for me because you want to make me happy Jessie. Why is that odd? They have one expeditor for deliveries and another for returns. What's so odd about that?"
"Ah – okay. Well I might love doing things for you, but I also have a partner so … let's keep this above board as much as possible, okay? There's the club committee to think about as well. We don't own the place you know."
She sighs. "You really need to think about your priorities."
"Uh huh. I've got to go – I need to arrange a flight out to see my Mum and then see about the restaurant. I'll call you later." I walk quietly down the hallway, get my shoes, leave the apartment, and close the door behind me - just as the sounds of small feet scamper past on the other side of the door. I hear Kate's voice and those of the kids, then I turn and go down the flight of stairs into the cool and noisy street below.

Marlies, that morning

Tomorrow is Alex's birthday. I'm battling with myself whether to send her flowers or a card or an email or to call her at the office. While the flowers are the most anonymous, they tentatively are the most explosive, suggestive … I don't know. Nothing else seems appropriate, and I guess if she doesn't like them, she can always give them away. I stop off at home, shower, change, then drive to the restaurant and walk across the street to the florists and order Alex a simple bouquet.
"No roses please – just something sorts of cheerful."
"Is it a birthday?"
"Yes."
"Then how about a birthday bouquet? It comes in a coffee mug and with a balloon."
This seems too cheesy for Alex. "No, just the flowers." I write down the address for the magazine I found on their website and add Alex's name.
"Does she have a telephone or office number?"
"Yes, but I don't have it in my head. Will it get to her anyway?"
"As long as she's the only Alex Rhodes then it should, yes. Is that cash or charge?"
"Can you put it on the restaurant's account?"
"Sure, no problem."
"Thanks Liz." I walk across the street to the restaurant and open the back door. Very hungry I go into the walk in, grab some eggs and cheese, take an English muffin from the bread box, and make myself some breakfast. The chocolate festival begins in four weeks – and I haven't done any preparation. David is going to have a huge laugh if I blow this. I take my breakfast into the dining room – scrambled eggs with cheddar cheese

over toasted English muffins – then fill and turn on the drip coffee machine I have stashed under the counter of the bar for times like this when I'm alone and lonely … and sit down to ponder the problem. I really want to do my tower of chocolate cruelty, but with Barb out … there must be something that hasn't yet been done in chocolate. Well, that I can publicly display.

The coffee takes time to run through, so I take advantage of this obvious down time to get some of the chocolate cups filled that I have ready for the grab and go counter. I go into the walk in and get the two containers of ganache we prepared yesterday – rosemary and dark chocolate infusion in one and lavender and white chocolate infusion in the other – pick up a large pastry bag and a #3 star tip – put it all on the counter and then unwrap the trays of chocolate cups we made. An hour later I´m still happily decorating chocolate cups, staff are arriving for their shifts, but I've never gotten around to pouring myself a coffee.

"Hey – how's things with Barb?" Judith's just come in, her big bag banging against the counter as she walks towards me.
"She's okay. I set up a phone card for her and David's coming by tonight. She'll be up again in a few weeks. What about you?"
"I don't know." I put the finishing touch to a chocolate cup as Judith reaches over and takes one. She tries it and smiles from ear to ear. "… mmm oh these are so good … "
"I need to fly out to see my Mum. I've been thinking of leaving Frank and Chris in charge of the kitchen. We

could close for a long weekend as well. Perhaps Tuesday as well as Monday. It would give them a chance to show their stuff. What do you think?"

"I'll be here. I think we should go for it."

"First thing though we need to order a new elevator. That'll be expensive … of course … yeah we'll be okay." I smile. "No panic."

***

Marlies, October 15

... I swear the battery on this laptop has a half-life of 15 minutes ... but let's not go there – I fear that my gut pounding, tear choking prose might make many of you nervous – therefore the tone of my discourse this chapter will be much cheerier, off key, bouncing, fluffy, jelly jammy ..... me? Me, I'm dead tired. Tired of eating over cooked fish in other people's restaurants and tired of repacking chocolate sculptures into bubble wrap filled boxes ...

...but I have a flight to catch kids – have to fly to Vienna to scare the straights with my chocolate perversions – scare the people, right ?– you know, next time you stick a wad of chocolate into your mouth then think of the 200,000 plus that work as slave labour to get those cocoa beans into the shops ... well, we'll see how this plays in the big city, right? Last year the small-town punters loved it, gobbled it up, literally walking about with the pieces in their grubby little hands licking them content as pigs in .... The big question is of course, will it play in Peoria?

Well, now I'm all out of licorice, the coffee maker is gurgling and screaming, and the Brunette's just padded barefoot past my field of vision with a croissant in her teeth so it's time to go. Let's keep this happy boys and girls – Vienna is a very long way away. It's almost not even western Europe, much – I mean, pull out your Atlases – it's teetering on the brink of the Ottoman sultanates. You need patience – you need a taxi and a train and another train, a bus, a plane, yet another train, and a subway before you are there. But damn is the coffee worth the trip ...

It's drizzling rain as I enter the Museum Quartier 21, snuggled in between all those temples, all that art, all that money, all that pretense and whispered critique and well – the organiser of the show confided to me over a beer at 2 in the morning of my arrival that only "serious art" makes it here. Serious art. So, I'm feeling pretty good. As you would, wouldn't you? As you would.

7:00 pm. There is a hushed silence as I enter the roped off area in a sparkly blue body stocking wearing nothing else but a pair of swim flippers and accompanied by six dwarves dressed in sackcloth and ashes. The block of chocolate awaits me in trembling anticipation beneath the hot lights. The crowd holds its breath as the music crescendos and I attack the chocolate block's girth with a vigorous urgency and a battery of instruments including an electric toothbrush, a hair dryer, surgical tweezers, nose hair clippers, an electric whisk all lending a virile and yet somehow unclear significance to the performance.

When it is done, I motion to the dwarves who wheel over the iron basket of glowing coals on squeaking coasters to my side. I remove one of the red-hot branding irons from the fire and as the halogen spots explode in intensity ram the branding iron into the middle of the chocolate sculpture where it sizzles, leaving my initials. Then all is darkness and silence. The crowd goes absolutely, fucking bananas ... Vienna. Eat at Treszenewskis Buffet. Wear Dorothy Strange.

Tear out your heart and cover it in marzipan. The coffees to die for and don't forget to bring back some chocolate.

I stare transfixed at Katrin's latest blog post. It sounds like the chocolate festival of my dreams. I turn around and watch the crew packing the baby rosemary and lavender plants into the boxes to transport them to the Strand. It's a cool idea, but certainly a blow torch or two would have helped make the evening news. After much deliberation Barb, Judith and I came up with a simple but elegant way to wow the socks off the festival jury while at the same time advertising our catering finesse. Taking a simple, tall shot glass as the basis of our idea – you know the type I mean – we filled one with rosemary dark chocolate ganache and the other with lavender white chocolate ganache. Then we plunged a small cutting of fresh rosemary in one and a cutting of fresh lavender into the other. Both the branches were safely enveloped in a small water pick. What we had was an interesting dessert and decoration creation - and after you ate the ganache the branches could even be planted - if they took root. When we ran a dozen of these up and placed them down the center of the banquet tables in the club for dinner, they looked elegant. We tried them in our grab and go, and on the dessert card, and were suitably impressed with the response. In the end we made fifty of each to ship to the Strand. "I wonder if people will think they're eating dirt?" asked Chris during our test phase. "Not with the white chocolate anyway." I replied. "We'll put out the word – 'Eat a dessert, plant a tree, save the planet.' Something like that … "

"What time do we have to be there?" I look at the clock – it's almost nine.
"Latest in an hour." replies Frank.
"Okay, who's coming with me? Frank? Chris?" I look around.
"Can I go Jessie?" I look behind me and there's Sarah – the apprentice who's been quietly biding her time in the pastry section with Chris. I look at Chris and raise my eyebrows.
"Chris? That okay? It can be one of you but not both."
"Sure, you can go Sarah – you put a lot of ideas into the event." Chris will make an amazing chef one day when she's on her own. I feel proud of all our crew.

"Okay, Sarah, grab yourself a clean jacket. I exchange my jacket for a new one and put in my special event buttons – the shiny gold ones – in the buttonholes of the jacket. "Blue team – move out!" Everyone chuckles, and Judith helps Barb hobble out the door – we pack everything and everyone in the van and drive off to the Strand a few blocks away as Judith and Barb wave us off.

The Strand Hotel, later that morning

An hour later we've unloaded and set up in the grand ballroom of the Strand Hotel. 'Not just a hotel, a lifestyle' – as their brochure claims. I can't resist tasting some of the other chocolate creations that are on display on little trays being handed out by a small army of elegantly clad hostesses. The ballroom décor is subdued, the ambience relaxing, however while the food performs well on the posters and cards laid out on the tables, as it is described in flowery tones to make your mouth water, it fails when asked to perform in my mouth. So, I feel really good about our entry as the jury members begin strolling through the room. The London Chocolate Week it ain't but for the region it's the best display of chocolate you can find. I see in the corner a large blue portable Costers' stand topped with their logo - standing at the edge looking on while her staff put the finishing touches to dozens of miniature chocolate cakes I see Kate.

I walk over to her and tap her on the shoulder. "Liebling, she purrs. you made it. Let me see your chocolate creations." I walk over with her and she looks them over. "Chocolate plants?" she asks questioningly. "Not plants, it's a chocolate ganache and you can plant the cutting. Nice idea eh?" Kate doesn't look convinced. "Dearest, leave the catering to me. Why don't you see about getting me a glass of champagne?" I walk over and get a few glasses – one for Sarah as well as myself. When I return Kate is at her stand chatting with the Mayor. I walk over to her and hand her a glass. "… so, we'd be more than happy to cater your re-election events your Honor – you have

my card." Hmm. It seems I was conveniently out of the way for that meeting. "Thank you. I hope you get a mention today."
I ring my glass against hers. "Oh, I plan on winning Darling." We smile at each other. I look around. "What do you think about getting a room here for the afternoon?"
"Is that all you ever think about?"
"Are you kidding? Of course, it is."
"You should watch your stand. Your little plants are attracting attention." I look over to see Sarah in heated conversation with one of the jury. I walk over and introduce myself. "Hello! Jessie Watkins, Marlies – what seems to be the problem?" Sarah scowls and one of the jury turns to me,
"Jessie, hello – I was just telling your chef here - the guidelines state that every part of an entry must be edible - your little trees are not."
I frown. "But of course, they are. Rosemary and lavender are both edible. In fact, they're both infused with the ganache."
The jury member nods his head and smiles, "Yes, this I know – the problem is that the tree itself is not edible."
"Well, that's debatable." I remove a few leaves from the rosemary and the lavender and put them in my mouth. "Yes, they are."

The man breathes in deeply. "I'm afraid that would leave the stem which certainly is not edible – nor is the water pick. I look at him, "You're kidding me. That's making too fine a point out of the rules."
"Well, it would fulfill them. I'm sorry, but we can't accept your entry if the entire chocolate creation is not edible." He walks away and confers with another jury

member as Kate comes up behind me. "Everything okay?"
"Kate, is everything edible on your chocolate cakes? The foil wrap for example?"
She sips her champagne and looks at me with her beautiful green tigress eyes … "Of course, Dearest – they're white gold, not foil. Completely edible. Didn't you read the rules?" She walks back to her stand and I turn to Sarah and raise my glass and smile.
"Sarah, you don't happen to have any poison with you, do you?"

The organiser was very nice to us in the end – let us show and retain our stand, but we were shut out of the prize giving – third place went to Micheal & Micheal who did realistic looking chocolate flowers in coloured chocolate, second place of course to Costers for their chocolate cakes, and first place oddly enough to a collection of edible but unlikely realisable walls of chocolate suspended from the ceiling on transparent cables from which guests could break off chunks. Nothing more than a grotesquely oversized chocolate bar I thought but there you go. Kate was happy – and if she's happy then I'm sure to be happy. We pack everything back into the van – not much is left over of the chocolates – even if they didn't pass muster for the judging, we did get a lot of interest in them from potential catering clients. We drive back to the restaurant and unload the van. "C'mon Sarah – I'm taking you out for a late lunch."
"Me?"
"Yes you –you did a good job and handled yourself professionally all morning. We're very proud of you – Chris says you're doing marvelously. Let's go - get

changed and grab your stuff." My mobile rings and it's Kate. "Hi Kate - congratulations."
"You left so soon – I thought you wanted to get a room?"
I laugh "Oh I think we both know that wasn't going to happen."
"I'm going for lunch. Join me." I look over at Sarah.
"Sorry, I can't - I've got a previous date." "With whom?"
"My staff."
"Oh, you can break that. I'm free, so you should join me."
"Sorry. Next time."
"Hmph. Well I hope for your sake there is a next time."
"I'll talk with you later Kate. Gotta go." I turn off my phone. Sarah is standing there with her backpack looking suitably impressed.

Marlies, that afternoon

I talk Sarah into eating at the Diner because it's a fun place I thought she'd like. Even though, between storm clouds, there was still a touch of the warm Fall sun. Perhaps a lunch on the balcony of Baxter's or The Mojo would have been more impressive. However, the tiny bit of sensuality that I felt building for Kate in the Strand thankfully died completely before lunch was even served. Sarah had a nice time and it was good to get to know her a bit better. I think she'll make a good pastry chef – she doesn't have what it takes to run her own show, but she'll quietly and efficiently put out a good product for someone who's lucky enough to get her. Perhaps we'll keep her ourselves if Chris moves on after she sits her exams next month. Now as I sit in my office in the early afternoon hours, I'm feeling tired and wonky. What in God's name did they put in the food? And why did I order battered sole with bacon? I want to sleep for a few hours now, not be productive - I feel padded - I wish I had something thick and brown, a habit perhaps, to cover my bloat. I feel as though it's expanding within me, whatever it was that I ate. Oh, my poor, poor stomach. I get up from the desk and walk into the dining room and extract a bottle of vodka – CCCP – from the freezer, pour myself a shot, replace the bottle and walk back to the office.

Downtown, later that afternoon

Anything to do with the body stress me. Sickness; the unknown happenings within. I get a yearly physical so I can see if my cholesterol level is okay but what if it's okay on just that day, they took the blood and then shoots back on up afterwards? I'd never know, would I? Doctors make me wary. Hospitals are the absolute worse. I´m waiting in the emergency ward once after breaking my toe even though I know they would just bandage it up and that´s that. Could do that myself, but I watch too much TV and I´m sure that there'll be a bone splinter that's waiting to break away and find its way to my heart and I´ll die. So, I go anyway. I wait three hours. It´s triage and I´m after the girl holding a stuffed turtle.

Dentists I don't mind so long as they give me a shot of Novocain. I am sitting in the Dentist chair now – some inflammation or another. It's a new guy, and the procedure is a lot different than I'm used to. No x-rays, no muzak, no gloves on his hands, and suddenly, he's drilling away! I´m wondering if maybe he´s forgotten about the Novocain, and then I´m struggling against the seat because the drill´s just hit a nerve or something pretty close and he seems actually even a little pissed off that I want a shot. I miss my usual Dentist a lot at this point, because he does everything by the book. Sure you´re there the entire afternoon but this guy seems to have some sort of quota this week that he´s a little behind on and he needs to get me in and out in ten minutes. My hair takes longer than this.

I'm not the best patient. I need to ease into going to the Dentist. I don´t want to go in and have him begin drilling as soon as I´ve sat back. I prefer the way here where you go in and familiarise yourself with the office, the Assistants, the rows of drills... and then you get an x-ray and you can know a few days beforehand what's going to be done and approximately how long you'll be strapped into the chair, then you make another appointment for a few weeks later. You can really ease into the whole thing. Sort of stretching out the pre-drill time in the same way that you take a Band-Aid off real slow like.

I like those sheets of plastic they staple in your mouth, and the reflective glass of the Dentist´s glasses so you can see what´s going on, the attractive Assistant, the window, everything. I need the gadgets, the machine that goes ping, all the sacramentals[18] that validate the profession. It´s all part of being Catholic. We can´t commune with God in the forest nor does it work for us standing about in a prefab church in the middle of an Iowa cornfield. We need the hundred and twelve cardinals, the incense, all the stuff. You know? So, I´m out of the chair and heading out of the Dentist´s office and I think that he´s been a little vindictive, because he´s frozen half my face and I'm not going to be able to taste a thing at dinner ...

Marlies, that evening

Dinner service is unremarkable except for a brief but telling moment with one of Judith's new service staff, Becky. We've got a vegetable gruyere terrine on for our evening appetizer served with an apple and onion compote and a few slices of fresh toasted bread. However, we left the bread up to the choice of the Diner – which is always a mistake. We should have just kept it at sesame or pumpkin bread – something obvious and simple – so I'm looking at the order and then at Becky because she hasn't specified what sort of bread she'd like, or rather the customer - "Sorry, what?"

"What type of toast do you want with the terrine?" She looks at me. "Ermmm brown. Isn´t all toast brown?"

I look at her in disbelief. "What sort of bread?" "Oh. Ummm ... sorry, I'll go ask." She sorts of blushes and goes back out to the dining room.

I look over to Judith who's smiling to herself and shaking the crumbs from the bread baskets over the sink. "Oh, that's just beautiful Judith - thank you very much for the new, comedy waitress …" Judith guffaws, and continues shaking out the bread baskets.

Jessie's house, later that evening

As I dodge the traffic back home that night, I make out Gwen and Dorothy coming down the stairs of the theater, so I honk and wave, but I don't think they really knew it was me. I've known Gwen and Dorothy ever since Freshman year but never see them anymore. Even though we live in this relatively small city you rarely run into people you've known for years – which is odd. They still live on the notorious Parkline street, a Greek street though they abhor the whole frat and sorority thing. Unfortunately, their house looks right into a frat house and after a few incidents of 'mooning', a method of interpersonal communication popular with some of the leading houses, they decided to paint the outside of their offended window black. Drapes just wouldn't make the sort of statement they were after. Drapes say, 'Oh, don´t do that you silly frat boys.' Black painted windows say 'Die!'. Gwen and Dorothy never were ones for mincing their words.

I spent some time at their place many years back - we were off to some party - and I noticed that up on the refrigerator was a photograph of the inside of that very same appliance. Instead of opening the door each time they wanted to look for a snack, they could just study the photo. This lent itself to choosing breakfast while they were doing their hair, drying off after a shower … it was a major time saver and saved electricity. Each time something was removed the item was blacked out in the photo. When the photo was completely black, they went shopping.

Kate calls me at home about nine that evening and rings my doorbell about fifteen minutes later. I've got an empty chip bag on my lap along with my laptop and two weeks of paperwork and, because I'm a fitness nut, a bottle of sparkling water. I can't be bothered to get up so I just yell – "Come in!" Now my remote control has a very finicky nature and must be constantly fiddled with, shaken, threatened, held upside down and the like for it to work. I'm lounging there half comatose in front of a painfully cheap sex movie from the eighties which they like to air some nights on VOX. So, before Kate comes into the living room, I'm trying to change the channel but to no avail. I try to turn the TV off, adjust the sound - I'm frantically bashing the remote against the side of the couch as she walks down the painfully short hallway. Panicking, I leap to the set and yank the cord from the wall almost toppling the set from its perch atop the pyramid of VCR, DVD, CD player and books on which it precariously wobbles

"Hi." she walks past me and grabs the bag of chips, kicking off her heels in the process. Her mouth being full of chips I don't get the kiss I had been hoping for.
"Hey back!"
"What happened to lunch? Haven't we had certain discussions about your lack of commitment, selection processes, your priorities …?" Kate screws up the chip bag and reaches over to plug in the TV again. Then she picks up the remote and turns it on with one click. To the last channel it was tuned to.
"Hmm, okay. Have you been watching pornographic films again?" Immediately the amazing trust I inspire in her rushes to the surface.

"Yes and no." she waits, undoing her hair, watching me with a raised eyebrow.
"Yes, it was porn, but it wasn't real porn. It was TV porn."
"Real pornography? There's a difference?" She turns towards the screen where a heavily made up blonde is gleefully sucking on another woman's breasts – "It looks like real pornography to me."
I take the remote from her and switch the TV off. "Yes. See TV porn you don't choose, it's just running, and you watch it or not and neither the quality nor quantity is very good. It's a cheap thrill. You didn't ask for it, it was just there, and you watched it …" She has her arms crossed and is feigning great interest in what I'm saying. ".. while on the other hand real porn, video rental porn, is much more discriminating, focused, and therefore bad. You have chosen to drive to the store with the intent to find porn, chosen to rent a specific movie, and paid money for it. It is intentional and therefore much worse. TV porn is like licking the icing on the cake while rental porn is cutting a slice and eating it before dinner. It's the mortal as opposed to the venial sin."
"Aha. Intellectual Catholicism. Look, don't try this rationalisation on me when I find you in bed with your apprentices okay? Like you don't get enough sex already you have to watch it on TV. I see you cooked …", she's pointing to my pant leg at a huge telltale pasta sauce stain ": is there anything left?" She turns to the kitchen and sees the bowl of salad I have prepared for her and the small casserole of lasagna which is gently bubbling in the oven.
I follow her into the kitchen and take a half bottle of champagne out of the fridge and begin opening it as

Kate opens the cutlery drawer and pulls a napkin from the stack on the counter. "You see how lucky you are to have such a nice person like me to cook dinner for you after a hard day?" She comes over to me and wraps her arms about my waist and smiles as the cork pops out of the bottle. "I'm not sooo hungry … what was that you were saying about sin just now …?"

Jessie's House, October 16

Ah ... fiber, bran, cholesterol. It isn't that I've become suddenly obsessed with intake so much as my intake system is beginning to grumble and complain and rebel in little ways. Better to give in to the forces that move you than face a lock-out. Or a lock-in which in this case would be a damn sight worse. I read that alcohol and tobacco combined don't help much in the stomach area either; though interestingly enough if you're talking gallstones you should drink a bit to help lessen the chances of getting them at all. I was given the exact opposite advice regarding my gall bladder and now am facing a ban on wine while my cellar faces a very long lie down. Good for the wines, bad for me. I wonder what normal people think about in the morning.

I flip closed the copy of Eating Well and put it beside the bed. Kate snores gently beside me. It's again far too early in the morning. I get out of bed and put some coffee on and then climb back into bed again to carefully snuggle against Kate's warmth - breathing in her fragrance, running my fingers across her shoulder - before getting dressed. I can't get over just how good she feels to hold. I stroke her hair and take deep breaths of the aroma of her skin.

Market Cafe, that morning

I run Barb down sitting at the market Cafe drinking a coffee with David. We nod at each other and Barb gets up on her crutch. "Still not 100% yet?"
She shakes her head. "The doctor said I should be really careful. They had to put a screw in it and everything." David stands up and tosses his and Barb's empty coffee cups into the garbage then gives her a little hug. He walks past me and nods with a thin smile, "Jessay …"
"Morning David."
"So, shall we get our order together? Should I support you or get a cart?"
"I'm fine – I could have done this by myself. I need the practice and you should be at home making Kate breakfast." Barb has always had a lookout for my wellbeing in matters of the heart.
"How do you know that Kate's at my place?" Again, I am treated to Barb's hooded eyes of reproachful boredom.
"Jessie, everyone knows Kate's at your place."
Barb is full of interesting but wholly irrelevant little tidbits of information like this. "Everybody knows? I sure hope her partner doesn't."
Barb and I go through the market collecting what looks good and then I drive her back to her place. I swing by the grocery to pick up some things for breakfast and drive home. When I open the back door, I hear Kate's singing and the sound of the shower coming from the open bathroom door. I open the fridge and take out a bottle of orange juice, pour a large glass and drink it, then begin putting away the groceries and place the espresso machine on the stove element which I turn on

to heat. When the coffee has run through, I heat two cups of milk with the steam arm, let them sit, and take the paper off one of the muffins – blueberry oat bran - that are still warm from the bakery, breaking off some which I eat leaning against the sink, looking out the window into the backyard.

I flew out to see my Mum three weeks ago to be there when she came back home from the hospital. [14] I turned up at the airport and suddenly felt incredibly old and alone – Mum was always at the airport to greet me and this time she wasn't. I took a cab home to find she was still in hospital, so I took one of the cars in the driveway – everyone has their own car and it seems at times that we don't have a driveway but more a car lot. I drove to the hospital and walked into my mother's room – large and sterile and there she was laying there surrounded by my weeping siblings and their wives and kids – though the kids were mostly ambivalent being both still hooked to the breast. Even Angie had made it in but on an earlier flight than I – but had left Nicki with Marta who was still not talking with me but had no animosity towards Nicki - and was now in the cafeteria downstairs. I chastised everyone on the spot for weeping and gnashing their teeth – what would Mum think if she woke up to this hysterical scene? So I went down to see Angie and we smoked our way through the hours of our denial on the wind swept cafeteria patio and drank weak boiling hot coffee from those damn stupid plastic cups from the coffee machines in the lobby when the cafeteria shut up for the night. It was a scary and dreadful time and the entire week I was in denial of my mother's impending death.

I didn’t say goodbye – I mean, I did obviously - I wouldn’t just get back on the plane – but I couldn’t say goodbye forever – I was coming back again soon anyway, wasn’t I? I didn’t want her to think I was resigned or without hope. I still have hope. Only because the alternative is not something I’d like to dwell upon. I don't want my mother to die. I don’t want to move to that next phase. I don’t want it to be me next. So, she’s holding on. We both are. My mother’s not going to go easily into that good night. She’s tough as nails but I don’t see just how she keeps going.

Jessie's house, later that morning

I hear the door of the bathroom open and the heavy patter of Kate's bare feet padding across the hardwood floor. She comes up behind me and lets the long length of her wet hair fall about me.
"Darling …" She purrs into my ear, "… what did you bring me?"
I turn and take her arms around me and kiss her.
"Mmmm. You are all wet and you … are … dripping on me!" I smile at her and she laughs. "I brought you some muffins. You like a coffee?"
"Yes, but I am very wet and very late – I have a meeting in less than an hour." I look into her eyes, see her dimpled cheeks as she smiles.
"Very wet …?" I put down the rest of the muffin on the counter, grabbing the belt of my bathrobe she's wearing and pulling it away.
She releases me with a cry, laughing, and walks slowly backwards out of the kitchen. "Hey! If you want to say goodbye to me, you had better be very quick about it …"
"Don't you want me to make you some breakfast?" She's backing up, shaking her head back and forth with a wicked grin playing about her face. "No breakfast? I thought I'd make you an omelet …" She's backing through the kitchen towards the bedroom as I take the whisk from the stand on the counter and brandish it in front of me, laughing all the while. "Here, let me show you …" and with a laugh and a shriek she turns and runs into the bedroom. We fall onto the bed and kiss, smiling at each other and laughing. "I want you so much Kate."

She smiles, "I want you – but I really have to go – hold that thought until tonight and fix me that coffee."
"Sure."

I get up and go back into the kitchen to finish the two lattes, sprinkle some cinnamon on top as Kate comes out of the bedroom brushing her hair and wearing a pair of my pajamas. Damn those pajamas look sexy on her … I must be getting old. Lately I dream a lot about renovating houses with generic women, or landscaping gardens with them. Once I dreamt of grocery shopping with a woman - just grocery shopping walking up and down the aisles with some kid sitting in the shopping cart. In the morning I was thinking, so who's the kid!? God knows what sort of disturbed psyche I must have to dream such stuff, and just how banal do you have to be to find women in men's pajamas sexy?
"Jessie, I have to be at home tomorrow - my partner is coming back with the girls." She throws her arms around my neck. "It's been a great, few days ... I wish we could do this all the time."
"Yes – tonight to begin with", I kiss her cheeks, "but later always - with more space – more bedrooms – the girls, you and I, space for Nicki when he's here. Kate, let's live together."
She breaks off our embrace. "I can't. We've talked about this Jessie. This is what I want, and I can't offer anything more than this." She goes into the bathroom and I can hear her brushing her teeth.
I call after her, "I know. You've said it before. But I don't accept it. Let's move in together."
She comes out of the bathroom, wiping her face with the towel and kisses me on the nose as she walks past. "I can't. I can't get divorced. What would people say?"

She takes her coffee and leans against the counter drinking it and looking at me.

"Who cares what people would say. You wanted to leave the university anyway – we're not employees there - I don't see how that has anything to do with it."

"Don't be unnecessarily obtuse Jessie. You know what I mean."

"No, no I don't – unless you how you think you're seen Kate. It's bullshit Kate - you stay with your partner for the sake of appearances. Brava ..."

"You're being tiresome Jessie. You don't have children and you don't know what it's like."

"Bullshit I don't."

Kate looks at me and finishes her coffee. "I have to go. Don't ruin a good thing Jessie – and don't bring my family into this."

"Sorry Sweetheart but your family are in this already. You may be in denial but if anyone ever asks about us, I'll not be. That includes your partner. If you had wanted a quick roll in the sack, then you should have called one of your admirers. This is very real for me Kate."

"I have to go to work." She puts her cup on the counter and goes into the bedroom to get dressed. I go into the bathroom and take a shower. When I come out again, she has left.

Marta's house, much later that morning

I walk over to Marta's. She's been home sick the last few days from work and I've run a few errands for her at the market, got some groceries for her, and picked up Anna's Halloween costume – a fairy princess of course - from the drycleaners. I'm sitting in Marta's kitchen while she makes coffee. Angie is already booked to be out of town at the end of the month and I'd like Nicki to have a good Halloween this year – last year he had to go with his Mum on a business trip and spent the night in a hotel room watching movies in Frankfurt - where they don't even have Halloween. Poor kid.

"Let's take the kids into the city for trick and treat. There is a boat trip along the river, and it's all decorated as a haunted house. Anna and Nicki would love it."

"I don't know if this is such a great idea Marta, you know I said Kate's kids might be joining us that night, right?"

"... Kate is married, where is her partner?"

"Her partner will be away that week and she has to cater the Board of Governor's banquet. I said I'd take the girls for trick and treat. Do you have any more coffee?"

"So, what is your point?"

"That I would be in the city with you – or to be more precise just with you ...."

Marta gets up and brings the coffee pot back to the table. "How stupid, it's going to the city with the kids – there will be hundreds of kids there."

"Are you trying purposely to be obtuse or do you really believe that?"

She pours more coffee into our cups and sits down, "What is this 'obtuse'?"
"Umm, silly, thick, not understanding."
She kicks me under the table very hard on the leg.
"You mean she thinks we will be sleeping together."
"Ow! Hey!" I take a mouthful of my coffee. "Yes, she probably thinks we're sleeping together already. Did you put cocoa in my coffee?"
"Yes. Do you always have this effect on women? This wonderful glamour? I know you are a great lover but ... oui … I cannot believe I am even talking to you knowing you touch her … okay - I don't feel the need to have you between my legs so your charm must not be that strong. Perhaps she is afraid of losing you."
"I doubt that – more likely afraid of losing her storage space at the club." I stir in some more of the cocoa into my coffee. "On the other hand, she doesn't like it very much when I admire another woman. In this regard you are much more mature." I smile.
"Of course – I am secure in myself. However, I too think have your head on a swiffel."
"Swiffel? You mean swivel."
"Swiffel, yes. So, you have looked at other women? Looking is not allowed? You have an affair with a married woman, and she is angry that you look at other women? I don't like this Jessie – but Kate, what does she expect? Ah you Canadians! In France a woman would kill a man for sleeping with another woman, but if they fought each time he looked at one … Ha!... I don't understand this puritanism."
"Kate might be German. I think." Mmmm cocoa and coffee is great together.
"Ah yes the Germans; frightened little men and bossy women who have sex with the lights out."

Hmm that's sort of true, Kate doesn't like the light on. I wonder if that's generally true. "Well it's my experience that most every woman likes to keep her man on a short leash. Having your lover go out for the evening with your children and another woman would not, by most standards, be acceptable. Do the French like the light on or off? "

"We only have sex during the day ... oui - you keep a dog on a short leash and one day he will bite you - give him a long leash and you still have him on a leash but most of the time he doesn't know it. Look, it would be a great time and be fun for the kids and you can tell your precious Kate I promise I won't succumb to your animal charms okay?"
I take a sip of my coffee and look at her, "Let me think about it."

University Campus, that afternoon

I swing by the student union building for a beer on my way to the club. I like dropping by even now and remembering what it was like to cook there, Rodd behind the bar … these were good days. Classes must be thin - the place is packed and filled with the din of voices and billiards and foosball and three big screen TVs. “I like that wraithlike post-apocalyptic look.” “What is his ‘want’ supposed to mean?” “It’s older English, noun instead of a verb it means his habit.” “Oh. Is ‘he made his made into the street’ older English ‘cause that’s what you wrote …” “How was the return lecture of Professor Twain?” “Like the second coming of Christ. Amazing what a suit will do for you.” “How do you want the tuna fish sandwich?” “I don't know - lettuce, mayonnaise, make it fun I guess.” “Where did you go yesterday?” “Oh, we didn't know, so we sporadically went to the mall” “Sporadically? How the hell did you manage that? That some sort of quantum thing?” “HAHAHA Spontaneously, I meant spontaneously!” “How´s classes going?” “Oh, I have to do this five-page lab report for Biology.” “Five pages? You could What’s App five pages. I’ve had footnotes longer than that.” “So, what´s it like to be single now, enjoying life without Cynthia?” “The SWC 4x4 is doing to all the major events!” “SWC?” “Semester without Cynthia...” “HAHAHA” “How much mayonnaise IS there in here?” “Hey, look, you said it was fun with mayonnaise!” “Where did you buy your sweater?” “Oh, at Lansdowne.”

The blonde ponytailed Freshman pledge … a Beta? Gamma? with a button nose, freckles, dark purple varsity sweater and baggy jeans made the statement as though it were where the Gods shopped. The cacophony of voices from dozens of students reaches me at the bar as I enjoy my beer and thank God I'm no longer in the thick of things.

The University Club, later that afternoon

I walk across to the club. The windows in the club kitchen haven't opened in more than a decade. This was one of the first things on my list when we took it over, and I've been at the university facility people for a month – and it's taken another month for Administration to decide whose responsibility this actual job might be. So, I called in a repair company and got an estimate, mailed it to all the vice Presidents I could find in the university who had the word facility or property in their title and ordered the work to be done. Today the repair guys are coming to do the work and waiting in front of the club I see two people in suits who probably aren't Bob and Andy the fixit boys … "Hi" I greet them "

"Hi, Jessie is it?"

"That's me. What can I do you for?"

"I'm Trisha Bentley and this is Micheal Andrews – I'm head of property and Mike's head of facilities."

I shake both the woman and the man's hands. "So, what's up?"

"Well, we both received your cost estimate for the windows and today we received a work order from the company."

"Yes, they're coming by today to repair the windows."

"But we haven't given an okay to this."

"And?"

"Well, you can't just order repairs on university property without the proper authorisation." "Really. Well, Ms., Bentley? Have you ever worked in a kitchen with closed windows? I don't mean cooking dinner – I mean for eight or ten hours? It's not very pleasant."

"That may be, but the proper workflow is that …"
"Yes, I think I can anticipate your thoughts here ... the windows in the club kitchen? they haven't been operable for more than ten years. I think, after ten years, the statute of limitations on even university bureaucracy have probably expired." I hold up my hand and continue, "See, I'm more of a doer than a talker, and I think Dr. Bleary and the club committee would be happy that the work's finally been done that your department should have taken care of a long time ago."
"I don't think I like your attitude at all. This is university property and … "
"Yes, but specifically University Club property. Why don't you contact Dr. Bleary to sort this out? I don't work for you – I'm more than happy to cook for you any time you're a guest of the club – however I'd prefer to do this with the benefit of some fresh air."
"Well you will have to take care of the billing directly with the club itself. We can't be responsible for any unauthorised repairs on campus."
"Uh huh. Tell me, do your office windows open Ms. Bentley?" They both just look at me and turn about to leave. "Have a nice day." I turn to unlock the outer doors and ring Dr. Bleary on my mobile. He isn't in his office, so I leave a message. "Dr. Bleary, Jessie here, I have the repair men here for the club kitchen windows. I think however you'll be getting a call from property management. Just so you know. A Ms. Bentley was just here to see me. Bye!" I close my mobile and collect a small stack of flyers and newspapers which have been left in front of the club door, open it to enter just as my mobile rings.

"Hello?" "Hello, this is the delivery gate – there's a truck on its way to you."
"Okay, thanks." "No problem." I hang up and see the truck coming along the main back road through the windows as I go inside the club. As I'm not expecting anything this can only be another delivery from Kate. I've only seen $100 so far for all the things she's stored and that handed to me in cash one day over lunch. I turn on the lights of the club and go to the bar, take out a bottle of mineral water and pour myself a glass. Then I turn on the coffee machine. We've got an afternoon workshop in the main downstairs room followed by cakes and coffee upstairs. There's a knock on the door and I turn to see a delivery guy from Remington Appliance - according to the logo on his baseball hat, on his breast pocket and on the arm of his jacket. – standing in the doorway. "Hi, I've got a delivery for you – from Ms. Morris."
"Hi, let me guess – something from Remington Appliance?"
He laughs, "Yeah, we're pretty well branded, aren't we?"
"You don't have the logo on your boxers well, do you?" We both laugh. "So, what do you have for me?"
"I've got twelve microwaves, twelve deep fryers, twelve salamanders … twelve of about everything …" he reads from the manifest.
"Okay, so it all goes downstairs. It's getting full. Come on, I'll show you."
We go downstairs and I show him the half full storage room. "No problem, we'll fit it all in." "I'm going back up – see you when you're finished." I go back to the main floor and find two men waiting for me at the door. "Hi, can I help you?"

"Yes, is this the University Club?"
"Yes, it is."
"We're supposed to pick up some wine glasses from you."
"I guess these are the wine glasses in the cellar … you have a truck?"
"It's on its way."
My mobile rings again and it's the delivery gate announcing the arrival of another truck. "Thanks." I close my phone. "Where are you from? Do you have any paperwork on this?" One of the men pulls out a much-folded paper and a pen which I read and sign, notice it's from a local restaurant supply house, and hand it back to him. The eighteen cases each of 72 wine glasses disappear as mysteriously as they had arrived.

The Office Bar, that evening

Each time I call Kate's number her phone remains unanswered. Fine. So, in the evening Bronwyn, Judith and I go along to 'The Office' to hear Darlene read from her new book. The bar located across from the train station was originally a turn of the century hotel which has seen much better days - now it's a popular venue for readings and local bands. Tonight, it's made up in a sort of Alice in Wonderland theme and the buffet features as its main centerpiece conceptual ravioli with almonds, mini swiss chard, and pine nut strudel. Yummy! Near the entrance is a collection of Papier Mache oddities on auction for the local Growing Chefs charity – so I bid $35 for a large, bright yellow Papier Mache clock with red cardboard hands for which I am mocked heartily by Judith. Bronwyn bids a cool $100 for a thick pink two-meter-high phallus.

At the foot of the staircase are girls dressed as ballet dancers in blood red tutus and stockings, while on the staircase above them are dozens of pale faced girls in black pillbox hats and body stockings blowing bubbles over the railing onto everyone. Beside me stands a well-known psych Professor wearing a flower arrangement on his head and, beside him, an art Professor in her very late forties sporting close cropped hair and wearing doc martens, who together with her recently-promoted advisee is showing everyone the ultrasound photos of their awaited baby.

Why this trend in art circles to negate one's sex? Men poncing about like scalded rabbits and women either stomping around like Hitler Youth or huddled in a corner like scowling anaemic laboratory rats, chain smoking themselves to death. Unlike Judith, who is dressed like Isadora Duncan or Bronwyn who is dressed like Catwoman. I always feel out of place at these events with my middle-class prejudices but then I'm long out of the Zeitgeist thing. If I was ever into it. Nietzsche wrote that without art, man is lost. I think man is lost regardless and is just using art to prop himself up before the fall.

"Men and women, I would like to welcome you." A tall blonde woman wearing an outfit of what appears to be blue aluminum foil raps the microphone for attention. The girls on the staircase begin blowing more bubbles and the ballerinas spin about as music roars out of hidden speakers ... *Black silk White skin Phosph'rous In the night - Fingers Wrapped tightly 'round the barrel Of a gun - Drip-ping blood wet lacquer succubus - Eros --- is Rhiannon the nightmare! …* There continues the gothic sound of a rusty electrified oboe accompanied by what could be a violin. The applause for the opening display is generous and the buffet is quickly stripped of its weight. There are a few speeches and then Darlene comes on stage. "Good Evening. I'd like to read to you the first short story from 'Not Now, Judith' - a collection of stories featuring waitresses all named Judith and who do not affect the stories in which they appear."
Judith groans beside me. "Oh, I feel just so honored …" I nudge her and smile.

The sky is heavy with the threat of rain. From my table at the front of the tiny coffee shop I look out into the darkening street. The sounds of the night find me here, as does a lot of unpleasant business. My meet is late. Experience has taught me that when a woman tells you to be somewhere at 7:30, she means 8:00. Inversely, if she tells you she's a size six, she means size seven. My coffee is cold, and I signal the waitress for more. The solid surety of my 'friend' comforts me as it weighs down beneath my armpit; Hey, these are violent times. I move over the half empty cup as the waitress appears. I read her name tag - Hi! My Name is Judith. This time the boiling liquid makes it into my cup and not over my sleeve. I take a long drag from the unfiltered cigarette. My thank you is harsh and raspy. She asks if I would like another piece of pie. "Not Now, Judith." She returns to the counter and I to my vigil.

At 8:15 a young woman enters the place; she's looking around even before she has the door closed. She comes over to my table. From her expression I know something bad is going to come out of her lips. I even know what it's going to be. She sits down.

'Hello, I talked to you earlier this afternoon?' I nod silently. 'You have to help me. I've heard that's what you do well, help people.'
I look at her a long time through the cloud of cigarette smoke and steam from my coffee. 'Yeh', I reply, 'I help people - but that's not all I do well Miss.'
Her attitude quickly changes. 'Look, let's cut the small talk, Ace. Word on the street says you're my man.'
I stare at her long and hard. 'If this has anything to do with a certain missing necklace, then the word on the street should have told you that I'm not.'

I stub out my cigarette and dig in my pocket for some bills.
'Hey!', she half rises and grabs my wrist. Her grip is cool and somewhat pleasing. I notice her lipstick for the first time; it is red, bright red, as red as the blood I knew I'd be wiping from my hands before this caper was over. I relax in my seat.
'You know about the necklace then?' She shakes her head and looks at me with big cow eyes. Eyes just like how Clarabelle looks at you in all those milk ads.
'You don't get my kind of reputation without keeping your eyes and ears open, Miss.' I pull out a cigarette, offer her one, she refuses. Everyone knew about the necklace. It was big news on the street, and it was bad news. 'So, what do you want me to do, Miss?'

I'm enjoying this part. The silent 'negotiation of my fee'.
'I want you to help me find the necklace. I lost it and if I don't recover it soon...' She begins to cry.
I smile. I can't resist restructuring my fee schedule.
'Hey, finding a lost spouse is one thing, finding a 'lost occult necklace' is going to be a little more costly.'
'I'll pay you whatever you want', she pulls out a bank book, 'See, my Grandmother deposited some money into my account.' I scan the page of the bank book. The broad is loaded.
I figure, what the hell, my social calendar ain't exactly bursting. 'OK' I rise. 'But we go now, you keep quiet and you do whatever I tell you.'
She nods and grabs her purse. I toss a fin onto the center of the table, tilt back my hat and dig my hands deep into the folds of my coat pockets. I take them out again so that I can open the door.

In the street I size up my next move. The skirt is right behind, not giving me any clues. 'So, do you want to tell me maybe which way I should go?', I toss my head to the side, my voice bitingly sarcastic. She looks at me, her eyes getting larger by the second.
'I thought you told me to stay quiet?!' She almost screams this and then begins shaking.
'OOOOOOEEEEEEOOOOOO...' a high-pitched whining noise emanating from her.
I turn and glare at her.
'That way', she points up the street towards the railway.
'Gee, thanks. ' I walk out into the street, checking both ways before doing so.
Ahead of us another couple is crossing the empty roadway. My client is lagging, so I hurry her on.
'Would you move your ass?' I run on ahead. She catches up, the woman ahead of us turns and looks at me as though I was something, she just scraped off her shoe. The goon on her arm turns too, thinking maybe I'm talking to them. My client bursts out laughing as we reach the other side. 'Would you mind sharing your joke with me?' I start up the sidewalk, not looking back.
'That woman thought you were such a jerk for yelling at me back there' she gasps as she rushes to catch up with me.
I don't have time for this. 'Yeah? Maybe she was thinking what a bimbo you are for being with such a jerk like me in the first place.' I grin widely.

We're looking all over the place. I know this is ludicrous. The necklace is probably around the neck of some moll who found it in the ladies' room in one of any of the dozens of little speakeasies in town. The wind is cold on my back. I get another chill when I look back at my client. She's walking with her head down rechecking my steps. The streetlight's glow betrays her two-toned hair colouring. 'I hope this chill ain't love' I muse to myself. The first rule in my business is never fall in love with a dame, especially when that dame is paying you. Though, the way her black roots merged gently into the brown...

She stops and begins looking frantically here and there.
'What's up?' I reach for another smoke.
'I don't remember if I was on this side of the street, or the other.' Across the street looms the construction site. The light of the moon reflected jutting steel girders and barbed wire. There is a musty, earthy smell in the air from the open pit beyond the hurriedly erected fencing. I put two and two together and as usual they still made four.
'You mean you could have been anywhere in the area?' I look at her in disbelief. She's been taking me for a patsy the whole time.
'I think I crossed somewhere along here', she responds sheepishly.
'Look Miss, I'm a busy guy. Exactly how did you cross?' I attempt to work out some sort of trajectory through which the necklace might have fallen.
'Oh, I don't know, I think I sort of ran this part, then skipped into the middle of the road and then did a back and forth sort of jig thing before coming to the side here.' She's in the middle of the road parodying the movements like some crazed marionette suddenly cut

loose from its strings. I follow slowly, savouring the movements of her body.

At the edge of the site, I hear voices coming towards us. With cat-like speed, I push my client into the mud and roll into a crouch, catching myself in the head on a large two by four. Dazed but still in action, my hand instinctively moves to my holster as I search the area for trouble. Across the street a couple of schoolgirls walk by oblivious to our presence. I relax.
Behind me the skirt is coughing on a mouthful of mud, scraping clean her outfit. 'What the hell are you DOING?!' she screeches.
'Hey', I look at her with weather worn eyes, 'You wanted to tag along. You're lucky I didn't accidently shoot you.'

I force calm on myself. This job is making me jumpy. Suddenly I get this feeling, I don't know how to explain it, kind of that feeling when you buy a pair of pants tagged with your waist size but you don't have time to try them on, and you just know that they've been tagged wrong ... My gut bunches into a fist and I push by the dame. She slips and tumbles into a large puddle. I walk over to a pile of dirt at the side of the road. On top of the dirt is the necklace. It's a little worse for wear, but the beam of my flashlight makes it twinkle merrily. I pick it up and wipe the grime off on my sleeve. I pass it over to my client, who has just caught up with me.

'This yours?' I grin, and reach for a smoke, confidence oozing out of my shoes.

'Yes!' She throws her arms about my neck and screams with joy. I back off. I know all about dames. One minute they're all over you, the next they're scratching your eyes out for not opening the door for them. She puts the necklace around her neck and instantly turns into a blonde. My heart breaks like a child's toy the day after Christmas. I hate blondes. She counts out the crisp bills that are my fee, and hands them to me.

Another job done, another night the city sleeps in peace. A light rain begins to fall, rustling the thick canopy of leaves above my head. The park is deserted at this hour, but I like it that way. I knock back a shot from my flask, feeling good. I hope she keeps her necklace tightly around her neck in the future - next time I might not be there, might not be so easy to find, the world not so easy to save. I flick my cigarette into the wet grass and hurry home.

Darlene closes the book and smiles out to the crowd. Everyone claps and cheers – it seems to have gone over well – I especially like the irony of the waitress having nothing to do with the story – I'll have to get a copy. We walk about unsuccessfully searching for Darlene as we finish eating our pasta from limp paper plates. Moments later she and Jorge emerge from the crowd, survey the event, and plant themself at our table - on our table as the two chairs we did find were a gift from the Gods. Darlene has a champagne glass in on hand, inside of which float her contact lenses and, on her head, sits an excessively large hat. Ted is wearing the sleeping Peg in a sort of bizarre backpack/camping cot contraption.

We all hug her. "That was a hilarious story – I love the style – and the fact that there's really no waitress in the story." Darlene beams.
Ted rubs his eyes, "Doesn't all this smoke make your eyes ache?" Judith, Bronwyn, and I put out our cigarettes though everyone in the place must be smoking. "Did you see the riots on TV last night? Just great. I have to go into the city tomorrow and there's unease in the local community."
I nod, "Last night's? Yeah. Crazy. Are people rioting because they're pissed about something or because they want free TVs and Stereos? If I were going to riot, I'd be knocking down the door of City Hall not Media Mart. What's that all about anyway?"
Darlene laughs, "You're such an idealist!"
"Yeah just an old-fashioned revolutionary."
Judith pipes up, "What would you do if you're walking down the street and there's looting all about you and oops there's a broken window and a nice laptop just sitting there for the taking, you going to leave it because it wouldn't target the issue at hand?"
"Um, am I being filmed, like on the news? Am I armed in this scenario?"
"What?!" this loudly from Darlene.
"No, I mean, sure if I was pretty sure I wouldn't get caught I would probably take it, but I didn't go downtown looking for a laptop it just happened to be there like you said. My point is that I think most people go with the laptop in mind and I would go with the issue in mind. I'm not going to run amok in the streets just on the off chance of getting an iPod."

The crowd seems to be getting larger and our space smaller. Everyone looks at each other and nods that it is now an optimal time to leave. Outside Darlene and Ted make their apologies for the sleeping Peg and walk off to their hotel. Bronwyn begs off further drinks owing to a late date.

“It’s almost eleven – who begins a date after eleven?” I ask.

Bronwyn smiles – “Airline pilot – doesn’t come in for another thirty minutes. I’ll need to fluff the pillows and polish the silver first.” She kisses Judith and I chastely on the lips and makes her way up the street home.

Judith and I walk to the restaurant and have a nightcap before going home. We talk about everything. That’s what I really love about Judith - talk. Talk is better than sex. Talk you can do when you’re old and not very sexy, or sick and not very sexy, or just not very sexy. You can do it anywhere, any time, and it doesn’t cost you any embarrassing moments. Not many at any rate. Talk is the new sex.

Jessie's house, later that evening

I get home to find Kate's car parked in front of my house. I find her sitting in the living room reading under the small lamp by the couch, Dressing in a pair of my pajamas and drinking a glass of red wine – didn't think I had any red wine left in the house. She looks up at me as I come down the hallway. "Did you have a nice evening?"

"What happened to you? If I'd been able to reach you, I'd have spent the evening with you instead of going out." I go into the kitchen and pour myself a glass of wine from the open bottle in the kitchen. "Another delivery came from you today and your wine glasses were picked up. I thought this was for campus. What happened to it?"

"I came over on the spur of the moment." She drinks some of her wine and puts down her book. "Don't worry about the deliveries - let's not waste our last night together."

She gets up and walks towards me, undoing the buttons on the pajama top. Damn are those pajamas sexy on her. How disturbed do you have to be to find pajamas sexy? Then she undoes and drops the bottoms, kicks them off, and envelopes me in her aroma.

That night or morning like at 2:30 a.m. the phone rings. It's Darlene:

"HI!!!!! I met Randy on the way to the hotel – she and I went back to the bar – we're here acting like lesbians. Rodd's here too."

"uh huh …"

"Who the fuck is it?"? This from Kate under the comforter.

"It's Darlene - she's being a lesbian. Rodd's there though – did you want to speak with him?"
"You're fixated on lesbians."
"Obviously … Darlene, why are you acting like lesbians and why are you telling me this because now I'm thinking about it, and it's like three in the morning you know that?"
"Ha Ha Ha!! Yeah so we thought it would be better that we didn't get picked up by any guys and it's having the opposite effect!"
"Yeah well I could have told you that would happen ... why don't you just leave … call me tomorrow …" I put the phone down, snuggle up to Kate's warmth and slide my hand up her thighs and over her backside.
"I'm sleeping. Do what you must but don't wake me …"

Marlies, October 17

It's eight in the morning the day of Chris's apprenticeship qualification exam, which is at ten. Frank, Barb, Judith, and I are sitting around the dining room with the coffee machine going full tilt and baskets of warm Danish and pots of fruit compote sitting on the bar. Even Sarah has come in to wish Chris luck. We're all helping her in the final moments of study by playing the traditional exam cramming version of kitchen Trivial Pursuit. "I remember when I sat my exams. I felt horrible afterwards. Got my red seal by eight percent, but it should have been more. I totally bombed on the meat and fish." I say.

"I couldn't remember anything about front of house." Barb adds.

Judith fills our mugs with more coffee. "There should be an exam for service staff. They should have the same system as with you guys. Blue seal you can work in restaurants but if you want to wait in hotels you need a red seal. Something like that … "

Frank, who sits his exam in December, reads off a card, "What's the cooking time for a whole turkey weighing five kilos?"

I look over to Chris who is looking out the window thinking, "… mmm 500 grams 20 minutes … let's call it three and a half hours?"

"Yep, close enough, three hours twenty minutes."

"What are the five mother sauces?" Sarah asks

"Oh, that's easy - Espagnole, Hollandaise, Bechamel, Velouté, and Tomato."

" What are the three temperatures reached when tempering chocolate?"

"Ummm … first 45, then cool to 25 then heat to 30. Approximately."
"What does the term Lyonnaise mean?"
"Oh, that's my favourite – it is a dish garnished with onions."
"What contains more saturated fat? Butter or Beef?"
"Oh. Ummm probably butter."
"Wrong they're about the same."
"Really?" asks Judith.
"Yep."
"Wow."
"What's the Danger Zone?" Everybody makes scary noises …
"Food held between seven and sixty Celsius for longer than two hours."
" What is the 80/20 rule?"
"Oh – I know this one … 80% of your food cost must be covered by 20% of your food sales." "Okay. I have a good one for you now. I'm going off the cards -" I smile and look off into space- "Ummmm okay - What are the nine basic knife cuts?"
Everyone groans. "Is this going to be on the test?"
"Might be. Definitely something on cuts will."
"Okay, well there's Tournée, Brunoise, Julienne, Batonnet, all the dices … three of those ... oh, then there's the fine Peytonnne … how many is that?"
I've counted on my fingers, "eight."
"Hmmm … I don't know the other one."
"Paysanne."
"Oh right! I never remember that one!"
"It rarely gets used. Maybe they put that on the test."
Barb has gone into the kitchen and returned with her hands behind her back. "I have a final question then we

should eat - I'm starved." Everyone agrees. "What did you most want to have all the time you were here?" Chris's eyes open wide - "Oh no! You didn't!?" Barb brings her hands out from behind her back. There wrapped in cellophane is a black chef's jacket and matching pants – Chris's name on the lapel of the jacket - and on top of this a large ceramic kitchen knife. Chris goes over to Barb and gives her a hug, taking the gift and smiling to everyone. "Oh, thank you guys so much! I really wanted one of these knives – they're so expensive though. I don't deserve this." Judith comes over with a bottle of champagne, opens it and pours out some glasses and then brings over a jug of orange juice. We fill our glasses and I propose a toast.

"A toast – to the first apprentice to come out of Marlies. Who will ace today's exams and then make us totally proud as she goes on to, as I understand Florence, where her Italian will be put to good use. Good luck to you – we'll miss you so much – you've left behind another apprentice who has learnt a lot from you already and we would welcome you back in our kitchen any time. Barb?"

"Yes, Jessie of course has said everything I wanted to say. To you Chris – good luck and don't forget us." Everyone claps and Chris is very teary eyed. "Thank you! I'm going to miss all of you."

I clap my hands. "Now – let's eat! I'm starved and we need to get Chris to the exam office in an hour."

I drop Chris off and then swing by the bus station to pick up a package my Mum's sent out to me. Sort of takes you back doesn't it? Getting a package on the Greyhound bus? Sometimes it's cookies, sometimes a jar of pickled gherkin, sometimes it's just something I left at home and she's come across and sends me to. The shipping office opens in fifteen minutes, so I go over and grab a coffee and sit on a bench to wait. Between buses the station is somewhat slow, but I was not to be disappointed as the first, faint strains of urban music reach my ears.

"How much is a phone call? Can you tell me that?! I need to call someone." A rumpled old man sitting on the bench behind me is drinking a coffee and nodding in my direction. I get up and check the telephone booth, but the information has been scratched off. "I think a call is 25 cents." A woman on another bench agrees, yes 25 cents. "Does anyone have 25 cents I could borrow? I need to call my daughter." No one else volunteers any coins. "I have a dollar." "Oh, I have a dollar too." responds the old man, "Doesn't matter …" In less than 5 minutes he's shuffled out the door just as the next bus arrives and disgorges its human baggage which begin to stream towards the waiting room.

I wonder if there are compounds, actual lockdowns where stereotypes are bred and let out to hang about the bus stations, museum exhibitions or the train stations of this world? I undo my jacket and get comfortable just as the metal grill of the shipping office is slid up and a smiley face sign is placed on the counter to announce they're open. I ask for a package for Watkins, produce my driver's license as ID and walk back out to the car. I unwrap the brown paper wrapping. It's a scarf. A long brown scarf wrapped around a steamed Christmas pudding which has been boiled in a glass topped with aluminum foil now slightly discoloured from being in boiling water. I smile. Nice.

Downtown, that afternoon

I drive over to campus to meet with Kate for lunch, parking behind the club. We leave campus and negotiate the traffic downtown in style. Kate drives through a red because 'it's usually green' when she drives down this street, turns left with me screaming turn right, right, the other left! and then shows me how well her BMW handles the sidewalks. Something you can only do in a BMW which, like Mercedes, have built-in right of way. Oh, and she has an onboard anti-smoking device so any time you push the lighter in it heats up and shoots out from the dash past your face and lands in the back seat. Really great when you're going down the highway. This is why I usually drive.
"Did you see that the campus map features your little red car driving around campus at five times the speed limit? I think that's hilarious. In fact, there's a moment when you almost wipe out a group of students walking past the science labs."
She does not find this amusing. "Yeah? Well, the web services people should think about which side their bread is buttered on before they begin pissing me off."
We are trying a new vegetarian restaurant on the river. Sitting in the converted house/restaurant/bar I cannot decide between the pumpkin goulash, spinach gnocchi or eggplant gratin.[16]

I ask the waitress "Is the gnocchi good?"
"Yes."
"Really good?"
"Yes."
"Really, really, very good?"
"Yes."

“Okay, then I will have the gnocchi.” She comes back. They’re sold out. This is why I usually don’t go out for lunch. After a disappointing meal of greasy quiche and an over-dressed salad I can’t bear to think what they might do with the coffee. Waitresses these days, do any of them have real names? Dietlinde, Joselyn, Gerda … Do they make these nametags up for the poor things? To be fair though, often the waitress's name is usually the most interesting part of these places.

Over coffee – me a double espresso and for Kate a latte - and I still can sit for a very long time just looking into her face. Even without my being blinded by lust, she is an extremely beautiful woman and God only knows what she sees in me. “You were in the right place at the right time Darling. We should do this more often, come out for lunch.”
“Kate, we never have time. This is the first time we’ve gone out for lunch in a month. I still don’t believe we’re here.”
“You like powerful women. Powerful women are busy.”
“Tell me about it – this I don’t know? Powerful women are as busy as they need to be - but you are as busy as you want to be. Sorry, but there’s a difference. Either I’m a priority or not.”
“You are so sensitive. Just like my partner. Why do I always seem to attract sensitive lovers?”
“Always? How many am I?”
“Now you’re being stupid.”
“No, serious …”
“Twenty-five okay?”
“Wow. That’s a lot?”

"Are you a Nun? How many women have you bedded Jessie?"
I gaze into the middle distance and rock my head a bit." Okay, probably about the same. Were these lovers before or after you were married?"
"None of your business- before."
"Then I'm pretty lucky." I look at her and drink my coffee. "You are beautiful." I take her fingers in mine and caress their length. She moves her hand and looks around.
"Yes, you tell me each day." She takes a sip from her coffee and bites off some of her biscotti.
"Is that okay? I mean, I don't want to sound like I'm mocking you."
She squeezes my hand and smiles, "It's fine. I like hearing it and I know you really mean it."
I lean over to give her a kiss at the same moment that the waitress drops off our check, so I wait.
"What are you up to today?" I pull out some bills, but she has already taken the check and put it beneath her coffee cup, "My treat. I have another meeting in an hour and then afterwards I need to get back home. And you?"
"Thanks. I have to go by the restaurant and then the club – we have the Alumni dinner tonight. I was going to meet with Marta and her daughter for coffee tomorrow by the way." I hate saying this, but I really have nothing to hide and even though I know she doesn't like Kate I want to be honest.
She looks at me while counting out the money for the check, which is a good trick, come to think of it, "She's really pretty isn't she?"
"I suppose. Yes."

“You know I don’t like her. You, don’t screw around on me okay?”
“What!?”
“No, seriously. You will only have one chance to screw this up. I appreciate that you are friends, but I don’t trust her.”
“Okay, sure, but there’s nothing in Marta not to trust. Besides, we never do anything with your girls when Nicki is with me, so what do you expect? Marta’s daughter and Nicki get along great.”
“I know you a little bit by now Jessie - you think something better is just down the street. It isn’t. It’s just different. Just decide what you want and stick with it okay? I’m not interested in being your friend – I want you as my lover – but I’m not interested in sharing you with anyone.” She gets up and kisses me, “I have to run across to the store, are you going to wait, or should I just go?”
Kate knows that Marta and I slept together. Maybe. So, she sees Marta as a threat. Perhaps I want to be with her more than I realise and Kate can feel it? Maybe she’s just paranoid ... Oops ... she’s looking at me and she’s asked me something. Shit. “…sorry, I was just thinking. Umm, no, I’ll go with you and then head out.” Good save. I get up and grab my jacket.

The University Club, that evening

On my way back through campus I pass Marta walking down the path from the food court to her office with a Tim Horton's coffee to go in one hand and one of their paper bags in the other. I slow down a bit and honk, waving to her. But she just looks at me and continues. She still isn't talking to me. I really miss her. I've got to find a way to make amends.

I've probably told the staff a hundred times about carrying wine glasses around the food. They move through the service area like gazelles on ice sometimes. My stomach tightens when I see the trays of wine glasses moving through the kitchen to the bar and I know it's always one glass away from tragedy. During our apprenticeship, especially in the bar in the summertime, the open ice bins were a tempting playground and always but always the highball glass at hand was the easiest way to scoop ice into the cocktail blenders. But you shouldn't, you really shouldn't go there.

Probably a dozen times a season an entire ice bin is emptied and dredged and washed and searched for that one miniscule piece of glass from a dropped margarita glass that managed to fly its way from across the bar and into the ice bin – and usually during the busiest time of the evening as well - oh and during the summer when the ice machines in the back are doing their darndest to keep up anyway it's especially frustrating. I don't know how many times we had to grab the set of oily keys hanging on the ring in the liquor room and make our way in the clapped out Trabbi to the nearest

McDonalds to beg ice during happy hour. That summer in Berlin with Barb and I begging tips during the weekend rush - biding our time until we could get away from the heat of the patio to the relative safety of the heat in the kitchen.

So even though I've told the staff a hundred times, probably even a thousand come to think of it – don't be a hero with the wine glasses in my kitchen – the telltale crescendo of a tray full of tall burgundy crystal glassware at 25 bucks a pop flying into the air and bouncing off the counter - exploding like little spider mines on the Ho Chi Minh Trail and sending their deadly shards about the place into unsuspecting salad and Appie trays and open pots of whipped butter and God only knows where we'll be fishing the little bastards out of for the next two months … So, the Alumni banquet is in full force across the walkway and we're hosting a private invite only chillout zone in the club for the Crème de la Crème of university Alumni on this side – mostly men and their slim, sleek, salubrious … daughters? Nieces? Dr. Bleary popped his head into the kitchen a few minutes ago with a beautiful young thing in tow and the tired but still funny line "Jessie, have you met my partner?" "No, I haven't Dr. Bleary." "Well if you do, don't tell her I'm here!"

There are two dozen on call staff waiting in the wings to replace the one idiot who couldn't hold a tray of glasses long enough to leave the kitchen and reach the reception area when it happens. Kablooie.

Then everything stops.

“Don’t anyone move.” I yell as I wipe my hands on my apron and with Barb hobbling in from the other end of the kitchen and Judith in my ear from the Alumni Hall we descend on the scene like vultures on carrion. “Jess, what was that noise?” comes Judith’s staticky voice from across the way in Alumni Hall. The hapless waitress is speechless as Barb informs her it would probably be better to go. The tall red head looks awfully familiar, but I can’t place her. “You just lost one of your waitresses. There is going to be a slight delay as I pre-empt our regularly scheduled service. We just lost a tray of wine glasses here in the kitchen. Just seeing what the damage is.”

Barb is diligently going through everything with Frank and Chris – who aced her exam in the end with an 88% - while I scan the service area for glass. Ten glasses on the tray, six unbroken, two broken stems – “Barb there are two glasses in bits around here.” Any food in the immediate area is binned. At the time we have three dozen Appie trays sitting out, just uncovered, and ready to go out. Fucking brilliant. Fuck. Barb already has Chris in tow to the back fridges to begin gathering ingredients for some new trays, though they will be sparse.

“Frank?” Frank comes over while the dishwashers clean with brooms and a vacuum - I learnt to have a vacuum in the kitchen early in my career. “Frank, can you get some bread sliced and make me some tomato and onion Concassée? We’ll run up a few dozen bruschetta, thanks.” He nods and disappears to collect bread from the back. “Judith? How’s it going over there?” I speak into the microphone hanging an inch from my mouth.

"Fine Jess. How about you?"
"We lost three dozen Appie trays because of the broken glasses. Could be anywhere."
"Shit. OK – we'll hold them off here with larger Martinis and spread the Appies we have here thinner."
"Thanks Du." It's pretty cool having this headset. Was a great idea of Barb's.

A few hours later we have the dessert plated and gone and being enjoyed across the way and everything seems to be back on track. Some of the early departures from the banquet have begun to show up in the club for cigars and brandy and chocolates and Barb and I have opened a couple of bottles of champagne – Bollinger of course - to share with the crew.

The risk of swallowing glass depends on the size and shape of the piece itself and the person swallowing it. Larger people have an easier go of it than skinnier people for example. Sometimes smaller pieces of glass can get stuck in the intestine and cause minor bleeding but it's unusual to lead to anything serious like peritonitis. Even larger pieces can cause some bleeding, but serious blood loss is rare – even ground glass - a favourite in the movies - has mostly no serious affect. At least this is what I read in my kitchen safety manual many years ago. It's what you want to believe, and it's usually what happens. Of course, you need to swallow the glass first and not have it lodge in your throat as you swallow.

The commotion at table twelve reached me over my headset as Judith called it in. One of the guests was choking and coughing up blood causing as much

drama as could be imagined at a black-tie event with white tablecloths. "Judith, I'm calling 911. Get Dr. Bleary to preach calm." "Barb! Call 911 to the Alumni Hall. We found the rest of our broken wine glass."
My heart rate soared, and I felt as if I just run up the stairs in the clock tower after smoking a cigarette. I did that once to fetch Alex's sweater one cool night as we sat up there watching the stars. Almost gave me a heart attack.

How a piece of glass made its way from the front of the kitchen into the back-prep area landing in the sugar of one of the Crème caramel ramekins as it was setting, I will never know. After going back and forth through the scenario I just do not see it - unless the 'magic glass' ricochet off the wall which seems a highly amazing feat. It's almost as though someone put it there.

Later that evening, after quiet has fallen, I am sitting in the club with Barb and Judith, Dr. Bleary and Dr. Barthe, the Alumni President – who both were responsible for organising the banquet - silently looking off into space and wondering what to do.
"Is Mr. Franklin okay?" I venture.
Dr. Bleary nods "Sure, yes – he's doing okay – he's very shaken up - but the piece was not swallowed – that would have been horrible – it caught in his tongue – poor man told me he thought it was a piece of candied sugar."
I shake my head. Tedd Franklin is an alum and President of the bank we do business with. This just gets better and better. "It's not your fault Jessie. I know you followed all the procedures anyone would have –

you did your best – it was just bad luck." Dr. Barthe says.
"Which will go a very long way to dent our business for some time to come." I respond.
Everyone looks about as Dr. Bleary nods sagely.
"There is that – but you've made a good name for yourself in the few months you've been on campus. I think people will be fine. Put out a nice letter and donate to the gentleman's favourite charity. There are ways to get over this. You didn't do it on purpose."
"I just don't get how the glass got into the back – the timing was too good to be true. If it had been in any other food, you would have noticed it immediately - candied sugar though – what a perfect place for it to land."
"Too perfect." says Barb.

The University Club, much later that evening

"Judith, do you have the contacts of all the staff from tonight? I want the name of the waiter who dropped the glasses."
She passes me over the list, stained with food and wine and much scribbled on and rumpled from use during the night. I scan the list as Judith goes down it with her finger. "Here it is Jess – Olivia Voder."
"It says here she works for Costers."
"Yes, we got some of their wait staff when we couldn't find enough of our own. Same pay – I didn't think there'd be a problem. The rest of them worked out fine tonight."
"Judith, who would most benefit from us fucking up tonight? Any names come to mind?"
Judith pauses – "Jess it's a coincidence. You don't think Kate would do something so stupid – that's crazy…"
"She didn't do anything – one of her staff dropped a tray of glasses – made us lose our beat – service not perfect – could have been worse – we were lucky - we might have had to 86 an entire course – how would that have looked? On the other hand, someone could have been killed. Like Bleary said, accidents happen, but it was a pretty convenient accident don't you think?"

I go into the little office and call Kate but she's not in – of course – her partner returned tonight. I email her - 'Hey - Let's have coffee tomorrow – major action here tonight. Thinking of you. Jess.' Then I drop a line to Alex. 'Hi – wonder if your email box is full and how you are and everything. I miss you at odd times. And I hope you're well. Jess.' Then I turn off the computer, pick up the staff list Judith left me, light a cigarette, and dial the number of the campus police.

The University Club, October 18

A large man with a braided goatee and a tattoo running over the back of his bald head is standing outside the restaurant when I arrive at seven in the morning. I almost feel sorry for him, stuffed into what is probably a triple X size jacket but which still fits him as tight as a glove. I park the car and get out at the same time as he begins walking towards me from the front of the restaurant around to the back alley. I shut the car door and lean against it as he lifts his hand towards me and shakes mine. "Morning Mark, how are you?"
"Jessie – hey – do you always get up this early?"
"Earlier usually. Like a coffee?"
"Yeah – thanks. "
"Come on in then." Mark and I know each well enough to exchange a few pleasantries - but a few months ago I was able to help him out by chance when his motorcycle broke down on the highway one night and as I was coming back to town. Normally the last person you'd pick up hitchhiking at night I recalled his face which is hard to forget from campus - he's a good guy and one good turn deserves another. I open the back door and we go into the kitchen. I turn the light on, and we walk through into the dining room. I switch on the coffee machine and take out some milk from the fridge behind the bar. "Make yourself at home."
"Thanks. Nice place – I should come in some time."
"You should indeed. In fact, you should come in and let me buy you dinner some time. You have a girlfriend?"
"I've got a partner - Stef - and three kids."
"Three kids? No kidding?"
"I know, I don't look like the type."

I laugh – "I bet your kids just love having you pick them up from school – who'll mess with them?"
He laughs. "Yeh."
I bring over two cappuccinos in big mugs and an ashtray. I offer Mark a cigarette which he declines. He takes the cup in his hand and drinks. "Mmmm this is great – thanks Jessie."
I light a cigarette and exhale the smoke away from him. "My pleasure – I think I have you to thank."
"It was a piece of cake – just like you thought. I found her at home and flashed my ID – told her the story about the poor guy and the piece of glass he almost choked on and she confessed without blinking. It gets better though. Olivia Voder is a Head Waitress over at Costers head office. She and Kate have known each other for years."
I'm beaming outside and furious inside. I can't believe Kate could be such a bitch. "I knew it!"
"Well, the story isn't that simple. She says she was told just to make a mess – something to upset the party – but she denies putting any glass in the dessert. I believe her too – she was almost wetting her pants – crying she was. She said that was a real accident. A freak."
So, Kate got much more than she had bargained for.
"Do you think I should go to the police?"
"I think that would be a bad idea – I exceeded my campus jurisdiction – she might think of this later but it's a bit late for that now. You got what you wanted – but you can't go to the cops with it."
"You're right, I guess. It's enough too. Man, I can't believe this woman." Mark nods his head.
"That's not all though Jessie. I discovered something else you might find interesting."
"What?"

"Kate's storing shipments in your basement, right?"
"Right … well she's ordering them, and then returning them all the time but … yeah."
"She's not returning them - she's selling them."
"What?!"

Mark nods. A buddy of mine and I were talking last night – he's got a truck stop down the road – he was asking me if I was interested in cheap tables and chairs, glasses, that sort of stuff. He's buying a lot of it real cheap and passing it on. Guess where he's getting it from? Right here on campus. There's something else. There are more bikers showing up too. Not the tourists, some of the local outlaws - and they aren't buying and selling catering supplies."
This is unbelievable. I bet this is the same truck stop Kate wanted me to go in with her on too. "I knew there was something weird about those deliveries."
"He tells me that he bought the supplies used from Costers. I'll bet that's the same stuff that's being stored in your basement. She buys it to replace hardware here, but just sells it further. No one's the wiser at head office. Kate's one motivated gal …." He drinks some of his coffee. "Jess, if you get any bulk deliveries of flour or baking powder, just turn them back ok?"
I laugh.
"Well, probably a bit far-fetched, but this is a university town, and the kids aren't using weed much anymore." He isn't smiling as I look over at him.
"She wouldn't …" I ponder.

We finish the rest of our coffee in silence. "Mark – I owe you – " I give him my hand " - anytime you and your partner and kids like a nice dinner you come in –

call ahead so I can hold you a nice table okay? I really appreciate this."

"No problem Jessie. Thanks for the invite. You want me to see if I can find out any more from my friend at the truck stop?"

"I think I've heard all I want to hear." I laugh, and we both get up and I walk Mark to the door.

"Oh, by the way, you know the Strand's opening another hotel in the trade and convention center at Christmas, right?"

"Yeah, I'd heard that."

"Well, I'll be moonlighting there when it's open. Maybe I can be of use to you? Comings and goings, I mean?"

"Thanks, Mark, yeah, you never know what info might be useful." After waving him goodbye I go into the office and call Kate's private number. She picks up the phone on the third ring. "Hi, Kate. It's me."

"I told you never to call me at home." Comes her whispered reply.

"We need to talk. I know all about what really happened last night firsthand from Olivia. And, I know you are reselling all the stuff you have in my basement." There is silence on the other end of the line.

"I don't know what you mean. I have to go. Call me at the office later."

"Fuck you Kate." I hang up the phone.

The University campus, that morning

I drive over to the bank to see Mr. Franklin – but he's still recuperating at home. I drive over to the florists and order some flowers to send to my Mum, then I swing by the Starbuck's drive thru and grab a muffin and a coffee – a pumpkin latte and a carrot nut oat bran muffin. I drive to campus and park in front of the lake where I sit for a few minutes calming myself and enjoying the sweet caramel flavour of the coffee and the warmth of the muffin. I love fall. There are the sounds of the leaves, the air smells different after the warmth of summer, it's cool and still sunny, and there is a sense of new beginnings – especially in a university town such as this.

I finish my coffee and drive over to park behind the food services buildings. I go up the stairs and enter Kate's office without knocking and shut the door. She looks up but otherwise doesn't flinch. She's got this smirk all over her face like it's all a joke. "What the fuck do you think you're doing Kate?"
She gets up and walks around her desk towards me – "It was an accident - you were lucky – how would a death due to negligence have looked at one of your caterings? Hmmm? You and your silly little restaurant … did you think you could just come on campus and take business away from me? What did you think would happen Jessie?"
She moves across the room, raises back her arm, and slaps me on the face, hard. The sound reverberates throughout the room. I rock back, she laughs, touches my face, and walks back behind her desk, opens the top drawer, removes a few sheets of stapled papers, on

top of which she places a gun. “Darling, you are going to forget all about my involvement in last night.”
“Right. Kate, you’re mad.”

She laughs - “Darling Jessie - it’s been so wonderful these few months and I’d certainly miss you between my legs, but you see we have a problem. I don’t really want you on campus, I never have, but as you obviously aren’t going to go away, I’m going to need you to behave.”
As she talks her words came out like a storm, and I stand in front of her feeling hunched and passive, as though I’m in a hail of pebbles. Kate lifts the gun and passes the sheets of paper to me across the desk. “Your darling Judith, Judith Merck as she claims to be, is not who she says she is. In Berlin, where you met her, she has a long arrest record – civil disobedience, customs infringements – it’s a nice read – and she has an outstanding warrant for her arrest for attacking a policeman during a protest shortly before moving here. Her hiding that criminal record is enough to have her resident visa here revoked and returned to Germany – and her real name is Ulrike Binder.”

I look through the papers in disbelief. Judith? Oh great - what is this? My life is suddenly becoming a made for TV film ... Kate continues - “I’ll pass this information along to the immigration authorities and your friend will be on the next flight back to Berlin if you don’t calm down, forget last night’s faux pas … understand my position - we talked about this remember? Why do you think anything’s changed?” She laughs - “Moving in with me and the girls? - Don’t

tell me you're falling for me? This is business Jessie – it's always been business."
"Where did you dig this up Kate?"

She smiles again and walks back behind her desk - "I have a very good friend in the Berlin police. When I was there this summer, I thought I recognised Judith on a post office poster of wanted criminals. I came by the restaurant once to be sure it was her. My friend was here visiting us with his partner as well. Perhaps you remember that night?"
I push the papers back over to her. "I can't believe you. I can't believe I ever slept with you – what was that all about anyway Kate – really all just business?"
"Oh, we both enjoyed that, Darling – and don't deny you don't enjoy that a lot. But it's business Sweetheart – don't be this way. I'm sorry, you must see it from my side – and isn't it anyway … exciting? Don't you want me still after all this? Wouldn't you like me, right now? Here?" She laughs, looking at me raising her eyebrow as she gently kicks off her heels, takes up the gun, and begins walking back towards me.
She's right, I really do want her. I don't understand why I still want her so much after all this. I move away, "Are you fucking crazy Kate? Get your stuff out of my basement. There might be a fire, flood - anything could happen. We're not insured for anything downstairs Kate – you know how easily accidents happen – or how stolen goods can suddenly become remarkably interesting to the authorities."

"Dearest, don't be stupid." Her voice coos as she walks towards me, holding the gun loosely in one hand, reaching back to undo the clip that holds her hair at the back of her neck with the other. As her hair falls to her shoulders, she is close enough for me to smell her, and then I don't feel anything else but desire. I start to tremble as she smiles and brings her fingers up against my cheek. Then she lowers her hand, walks past me to the door, shuts it and presses the lock. She returns to me, coming so close our noses are almost touching. "You're fucking mad Kate. Put the gun away." She smiles at me and takes the gun in both hands. "Does it scare you Jess? Does this … paperweight … scare you?" She raises it and presses the cold metal against her lips. It smells acrid and sinister. Then she tosses it onto her desk where it lands with a loud thud. "It's not a real gun. Why do I waste my time with you?" "Now, some rope I *do* have if you like …" She looks back at me and laughs, walking slowly back behind her desk.

I leave Kate's office much later, and barely able to walk. Crazy. A crazy woman. Her breath still in my ear, the smell of metal in my nostrils, and her aroma smeared over me like a sticky gel. I can't believe myself. I walk unsteadily down the stairs, out of the building and, determined to make some retribution to my conscience, leave my car and jog quickly back towards the club, down to the basement, dropping my keys twice before I manage to open our storage room – which is of course now completely empty.

Marlies, later that morning

I get back to the restaurant and take Barb by the arm.
"We need to talk. Where's Judith?"
"She's not here."
"Hmm, weird, her car's out back." We go into the office, I shut the door, and explain everything to her.
"Wow. Judith's a terrorist." She shakes her head.
"She's a dark horse … I told you to stay away from Kate though. What a bitch."

I light a cigarette and blow out the smoke. "She's not a terrorist Barb. Fuck. They have strict laws in Germany – but hitting a cop? That doesn't go over well anywhere. You don't need to remind me about Kate."
"So, what do we do? Tell Judith we know?"
"Mm hmm – yep we should. Then we can decide what to do."
There is a knock on the office window and there is Chris. I open the door. "Hey! You're finally off eh?"
Chris, Barb, and I hug.
"Yep, I'm going to the airport in a few hours. I wanted to bring you something on my way." She removes from her bag three packets of biscotti. "I made these for you. They are my mother's recipe. It's not much, but she was very important to me – she's why I want to go back to Italy and cook – as a tribute to her."
I take the bags and pass one to Barb. "Thank you, Chris. That's thoughtful. Be sure to stay in contact. I'll definitely want to come by so you can cook for me if I'm in Italy anytime soon." "Bye Jessie, bye Barb – say goodbye to Judith for me? And thank you both so much for everything."

"Goodbye Chef." I shake her hand and use the title she has earned that she never heard from me before in addressing her. She smiles broadly and walks back along the kitchen, looking around it and then leaves through the back door.

I look after her and then to Barb. "Hmmm … I wish I were twenty years younger starting all over again. It's never the same is it?"
Barb shakes her head. "Nope. I remember how it was, learning to cook, all that excitement, beginning my first post. It's like the first time you kiss. Your first love … "
"I know … Oh well." I look at my watch, "Hey, where is Judith anyway?"
"Should be in any minute."
"Okay, then when she comes in let's talk with her."

However, we're still calling about looking for her an hour after lunch begins. Judith doesn't come in and she doesn't call and I'm sort of laughing to myself thinking of all the times when this could happen. I mean really, not now Judith. …

Marlies, that afternoon

There is still no sign of Judith as the afternoon begins and both Barb and I begin to panic.
"I'm calling the police." Barb says to me as she comes into the office, wiping her hands free of chocolate shavings.

"You're always calling the police. Relax. Hey, don't get chocolate on my shoes ..."
"Sorry. Something's wrong."
"I know, but we can't call the police just yet." I think about it and find the number of the Inspector who handled our brick incident. I dial his number but am rerouted to the station desk. "I'm sorry, Inspector Peters is away from his desk. May I help you?"

"Could you please ask him to call Jessie Watkins at the following number? 474 39219? I'm calling about a recent incident at my restaurant which the Inspector investigated."
"I'll let him know when he returns."
"Thanks." I hang up.
"'Your' restaurant?" Barb rifles through the desk drawer looking for some licorice.

I remove a stack of papers and fish a somewhat flattened, half open bag of licorice out from beneath some menus. "Okay, 'our' restaurant. You want me to call them back? If Judith isn't in for dinner, we'll get worried then. Let's go over to her place okay?"
"Okay. Let me just get my things."

Judith’s apartment, later that afternoon

We change, lock up the restaurant, drive the ten blocks to Judith’s apartment and park in front of the building. We get out of the car and walk to the row of buzzers in front of the main door and press the one with Judith’s name on it. There’s no answer. Barb waltzes in through the main front door. “See anything?”
She shakes her head, “Just a dying rubber tree plant.”
The clouds have been building up all day and the first few drops of rain begin to fall as we stand there.
“Come on - I’ll drive you back to the restaurant. I’ve got to pick up Nicki from school.”
“Where’s Angie this week?”
“She’s at home actually – she sprained her wrist at the gym, so she’s been resting.”
“Oh … “

Downtown, much later that afternoon

I swing by the restaurant and drop Barb off by her car and then drive to Nicki's school. The rain has turned heavy and now bounces loudly against the windshield. I make out Nicki dashing across the road from the school grounds and open the door for him. I take his umbrella and toss it behind my seat and haul his knapsack onto the back seat. "How was your day?"
"Hi! Yeah, fine." As we stop for the red light on the corner, I see Marta crossing in front of us struggling with both her bicycle and that of Anna - both soaked to the skin. Why she never uses an umbrella I'll never know. And who rides their bike in October? As they reach the curb on the other side the soggy paper grocery bags in her basket give way and a cascade of pasta, oranges and small jars of caramel sauce fall almost in slow motion to the street. I'm surprised - I mean I thought the French were good cooks. Is this how she's been eating since we stopped talking?

I put my hazards on, turn the corner, and pull over to the side of the road - Nicki and I get out of the car and run over with an open umbrella. Marta is trying to pick up the groceries, bicycles, and Anna at once and failing. I pick up a packet of frozen ravioli and pass it to her. We just stare at each other, the rain covering us.
"Hi. Since when are you eating frozen ravioli?"
"Hi. Since when are you caring what I eat?"
"I … "
Nicki pipes up, "Hey we're getting really wet here you know!"
I look over and see he and Anna are looking at us.
"Then go to the car." I turn to Marta, "Come home

with us and get dried off." She looks at me, and I brush the rain drops off her nose with my finger.
She moves her head away. "I'm fine Jessie. Go to Kate."
"Marta, I'm sorry. I've really missed you." Nicki and Anna are sitting in the car playing with the radio, turning the volume up so I can hear it clearly. "Hey! Turn down the volume Nicki!"
She sighs. "Me too – I have missed you both. I'm sorry. It is your business, but I'm disappointed in you."
"I know. Let's have dinner again. Soon. Tomorrow. We'll make pasta."
"Who'll make pasta? Oh, you? Please ... I've seen what you do to pasta - I'd rather just get it out of a jar." We gather up the remaining items and carry them to the car.
"What do you mean, what do I do to pasta? What? The French have a special way with pasta now?" I open the back and put Anna's bike inside. "Can you bike home? I'll take Anna, and you're already wet. There's no space for your bike."
"Oui ... Anyone knows that you must dry the pasta for some time but you just ..."
"I don't believe you, what's this thing about the way I cook now? I'll have you know that …"
"Also, Cherie, while we are on the subject of your failings, I have always wanted to tell you - you dress like a pregnant woman …" she laughs and calls back as she bikes away in the direction of home.
I drop Nicki off at home, make sure he's got enough homework to keep him busy and that he sees the chicken I've prepared for him and left in the fridge. Then I drive to the restaurant. Unfortunately, Judith never shows up that evening either.

Jessie's house, October 19

At seven my phone rings. It's Inspector Peters, we of course can't do anything until Judith is missing a few hours longer. "I really have the feeling that something's happened to her. She would never not show up for a shift without calling. In fact, she's never missed even a shift in all the years we've worked together. She doesn't answer at her apartment nor her mobile. Her car's parked behind the restaurant. It's not normal."

"I can understand your concern, unfortunately we can't do anything until tomorrow. It could really just be a coincidence."

Now I wonder if somehow, she found out what Kate knows – or worse still that Kate simply called the police. But then the Inspector would have her name on the wire already and Kate would be without a card to play. Of course, it wasn't something I could bring up.

"Then you don't know Judith, Inspector. This is not her at all."

"Call me back if she hasn't made contact after lunch."

"I will. Thank you, Inspector … Ah! Wait, please, sorry, I have a question. What if I were threatened by someone using a fake gun? Would that be something you might be interested in?"

"Well, probably. What do you mean by a fake gun exactly?"

"A paperweight, which looks like a gun."

"Well, I think it depends also what you mean by threatened. Did someone try to rob you?"

"No, no, it was something else. But, well, there are no laws about paperweight guns I suppose?"

"I think it comes down to how it was used. Do you want to give me any more details? Who? When?" The Inspector probably has more important things to do.
"No, I was just thinking out loud, Inspector. Sorry for taking up more of your time."
"Ok then, Goodbye, Jessie."
"Goodbye."

I hang up and message Barb, then go in search of breakfast. I'm feeling hungry but when I open the fridge nothing attracts my eye. Somehow the fridge at home when I was growing up always had a lot more to eat in it – half chickens, roasts, cakes – my fridge seems to always just contain yoghurt and cheese … wine … no leftovers. I really miss leftovers. But then, I never make enough food to have leftovers. I wonder if there's a market for leftovers. Housewives could sell their leftovers to singles. I turn on the coffee machine and make myself a coffee, then find a still somewhat toastable bagel in a brown paper bag, with the apples, onions, potatoes, and garlic near the window. I really need to get some groceries.

While I'm drinking my coffee and picking at my bagel – raisin with a thick layer of goat cheese – the phone rings. It's Barb. "So, what are we going to do? We can't just sit here and watch the clock." She sounds frantic.
"I know – but we've tried everywhere. Something's happened to her – but the police can't help. We've called everyone, checked everywhere. We're sort of screwed. Let's talk at work. Coming in early?"
"Yeah, of course."

Marlies, that morning

Barb's already at the restaurant when I arrive an hour later with a box of muffins – twelve of the daily assorted but with Judith missing I really don't feel like going into the varietal details. I open the back door and go inside, then walk into the office where Barb's sitting in front of the computer surfing the missing person websites. "Hey. I brought muffins."
Barb points to an open box on the shelf. "I bought doughnuts, but there aren't many left"
"Oh, good. We should be completely wired by lunch. Did you make coffee?"
Barb nods. "Should be ready now. Bring me one?"
"Sure. What are you doing?"
Barb's typing feverishly. "I've uploaded Judith's photo and I'm posting a missing report on all these websites. Maybe someone saw her."
"Hmm maybe not a good idea if one of those websites is seen in Europe?"
I look at the clock. "I'm calling Inspector Peters at noon. That's 48 hours then."
"Okay. That's a stupid rule too."
"I know." I go into the dining room to get the coffees, a Boston cream doughnut in my hand from which I take 3 large bites before it's gone. Delicious.

Sometimes I wonder if I'm really a chef. As I enter the dining room, I'm just in time to see something being pushed through the mail slot in the door. It lands on the floor with a soft thud, I go over, see it's the same as Judith's missing wallet, pick it up and quickly unlock and open the front door and look up and down the

street. A woman walking a dog is the only person I see so I call out. "Excuse me? Hello?"
The woman stops and turns as I run up to her. "I'm sorry, but did you just put this wallet in our mail slot?" I hold it up in my hand.
"Oh yes, I did, that was me." She begins walking back towards the restaurant, so I walk towards her. "I saw it laying on the ground behind the telephone box there and opened it up. There was a card inside that had the name of your restaurant, so I put it in your mail slot. Thought it must belong to one of your staff."
"Thank you, it does." She smiles and pulls the leash and progresses with her dog back along the street. I go back inside, make Barb and I a coffee each and go into the kitchen to the office. "Hey, someone found Judith's wallet outside the restaurant. She must have lost it."
"Maybe she left it as a sign." I nod my head, I'm big on 'signs'. "Sounds good." I go through it. Nothing seems out of the ordinary. "Well, there's no note in here anyway. I'm calling Inspector Peters." I pick up the phone and dial the number on the card I pull from my pocket. I explain the new development to him and when I hang up explain to an excited Barb. "Okay, so they're treating it as a missing person now, and he's going to send someone over to look about and collect the wallet."
Barb looks at the wallet. "You know, it's too bad so many people touched it – perhaps someone took it from Judith as they were wrestling her into the van and their fingerprints were on it – that might have been great evidence."
I look at the wallet and at Barb. "What van?"

"There's always a van that comes screeching to the curb and men open the sliding door and grabbing the victim before racing off again."
I look at her "O … kay … but I guess you're right about the fingerprints. Blew that one, didn't we?" I drink from my coffee and place the wallet on the desk. "Can I have another doughnut?" Barb drinks from her coffee, watches me, and wordlessly passes me the box.

Two uniformed police come by the restaurant about an hour later, followed by Inspector Peters another thirty minutes after that. We tell him all we know except for the bombshell Kate has squirreled away in her office.
"It's a bit odd. We'll keep our ears open and check in with all her friends."
"What about Sammy and the stalking incidents, Inspector?" this from Barb.
"We still have no information on his whereabouts. Nothing yet came up in our search for him. However, as he hasn't committed a crime that we're aware of we can't put out a bulletin for him. I'm sorry. I'm sure your friend will show up. But we'll begin a missing person's search."
"I seem to recall that he had a girlfriend."
"Do you know her name?"
I shake my head. "No, sorry. I know she just finished her Master's in Shakespearean Music. Can't be many of those at the university."
"Okay, good lead." He scribbles this in his notebook and replaces it in his pocket.
We walk with him out the front of the restaurant and down the stairs to the street. I shake his hand "Thank you Inspector."

He shakes Barb's hand, "We'll call you if we hear of anything. Oh, Jessie, was there anything further about that gun you were telling me about?"
Barb's eyes open perceptibly wider as she looks at me.
"No, no Inspector, nothing more."
After he drives away Barb says, "I know Sammy has something to do with this. What was that about a gun?"
"I think so too … oh, nothing – I was just asking about replica guns." I light a cigarette looking up and down the street. "I really wonder where Judith is. I hope she's okay."
"Replica guns. Kidnapping. We will be receiving stolen goods next." Barb walks away and I am left with a growing sense of dread.

The University Club, that afternoon

I drive over to campus – Barb has the ball at Marlies for lunch while I do twenty VIPs of the President's office who, I have been informed, 'must have the best', which is what I try to give everyone but okay, so I'll try harder at lunch today. At a time of economic crisis - brought on mostly by mismanagement - one hears more and more that there will be some new money - a sponsored chair or a sports complex announced at the end of the day. So, I spent a lot of time going over a menu and pairing it with a nice selection of wines with the President's Assistant. I just hope that all this work generates more than the new park benches which is all the university got from Citibank last year. At least our catering bills are being paid which, in my world, is all that really matters to me. I've got Alissa in to serve and I brought Sarah in to help me in the kitchen, leaving Frank with Barb back at the restaurant. If I can be honest, I don't like working with men in the kitchen. Women have a better touch.

The group arrives downstairs and Alissa is serving drinks and some canapes while I survey the group from the bar while I'm getting a bottle of Remy Martin with which to flame the duck. There are two women in the group, both who sadly decided to dress as they thought men would dress if they were women the last university President who retired the year previously, the recently retired Dean of Schools, two faces I know sit on the board of governors, the rector, the President of course, the VP of Academic Affairs and then someone who I know I've seen before but can't place … oh! the Mayor. Didn't vote for him … then there are

half a dozen men who are being fawned over – these must be the money men.
"How do they like the canapes?" I ask Alissa.
"They smell delicious. No one's complaining – what's this one again?" She points to a small puff pastry flower with glazed honey and poppyseeds on top.
"It's a baked Georgian cheese."
"I've heard them say they like that one a lot."
"What do you think?" Prior to service of course I get the staff to try everything we're serving so they can explain it to the guests.
"Yeah, probably my favourite as well. Though I really want some more of the meat in filo."
"I'll keep some for you upstairs next time."
"Thanks."
"Okay, then lunch is served in about fifteen minutes."
"Okay." I
go back upstairs through the crowd, nodding greeting to faces I know, receiving some smiles of compliments on the food and catching strains of conversation as I go - "… six faculty members plagiarizing research material …" from the Ombudsman to one of the two women who looks somewhat familiar … "St. Petersburg eh? the girls there are amazing … when I was there last year … Hahaha!" … that to the Dean of Schools from the retired President … "… student was asked for suggestive photos of herself by that new fellow - the bald prof …" and that, slightly more hushed from beneath the stairs, as I go up, from the Rector to the Provost who I know chairs the EQ committee – so someone's been abusing their power again!

Alissa and I are serving a late round of coffee and chocolates. The group of visiting moneymen have already left stroked and toasted and accompanied by the President and a few others after a satisfying lunch. A late Fall sunshine streams in through the windows over half a dozen stragglers. During lunch I've placed one of the women who remain as VP of University Development, in charge of student housing, campus activities and the like. I recall her now from my student days, Randall … I don't remember her first name but since my day she's made herself over and cut her hair sadly much shorter than it was. "… our contract for the facility on Pandora street was for twenty-five years from which only five now remain and we must decide to renew or not. I don't see there being any point in throwing good money after bad – the renovation costs would be better invested elsewhere. We should close it down."
"So, we let the space stand idle for five years?"
"It would be cheaper – it's not fully occupied as it is."
"Student housing is a sensitive issue – we have waiting lists of graduate students and the next housing complex will be two years in the making … how many students live in Pandora anyway?"
She waves her hand in front of her. "Less than a hundred …" There are whistles of concern at this number. "… look, we offer student housing, but we're not under any obligation to provide it – we house as many as we can. The costs to upgrade - half of the rooms on Pandora street need to be completely renovated – almost 20% are empty – we have too many smaller housing units which offer cheaper apartments – Maffey, South, Trenton - we're in competition with ourselves. No, the money can be better used elsewhere.

I'm in favour of shutting down the entire complex at the end of the academic year and seeing if we can find someone to take over our lease. If not, then, as I said, it's cheaper to let it sit idle. Students always find a place to live." There is much head nodding and murmurs of agreement. The woman blows out a cloud of cigarette smoke and signals to Alissa, unbeknownst to the woman herself a grad student, "Honey, you don't happen to have any more of those delicious little truffles, do you?"

"What a bitch. Oh, this is going to the student government." Alisa furiously pulls on her sweater over her head.
"You don't live on Pandora street, do you?" I'm nibbling on a truffle and leaning against the bar downstairs an hour after our guests have left.
"They, these are really awesome. Bacon fat instead of butter – way to go Jessie."
Alissa smiles. "That's why you're the Chef."
"Well, to be honest, Judith was the inspiration – she's always eating bacon." I wipe my mouth on my finger.
"So, I don't live on Pandora street, but I know a few people who do." I take my cigarettes from the bar and light one, offering Alissa the package from which she removes one. I light it for her.
"Well, just don't say you got the information from here. Admin would be thrilled – you know how people talk after a few chocolate bacon truffles[15] …" we both laugh.
"See you Jess!"
"Bye … "Alissa leaves and bumps into Lidia as she goes out the door. "Hey, you." We give each other a hug. "You like a drink?"

“Is a goat smelly?”
I look at her and laugh. “Umm I don’t know – is it?”
“They stink.”
“There’s something I’ve learnt today.” I pour us two glasses of scotch on ice – sorry but it’s not cold enough outside for me to drink it straight- and we go over to sit in the comfy chairs. Lidia blows the smoke out of her mouth and leans forward on her elbows. “Cheers.” We raise our glasses.
“Mmmm, not as smelly as a goat.”
“I hope not! That’s Laphroaig!” She puts down her glass and leans closer across the table. “Jessie, I’m leaving. I got accepted at Exeter.”
“Wow. Oh wow, that’s great! Congratulations. When do you leave?”
“Tomorrow. The plane leaves tomorrow and the next day I will be working in a little office for the next sixty days until the spring semester begins. Then I will study again. I was really incredibly lucky to get into the program after all.”
“Tomorrow?! So soon? Why didn’t you tell me earlier – aww - I’m really going to miss you. I didn’t really get to know you as much as I’d have liked to – but I’m glad you got what you wanted.”
I stare out the club windows, what do I want ... that’s an interesting question ... I watch the people working in the garden, tearing up the dead vines and clearing up the detritus of summer. Pumpkins fill the spaces where once tomatoes and zucchini clustered and grew.
“Are you okay?”
“… Oh, I’m sorry Lidia.”
She looks at me through the cigarette smoke. “You were pretty busy – work, the scary lady .... I would have liked that we had hung out some more. But I have

to leave." She puts out her cigarette and places her hands over mine. She leans forward and gently kisses me on the cheeks, which I return with equally gentle firmness. *here... Just now ... Brain to rational thought center: we need more power ...* I pull back slowly and look at her. "You're completely amazing kiddo." She smiles and strokes my cheek with her long fingers. "Thank … you …" I pull back ever so gently, smile at her and change gear. "That was nice …"
"Aha."
"I'm sorry."
I light a cigarette. "Would you like something else to do?" I wave my empty glass, but she shakes her head. "I really need to get packed. My room, you have no idea how many years of detritus is washed up in my room." She lights a cigarette. "I think I'll be throwing most of it out."

I come back from the bar with my drink. "Maybe you can save something for me?" She rests her elbows on her knees and blows smoke out across to me. "You don't want to sleep with me but … you'd like a pair of my socks perhaps?" She laughs deeply and mercilessly.

"Ha ha - no - no I meant a book, or something … I think we both knew sleeping together was never going to happen, Lidia. It's not that I don't like you – it's ..." Lidia raises her eyebrows. "You're somewhere in my heart like a sister. You're really special." She smiles at that. "Jessie, you are a poet, as well as a waiter. Brava." She stands up – "I should go pack."

I stand up and with arms around each other's waists and walk to the door, and then outside along the path and up to the main walkway without a word. We hold each other and hug tightly. And then she smiles and laughs, "Bye Jessie," and then spins a bit, catching a few of the dry yellow leaves that are continuously falling from the oak trees that cover the campus.

"Email me sometime." I say and she waves, and then she is gone.

Coffee Shop, October 20

The phone in the club office rings, then goes silent, to be followed shortly afterwards by the phone in the restaurant - but I'm not answering either of them. I'm sitting in the coffee shop around the corner from Marlies reading the Bugle – Voice of the Wildcats –the university's student newspaper which leads today's edition with "Pandora Street Closed? Randall says No Comment!" I laugh – oh Alissa – great job … and wonder how long I'm going to have university admin on my back now ...

When my mobile rings, I do answer that, wiping chocolate pecan date muffin from my lips and almost knocking over my coffee grabbing for a napkin.
"Hi, Jessie here."
"Jessie, Hi, this is Mark."
"Mmm … Mark, Hi. Sorry, just eating. How are you?"
"Great, thanks. Listen, I wanted to call about the truck stop thing we talked about."
"Yeah? What's up?"
"Well my friend there was telling me a big delivery of kitchen equipment showed up the other day – nothing he ordered – just a big semi that's been parked in the lot, and handing things out of the back now and then. When he checked it out, one of the outlaws handed him some cash and thought he could turn a blind eye."
"Oh, that IS interesting. All the stuff from my storage room was taken away a few days ago as well. So, she's selling it right from the back of the truck now. She's totally lost it. Is your friend calling the police? Should I?"

"No, I think we better let it lie. I just thought you'd want to know."

I think about this for a bit. "You know, I could use a new salamander for the kitchen. Perhaps I go over and see what's available."

"Well, play it really cool ok? Do you want me to come with you?"

"Do you want to? Would it help?"

"Well, I look the part more than you," he laughs "and it would explain why you're even there."

"Sure, sounds good. When?"

"Any time. Now? I meet you there?"

"Ok Jessie, then, in an hour. See you there".

"Ok, an hour." I end the call and begin to really worry about the delivery forms I signed for Kate.

Truck Stop Diner, later that afternoon

A kitchen salamander will set you back about 700 bucks, but the one I got from the back of the truck just now only cost me two. 200 dollars for a new salamander still in the box. Buggers are heavy too. I can't fit it in my car, so we stick in in Mark's, and then go inside for a beer. I've never been in the truck stop before but have passed by many times. Always been curious. As we walk by the front window of the place, a dozen baseball caps can be seen inside slowly following our progress past. 'John Deer', 'Tool Time', 'Eurest', 'Caterpillar' – the logos pan right like one of those moving billboards we had before everything went digital.

We grab a booth near the door, order two beers and burgers from the waitress, and sit back. Mark lights a cigarette from a crumpled package of unfiltered Luckies, and offers me the pack, but I shake my head. "What do you think?" I ask. Mark inhales and exhales slowly, looking out the window and scratching his beard. "Well maybe you should lose the salamander in the river somewhere," he laughs "but at least now you know where all the stuff went." I have to admit, the outlaw bikers here and there, the guy selling stuff from the truck, Mark standing shotgun, getting a huge bargain on a brand new salamander – though this latter thing is probably only something a chef could appreciate, for anyone else imagine you got a brand new 700 dollar TV for 200 bucks. Still in the box. – I must admit that it was pretty damn cool. Stupid, but cool. At least I know where all the stuff went, and what Kate was doing. I don't know why of course. How much money could she be making, and what about the risk? It doesn't add up.

I notice the front door open, and three large bikers enter. They begin to walk past, as one slows down and turns to us. "Hey Mark." Mark looks up, "Hey Terry." The bikers continue past. "That was uncomfortable." I look at Mark. "I thought he was going to beat me up." Mark chuckles. "Not all bikers are outlaws Jess." "I wouldn't have expected a Terry. Perhaps a Duke or a Mitch." Mark laughs. "He only goes by Terry to his friends. Everyone knows his as Mad Dog." I raise my eyebrows in surprise. "Really? That's more like it." "You also know me as Mark, but my biker name is Snake." "Really? Pretty cool." Mark laughs loudly. "I'm shitting you Jess." "Oh." I feel disappointed. Our beers and burgers arrive. I am famished. I take a long drink of the cold lager, wipe my mouth on a napkin, and pull the burger towards me. "Are these any good?" I ask Mark. He stubs out his cigarette and pushes the ashtray off to the side. "No idea to be honest. I've never eaten here before." He takes up his beer and drinks about half of it in one. Then he picks up the burger, lifts the top buns and peers inside. Satisfied, he takes a large bite and chews. "Seems fine." He says and wipes ketchup from the corner of his lip with his thumb.

The burger is good, not as good as some I've had, but good. The best burger I think I ever had was probably in Germany, oddly enough. It was a long time ago. The burger was cooked medium rare, the meat was salty, peppery, and juicy, and it sat in between two freshly baked brioche halves. Just enough bun to hold the burger and add to the flavor and aroma, but not enough bun to fill you up too fast. It was excellent. the fries were crap, but the burger was good.

The worst burger on the other hand, and there have been many, but the worst was probably one I mistakenly got at the McDonalds in the Marseille train station in France, also a very, very long time ago. I took one bite, and here I am lucky that I always look at what I bite into while I am chewing but before I swallow, and I see the patty has not been fully cooked and is in fact still bloody. A half raw frozen meat patty. Deadly. I spat it out onto the paper, waited back in line, and gave it back. Funny thing is, they asked if I wanted a replacement. I didn't even take my money back. I went across to the bar in the station and bought a scotch to wash out my mouth. Horrible. Now, I could tell you stories about other crap food experiences, but I'm going to take you back to the truck stop.

"I don't get it. Kate orders stuff from her supplier. Then she sells it. For next to nothing. Where is the upside? How much money could she make, and for what risk? I don't get it."

I take another drink from my beer. Mark is looking at me. "She might be in the middle you know. Maybe she didn't initiate it. Maybe someone at head office? Maybe all this stuff is factory seconds. Maybe none of it even works. There is a lot we don't know." Mark takes another bite of his burger and talks as he chews. "200 bucks doesn't sound like much, but if there were a hundred pieces, that's twenty grand. If she gets half, it's still ten grand. When is the last time you had ten grand in cash?" Mark is right, but it still feels wrong. "I should try the salamander to see if it works." I muse out loud. "You should try the salamander to see if it works." Mark nods.

"So, what do I do?" Mark finishes chewing and looks around, picks up his beer and finishes it. "I don't know Jess. What do you want to do? You could go to the cops, but you might have to explain how you know about this and why you now have stolen property. You could do nothing. You could go see Kate." He lights another cigarette, and inhales deeply. He exhales and raises his empty glass to order another beer. "You want another one?" My beer is still half full. "No thanks." "I think you should probably go see Kate."

Downtown, much later that afternoon

I park down the block from Kate's house, where I can see her flat, and wait for her to return. I don't have to wait long. Her shiny red BMW pulls out from the intersection behind me, and roars past. Kate glides into a reserved parking spot in front of her apartment, shuts off the engine, lifts the roof back into place, and gets out. For some reason I don't even wait, I just climb out of the car, and before I can call out, she gets quickly back into her car, backs out with a screech, and zooms away. She must have seen me. Where is she going?

I quickly get back into the car, and try to restart the engine - which, even on a good day is trial and error. I have absolutely no chance to catch Kate unless she hits a red light. I accelerate out of my spot, hear a honk and a screech behind me (I never check my mirrors), wave an apology out my window, and shoot off down the street. At the intersection, I take a left, then put my foot to the floor, scanning ahead for any sign of her.

I am in luck. Kate is three blocks ahead sitting at a red light. I manage to get another block when her light changes and she accelerates fast down the next city block. I do my best to keep up, but she herself should know I don't stand much of a chance, so she needn't speed. My luck continues to hold when a bus suddenly comes out of the street ahead of Kate, forcing her to brake hard and swerve into the incoming lane. She does a poor job of it, instead going up over the curb and giving me time to close the distance between us.

There are honks from other cars as Kate guns her BMW down the next block via the sidewalk. She jumps back onto the road at the next intersection, revs her engine, and takes the next right with a screech of her tires. Now I slow down a bit, as I've probably lost her in the maze of city streets.

I come to the intersection and turn the corner, when to my surprise and horror I see Kate's car crashed against a lamp post. The trunk open, the street quickly being littered by hundreds of paper cocktail napkins, a few chafing dish sternos rolling about, and a few dozen Forster flyers. I drive up near her, stop, and jump out of the car.

Kate opens the drivers' side door and gets unsteadily out of the car. Had she been carrying a passenger it would have been bad for them. I was a passenger in that car. Ouch! There is very little space inside for error. Kate brushes her hair out of her eyes and looks at me. Not far away I can hear a siren, and people are coming down the street to see what they can do. Or not do. Or film, as the case might be.
"What the fuck Kate, are you ok?!"
Kate laughs, and leans against the open car door. "Oh Jessie, you know, I forgot to pick up my dry cleaning, and they close in 5 minutes …" she looks at her watch, which has come undone and lies at her feet on the ground. "… well, they're probably closed now".
"What? Is that why you drove away? I was waiting for you at your place. I was at the truck stop. You're selling stolen goods Kate. You fucked me around."
Kate laughs, guffaws. Comes over to me and holds onto my arm. She is so beautiful. "Jessie," her voice is

hoarse, and her lip is bleeding. “Fuck you.” She laughs. “Fuck. You. I don’t know what you think you know or don’t know, but just forget it. Leave me alone. Your signature. I have your signature. This is …. this is the price you pay for having me … had me …” She puts her fingers up to her lip and looks at the blood there. Then she looks back at me and shakes her head. “Stay out of my business Jessie. Fuck off.”

The sirens have grown much louder and then suddenly stopped. A police cruiser arrives, closely followed by a firetruck. People are crowding about on the sidewalk, and one of the police officers comes over to us. A fireman removes a fire extinguisher from the truck and sprays the crumpled hood of the BWM. This is one of those moments you see very often on television but rarely live. It feels very … real. “How are you folks doing? Can we move away from the car please? Who’s the driver?”
Kate turns to me with tears on her cheeks “... Leave Jessie. Just go home.”

***

Jessie's house, November 11

'Hating but missing you. You do not deserve the latter. Though you probably don't believe it – I'm missing you ...' Kate's email flashes over the screen of my notebook. At once I feel happy and scared. I have heard nothing from her since the crash. I went through many panic attacks thinking about my signature on the things Kate stored with me. There have been, however, no visits from the police, or from outlaw bikers, or from the university authorities. I almost thought I had Kate out of my system, but the tightening in my stomach assures me that I have not. As soon as I see her name on the screen, I think of how badly I want her.

One eye on the screen and one eye watching Nicki talking to my Mum on the phone. I like doing this because I can see how he is when he's talking to me on the phone. He's very animated as he dances through his little talk. "Yes, No, Wellllll, I don't know, Yes, oh you know what?! …" Children seem to carry on these monosyllabic conversations. I wonder when this will end, this ability to translate entire afternoons into single syllables? Or does it ever end? Come to think of it when I have a lot to say, often when I have a lot to say but don't want to say it, one syllable words seem to just bubble to the surface. I smile to myself, get up and close the laptop.
"Hey chief, say goodbye, I need to talk to Nan now."
"Bye Nanny! I love you, mmmmmmwwwa!" How do you write the sound of a kiss? I know it was "SMACK" and "SMOOCH" for the longest time, but I

must tell you a kiss has never sounded like either of those to me.
"Get washed up for dinner okay? - and could you grab us some drinks?" I take the phone, "Hi Mum."
"Hi Jess …" Oh, she sounds horrible. Probably one syllable words are easier on her ears. This big wave of guilt rushes over me. I still feel guilty, that it's somehow my fault, that my mother, as sick as she is, lives on the other side of the country – that Nicki is being exposed to her illness at such a young age – that Angie isn't here, that he doesn't see his Dad ... it just goes on and on. Guilt. We raise our children with this big cloud of guilt hanging over our heads. Well, those of us lucky enough to have kids or pathetic enough to dwell too much on the pain of life rather than just getting on with it. I'm sure things like going to university and making your own pesto lay in direct relation to how you bring up your kids and how big your cloud of guilt is. I mean, I doubt very much that your average Welsh coal miner worries much if they're going to psychologically damage their children when they yell at them for tracking mud in across the living room.

"How are we doing Mum?"
She laughs a little. "I've felt better, you know?" I can hear one of the girls in the background. My younger brother and his partner have moved back into the house with their boys so they can help Mum around the clock. My brothers are good people. Angie and I just seem to sit on the sidelines feeling guilty. "Jessie, I want to know if there's anything you want, after I go. I need to write this down, for the doctor."

“Mum I don’t want anything. I don’t want to talk about this.”
She coughs and I can hear her drinking something.
“Jessie it’s okay, don’t be such a child.”
“I’m not being a child. I’ll come out and if there’s anything you would like me to have then I’ll show you okay?” She sorts of wheezes. “Mum? Are you okay?”
She coughs again and sort of laughs, or something.
“Give Nicki a hug for me. Tell Angie, tell her that she should take care of him better. Tell her okay?”
“I will Mum.”
“Thanks for calling … I love you.”
“I love you too Mum, talk with you tomorrow.”
Megan takes the phone, “Hi Jess.”
“Hi Megan, how’s it going?”
“The doctors don’t give her much time – they say she could go anytime.”
“They said that about Grandma and she lived to ninety-two.”
“She didn’t have cancer though.”
“No, that she didn’t, though she smoked, and Mum never did. Sort of unfair.”
“Where’s Angie?”
I blow out a lungful of air … “Hmmm I don’t remember – I think she’s in Seattle this week. I lose track.”
“Tell her to call when she gets back.”
“I will.” I look at the clock. “She’s going to call in half an hour anyway if I recall correctly.” “You should come out again.”
“I will. Give her a kiss for me.”
“Bye.”
“Bye.” I put down the phone and hear the TV in the other room. I go through the kitchen and peer in. Nicki

has the table set and drinks on the table, he's in the living room watching Sponge Bob. Nicki's the greatest kid in the world so I guess he can live with the stress we're all going through at the moment. Perhaps letting go and letting him make his way in certain ways makes me confront my own fears - helps me get on with my own things. I know I always have this in the back of my mind when we go to the waterpark together and I'm standing at the top of the 'Black Hole' water slide and he's waiting for me to sit on a stupid little rubber inner-tube with him, let go and jump into this dark metal tube and plunge to my almost certain death. I guess that's the wonder of childhood, never thinking you're going to get hurt – and getting hurt, in any of the myriad ways it can occur, is one of our most ardent fears as an adult. "Hey, let's eat. Your Mum's going to call soon."

Jessies house, that evening

After dinner and the phone rings just as we're doing the washing up. "Nicki, can you get that please?" Nicki walks over and picks up the phone, "Watkins residence… Hi Mum… yep, we just ate and now we're doing the dishes… when are you back? Oh. Okay. Sure." He holds out the phone to me. Jess? Mum wants to talk with you." I wipe my hands on the dish towel and take the phone. "I think there's still some chocolate ice in the fridge. Why don't you grab some to eat while you're doing your homework?" Nicki wordlessly goes to the cupboard and takes out a small bowl and a spoon from the drawer and then digs through the small freezer beneath the fridge. "Only if you want ice cream though. You don't have to."
"No, no I want some."
"Okay." I turn to the phone. "Hi Angie."
"Hi Jess. How's it going?"
"Fine here. Mum's doing bad. Megan just called. We have to go see her."
"Jess, I'm going to be late back. We're flying from Seattle to Los Angeles now for another meeting. Short notice I know but I won't be back until the end of the week."
"Not tomorrow."
"No."
I sigh. "Okay, but as soon as you're back we have to go see Mum. You'll need to bring back extra duty free for this sis." I try and joke.
"I've already got you an amazing limited-edition carton of Dunhill signed by Christopher Hume."
"Excuse me? Who is Christopher Hume when he's at home? The President of Dunhill? Never heard of him."

"He's the publisher of Chocolat!"
I'm silent for some time. "Oh. The magazine or the chocolate company?"
"I don't know. I think the company. We ran into each other at duty free and I recognised him from an article in the Economist. I thought you'd be happy!"
"Okay, I'm happy. It's a weird story to tell people. Thanks."
"Okay, have to run! Thanks again Jess."
"Bye." I hang up the phone and go in to see Nick.

"Your Mum's going to be a few days late. We should go over and pick up some of your things from home okay?"
Nicki's bent over his homework. "Okay." I pause at the door and then turn to go.
"Jess?"
"Yes?"
"Mum loves me, right? I mean, she's never here. I'm always with you."
I walk over and run my fingers through his hair.

"Nicki, your Mum loves you very much. She works an odd job, but she loves you very much. And I'm more than happy that you're here." I rub his shoulders and point out a mistake he's made in his homework. As he's erasing it and filling in the correct answer I say.

"When you're older you'll find that people you really love, well you expect them to know you love them even when sometimes you don't tell them, or you're not always around. It just gets harder when you get older to spend time with all the people who need you."
"I was sort of looking forward to getting older."

I laugh and mess up his hair as I turn to go back into the kitchen. "Enjoy the time now my friend. Growing up is like math. Each year it only gets much, much harder."

Marlies, November 12

I'm cleaning up from lunch and thinking about the dinner specials. I see Kate's name flashing on the screen of my phone as it rings. I take her call like I want to throw up. What feelings, such terror. "Hi."
"Hi yourself. You don't deserve me calling, but I'm taking you to lunch. I'll be by in five minutes."
"Kate, I can't – I've got a hundred things to do right now."
"Darling, I'll be by in five minutes. Just be ready."
I put down the phone.

I start putting on my jacket when my phone rings again.
"Hello?"
"Hey Jessie, it's me."
I haven't heard from Jean in ages. Jean is also a chef and runs a cool little bistro with probably a hundred types of beers on tap. A good person to have with you on the line during a rush.
"Hi me, what's up? Long time no see."
"I've been catering. Everywhere. Don't ask. Listen, I wanted to know if you have a good bread recipe that doesn't require yeast. I'm out."
"Out of bread, or out of yeast?"
"Ha ha"
"Hmm … I thought you were the sour dough Queen?"
"No time, I don't have any starter left."
"Have you tried wheat beer? Pizza dough style? Roll it up, let it rise. Toss in a bit of baking powder. Works for me most of the time."
"Yeah? Sounds good … wait a minute."
I hear something crash, and then yelling.

"You ok?"
"Yeah fine, I'm in the van, and there's a wasp in here. I was just curling my hair too. Damn curling iron fried out."
"In the catering van?"
"It's good. Now there's two wasps! They're coming in from the patio."
I hear her inhale and slowly exhale.
"Are you smoking again?"
"Since weeks."
"Ouch."
"I won't die healthy. Neither will you. Haha. Jess, what do I do? You have to help me!"
"Ok, ok, is anyone there with you?"
"No. I´m all alone!" Her voice starts to break.
"Calm down. Do you have a can of bug spray?"
"Yeah, but it´s back in the kitchen."
"Ok. How about a stick or, like, a big ladle?"
"Wait. I have a tennis racket"
"You have a curling iron and a tennis racket. In the catering van? Ok, Take it and swing it back and forth in front of you. They'll be scared off."
"Hey! These are big wasps. They´ll attack me! Oh my God, it's after two - I'm late for the bank, I gotta go!!"

The line goes dead. Jean's funny. Great chef though. I put the phone in my pocket and walk the length of the kitchen to the back door. "Barb!" I yell "I have to go out …"

Lunch with Kate, that afternoon

Kate picks me up and we drive wordlessly into town to a small German schnitzel house on the river I've never seen before. We get out of the car. "Never seen this place before…"
"Dearest, there's a lot you haven't seen before." We walk into the restaurant which is both surprisingly authentic looking and surprisingly busy. The first thing that struck me about German in school were the words that meant one thing to me in English but something completely different in German. Like, 'Wild Konditorei' and 'Avant Garde Schmuck'.

Because of my LitCrit classes, this constant deviation between symbol and meaning will be my cross until the day I die. Japanese is an easier language to grasp than German. This is true trust me, as I learnt Japanese quickly. Japanese is phonetic, and really has no rules of grammar (this is a relative statement for all Japanese teachers reading this; *comparatively* no rules of grammar then, and what there are I learnt quickly) German is empty (*leer*, which is what my German textbook does whenever I had to crack it open) without grammar, something I was never really good at in grade school.

I will never master the 'ch' because I´m English and not Scots. I can still copy out my katakana and hiragana without a break, but I couldn´t list three German verbs in the passive present tense. In fact, I couldn´t list three *English* verbs in the passive present tense. What is the passive present tense, and why is it taught in English and not in Physics? *Heisenberg* would have understood the present being passive, non-existent, but then he was German and so probably a lousy example.

"So, what's up?" I get straight to the point in hopes of avoiding the effect Kate has on me simply by the amount of her scent I've already breathed in.
She leans forward on her elbows towards me. "Last week I thought I was pregnant."
Pure terror. "And …?"
She laughs, "Don't look so frightened. I'm not. But it got me thinking. I'd really like to have another baby."
"What does your partner say about that?"
"I have no idea. I don't think I want another child with them. There are other ways."
"Yes, a few - why are you telling me this?"
"I don't know. I told you, my scent is in the air and I'm waiting to see what it brings me …"
"Kate, last month you tried to put me out of business – now you're asking me what I think about you having more children? I don't see the connection."
There is a brief, fleeting nanosecond when Kate's face registers fear – when in her eyes and around the corners of her mouth there registers a defenseless expression of fear and loneliness. - like she's chubby and thirteen and facing her first day of high school. I've never seen this look on her face before. And it is immediately gone again.
The waitress appears and Kate speaks to her in German, ordering our drinks, I assume. I understand the words 'wein' and 'bitte'. They laugh and chat a little bit together and the waitress leaves.
"You speak German?"

"Natürlich. My partner is German. I lived there for some years."
I laugh. "Hmm, what can't you do?"
She looks down at the menu for a moment and then looks up at me and smiles, "Really not that much Dearest."
"Kate, where would you put another child in your life?"
"In a basinet." She shuts the menu. "I was just asking. I'm going to have the schnitzel. It's very good here"
"Okay, then I'll have schnitzel as well." Our drinks arrive – we're both having a glass of rather late Federweiss wine and some Bergkäse to begin – and we place our orders. "How do you know about this place? I must have driven by a hundred times and never seen it before."
Kate sips some of her wine. "My partner and I used to come here a lot."
"Aha. So, where are we going Kate? What's the plan? It's been nice, but I still can't stop thinking about you, wanting you - even after what happened with you and my storage room … I … what do you want?"
"You know what I want Jessie – and I thought we weren't going to talk about that other thing. I told you. It's over. It had to be done, and now it's over. If you want to be with me then you accept that."
"I feel sort of stuck as to what either of us really want from this. Sex of course, but I want more than that. Do you?"
"I'm waiting to see what you do. I have what I want. I'm waiting to see what you do. Impress me. Take me out of myself."
I breathe out - an exceedingly long breath. "I would like to be with you, all the time. I don't want to be

thinking about when I can see you and when I can't. I want to live together."

"Then you'll have to be very patient." Our food comes – huge, thin, golden veal schnitzel still gently bubbling with fat, and between us a porcelain dish of potato salad made with apples, and sliced potatoes in meat broth. Delicious. We order another glass of wine. "Get on with your life. Don't wait while I decide what I'm going to do."

She finishes the wine in her glass and moves it to one side. "And I'm going to watch you while I'm deciding." She cuts off a slice of meat and puts it between her lips, holding it there for a second, "Dearest, I have a life – it's not perfect, but with children it's safe and it's complete. So, if you're asking me to change, then it isn't a question of what you do specifically for me, but what you do without thinking about me that I find interesting." Then she places the meat into her mouth, closes her lips and begins to chew. "It's how this all began." She looks at me and picks up her wine glass.

Marlies, later that afternoon

Back at the restaurant Barb informs me that the walk-in is on the blink. We look at the thermostat which reads four degrees and the thermometer inside which reads ten. "Great. We just got the dairy order in. Did you call Pape?" Don Pape is the local refrigerator and freezer company and usually have no problem coming in on short notice.

"Yep, but he's on another job. He'll call back."

"Why don't we raise the temperature of the freezer and move things in there?" Barb suggests. "What do we have in there?"

"Nothing really. Ice?" We open the walk-in freezer and see that indeed there is mostly bags of ice and the odd container of homemade ice cream.

"Great idea. It should keep things cool if Pape can't make it today. Honestly, Barb sometimes I could just eat you up."

Tonight's blackboard menu is slow cooked roast lamb stuffed with prunes and spinach or sea bass pan fried with a bacon and onion breading. Then we have some amazing pumpkin fritters with apple and cabbage coleslaw and end of the season tomato soup with onion and cheese biscotti standing in for the croutons - and yes, we always have a camera in the kitchen for our Instagram moments.

"You know, if Judith doesn't turn up soon, we're going to have to find another Front of House Manager. We can't run the place just the two of us."

Barb's writing out checks to some of our suppliers and ticking them off on the bills. "I know. I'm not cut out to be a waitress. We're lucky we have the girls." As I update the online order form of our wine merchant with one eye, I watch a YouTube report on airline security with the other. It's not very convincing, because it´s about how easy it is to plant a bomb on a plane and how difficult it is to survive a crash with all these idiots trying to retrieve their floppy hats out of the overhead while burning jet fuel tears its way up from the tail section. The presenter offers a serious, and terrifying, statistic that you had a better chance of surviving a crash if you read the safety card, based on a poll of people who survived airplane crashes. This sounds logical at first, until you think whether the dead people read it.

"How would they know? Not very comforting now is it? I bet there are a few dead people saying, hey I read the damn thing!" Barb mumbles her agreement.

"Remind me again why don't we do online banking?" Barb looks up at me. "Because the bank misplaced an 1100-dollar online transaction once and we got stuck with a bailiff on our doorstep threatening to take our Hobarts … remember?"

"Oh, right …"

"It took almost a month to sort that out."

"Barb, I just typed in your name in this word document and it's come up 'unknown word' on the spellchecker."

"Ha Ha. Why don't you go make us some coffee Jess? It's going to be a long night."

Downtown, that evening

It was a busy dinner – only the sea bass didn't go over as well as I had expected, so I made a portion each for Barb and myself. After sharing a half bottle of wine – an Okanagan Valley Ehrenfelser - Barb goes home and, after dropping Nicki off at a friend's house for a sleepover, I meet Rodd, Tina, and Bronwyn at the Diner. We're picking at the unhealthiest hamburgers and fries before heading out to the watering hole to listen to Rodd's favourite local band, 'Septic Flesh'. A sign hanging on the wall requests of patrons 'If you′re allergic to anything on this menu, please tell us BEFORE you order and not AFTER you choke'.

Tina's experiencing some difficulty opening the ketchup wearing mittens - which she has on to protect her new acrylic nails which were done just this afternoon, Rodd explains to me with a shrug. "Why have them done if people can't see them?"
"I want to look nice."
"Oh." Rodd and I are reminiscing about different truck stops that we've eaten in, especially that one in Montana when we had to run out in the middle of lunch because the wind had blown the tarp off the rig and it was now on its way back down the highway (the tarp, not the rig). A tow truck slowly passes the window, its victim securely chained to the back. Jokingly Bronwyn says, "Hey, Tina, there goes your car!"
Tina looks out the window and stands up, knocking her cola onto the table and onto most of us. "Hey, that IS my car!!"

Getting your car towed in town is bad, very bad. The towing company is made up of 'good ol'boys' who own big dogs fed on nothing but Chinese food so they're always hungry. They operate out of a compound fenced with rusty chain link topped with Israeli 'ribbon wire' which they patrol with baseball bats. It costs you double what it would to have your car released from them than it would in any other city in the northern hemisphere, even Paris. We each order a beer now that we won't be driving to the bar, but there's no Coors Light because of the tang of white supremacy hanging over their product now so we settle for Becks.

We come out of the bar about midnight, our ears still ringing with the metal of 'Flesh', to find it has begun to snow. We walk through the light cast by a streetlamp and Bronwyn stops to watch the stream of snowflakes caught in the cone of light where she stands. The snow is falling in ever larger flakes and is beginning to blur a lot of what is in the distance as we watch for the arrival of the bus. I hear Rodd and Tina's voices but I'm watching Bronwyn, and I'm not really listening to what they're saying.

Bronwyn wears snowflakes the way others wear mascara, but with an easier grace, almost an absence of care. The mascara is falling in buckets, but it's falling slowly, gently, almost falling backwards in the same way that a wheel seems to stop rolling and then begins to roll back on itself in that time dilation effect - and Bronwyn silently spins around the street lamp and through the falling snow like time was her playground, the drifting snow stretching back up into the sky for eternity. Bronwyn catches me watching her and smiles and then calls out and waves goodbye to us. “Have to run! ‘Night!”

Rodd and Tina have made it to the bus stop, Tina using her hairbrush to wipe off the snow from the seats in the shelter for Rodd and her to sit on. I make my parting words and turn to walk back to the restaurant where there are growing stacks of unfinished paperwork to be done. “It was nice – see you guys again soon okay?” While I’m waiting on the corner to cross the street, I notice a man urinating in the parking lot across from me. In Italy I once saw a man sitting on the side of the street casually open his pants and urinate into the street as dozens of people walked by him and politely walked around the puddle of urine he made. Without a word. He just whipped it out. Someone should tour the world, taking pictures of the vagaries of urinating men and turn it into a coffee table book of full page black and white pictures. I’m sure there’s some money in this somewhere.

Jessie's House, November 13

It doesn't take me very long to decide what I'm going to do. Who knows when I'll get another chance to go to Nice anyway? Bugger it. I've made up my mind. I'm going to the food show. This is great! I feel like the weight is finally off my shoulders. I rummage around in the junk basket I keep on top of the fridge for my Mastercard with its last remaining emergency 1500-dollar credit and pick up the phone to call the ticket desk at the airport. Some people have junk drawers, I have a junk basket. My drawers are all filled with cooking utensils anyway. There are three seats left on the morning flight to Paris connecting to Nice. I put down the phone and feel a rush of exhilaration. Grown up decision making! Super!

It's just turned noon, and I'm thinking of making some lunch when I hear a car honk, and the sound of a key in a lock as Nicki comes in the front door. "Hi Jess!" he calls.

I walk into the living room. "Hey, how was your night? Hungry?" I take his sleeping bag and drop it onto the sofa.
"Mm, yes. We had an early breakfast."
"Pizza?" I saw they opened a new Joey's downtown.
"Sounds good. Let me use the bathroom."
"Sure." I grab my car keys and check the fridge is closed and the stove off. I can't tell you how many times I've come back home and found the fridge door ajar and the inside full of frost – or a stove element is still on. Anyone else have this luck?

Winter is starting. As we drive downtown there is a definite lessening of green, and the sun is angled lower, reflecting off the windows of the many three and four-story buildings that make up our city. I find a place to park a block down from Joey's, and as we walk there, we stop in front of GameStop to check out their latest window display.

"It must take weeks to paint all those figures." Nicki likes the fantasy figures used in the Warhammer game. "It would probably take me weeks just to paint one." I crouch down and look at the array of figures arrayed in grueling battle in front of us. "I used to play Dungeons and Dragons when I was in school, but this was before any figures. We just used paper and pencil, and our imagination." I remark. "I did like the plastic figures that came with my model tanks though. Probably easier to paint than metal. Certainly not as tiny." I think back about all the hours I spent in my youth building models and painting them. "Come to think of it though, the father of a friend of mine had a complete Waterloo diorama set up in his basement. Hundreds of hand painted cavalry and cannon. I remember it was pretty cool. You need the time though." I stand up and we head off to Joey's.

We get a booth near the window and order the largest Texas style pizza on the menu. "It's cool they opened here. The last time I was at a Joey's was last summer on vacation." Nicki comments.
I look around and nod. "Yeah. I like Joey's. I'm glad they didn't turn it into a 'Friends' theme though."
Nicki laughs. "Yeah, there would probably be only warm drinks because his fridge was broken!"

"Haha! Yeah, or there would be a duck or two walking around." 'Friends' was a great show. Too bad it had to end. So many of those great shows ended, as I guess they needed to. Sad.

Our pizza comes and we dig in. I love Texas style pizza, but normally I make it myself when I can. I love the smell of yeast dough in a warm kitchen – it's not difficult to make and you get to have exactly what you want on your pizza, and the crust exactly as thick or as thin as you want. We have a Tarte flambée on the menu occasionally. I really like them old school – just some sour cream, perhaps some onion and the tiniest bit of smoked ham. We did it with grapes once too. It's excellent with Gewürztraminer. Funny name though. You expect this flaming tart to arrive at your table – or better yet, one that explodes into flames as you cut into it. "Good?" I nod at Nicki, who nods back, chewing happily.

"How is school?" Nicki nods and grunts.
"It's ok. Thanks for all your help with my project too. I got a B." Nicki takes a big gulp of root beer and wipes his mouth.
"Cool." I mimic him with swig from my cold IPA. "An interesting project. You should do more of that sort of thing. It'll be useful later."
Nicki frowns. "Really? Health? How so?"
I laugh. "Ah yes, youth. You never think you're going to get old. You will, so if you eat right and exercise now, it might be easier for you later."
"Oh yeah, Mum says that all the time."
"It's true. Think of your karate. If you practice you get and stay good. if you don't then you don't. Simple

logic." I bite into another slice of pizza. "If you eat well and exercise, you're priming your body to fight what's coming up later."
"Eating pizza won't help." He winks.
"Eating crap pizza won't, but if you eat good pizza, and perhaps not pizza every day, then you'll be ok." I flick my finger at his nose, and he laughs and backs off. "I liked the project because it showed you how all the pieces fit together."
"Well, thanks." He eats another half slice and then places the rest on his plate. "Whew! I'm stuffed." he takes another drink of root beer and sits back. "I think I eat a lot better than some of my friends any way."
"You'll be ok. Just don't forget. You eat garbage, you become garbage. Just make sure your Mum cooks. You could cook too. You know enough from living with me all this time."
Nicki nods. "I like to cook." He takes his phone from his pocket and begins to play a game.
"You want dessert?"
He shakes his head. "No thanks. Full."
He is lost to his game, so I finish my beer and call for the check.
"Hey Nicki?" He grunts. "Nicki."
He looks up.
"Your Mum is coming back on Monday. We need to tidy things up at home. I'm going to be in France, so it will be a few more weeks before you're back at my place. See you have everything you need, ok?"
Nicki nods and goes back to his game.
I worry about him, and hope Angie is able to spend more time at home than on the road in the coming months.
"Hey, you want to grab a movie?"

Nicki looks up. “The new Star Wars? It just opened.”
“Sounds good. We can grab some M&Ms for dessert.”
“Cool!” Nicki stuffs his phone back in his pocket, and we leave the warmth of Joey’s for the cooling, Fall air of the street.

Marlies, November 14

Since brunch prep began Meredith's noticed a subtle buildup of police vehicles in the immediate vicinity. She comes into the kitchen and calls to Barb and I. We wipe our hands and I grab a muffin fresh from the oven – apple date with walnuts - and walk into the dining room, looking out our front window. A canine unit sits outside the hairdressers, a squad car waits outside the art store and another goes slowly past the front window where we stand. Two unlikely looking men in jogging suits stand in front of the florists looking into the window.

We look at each other with raised eyebrows. "This might have something to do with the two crackheads I almost ran over in the alleyway last night when I left …" Her theory still hanging in the air, we hear shouts coming from across the street and see a swarthy young man unseasonably clad in only his shorts running out from the back of the cafe followed by a converging group of city police. A cruiser speeds by coming from the alley behind the restaurant, an M16 toting SWAT leaning precariously out the window like you see them doing on TV and wish you could try because it looks pretty cool, and cuts off the man's escape – just as he raises a gun and starts waving it in front of him.

Meredith sips her tea and Barb picks at my muffin as I stare bug eyed. "Hey! That's Sammy! ..." Meredith points and calls. There's more shouting coming from the direction of the art store. The police are attempting to handcuff another man as he lays face down on the pavement. Staccato notes ring out, there are some screams. Meredith drops her cup onto the freshly laid table beside us, spraying half of the tea down my pants and into my shoes, Barb rushes to lock the front door, gun shots ring out, and our front window implodes. We dive for cover beneath our beautifully set tables. There are more sirens, the screeching of tires and a final definitive series of shots.

“What the fuck?! ...” Barb swears, and Meredith and I pick ourselves up from the glass covered floor. I stand up and look out my empty windowpane. “Not again! Shit!!!” Barb’s still on her knees searching for her glasses which I pass to her. “C’mon, we have to go outside to see what’s happening.” she calls, popping a stick of gum into her mouth, “Let's go.” She stands, and we peer out the windowpane blinking against the sun as we survey the street scene. Barb goes to unlock the door. “C’mon!”, she insists. I look at Meredith and quickly scramble to my feet. Sammy is lying on his side holding his leg covered by the police as a paramedic attends to him. The street is a hell of a mess. Sundays were never like this.

There’s a sense of ‘the cleanup’ that’s played out in every police drama. You know, the camera pans back and across the street, people are led off to awaiting squad cars, while the narrator drones on in his monotone voice about the harsh reality of senseless urban crime. We walk down the front stairs of the restaurant and carefully into the street. The police seem to be mopping up the last pockets of resistance. Meredith pulls my sleeve and I look across to the flower shop. Then I pull on Barb’s sleeve. Wrapped in a blanket and being guided to an ambulance is the unmistakable figure of Judith. Speechless we just stare. Then she sees us, timidly waves, and smiles.

The Police Station, that afternoon

Barb and I are sitting with Judith in the lobby of the police station a few hours later. A female Constable has just brought over a carboard tray with three coffees, some sugar, cream, and plastic stir sticks for us and placed them on the small wooden table beside a stack of community awareness pamphlets. "Inspector Peters would like it if you could stay for a few more minutes while he finishes off the paperwork and then you'll be free to go?" Judith nods.
"That's fine, thank you Constable." I reply. She smiles and leaves. We sit there in silence. I make a coffee for Judith and place it in front of her. She looks up at us and smiles, then laughs. "So. Miss me?"
Barb gets up and goes over to Judith and hugs her while little tears roll down her rosy cheeks. "We thought you were dead. It was horrible."
I reach over and hold onto Judith's free hand. "Don't ever stay out that long without calling. We were worried sick!" We all laugh, and I get up and join in the hug of our terribly missed friend. "Can you tell us what happened? Feel up to it?"
"Yeah, I should, I've already told the story once to the police. I probably have more details now. I don't know."

"I was coming out of the restaurant – you had both already left and I was locking up. I came down the stairs and was about to go around back to my car. I had my wallet out of my bag trying to find my keys when someone grabbed me from behind and covered my mouth with a glove or something. I couldn't scream. Then someone else grabbed my legs and they carried

me across the street into the back alley and into the old cafe."
"Doesn't anyone see anything on our street? It's incredible!" says Barb shocked. I nod my head. "They had me gagged and tied up inside the cafe all that time. I couldn't even talk. When I saw Sammy, I got scared. But it turned out he just wanted me for himself. It was totally weird. His friend and he were always arguing, I couldn't understand what they were saying, and sometimes Sammy's friend would leave for days. Sammy just sat there watching me, reading, cooking for me. At first, I'd just scream when he took off my gag so I could eat. Then he stopped feeding me. So, I gave up. I knew I'd get free some time."
"Ermm … what about the bathroom?" asks Barb.
"Oh. Thank God, I thought you were going to ask about … something else Barb." Judith looks at us askance. "You two just don't change …"
"Sorry."
"Yeah, sorry."
Judith sips from her coffee. "Ugh this coffee's crap …"
"Mine's okay …" says Barb as she winces into the cup.
"So, to answer your question Sammy didn't touch me. Oh, he stroked my hair and my face and my hands, but that was it. The bathroom was a bit difficult but … that's a long story… I really missed you guys. I was so close! It was the weirdest thing I've ever gone through."

At that moment Inspector Peters comes along the corridor with a file folder in his hand. We stand up and each shake his hand. "Hello Jessie, Barb – sorry about your window again." He opens the folder and puts it down on the table, taking a pen out of his pocket. "If

you could just sign here, and here …" He points and Judith signs. "If you need anything, here is the number of the crisis counselling center."
"Thank you." Judith takes the card from him.
"Inspector, how did you find her in the end?" The Inspector smiles. "I'm surprised you didn't figure it out yourself though Jessie. You're a chef and the cafe where Judith was being held is right across the street from you."
"And?"
"It's been closed for how many months?"
"I don't know, probably almost a year now. Why?"
"You wouldn't think it strange that there was smoke coming out of the kitchen chimney sometimes - any time?"
I had never noticed. "Yeah, I'd find that pretty strange."

The Inspector smiles. "Last week the building owner noticed it when he was driving down the street, found a new lock on the door, thought it might be squatters, so he called us. It was a lucky break for us all."
"Wow. Thank you again Inspector."
"Yes, thanks – we're really glad Judith's back again."
"Okay." He smiles and we shake hands again and he leaves.
We head out of the station. "I'll be so glad to get back to normal life again." Judith says as we walk to Barb's car on the corner.
Barb opens the door for Judith, and we all get in. "Oh, I wouldn't get your hopes up about 'normal' just yet Sweetheart."

Marlies, later that afternoon

Back at the restaurant, I feel the time that remains for the three of us to be together slipping by. I think Barb can feel it too. We can't look each other in the eye and Barb's drinking her wine in nervous little sips. I'm on my second package of cigarettes. I've told Judith everything I know from Kate. Judith sits, stunned, one blow coming after another. I feel so sorry for her.
She doesn't look at us. "I didn't want to lie to you. I love you guys ... being with you here is … amazing. I had no choice."
"Is it all true then?" "Most of it yes. I changed my name – rather that than get arrested – I got out of the country – I've demonstrated a lot – against the G7 security council, animal testing – the usual – and why not? In Germany there are a lot of instances where an event cannot be protested. You get arrested if you do."
"Nazis!"

Judith smiles. "No, not Nazis – we don't have any love for that part of our history. This is just the same ignorance in many countries. The government run the police and the police … well in some instances the police are there to serve and protect the interests of the government, however the anti-protest law wouldn't go over well here. There was a demonstration – I wasn't there - I was away and had just arrived back in town by train. It was late and I was waiting for a connection. There were still police walking about in small groups, and some people who were standing on the platform. There was one girl, she was sitting on the platform with her boyfriend perhaps it was, anyway with this boy – he was drunk. There were two police with them, a man, and a woman, trying to get him to move along, to get up. So, they picked him up to carry him away. He resisted. He was very drunk or very stubborn. Any way he resisted, and they pushed him up against the vending machine there on the platform.

Of course, everyone is looking away but the girl, she's yelling at them. I got so angry watching this whole scene – the girl pushes at the woman from the back, following as they took her boyfriend away down the platform. The woman turns to her and simply hits her, right on the nose, and it's bleeding and she's standing there in shock looking at the blood on her hand as she wipes her nose. So I yell over and they tell me to mind my own business so I run up to the woman, call her a pig and as she turns I wind up and slap her across the face as hard as I possibly can. She just stares at me. Then I ran.

I ran all the way down the platform, and I was very lucky. The man is still holding onto the boy and the police are too well padded to run very fast in riot gear, but she chases me, trips on a cable laying around from all the construction on the platform, falls and I get away. Of course, this has all been caught on the station surveillance cameras and as my picture is already plastered in the police files, they're at my door the very next day. But I was at work and my roommate called me, so I just left. I went to a friend's and we drove to France. Then I flew here. It was lucky. I had already planned to come here anyway so I had a visa. I just worked under the table and changed my name. A waitress is pretty hard to find if she wants to be." She drinks from her glass. "It's funny, not even the driver's licenses here are followed when you move from province to province."

Barb and I sit there with our mouths open. "Oh man."
"Kate made it sound a lot worse."
"Well, it's still assault. They'd arrest me if I were back wandering around, I can assure you. Assault, interfering with an arrest … there's probably a few things. I don't have a clean record to begin with."
"You followed your conscience. You weren't out murdering people. There's a big difference." Judith drinks her wine. "The law is blind."
"Oh, thinking of France – I'm going to Nice for the food show the first week of December."
Judith and Barb look at me.
"It's not always about you Jess."
I lift my hands in defense. "Ok ok, just, you might want to know."
"Bring us something, we'll overlook it this time." Barb blows me a kiss.
"We have to do something. Kate's going to hold this over my head. Even if I get out from under her she'll use it one day as revenge."
"So, you're suggesting I become a fugitive because you slept with Kate."
"She might use it simply to force us off campus."
"Let her."
"Maybe you could sleep with Kate."
"What?!"
"Sorry, kidding."
"I'm not afraid of Kate. Fuck her. We've got the information about her deliveries. I even made a copy of the last one which might be enough proof for Costers' head office."

"Does she know?"
"Nope."
"I'm sticking with you guys."
"Yes. We'll get you a lawyer."
"This could get serious - you know, that right?"
"Yep."
"Oh man …"
"We need to keep Judith here. She's our best friend."
"You're right."
"Besides, I'm pregnant and you'll need Judith to help you in the place full time in a few months." Barbara says matter-of-factly. We look at her. The stem of my wine glass snaps in my hand. Judith starts to cry. Now Barb's starting to cry as she looks at us both nodding her head and smiling in glee, "David and I are expecting a baby! We're going to get married! I'm going to have a baby chef!"

Jessie's House, November 15

"Thanks. Thanks for calling. I'm sorry I wasn't there." I hang up the phone and look around the living room. Do you ever get the feeling that you've been duped? No? Well then, I tip my hat to you good folks because this clown's shoes have just been properly scarred. It's a funny thing about time zones - I always thought the world couldn't end today because it's already tomorrow on the other side of the world. But I guess it can.

The world ended for my mother about nine this morning but for me it was only about six. She should then still be alive for another three hours, shouldn't she? … that would only be fair. I light a cigarette and rummage through my cd collection and pull out my saddest music - music to weep profusely by – that hasn't seen light for some time. I put it into the cd player and fiddle with the numbers until I get to Send in the Clowns sung by Renata Scotto. Then I turn the volume way up, walk over to the sideboard. I finger the photograph I had framed and wrapped in Christmas paper that sits there ready to be sent off. Of us kids with our mouths open and tongues out grinning at the camera one summer holiday long ago. I wanted to give it to her for Christmas. I thought if I wrapped it, if I had a present for her, that she'd live to open it. I unscrew the cap of my most expensive bottle of scotch and feel utterly sorry for myself.[17]

***

Marlies, December 2

"I said, I'm going to the Food Show in Nice. You didn't want to go together so I'm going to fly down with Marta. Her parents live there. I'm tired of waiting for you to decide what we're doing."

"What?! You are unbelievable. What have I told you about your priorities?" She sighs deeply. "I told you I can't go with you. Costers stipulated no guests. I can't bring anyone along with me."

"How would they know? We could have gotten a hotel to ourselves, I'm paying my own fare, what's it to them if I go to the show at the same time as you?"

"Sorry Darling but I'm not going to risk having them know I'm there with anyone."

"Well, I'm going anyway. I haven't been to a food show in ages and I've always wanted to go to the Cote d'Azur. The food market in Nice is one of the best in the world."

"You're incredible!"

"And you're ridiculous … and a thief! Don't get all high and mighty on me Kate."

Kate ends the call and I turn off my mobile. Judith's on her second roast chicken, the juices covering her hands and glistening on her lips as she tears the meat off with her fingers. "So, she's really pissed off eh? I can understand you want to go to the food show, and she must see that is as important to you as it is to her, but she doesn't have someone going with her. Isn't it weird going somewhere hot and sunny just before Christmas?"

Barb rummages through the bag of French fries for some more of the crispy ones and then dips the few she finds into the small lake of ketchup on the paper's edge. "It is a bit odd - and, I mean, you're having an affair – it's not like either of you owe the other any trust at all. You threw that out the window. But she's a complete egoist, so of course she's pissed. I thought affairs were supposed to be exciting – you two go on like you're married to each other."
"Why is it a problem if I go to Nice with Marta? There must be thousands of people travelling there for the show. How is this my bad? Kate could take her partner with her if she wanted to. For all I know she might even have arranged to meet someone at the conference ..."
"Wow, this trust you guys have going. It's eerie." Barb chews her fries and looks at me. "You're not still involved with Kate, are you?"
"... Of course not. Like I shouldn't travel with her because there's only the danger of forbidden sin and unbridled sex awaiting us?" Barb snickers and Judith raises her eyebrows. "Look, neither one of us is ever happy doing less than 100% what we want. I want to go to the food show and preferably not alone. Kate never wants to go anywhere together in case we're seen, so my choices are few."

Judith sucks up water through her straw and spears some of my chicken with her fork. "Have you specifically asked Kate if she'd go away together?"
I gaze into space. "Well, not specifically ... it's always implied."
"You should ask." Barb slurps down the last bit of cola in her glass. We're all eating like complete pigs today;

I don't know what's gotten into us. At least Barb has an excuse, being pregnant … "She'll say no, but you should ask anyway."

Marlies, that afternoon

Not every moment in the life of a chef is spent behind a hot stove. You've noticed right? I'm now painstakingly devising the best PowerPoint presentation I can in thirty minutes for the Chamber of Commerce, of which most businesses in town are members. Now, while I had this done in my mind and in the bag weeks ago, I did not actually physically begin until last night and now I'm feverishly trying to gather my thoughts on screen. The thing that endears me to presentations is the pauses. There need to be enough, and they need to be just the right length, and there needs to be a great full screen image to go along with every one of them. "… this is chocolate … pause … and this … pause …even this … pause … and these …" yes, the slides are coming together nicely... but what do I say to accompany them?

Brian Fairfax, Chamber of Commerce President for the fourth year running and owner of Fairfax Ford which to be honest has been in the city for about as long as Fords were sold, asked me to give a small presentation to a group of scouts from a large and to remain nameless chocolate company who would like to locate at the edge of the industrial park in the south part of the city on the other side of the freeway. It would be amazing for business to have a large but nameless chocolate company in town and to this end I am devising the PowerPoint presentation – to sort of show how us small business people would just love to have them locate here instead of somewhere we couldn't drive to.

Chocolate, chocolate everywhere … we buy it, drink it, eat it, wear it, fantasize about it … maybe I should leave that last slide out. I sit back and stare at the naked model felating a strawberry, dripping dark chocolate onto the white background … it works for me … I copy and paste Marlies logo and our internet address on the bottom left hand corner of each slide and then do the same on the right hand side with the chamber logo, save, export onto the USB stick and … the computer freezes. Fuck! Fuckfuckfuck … beeeeeeeeeeeep. The dreaded beep noise which means you had better have saved everything because your computer is shutting down for no reason other than to completely piss you off. So, I wait, turn the computer back on, save onto the stick again, and put the stick into my pocket. Then I go out back and have a cigarette. I push open the back door which seems to become harder and harder to open each day. "Don't get up Charlie." I motion to Charlie who sits back down again on the rusting garden chair that is propped up against the back wall. He smiles and gives me a limp but caring salute.
"I got you JFK."
I look at him. "Excuse me?"
"JFK. You asked me if I had the movie."
"Oh! Right! You got it?"
He hands me a USB stick. "Thanks Charlie. I haven't seen this in ages. Can I take it with me?" Charlie nods. "Sure, bring me the stick back when you've downloaded it."
"Thanks." I put the USB stick into my pocket and finish my cigarette.

Now while you think I'm going to put the wrong USB stick into the laptop at the presentation and a porn flick instead of JFK automatically starts, it doesn't come to that. Life isn't that obvious. After everyone is contentedly sitting around the conference table in the Chamber of Commerce offices satisfyingly digesting a good lunch and a few extra beers I stick the correct USB into the laptop and the presentation goes off without a hitch. Even the strawberry-fellating model covered in chocolate goes over a treat.

Kate's house, later that night

That night, after a late dinner of fresh fish grilled with garlic, a mixed salad with olives and goats cheese, and ciabatta – there will be plenty of time for heavy winter meals soon enough - Kate and I are sitting over our wine. I'm exhausted from work and swaying between the feelings of sadness about my mother and the tension in the room between us - we haven't slept together in weeks and Nice seems to still be a sore point. We pick at cheese and nuts while the candles burn down on the big dining room table. I'm flipping through an article in The Atlantic on the politics of cocoa she's given me to read to source my opinion. Which I guess is a loaded gun. I finish it and put it to the side,

She places a nut in her mouth and looks at me. "What did you think?"

"Nothing new. If you think cocoa is produced without the help of slave labour then you probably still think that IKEA furniture can be put together without tools ..."

"You've been reading that article for the last thirty minutes. Do you agree with what they write? I disagree with their conclusions. What about going to the theater the week after next Jessie?"

I'm silent. Pensive …

"Are you with me Dearest? If you're going to fall asleep then you could have stayed at home."

"Hmm? ..." I am somewhere. Where were we anyway?

"Yes, yes. Sorry, I've really had the worst possible day, Kate. What were you saying? Look, I'm sorry about earlier as well. I just want to go away together."

"I was asking you if you wanted to watch to watch this

theater channel together?"
I put down the newspaper I had taken up from the pile on the floor. "Sorry, I was reading about this exhibition of Rasputin's penis in St. Petersburg ..."
"I'm not going to St. Petersburg. Theater Channel - Lion King or Stardust Express?"
"Ummm, La Boheme is playing in town actually and I'd really like to see that … I am not going to watch Stardust Express. I disagree with the article's conclusion as well, but I should read it again in the morning when I can concentrate. Wait, we agree on something? This is a disturbing development. I think I'd rather disagree then …"
"Lion King it is." Kate orders the program, and the Channel loads.
I empty my glass and steel my nerves. "Listen, Sweetheart, I was thinking about us. Why don't we go away somewhere – with your kids, we could have a nice holiday together – we could go skiing?"
"Du … when I'm back from Nice we'll talk about it. You know how difficult it is."

I look at her. "How about we go to bed so I can show you again how simple it really is - because it's really remarkably simple Kate - do you want me or not? I'm not just interested in the sex. I want you, and your kids. I want the whole package. I want you to take this seriously."
She looks out the window and takes a mouthful of her wine. "Jessie, I never wanted anything more than an affair. It's you that's taking this too seriously."
"Kate, how is our affair not serious? You were just asking me about having a baby together. What would

you do if your partner found out about us? Did you never think he might leave you? He'd have your ass."
"He's not interested in me; he's interested in the children. We haven't slept together in ages, and I'm sure he has other women. I don't think he'd take you and I very seriously if he did find out."
"Why?"
"Don't be obtuse Jessie."
"Not in his league?" I get up and go into the hall and grab my jacket.
"You know what I mean. Where are you going?"
"I have to go. Dinner was nice, but I need to pack."
"Du, stay, I want to see you before I go to Nice."
"Kate, I told you before, I'm also going to be in Nice. You can see me there."
"With Marta. Yes, you told me. Very cosy."
"Then you do listen once in a while." She just stares at me as I put on my shoes and leave the apartment, slamming the door behind me. I hate Lion King anyway.

Off to Nice, France, December 3

The phone rings. It's Marta. After getting home from Kate's I opened a bottle of vodka and began to pack. I managed to fall asleep mid-process and now I've woken up with an hour to spare before we have to leave for the airport. They wait in the taxi which idles in the driveway while I drag myself through the 20 centimeters of snow which has fallen overnight and, as we are off to the south of France, I am not remotely dressed for. The driver takes my bag and deposits it in the trunk as I get in, smiling sheepishly to Marta, who looks at me, mutters 'merde … ' beneath her breath and turns to look out her window as I dig out the snow from inside my shoes. Anna bounces on the seat hysterically happy, "We're going on an airplane Jessie!"

We arrive at the airport, check in and manage to get three seats together. I still feel a little drunk … pathetic isn't it? I even drop the bottle of wine Marta entrusted me with for her parents on the floor in front of the check in counter - my carry-on bag looking like a dead animal laying there in the slowly growing pool of red. Marta asks the counter attendant if there's a cleaning crew and ten minutes later this old woman appears with a dustpan and brush. How dry did they think the wine was?

I go to the bar and buy myself a vodka and an espresso while Marta and Anna visit McDonalds, and then I walk over to duty free for a carton of Rothman's International which I like to treat myself to when I can. I buy a jumbo box of smarties for Anna and a bar of

Lindt chocolate with hazelnuts for Marta because, well, I'm not completely thoughtless. She takes great pity on me during the entire flight and keeps Anna happy with a small stash of new toys from her carry on with one hand and me happy with a supply of miniatures she buys from the stewardess with the other. "I don't deserve a friend like you. No one does." I lean on her shoulder after the lunch trays have been cleared. "Tres bien Jessie. This took you a very long time to realise. I don't know if I should take it as a compliment that you are drunk as you say this …" She's hard but fair the entire trip.

After the delayed flight, the two time zones, turbulence at times which was making the cabin crew blush, the four drunk American guys running up and down the aisles in their socks, the Indian family arguing over their seat assignment, the smokers actually trying to light up and being yelled at by the stews, it was quite relaxing having Marta there with me. At some point Anna absorbed herself in the movie and Marta curled up and went to sleep, her bare feet gently digging into my right thigh. When the Cote d'Azur comes into view in the distance two hours later, I'm in wonder. It is the combination of sunshine, the beach below us, and the coffee that Marta charms from the stew before they close the inflight service that gently pulls me out of my pathetic state. I'm about to step foot on the Cote d'Azur. Nice. St. Tropez. Cannes. Monaco. Wow. Mum would have loved to have seen this.

With promises that I'll call the next day, Marta drops me off, pointing me in the direction of my hotel in front of the Nice train station before she and Anna take the next local train in the direction of Beaulieu-sur-Mer where her parents live and run a little hotel. When I get to my own hotel, 250 meters down the street, I am faced with a sign that the hotel is closed for the season and would I kindly walk another 50 meters to the right where the hotel has its winter quarters. This takes me to what at first glance appears to be an off-season discotheque. I wish with all my heart that I'd gone with Marta. I check in and go up to the third floor and then squeeze myself into my small room overlooking the roof of another building. I open my knapsack and pull out my notebook, find the number of the Meridien Hotel and call.

"Hello, yes, could you please put me through to Ms. Morris's room? Room 500 is it? Merci … Hi Kate? It's me, Jessie."
"Darling, how nice of you to call. How are things back home?"
"I don't know, I'm in Nice."
There is a pointed silence. "What? You're here?"
"I said I was going to come. What did you think?"
"I told you not to come Jessie. Why would you bother – I won't be able to see you. This is business."
"Well, I know you've probably forgotten but I'm actually a restaurant owner and a chef, and this is a food show so I'm sure they'll let me into the events …"
"That's not what I meant. I don't want anyone back home knowing we were here together. We discussed this Dearest."
"No, we never discussed it. You dictated it. I'm here and I'd love to see you. Really. I'm going to the show

anyway, so perhaps we can have a coffee together – you know?"
She sighs deeply, "I'll call you. What's the number at your hotel?"
I look around and then think, she won't write it down anyway so what's the point. "Good question. I'll have to get back to you on that." I yawn loudly and deeply.
"Dearest I have to go - we'll chat later." Then she hangs up.
After flying all this way, this isn't exactly what I had in mind. You'll have to excuse my reticence. My pensive murmuring. My self-indulgence. But I feel a bit sad. I sit on the bed, roll over onto my side, and fall soundly asleep.

Nice, France, December 4

I'm not going to let my excitement of being in Nice be undone by either a crap hotel or Kate's ego. I awake shortly before lunch, shower, and dress, and walk out down towards the seaside, stopping in the middle of town for a Salade Nicoise and a 'Blonde' … beer at a little bistro filled with tourists. Amazing to be sitting in an outdoor cafe the first week of December. In the south of France. Mum really would have enjoyed this. Just a little note about your hotel. Do not eat in it. Hotel dining rooms in tourist areas operate on the principle that if you're eating in your hotel you are either too boring, lazy, unadventurous or scared to eat the local cuisine. And they cook accordingly. Would you book a week in Paris and then eat at Burger King? No.

After my meal, a cigarette, and another blonde I walk down to the seaside and along the Promenade. I see the Meridien and cross the street. Nice hotel. Makes mine look like a cheap brothel. I go in and up to the Front Desk and ask to speak with Kate. They dial through to her room but she's not answering so I leave a message.
"Could you tell me what room Ms. Morris is in please?"
"Certainly, that would be room 500."
How did I forget that? "Thank you."

I walk back through the lobby and towards the main ballroom where the Meridien, as the main venue for the food show, is holding their workshops and talks. I stop in front of the posters listing the discussion panels and cooking demos, the talks, and the readings.

Scanning down the list my eyes go immediately to the name of an old acquaintance. Katrin Lawson. Oh wow! Katrin Lawson of Dandelion Marmalade is here and has a talk in … thirty minutes? This is too great. I note the name of the conference room and go in search of the registration table.

Meridien Hotel, Nice, that morning

55 euros later I have a badge and an info package. Boy are these euro notes funny looking. A bit big too. Like play money. Weird. 'Jessie Watkins, Chef Owner, Marlies' is printed on my name tag which I wear on a red white and blue lanyard around my neck. Cool. I walk to the conference room and take a seat in the half full room near the front. Katrin walks onto the stage right on time and everyone applauds. She looks exactly like her picture. Middle aged, stout but not fat – firm – commanding, but gentle, taller than I had expected with shoulder length dark blond hair held up with a clasp – she's wearing jeans and running shoes, a white polo shirt and a small set of pearls. Her hair is up, and her glasses sit on the edge of her nose. I laugh a bit to myself. She looks as if I had taken Barb and stretched her a foot.

Katrin is introduced and the title of her talk, 'Taking the Bite out of Social Networking' appears behind her on a large wall screen. "Good morning. My name is Katrin Lawson, I'm currently living in Germany where I work as a food consultant. I'm also a chef, a Mum, and my blog, when I have time to write it, is Dandelion Marmalade." There is a moment of laughter from the audience and from Katrin as she looks at her notes and the audience applaud.

"If you find yourself in the wrong talk, you now have the chance to leave. I believe there's a talk on the politics of chocolate going on next door …" She smiles and there's more polite laughter. She turns around and looks at the screen behind her as the title changes to a slowly animated selection of restaurant logos. "I'd like to talk today about social media and how it affects your audience, the millions of foodies and cooks who enjoy the food we prepare for them in our various businesses around the globe every day. They are educated and knowledgeable, have disposable income, a discerning palate, and can themselves cook.

As if that weren't daunting enough, internet blogs and food channels are making them even more demanding, expectant, and knowledgeable than they already were. So, what does this mean for us? What the heck is social marketing to your average restaurant owner? How does the speed of the internet take the old adage, 'One happy customer tells two friends but one unhappy customer tells ten friends', and with a simple mouse click and changes ten friends to three hundred friends on foodbuzz, or twitter, or facebook? …"

Katrin's voice continues as the slides behind her change and I look around the room's hundred odd faces. Until now I hadn't thought that there were obviously other people around the globe reading Katrin, that it wasn't just me. I had taken her words and imagined they were for me alone. I smile to myself and lean back to listen.

When the talk is over, there is a small crush at the stage to meet Katrin, so I wait for a bit, and then walk out the conference room and around to the casino and peak inside – it's early and there isn't much going on - I'm really tempted to play some poker or black jack but feel totally out of place in what I'm wearing. I wander back around to the bar for a drink and look about for a free table. Far in the back, framed between two large palm trees, I see Alex. I guess I should have known she'd be here – and that of all the hotels catering to the food expo she'd be at this one. I walk slowly around the edge of the bar to get closer without her seeing me.

She's sitting alone with her laptop open in front of her as she types, a half-eaten lunch – a basket of shrimp and French-fried potatoes with coleslaw - sitting cold and forgotten behind the open screen. She hasn't changed at all – still eating on the go and not even that well. I wonder when she last ate a properly cooked meal. She's still somewhat harried looking and her hair's up in her ubiquitous ponytail which is still how she looks best – but there is something less grown up in her features now. She doesn't look as steeled. I think she's been beaten about a bit by life in New York.

I walk over to her and stand by her side. In a phoney French accent I ask, "'As Madam perhips fineeshed vit er shreemp bas ket?"
She looks up "Excuse me?" Then she stops typing and sort of rocks back in her chair. "Jessie. Oh my God. What are you doing here?"
I smile at her, "Hi Alex. Same as you – here for the food show."
"Wow - sit down." She moves over her laptop and picks up a stack of papers from the chair beside her. "You know, it's strange, I just ran into a woman coming down in the elevator – she works at the university and when I mentioned you and your restaurant she seemed to know all about you – small world huh? Kate something – you know her?"

"Ahh – yeah. Yes, I know Kate. That's a long story." I look around, "Is she here?"
"No, she was leaving the hotel for lunch – there are events all over town this week – the whole place is bopping. She seems like a bit of a bossy cow if you ask me – total control freak, didn't like her much." That's no great surprise I think to myself. "I heard the University Club is going really well too. That's amazing Jess – congratulations."
"It's a long story – since you left – a lot has happened." I shake my head and light a cigarette. "You have no idea." I laugh.

She takes my hand. "I'm really, really sorry about your Mum Jess. That really sucks."
"How did you hear?"
"Megan called me."
"She called? Wow. Well, thanks. I think I'm still in denial. I really don't want to think about her this way. I never said goodbye – there was a lot of unfinished business. Well, you know me – you know my family …" She nods. "I think she would have liked to have seen you again though – she mentioned you often."
Alex squeezes my hand. "Are you happier - I mean, with everything else - the business?"
"Are you?"
She smirks. "I love my job … Are you seeing … anyone?"
"Not Lori if that's what you mean …" I think about that and remember Lidia's words. "… I'm not seeing anyone I like – "I laugh "Yes, but it's … it's not like it was with us. Let's put it that way."

There's a pause in which we look at each other and then quickly away again. "Look, I have to finish this article and mail it out. Let's meet for a drink later – in an hour? Call me – I'm in room 516."
Great - the same floor as Kate? "Sure - why aren't you out enjoying yourself – everybody else here is. Isn't that the life of a food critic? Restaurant openings, parties, life on the road?"
"Ha! Ha Jessie! I wish. I'm still the rookie – if I don't impress my editor with some amazing work then I won't be sent to a big show again. We'll see each other later. Oh, before I forget- I'll be in town before Christmas – the magazine's sending me to cover the Strand's new hotel opening." I get up and look at her – it feels like it's been years instead of months since I saw her last. "Wow. Then maybe I can make dinner for us again?" We look at each other without a word. "It's really good seeing you again Alex. I'm proud of you – doing what you wanted to do - and I've missed you."
"Thanks Jess. It's nice to see you again too. I've missed ... us." She smiles but, I don't know – somewhat vaguely, which is fair. I haven't thought about Alex for some time – I mean, of course I have but life goes on and I've been so obsessed with Kate that in many ways she's sort of slipped my mind. Now here she is, and I get the sudden realisation how good it was. Safe. Relaxed. Going somewhere steadily instead of the chaotic and violet passionate moments I've been living lately. And suddenly I miss her a lot. I kiss her on the cheek and leave the bar.

I walk back to the conference room but Katrin is gone and people are taking their seats for the next talk. I look at the sign beside the door – "Lifelong Learning,

Lifelong Cooking". Oh boy ... I go out the front doors of the hotel and walk along the Promenade basking in the sunshine. I cross the busy four lane avenue and go down onto the pebble beach and walk towards the coffee bars close to the water whose gaudy lights are bright enough to be seen in the daylight. I love the sound of the pebbles moving and crunching as I walk on them. I stand and watch the waves gently coming in when the tinny reverberations of my mobile break the spell and I open my mobile. "Hi Kate. Where are you?"
"I can't believe you actually came to Nice Jessie."
"I said I would. How are you enjoying yourself?"
"It's all work. You have no idea."
"Yeah, I've heard that before somewhere – how's things?"
"Fine. I'm out with people in town – a lovely little bistro near the market."
"Can I see you?"
"I'll call you when I get back to the hotel and we can have a drink together."
"I haven't eaten yet – I could come by the restaurant."
"Jessie – there are people here I know. You're always so physical – I don't want anyone getting the wrong idea."
"What idea would that be Kate, that we're sleeping together - aren't we? Remember when we first met, I was with you and your friends in that Tapas bar – your hand was on mine resting on your thigh beneath the table – you even kissed me - it was clear to everyone that we were in each other's pants. Well we're not even in the same country now Kate."
"I told you not to come Jessie. I told you we'd talk about things when I got back."

“I came all this way and I’d like to see you. What’s to talk about?”
“I told you – you’re too sensitive.”
“I want you. Maybe that’s too much for you.”
Kate laughs her tinkling little laugh. “Oh Jessie. We’ll talk later. I’ll call you when I get back to the hotel and you can come over. Be awake and ready for me though! I have to go.” There’s laughter in the background and then she ends the call. I feel like a complete idiot.

My phone rings again as I put it into my pocket.
“Hello?”
“Hi Jessie? It’s Alex.”
“Wow – you still have my number?”
“Of course. Don’t you still have mine?”
“You changed it the day after you left – don’t you remember?”
“Oh, right. Sorry. Listen, something’s come up - I have to meet some people from another magazine – I’m going to have to move our drink date a bit later, how about tonight? Can I call you then?”
“Umm, okay –.” That’s sure to be the time Kate calls.
“Thanks Jessie – see you later!”
I shut my phone off, look around the beach, and then at my watch.

Monaco, that afternoon

It's only two. I turn and make my way back up the streets to the main train station. Fuck it. I'm off to Monaco. I walk up to the train station, find that most trains go from Nice to Monaco anyway and so buy a day ticket and then jump on the first train I find pointing east. Thirty minutes later I'm standing on the platform of Beaulieu-sur-Mer. The train I took only went that far and the next train to Monaco arrives in forty minutes. Brilliant. Beaulieu-sur-Mer is a beautiful little town wrapped around one side of a sandy cove. There are a lot of little hotels and houses and restaurants and then a small beach which I walk around. Very few people anywhere. I wonder where in this town Marta and Anna are? I walk along the beach throwing rocks into the water and trying to hit the waves. The sound of a train reaches me, and I panic a bit, begin to run back to the station, but the train is obviously not mine and zips by fast in the opposite direction. I sit on a large boulder and look out over the water and the little town.

Thinking I'll have a coffee I get up and walk back along the pebbles which rattle beneath my feet as I walk. My eye catches something white to my left and I stop, bend down, and retrieve the most beautiful fist sized white rock pitted with hundreds of small holes, inside of a few still sit tiny barnacles. It's beautiful. I take this with me and walk over to the nearest cafe and sit on one of the small metal tables arranged outside on the street side. "Cafe au lait, s'il vous plaît." The waiter nods and goes into the restaurant, returning in a few minutes with the coffee sitting upon a small tray with the receipt tucked beneath the saucer. I miss every country having its own currency. Now it's all euros as I expect one day it will all be a single currency. How boring.

I break open the small plastic wrapped ginger cookie and nibble it, getting hungry but wanting to wait for Monaco before eating anything more. I take out my mobile and the piece of paper Marta wrote down her number on yesterday. I try the number in various combinations, but each time hear the irritating squawk informing me in French that either the number is incorrect or thanking me for dialing into an answering service which will now charge my account the minimum three minute connection fee. I put my phone away, look at my watch, leave three euros on the small silver tray, and walk back to the train station. "Merci", I wave to the waiter as I walk back along the embankment and up the street.

The train gets into Monaco and I'm surprised to find the station underground and serviced by a long and unattractive cement tunnel. I walk its length and exit onto the street across from Port Hercule which is filled with large yachts. At the far end of the Quai Albert I can see the unmistakable signs of what a Christmas market at the end of a short row of restaurants can only be. I'm completely starving so I go into the first place my eyes fall upon, Bistro Tartine, which has a patio area with large wooden umbrellas, and order a glass of their house white wine – 2008 Côtes de Provence - with a squid and goat cheese Brandade and a basket of warm bread. Amazing.

After lunch I walk up the path to Monte Carlo, lean out across the ramparts and let the breeze ruffle my hair as I stare out across the city and the pale blue Mediterranean. Mum would have loved to have seen this. With her in mind I walk around the palace to the Cathedral in the back and go up into its busily ornate interior. I purchase two of the larger candles each with a blue crest attached to the front, stick them onto the metal rack where many less significant candles burn, and light them with a taper. Then I sit in one of the pews marveling at the interior and wondering about Grace Kelly and all the magic that was Monte Carlo and the French Riviera. At least today I didn't run into more than a dozen people in the streets. Where are the paparazzi and the frazzled celebrities dashing from hotel entrances to the hushed interiors of patiently waiting limousines? I feel somewhat cheated, but the lunch was incredible, so I decide to go back to the bistro for a coffee and their chocolate raspberry tart …

Nice, later that evening

Shortly before ten in the evening I'm back in my hotel room and have just turned on an old episode of Mad Men dubbed in French when the phone rings.
"Hello Darling."
"Hi Kate."
"Dearest I'm not going to be able to see you today after all. I'm just too busy. I'm sorry."
No surprise somehow. "Uh huh."
"I hope you're having a nice time here though - you should go out instead of just sitting in your hotel room."
"Well, I was out – I took the train to Monaco and had lunch - and then I came back because you were going to call, remember? Look Kate, whatever – you have a nice time and I'll see you when I see you." There is a lot of laughter in the background again, and I put down the receiver. I go back onto the bed when the phone rings once more. I wonder if it's Kate again. I crawl over and pick it up anyway. "Hello?"
"Hi Jessie, it's Alex." This feels much better.
"Hi Alex, what's up?"
"I'm out with a group - we're in this bistro near the market. Why don't you come over and we can have a drink and catch up – there's someone here from Chocolatier as well!"
Chocolatier magazine? It would be cool to meet them, but there's something oddly familiar about the laughter in the background. "Alex, the woman you met, Kate, she's not by any chance in your group, is she?"
"Kate Morris? Yes, she's here – you know, she's starting work with us in a few months – my boss

offered her a job. How did you know she was here? That's weird."
"What?! Kate is going to work for the New Yorker? What about Costers? What about …" I stop before I say what about me. ... "What's the name of the restaurant?"
"Umm … hey! What's the name of this place? … Le Safari - it's right in the market. It's got a blue awning and we're sitting outside."
"Okay, I'll see you soon."

I put down the phone and get my shoes on, go out the front door of my hotel and walk along past the train station and then turn down Avenue Jean Médecin, through the little park and then across the main avenues and into the old area of town which is alive with little cafes and restaurants, each very similar to the next. I walk along the stretch of patios and cafes all spilling out groups of laughing guests until I see Le Safari on the right-hand side and stand at a safe distance. There is a table with about twenty people outside. Kate is unmistakable. Alex is more hidden but after some time I see her. I hesitate, and then it's clear I'm not going to join Alex with Kate at the same table. And it's obvious that Kate's 'working' too much now to bother seeing me. Fuck it.

I'm bound by beauty, bound by desire, bound by yearning - this is simply too much pain for the Cote d'Azur. If I'd wanted to suffer, I would have gone to the Praia de Rocha. After a few minutes brooding in the shadows I turn and make my way back to my hotel. As I'm opening the door the phone by my bedside rings, but I don't pick it up. Then my mobile vibrates and rings as someone sends me a message, but I just turn off the phone without reading it. At about midnight I'm still watching TV when there's a knock on my door. I don't answer it. There is a rustle beneath the door and a slip of paper slides beneath it. I carefully get off the bed and walk over to the door, bend down, and pick it up. It's a note brough up from the Front Desk. 'In town staying at the Meridien. Anna at my parents. Call me room 542. Marta.' God damn it - doesn't the Meridien have any other floors?

I go back to the bed, turn my phone back on. There's a text from Alex but nothing from Kate. I message Alex back 'Sorry – could not find you and my mobile battery died. Breakfast at 9?" Then I call Marta and get her on the second ring.
"Jessie? Were you asleep?"
"Yes, sorry. When did you get into town?"
"Just now. Anna was having such a lovely time with my parents that I took their car and drove back into Nice. It is too sleepy at my parent's. When are you flying back?"
"Tomorrow after lunch. I took the train to Monte Carlo, stopped in your little town. It looked lovely."
My phone beeps a message.
"Oh, couldn't you stay a bit longer? It would be nice. Why didn't you call me?"
She's right, it would be. "I couldn't figure out the telephone codes and the train to Monte Carlo was just leaving I can't stay any longer, I must get back for Mum's funeral. I should at least be there for that."
"Certainement, Jessie. Why is it so late? It's been a month already." I read the text and see Alex is good with breakfast at 9.

“She was already cremated. The family is spread out everywhere though – for Mother’s Day we’d always send a world map with photos of where everyone was. But we’re getting everyone together at least this once to spread her ashes onto the ocean, near where she liked to walk. Right now, she’s in an urn in the living room, above the fireplace. It’s too odd. Look, how about breakfast in the morning? But at ten – I’d like to sleep in a bit.”

There is a pause. “You want to sleep in? You never sleep later than six.”

“The air here’s different.”

“D’accord – I will see you in the morning.”

“Of course - Good night Marta. Thanks.”

“Good night Jessie.”

Meridien Hotel, Nice, December 5

True to Marta's word I'm up before six. I go for a walk down the avenue, past the road cleaning and delivery trucks and along the mostly empty seaside. I feel as though I could walk all the way to St. Tropez. The sun is spreading across the beach and there are already a few people about – the seagulls, joggers, the dog walkers, and me. At seven I still have two hours before I should meet Alex for breakfast, but my stomach is already grumbling. I could do with a coffee and a cigarette. Recalling the coffee served in the discotheque bar of my hotel the previous morning I head to the Meridien for a more civilised one.

Sitting there later over my espresso, playing with the remaining croissant crumbs wondering if I'm ever going to see Kate before I fly out, I notice Katrin Lawson seated a few tables away. Her photo on the seminar posters must have been taken in the hall; the resemblance is unmistakable. I get up, take my coffee cup, and walk over to her table. "Hello. You're Katrin Lawson. Dandelion Jam?" She looks up at me, with her coffee cup poised at her lips and smiles weakly. "Jessie Watkins - I'm sorry - I'm a huge fan of your blog. I've been reading it for months now. It's … you're brilliant."
She smiles again and puts down her coffee. "Hi Jessie, thanks. Nice to meet you. I'm glad you like the blog. Are you in Nice for the show?" She motions to the chair next to her.
"Oh, I don't want to bother you – I just wanted to say hi and tell you - well that I'm a big fan."

She shakes her head and pulls the chair back. "No, come on, sit down – you've come this far, so join me." I sit down next to her and smile at her - she's beautiful. I can't believe I'm sitting next to her in real life. She places some jam – apricot? certainly not dandelion - on her croissant and bites into it. "So, are you a chef or …?"
I nod – "Oh right yes, I'm a chef. I have a restaurant – well two, sort of. I came here for a bit of a holiday and … well and for some personal reasons."
Katrin snorts and smiles, wiping crumbs from her lips – "You're a chef and came to the largest food expo on the continent for personal reasons?"
"Yeah, that sounds stupid. I came here to see this woman – she runs the University Food Services back home – it's really for her that I came to Nice I think. We're sort of together – well – she's married actually but we've been having an affair for the last few months. And, okay – there's a good friend of mine here as well, we flew in together. She and her daughter are here visiting her parents." I pause and look down into my coffee cup as she looks at me. "… mmm and there's my ex –she's a food critic and writes for the New Yorker – she's here too I just discovered ..."

Katrin nods approvingly, her eyes wide as she spreads jam on another croissant. "When do you have time to run a business? You should get out of food and write novels …"
I laugh. "Yeah, that would probably be easier. My life now – it's pretty fictional …"
She looks at me and bites into her croissant, chews, and wipes her mouth. "What's the name of your restaurant?"

"Marlies."
"Nice name - So are you enjoying the sights? Nice is wonderful." She sits back and looks out the window towards the Promenade and the seaside.
"Oh yeah – the market, the little side streets, the restaurants … I love it here. It's almost Christmas and I'm just wearing a shirt and walking along the beach – and there are little Christmas markets about the place – it's pretty surreal." She nods. "I went to Monaco yesterday – they even had a big plastic tent thing filled with artificial snow and an ice-skating rink right on the harbour with all the yachts and palm trees. Now that was odd. Ice-skating inside and watching the sunshine of the Mediterranean on the other. Monaco was beautiful."
"Mmmm", Katrin nods, munching croissant, "I wish I had brought my kids – they would have loved it. But there was only budget for one and we've been travelling most of the year anyway."
"I heard your talk yesterday by the way."
"You liked it?"
"Mostly."
She laughs loudly. "That's being honest. I'm still a bit jet lagged, and I forgot my notes at home – had to adlib everything I wanted to say when the screens came up and forgot most of what I wanted to say. The questions were good though."

I smile at her. "Katrin, may I ask you a question - not food related? I get the sense you might be able to give me some advice – I mean, from reading your blogs and all you sound like you really have your feet on the ground."

"They wouldn't work well anywhere else, now would they?" We both laugh at that.
Katrin's looking at me. "So?"
"Would you invest time in something you probably can't have – or would you invest in what you probably can have?"
Katrin looks at me and then drinks from her coffee cup. "You mean your love life?" She smiles, I nod. "Well, first things first. You said you met your ex here? So, you could go up to your ex and say – 'I've been an idiot and I'm sorry so let's try again.' Second, you realise that … this woman you're having an affair with …"
"Kate."
"Kate … is unlikely to leave her partner for you, right?" She takes another sip of her coffee, shaking her head, "And third, your friend, that's a huge step into a very demanding relationship – which is fair – you don't want to ruin a good friendship. How does she feel about you?"
"We've slept together."
"Mmm, okay, this gets better." She pours herself another coffee from the thermos on the table and moves it towards me, but I shake my head. "You should find a good agent; this is movie material."

I laugh at that. "The thought of being with Marta scares the hell out of me." Katrin laughs. "Maybe you need a good scare to get your head together. This sounds like an easy decision Jessie – why are you making it difficult? Perhaps you need a change of perspective. Focus on your cooking more – open a third restaurant, take up jogging … Do these women know about each other?"

"Mmm ... yes – and all three have rooms up on the fifth floor ... I'd like to know how you find this an easy decision."
"Because I've got a room on the fourth floor .... Ha Ha! … Jessie, I've let love go because I was stupid, scared or lazy – and sometimes I've just followed my libido. Now I feel incredibly lucky to be with my partner – and I hope there are no changes on that front - I'm in a good place in my life." She smiles. "… but it's nice you think I might have the answers." She sips from her orange juice and gazes into the distance as the wait staff tend to a large group seated at the far end.
"Maybe people in food are too wound up in the process of making other people happy that they aren't very good at making themselves happy."
I drink some of my coffee, "But you're happy …"
"Oh, I'm happy - I'm fine … But what I'm saying is that it doesn't mean I couldn't have been happy with someone else. So – who knows. Don't do what you think you should - the world has enough self-sacrificing heroes suffering in silence." She laughs. "Jessie, give in to what scares you. Life is short. You'll sleep better … you'll use less salt in your food too … your customers will thank you." We both laugh at that.

One of the event hostesses, a slim brunette in a burgundy Chanel suit, comes over to our table and excuses herself. "Ms. Larson?"
"Lawson." Katrin corrects her.
"Ah oui, of course, I am sorry – Ms. Lawrson – there are some people here from the press who would like to interview you – if you would be so kind?"
Katrin wipes her mouth with her napkin and stands up. "Well, that's my flight."

I follow as she reaches out her hand. I take it and we shake. “It was amazing meeting you Katrin – thanks.”
“You’ll be okay Jessie. Thanks for confiding in me – it’s nice that some people like my blog and think I have the answers to more than just their failed recipes. I don’t, but it’s nice to know.” She smiles and walks off with the hostess to the hotel lobby.

Nothing like being confronted with a solution to give you strength. I take out my mobile and send a text ‘Decided to leave Nice early. Sorry. Call you when home. J.’ I walk in the direction of the hotel elevators, change my mind, and walk over to the Front Desk.
“Excuse me,” the Front Desk clerk raises his head and smiles.
“Yes, how may I help you?”
“I’d like to leave a message for Ms. Morris, room 500 please.”
“Of course,” he slides a pad and a pen over to me. “Do you need some paper?”
“Thank you, excuse me for a minute please.” I take up the pen and the pad and move to one of the tables in the lobby.
What should I write? Perhaps something brief. Profound, stunning, unforgettable, but brief.

Kate, congratulations on your new job! I envy you the chance to work for the New Yorker. I will look for your first article with great anticipation ... I crumple this up and try again … *Kate, I hate you and I’m very glad that ...* This is not going as well as I had hoped. Brief certainly, but far from profound. I tap the pen against the table and look out across the street.

Kate, I am off. You are an addiction that has become unhealthy. Like an addiction, having you was never as good as wanting you - and sooner or later either the props or the tension between us will cause actual pain instead of excited bother. If you are bruised, the only way to feel anything is to bruise deeper. There was probably a better way for all of this to have happened, but I suppose that wasn't completely up to me. Good luck in New York. Jessie

I look at this and read it through a few times. I shake my head, take up another piece of paper and try writing my name with a y, and then again with one 's' and an 'i', fold the note over twice, and write her name and room number. I get up and walk back to the Desk. "Thank you again," I give the folded piece of paper to the clerk who nods and smiles, then I head back to the elevators.

I push the call button and wait for the doors to open. I step in, press the button to the fifth floor and lean back and wait, music playing in the background. The doors ping open and I get out, looking at the room number listing on the wall in front of me before I march off towards her room, looking left and right until I find the right door - and then I knock. She opens the door – she seems somehow neither surprised nor delighted – she seems resigned as she leans against the door jamb holding a crumpled newspaper in her hand.

"Oh. It's you." She smiles crookedly.
My heart is thudding against my rib cage and I feel odd, but I simply say it before the moment passes. "Look, I'm – I wanted to tell you that I love you …." I

pause and we just stare at each other. "That's it. Just that. I love you."
She stands there looking at me without saying a word. I point to the papers in her hand. "I said I love you – check your script."
The telephone rings and she turn to look back into the room, then back to me. "You love me."
I look up and down the hallway and shake my head a bit, smiling. "Yes."
She stares at me and I have the feeling that she's simply going to turn around and shut the door on my face or … – but at least it's out there – in front of us – and it's her move. She looks at me and I can see fear in her eyes. Confusion.

She stares for some time and breathes in and out on the verge of indecision. Then she looks down at the papers in her hand. "You love me … Oh! Right, yes I didn't see it there – there's red wine or something spilt over that part of my copy …" She reaches out her free hand and takes my arm, pulling me gently across the threshold of her room. We kiss like it's the first time we'd ever kissed. We slowly break apart, our noses brushing, and she's looking into my eyes and I can smell the warmth of her breath. She leans her head over my shoulder and chuckles. "I was really just expecting room service when you knocked."

I let her go and walk over to the window of her room noticing her clothing strewn about the place - on the bed, hanging over the chair, on the floor - as I'd seen it in another room, far away. I look out the window. She has an enviable view overlooking the sea. I turn and smile at her. "Really? Great, I'm starving … "

Epilogue

University Club, January 8

The Admission Committee meeting adjourned, the eight members have moved from downstairs and are seated along one of our banquet tables next to the window enjoying their dessert – white chocolate celeriac mousse sandwiched between dark chocolate wafers and topped with caramelised ginger – and coffee.

"This has been just a superb lunch – Jessie? Thank you!" There is a small round of applause as I serve coffee together with Alissa and smile in response. "Phil Bleary knew what he was doing when he turned the place over to you. The food wasn't this good even when we had a regular chef. Of course, that was before we had the new kitchen." David Ikram, the Associate Vice President of Student Marketing looks around the table at his colleagues, who are nodding their heads. "Why can't the food be this good in the serveries? I'm going to talk to the Food Committee about that …" Dr. Isabelle Sanders, the only faculty member on the committee, gently waves a spoon between her fingers, smiles in agreement and says to me, "Do you also cater weddings? Can we do a wedding in the club? My son is getting married soon and everywhere in town is booked solid."

I replace her coffee cup which I have just refilled. "I can cater a wedding, Dr. Sanders, but I think

organising an event is something you'd need to have okayed with the club Secretary."
She looks rather horrified at this suggestion, "With Rob? Oh no, he's just never here – I don't think I've had an email from him all term." She looks across the table- "Mary? Is Robert Murphy still about? Have you seen him?" "Rob Murphy left three months ago for Ireland." replies an incredibly old man in a rumpled suit seated at the head of the table.

Frank Masters is the oldest living member of the university administration – and sits as an honorary member of any committee at any meeting he chooses to attend. "I'll be eighty-four next month, but I can tell you the whereabouts of any faculty member, even, "he smiles and digs into his dessert, "if they are somewhere, they shouldn't be." There is laughter around the table, as everyone eyes each other somewhat nervously.

I take this to mean that, yet another Professor has been caught in flagrante with a colleague, grad student, or worse, undergraduate. "Not much gets past these old eyes, or ears… does it, Pat?" All eyes turn to Pat Gropple, acting Vice President of Student Services as she confronts the remark. "You should drink your coffee before it gets cold Frank. If you are alluding to what I believe then I would appreciate your remaining aloof from such comments. If you don't mind."

"I'll see about talking with the committee myself, Dr. Sanders." She thanks me and returns to her coffee. As I move along the table. Frank Masters grunts, and everyone returns to their desserts. "What about the

Dean's suggestion of reducing the GPA requirements for merit scholarships? Allow more students to apply? I've been thinking that we might be discriminating against those students who, while not exactly lazy, aren't as motivated or capable through whatever extenuating circumstances – I don't think we should appear prejudicial in any way by accepting only elite applicants each year?"
Vice President of Undergraduate Admissions Sally Freeden is stirring her coffee loudly as she tosses this gem out to the group. "You mean we're discriminating against lazy students?"

Pat Gropple counters, "Why is this a bad thing? What does the word 'merit' mean to you?" "We're only discriminating against lazy students if the basketball team is discriminating against short people." Comes a comment from the other end of the table. "Vertically challenged." Retorts another. "Why don't we just offer scholarships to anyone who applies? Then we'd not be discriminating against anyone." "What about exchange students from underprivileged nations?" "I think we're missing the point …" replies Sally Freeden "I think if we continue offering subsidised room and board …"

There is a loud banging of a spoon against the side of a coffee cup, which silences everyone. "If I may add my two cents? I'm finishing a very enjoyable lunch and would like to do so in relative peace. I would like to remind everyone that our meeting has already adjourned, so let's keep shop talk for the next one." The speaker leans forward "And, has anyone yet congratulated Jessie on the new Food Service contract they have now since Costers left us?" There are hurried calls of congratulations, which I nod and accept, happy in a nervous and surprised way. The committee chair, Student Admissions and Financial Aid Vice President Carlotta Sims, leans back again and smiles at me as I look her way. I smile at her and nod, lifting my hand as I leave the room. As I pass the sideboard, I notice the latest issue of Food & Wine.[19] I pick it up, and head back to the kitchen.

Notes

1

Our contract with the University Club began last August. Bleary and his partner are regulars at the restaurant, and one evening he took me off to the side 'for a word'. "Jessie. Becks and I just had a wonderful idea. There's an unused kitchen on campus I think you might be interested in. For catering and things."
"Really? Where? Costers has all the facilities contracted and runs all the on-campus catering." "Well, that's generally true. There is one space their contract doesn't cover."
"Oh? Where's that? Wait … not the barbecue pit in front of the student union building …"
I smile and Bleary laughs, "No hahaha – of course not – I mean the University Club."

On Bleary's suggestion Judith, Barb and I sat outside on the sun warmed stone benches of the McClurrsen Campus Center and waited. Judith and I nervously chain smoking while Barb, who had quit smoking the month before, had crumpled up the first empty mini Tootsie Rolls package of the day. The first cars filled with students, bits of furniture protruding out their open windows, had begun arriving for the new term. The freshmen have the most belongings – mostly brought from their bedrooms at home. The juniors and seniors are identifiable by their simple knapsacks and laptop bags. The odd exchange students trundle oversized suitcases with the occasional missing wheel over the long, wide stretch of concrete that separates the cluster of student service buildings from the green on one side and Alumni Hall on the other. The concrete beach. Bleary walked towards us from the ivy-covered Stevens-Last building which houses administrative offices. He saw us and waves. We got up to greet him as he comes closer. He had a big grin on his face. Bleary talked firmly and loudly as he opened the club doors and ushered us inside. The club faces north and never gets any direct sunshine, so the space was quite cool despite the August heat. He turned on the lights and showed us around the elegantly equipped space with its leather sofas, frosted glass tables, and hardwood floors. "There are two floors – this one where we usually meet has the bar, as you see. Then there is the upstairs where we have a small gallery, library and of course the dining room and kitchen. That, I believe is what you are most interested in."

Our eyes adjusted to the change in lighting. I think we would be *extremely* interested in the bar which offers five shiny brass taps of various draught beer. This sits in front of an impressive display of red wines behind a latticed wooden door and a glass fronted wine cooler along the back wall. We follow him up the staircase anyway. "The club was renovated during a time of lax budgetary control and, ahem – shall I say, more generous support from the membership. In those days it was the Faculty Club before we were requested to open our doors to the entire university staff. Sadly, we don't have as many members as we used to. Faculty, I must say, prefer a certain clubby aloofness. The club is now mostly used for meetings and rented out for weddings. Politically correct thinking has left another victim in its wake." We reached the second floor. Floor to ceiling windows overlook the campus swimming pools, playing fields, orchards, and community gardens

– the latter run by students and the local farmer's market co-op. People were working in the garden and a small tractor drove by pulling boxes of fruits and vegetables. "A lot of what is produced here is purchased by Costers, and some of the proceeds given to the garden club. It's a good program – the kindergarten has a piece of the garden as does a local senior care home." We nodded our heads. I bet Costers get this stuff at a knockdown price … This room has a hardwood floor. Leather chairs surround low, wooden tables covered with recent issues of The Atlantic, New Yorker, and Food & Wine. I picked up a copy of the New Yorker and flipped through it. Barb and Judith admired the watercolours ranged along the walls between the bookcases. As Bleary opened the far doors he turned, "We like to support local artists as much as possible. These are by Larissa Kühler. Next week we are replacing them with photographs by … oh yes - Konstantin Mihov; perhaps you've heard of him?" We shook our heads – this is a town bursting with young artists.

"We do the same in the restaurant," said Judith, "Last month we had photographs by David Meekison and next month we have drawings by … Jen Frankel?" I turn to look at Judith, who nods, "Yes, Jen Frankel. Customers like it, and we can regularly decorate the walls with something different."

"Really?" Bleary's eyes lit up. "I do like Ms. Frankel's work. I seem to recall a drawing of hers entitled 'Draw me what's an Obi'. I met her at a show in the Hamish Gallery last spring – a delightful woman." The doors to the dining room opened, we entered a well-lit carpeted room filled with about a dozen tables each with four high backed chairs. All the tables were empty except for a small white porcelain bud vase sitting in the center. Three large, potted plants in bloom stood against the picture windows on the left-hand side. On the right wall framed prints advertising past exhibitions were ranged above an exceptionally long conference table. At the back of the room there is a silent and hauntingly empty open kitchen. “We only do luncheon once a week, on Thursday usually.” Bleary informed us as he walked between the tables. “It used to be daily, but then we lost our stipend from the university. Money doesn’t stretch as far as it used to. Though, I wonder about some of the projects we do find money for when it is politically expedient to do so.” He had his hands in his pockets, looking out the window and gently rocking on his heels. “It would probably surprise you to know, Jessie, that some of my colleagues have found it necessary in next year’s budget to again allocate $80,000 simply to entertain the students in their residences. $80,000! Incredible. When I was at university, we never had a social budget. We contributed ourselves and made do. I must say, we never suffered.” I nod to him. Our student budget was considerably less. But our residence was off campus. In the food chain off campus housing ranks even lower than even the Freshman class. Eighty thousand dollars is a lot of pizzas.

“No. Students are coddled these days I tell you. Coddled. Then they go off into the world and complain how no one cares …” He muttered as he looked out the window. “Ha. Retribution. Well, we do them no favours in this regard. Of course, eighty thousand is just a drop in the bucket compared to the six figures we

spend on our graduation ceremonies each year …" He turned back from the window.
I looked at him and smiled, "Six figures? What's the catering end of that?"
He laughed and walked over to me patting me on the shoulder. "Hahaha! Always with a keen eye for potential business eh Jessie?" Judith and Barb were standing transfixed in front of the kitchen. I had half an eye on it and half a polite eye on Bleary. There is something quite spooky about an empty kitchen. I notice this every time I come into work first or leave last. A kitchen is meant to be full and busy and loud - when it's empty and closed it feels abandoned and unnatural. "But I think," Dr. Bleary came out of his reverie, "I think you came here to look at the club's kitchen and not hear me ramble on." He followed us into the kitchen, flipped the light switches, and the kitchen sprang to life. It was incredible. Costers would have a fit if they knew this kitchen was sitting idle. Even without the lights the three of us easily made out the unmistakable lines of the stainless steel Bulthaup design. I couldn't recognise a Hugo Boss shirt, but I can recognise kitchen equipment the same way most women can recognise a Prada bag.

Judith ran her hand over the cabinets set flush into the tiled walls, the row of spotless salamanders between the hoods and the ceramic plate warmers set into the countertops. Barb walked along tenderly caressing the arrangement of two sets of six stainless steel gas burners with one hand as she went. A meter-wide rock broiler sat beside an equally wide mirror-smooth grill area. Judith slid open one of the cabinets to reveal dozens of white, oven safe ramekins of various sizes.

She caught her breath and turned to me with big eyes. I opened a few of the drawers to find a full inventory of Henkel knives and utensils. Cleaned and ironed aprons and jackets were stacked on a tall shelf sharing space with KitchenAid mixers and sticks. There wasn't a dry pair of underwear among us. Only Bleary seemed unmoved. "We had the kitchen renovated and outfitted a year ago. Our Treasurer left for America taking with him a considerable amount of the club funds. A very charming man but a rogue of course. He used ten thousand dollars of the club's funds to 'short financials', I believe the term to be, and made a fortune. He sent us a tenth of the money he had pilfered with the stipulation that it be used to upgrade our kitchen facilities. Well, I thought that particularly good of him. He could have walked away with the entire amount. I don't know how we would have gotten the money back from him. We had made a profit we could never have otherwise realised - so we left it at that. We sent him a photo of the new kitchen, but it was returned 'address unknown'." Judith, Barb, and I smiled and nodded our heads as Bleary rationalised the crime.

"Anyway. I don't want to take up more of your time than necessary. I know you have a restaurant to run. Jessie." He turned to me, "My assistant, Robert's idea really, but what I was thinking was this - you and your team take over the kitchen here – expand onto campus. We haven't had an active Food Service here at the club for donkeys. Ages, years …" He explained to our bewildered expressions, "… so why don't you take the place over? Make something of it? We have our own small staff - you could absorb them in some way - you would have carte blanche. All we would expect would be that some of the profit makes its way into the club treasury. Something like forty percent?" He looked at us expectantly rubbing his hands in front of him. We were speechless.

"Well, I know you probably want to talk about this amongst yourselves, and I have to get back to my council meeting." He looked at his watch. "Why don't we talk about this later on the phone?" We left the upstairs and made our back way down to the first floor. When I could unglue my mouth, I spoke. "Dr. Bleary. This is an amazing offer. Thank you, but … I don't know what to say." He shook his head and smiles like a man who has just given a favourite grandchild a large teddy bear. "What about the contract with Costers? I don't think they'll be very happy about this. It's probably against their contract anyway."

He shook his head again, knowingly. "Our bylaws clearly state that we may not only accept off campus catering, but we may also offer on campus catering – it doesn't stipulate where or how. We were catering a few functions before Costers arrived, when Food Service was still carried out by university staff." He closed the doors and locked them behind us as we emerged into the glaring sunshine. "I had a word with the Vice President of Finance about the matter yesterday and he sees nothing in the Food Service contract that disallows the University Club offering catering how and where we please. Costers might not like it, they might scream bloody murder, they might even send us a strongly worded letter – but legally they will just have to accept it."

A small alarm rings, and Bleary pulled from his jacket an impressively new iPhone. “I must unfortunately leave you now – I am honorary chairman of the faculty committee, and today my esteemed colleagues will be discussing ways in which we can attract students to our new transdisciplinary programs. Though how a humanities student is to find satisfaction in combining an interest in Victorian literature with daily lab rotation dissecting mice is beyond me. Humanities was humanities and engineering when I was at school.” He let out a long sigh and looked at us, and then smiled. “So. We don’t want to keep the Deans waiting.” He nodded and shook each of our hands before marching off.

Still speechless we wandered to the food courts and found a table in the sun overlooking the small lake beside the university’s ‘concrete beach’. The lake was once a swimming pool, now half filled with rocks. Who would have built a 30-meter-long rectangular lake? We sat lost in contemplation sipping our drinks – Starbucks mocha cappuccino, Starbucks skinny latte with cinnamon, and Starbucks Very Berry iced tea - and smoking feverishly. “I think I heard some rumours about the Treasurer …” Barb looked off wistfully into the distance. Judith laughed, nodding. “What do *you* want to do? I say let’s go for it.” I drank some of my coffee and swirled the foam back from the sides of the cup. Judith lit a cigarette, passed it to me, lit another for herself and reached for her drink. “I don’t know Jessie. How do we run two places between the three of us?”

I’d been thinking this over even before today, almost like a dream of avarice - “We start small. No one would expect that we open the place immediately for

daily lunches – but we could do the occasional dinner in the same way we do our catering now. What do we have Barb, four or five events a month?" Barb nodded her head in agreement, "Then it will probably be double that – which we can still handle." Judith and Barb were silently calculating overtime and costs but they're not frowning which I took as a good sign. "We run as many caterings as feasible using our existing staff, bring in a couple more on call if necessary. For the first while, until word gets about, we'd be able to run things smoothly. Then, well we cross that bridge when we get to it. If it works, we can talk to the university about using our name – 'Marlies at the University Club' or 'Marlies Campus Diner' or something. Hell, look around – Pizza Hut, Starbucks, Burger King – they're all here." Barb pointed at me, "Yes, but they're here as a part of Costers' contract. Not solo." "Yes," I pointed out, "But we both know that Costers pays a hefty percentage of sales – sometimes as much as thirty-five percent – to have them here. Their brands attract students who in turn eat Costers' food. And we, darlings, are a brand."
Judith and Barb were nodding. I leant on the table and looked at them in turn, "Imagine what we could do in that kitchen. We'd be in effect expanding at *no* extra cost – the club covers the overhead and we give them a piece of the profit. We'd have our foot on campus unlike any other caterer in town."
Judith raised her hand, "I'm in."
Barb looked over at her and then at me, sucked up some of her iced tea through the straw. "Let's do it."
I leant back smiling in glee, "Kate is going to just shit!"

2

I bought Marlies six years ago. A year out of chef's school and like the rest of my class pretty sure I'd be splashing the front covers of glamourous, international food magazines. Marlies was well established, and the owner wanted to retire. I had apprenticed there for a summer and we had gotten along very well, Marlies and I. When the owner decided to sell, she was happy to sell it to me. With 28 seats Marlies was the perfect size for a startup. A small garden overgrown with wildflowers and herbs ran along one side with a few cast iron tables and chairs. The perfect place to sit with wine, hummus, and olives on summer evenings. Two years into the project, I was working without much sleep, a single magazine portrait but no cover shot to my name and was sinking all my cash into repairing a kitchen in desperate need of an upgrade.

One day after a busy lunch my old roomie, Barb, walks into the place with a much more level head on her shoulders and three years in Paris at Le Cordon Bleu. Barb and I together proved much more successful together than I could ever have been alone. We began selling the crowd-pleasers as take-home items from a storefront grab and go, ran a strict blackboard menu - to keep down inventory and ensure seasonal items - and focused on covering all our overhead and loan payments with out of house catering. In two years, we were out of debt.

3

X position? It's nothing kinky. Check your restaurant bills every so often. Occasionally you see it on your receipts from the mall too. You might have wondered what that X at the bottom meant. X position on the register is used for training staff on the register and doesn't add the items to the Z or account of the register - which means that it doesn't add to the final daily total and there's no trace of it for the tax boys. A lot of places either have one waitress using the X key and building up the slush fund for the owner to pay the dishwashers under the table orrrr … some floor manager or headwaiter run a few bills through on the X key themselves. Depends on whether you need a master key or not. On most older machines you don't. More locks don't make for a safer store.

I've worked in countless places and I have yet to find one that isn't being ripped off by its employees. Someone long ago and much wiser than I said, "Give your dishwashers two bottles of wine a night or they will steal three." We don't have a big enough operation to satisfy a slush fund, but a truck stop - truck stops are happening.

4

Kate loves her children, but she has no more love for her partner. In the beginning, their brash and dominating figure intrigued her - now it merely repulses her. And why, she wonders, are their hairy feet the first thing that come into her mind? Why not their boorish laugh, or incessant chatter? Or their bad breath? She is simply tired of her partner and wishes for a fresh start. Not for the first time Kate wonders if she married simply because they were the only decent looking one she had met who was remotely taller than herself. Or was it that they were a banker and a good catch? She doesn't know any more. Kate doesn't want much of what she wanted twenty years ago.

Kate has been open to an affair for some time now. The right man in the right place at the right time. Or the right woman. A good fuck is a good fuck she thinks, and both sexes have always intrigued her. Kate sighs. She and her partner have separate bedrooms and have not shared a bed for over a year. She is only forty years old and expects to find lovers and perhaps another partner - though, she thinks, the latter is not a necessity. Before she married, she had lovers of both sexes.

Kate wears her shoulder length hair tied up behind her neck with a black ribbon – as she always has, since she was in school. Some things never change, she thinks. She has piercing, grey blue eyes and pale, full lips; she thinks herself a very good-looking woman – though much taller and broader than average. Paired with her forceful character she knows she is probably too much for most potential lovers. Though, she is not interested in *most* lovers.

5

Alex and I met a month before graduation. Lori and I had just gone our separate ways, and I had spent a year without meeting anyone remarkably interesting - except for a Professor with whom I shared a triangle with another student. Both she and our prof were caught in flagrante in the seminar room by the department head. They were both very quickly let go for violating the university's 'standards of academic and community integrity'. These standards are regularly flouted, but sometimes you need to provide a scapegoat to feed the PR machine. There was much talk of a more lurid reason for their removal - said department head and said Professor were married and the student was also seen in and out of the department head's office at all hours. Or so went the gossip.

So, one night I attended an ironically themed 'off campus farewell meet and greet' at a big graduate student house – one of the last of the old kind in a big old gingerbread style house along University Road. Single family dwellings at the turn of the last century, they were recently all torn down and replaced by simple three floor student residences with live in staff but no bike sheds. Development and improvement. Alex was standing there, arms crossed, sipping a beer, smoking, looking somewhat bored. She was wearing red flip flops and a much-worn green summer dress. I didn't notice her right away because I was looking for the sour cream and onion chips and we sort of bumped into each other.

"Hi."
"Hi."

"Got a light?"
"Sure."
"I'm Jess."
"Alex."
"Have you seen any chips about?" When I saw her smile my stomach did a few gentle flip flops and I was wishing it was Freshman year all over again. She lit my cigarette and we chatted as one does at university events, jockeying for position.
"… hahaha ... yes, I know what you mean. I just read a critique on the dangers of translating poetry from its original language. Rilke had written a poem, in German, on the Last Supper in which he describes the apostles as ′gathered about Christ′. In successive translations this digressed into the apostles ′being about Christ′, ′lying about Christ′ and eventually ′lounging about Christ′ with an allusion to couches upon which the Holy Party had stretched themselves out."
"Hahaha!" Alex had just completed a double major in journalism and theater. I'd been taking the most trivial classes - but the best I could get into at the last-minute. I was always late registering, being away on the coast working each summer to pay tuition and never getting back home in time. Alex had been taking great courses in 'Ethics and Morality', 'The Politics of Irish Theater', and 'Elizabethan English Literature' actually *taught* in Elizabethan English. Alex was a bit Goth looking at the time. She wore a big silver cross around her neck. She had jet black hair, very pale skin, and a Triskelia tattooed on the back of her shoulder. She appeared to me somehow *underfed*. Perhaps I felt drawn to her out of some desire to feed her. I thought she also bore a strong resemblance to a squirrel. She

had a sort of pointy squirrel-like face and big eyes and she wore her long hair in a messy ponytail – a style I rarely ever saw her change over all the years we were together.

"So, Alex, graduation, what are you going to do?"
"You mean after graduation or do you mean this weekend?"
I pause but a moment. "This weekend."
We never looked back. Knowing the job market was a black hole for LitCrit majors and as I had already been badly bitten by the food bug, I was off to culinary school. Alex was off to grad school in the big city. Over the next year of weekend and holiday visits Alex too became a foodie and began writing food critiques for some local magazines. It was wonderful and cheesy, and the sex was never wrong. We simply fit together. Now I'd gone and fucked it all up.

What you must know about me is that, like a lot of us in the food business, while I'm great at food I'm really, really crap at relationships. Now, if you're reading this, are in the business and have been together with the love of your life since day one, then please forgive my sweeping generalisations about our ilk. I call'em as I see 'em and I'm not writing this for youse to love me. I'm what past partners, lovers, employers, even family members for that matter, have aptly termed "self-sufficient". That doesn't mean my need for affection, care and surprise birthday presents is any less than the next person though. Last week, an ex-girlfriend of mine, Lori was in town. My hormones kicked into high gear as soon as she called. We had remained in contact and were always flirty. So, when she said she was coming to town, I was stupid enough, or drunk enough, to text her back with no great subtlety. Actually - like you're reading this right now - in black and white - 'I'd really love to sleep with you again'. Then I come into the dining room from the kitchen the next morning and there's Alex, with my phone in her hand. *Reading*.

The fact that she's going through my messages is strangely not the point. If I have something to hide then she has every right to stumble across it – even probably look for it, for that matter. This is all painstakingly explained to me a few days later by Judith. In some corner of my mind I can see her simple logic – but to be honest, if I had wanted to hide something, I would have deleted my messages. My sister Angie explained to me later that in some deep, dark, backwater of my psyche I obviously wanted to be caught and there remained only the variable of when to enter the equation.

This was all purely academic as I stood there that morning, the coffee in my cup almost freezing as Alex looked up at me with big, sad eyes. I knew that I'd totally and completely screwed up. I felt so angry at myself for being such an idiot that I pretended I didn't know was going on. Nice touch eh? I took a sip of my coffee and lit a cigarette. "What's up?" I couldn't imagine what I would have said had I slept with Lori. I don't know how to describe how mind boggling huge this mistake in judgment really was. If you can imagine preparing custard cremes for let's say, a room full of food critics, and then as you were about to serve them realise that instead of sugar you had used salt, and your wait staff had all walked out and you were naked and the police were on their way to arrest you then you might understand how I felt. The tension between us was horrible - filling the room like some terrible balloon – massive and expanding. Alex didn't say a thing. She got up, pushed by me, left for work, and didn't take any of my calls.

When Alex came back that night, she left her car running in the driveway, which told me volumes about how pissed off she was at the world being somewhat more than a weekend environmentalist. I'd taken the evening off and had dinner ready – grilled chicken breasts with a tomato and yellow pepper Concassée, some shoestring potatoes and a small Greek salad with garlic stuffed green olives marinated in walnut and parsley pesto - even though I knew she wouldn't be eating any. She came in the front door, ignored me, grabbed one of the many empty moving boxes stacked in the hallway and slammed it onto the floor like she's some pro wrestler on Saturday afternoon television - twisting and tearing and forcing the helpless cardboard box into shape. Then she dragged it into the bedroom and began gathering her clothes from the bed, where they hung on the chair in the corner, from the floor – wherever they lay. There really weren't many in the closet - that's how Alex was – cute but messy. She began tossing everything at the box.

I walked into the bedroom with a cool vodka tonic in my hand. "You want a drink?"
"No."
"Do you want to talk?"
She turned to me with an exasperated look on her face. "I'm leaving. You don't want me, you want Lori.

What's to talk about?" Clothes were flying through the air and piling up about the box like a bean bag toss at the fair.

"Look, I didn't sleep with Lori. I wanted to but I didn't."

She walks over to me smiling, and inside I cower slightly. "Oh. That's okay then. Then I'll just stay here, and you can think about Lori while you're fucking me." She swings back and slaps my face hard. "I could forgive you sleeping with her on some stupid drunken whim. You wrote the bitch about it. I can well imagine how pathetic she thinks I am. Do you have *any* respect for me? You still want Lori. Perhaps one day you'll get your wish so there's no point planning anything else together is there? One day you might suddenly give in to your desires and sleep with someone else right?"

I rub my cheek and walk over to the box and begin putting the clothes that lay about it inside. Alex leans over and tears them from my hand. "Leave my fucking things alone!" My Catholic school education has finally caught up with me. What did they say about mortal sin? 'If you want to go out tonight and commit a mortal sin save the gas money - you already did!' I'm trying to be sensitive, but I feel totally defensive – wavering between postures and wondering how I should be holding my glass. Probably even having a drink makes me come off as far too at ease with the situation. I put the glass on the dresser and stick my hands deep into the pockets of my jeans. I think, by now the chicken breasts are going to be completely over cooked …

"Look, there's always that risk Alex, but so could you. There are no guarantees. Hell, there are dozens of people I'd like to sleep with … err … BUT during the time we've been together I haven't slept with any of them. Only you. I think that's pretty good." The words just sort of tumble out of my mouth, end-running my brain completely. She laughs, sort of a choking sound, then she bursts into tears, sits down on the bed, stands up, drags the battered moving box to her car. "How many of them were you thinking about each time we fucked?" I watch her, not believing that I'd hurt her so much. Why couldn't I rewind and begin again? Shit. The TV is hers, so I unplug it and take it out to her still idling car which by this time has drawn a few passersby. "What are you looking at?!" she screams. They look about and wander away.
"Alex. I'm sorry."
"Jess I thought we had something that I could rely on." She pulls the TV from my hands and almost loses it on the ground before stuffing it into the backseat of her car.
"Look, I was wrong – stupid – but I'm not going to lie to you and say I will not ever want to sleep with anyone else but you. I haven't but I can't guarantee I won't. I accept the same from you. If you want honesty that's as honest as I can be."

She stands there looking at me. She slaps me again – but *hard* this time. Then she gets into her car and drives away. The chicken breasts weren't bad, but the shoestring potatoes were a complete write off.

6

Recycling is stressful for me because I know, as you do, that no matter how many different recycling containers you separate your garbage into, it all goes onto the same pile at the dump. Besides, recycling is supposed to make you feel better, that you are doing your part, making a difference. Very Orwellian I know but then I don't believe anything I read in the papers anymore either so there you go.

I once spent an hour walking about town with a bag full of batteries in my hand looking for a battery-recycling bin. In the rain. I´ve got a plastic carrier bag in my hand and the battery acid is like foaming out the sides ... It's so much easier to throw it into the bin. It's even a little exciting to throw all the garbage into one box – like stealing those miniature glasses of jam from hotel buffets. No rinsing out the glass or the plastic, no peeling off the tinfoil cover from the yoghurt container, no sorting out the cereal box into plastic and paper; just all into the bin. Plonk.

7

Since their first meeting, Jessie and Kate have seen each other regularly – at the market, getting a morning coffee at Starbucks, and lining up for falafel to go from Don's. Don has a truck that serves wraps, kebab, and other Turkish delights.

Twice Kate even came into Marlies for dinner. Jessie finds these meetings somewhat odd. Jessie had never seen Kate before that first meeting in her office with the petit fours and the polite conversation. Either Jessie had never noticed Kate, or she was going out of her way to be more noticeable. Kate was always charming, but as Jessie feels a desire for Kate subtly building, so does a sense of wariness.

8

I hate Sundays. Sunday the sorority crowd come in with their parents and boyfriends. This used to happen only to the Strand or the Courtyard hotels, but more and more the buffet crowd has slimmed down and begun to favour a la carte – throw in our garden and regional wine card, and within a very short time we became pretty popular for brunch. I don’t mind the extra business; it can be just a bit too *tediou*s at times. Judith bowed out of doing brunch right at the beginning as it meant getting in at nine instead of eleven in the morning. Barb and I have always had no problem getting up at four. We had no time for the sorority girls and frat boys while at university and we have found little since then to change our minds on the species. The girls know each other of course and if you aren't in a rival house you will probably get a kiss blown across the restaurant or a big goofy smile from a boyfriend. However, if you happen to be a Beta, and a Gamma were sitting right in your lap, they wouldn´t pass you the salt without knocking some into your eyes first. The parents are the most terrifying. Often when I’m circulating in the front of house, I’ll catch sight of a father with his platinum Amex tipping his waiter twenty or thirty dollars simply for calling him *Sir* and putting up with his amusing habit of calling them *Son*. Hey, if I were their son, I wouldn't be serving them - I’d be sitting down there between Bitsy and Christi wondering when the conversation is getting around to my allowance. Jeremy, one of our regular brunch waiters once confided to me, “You see more cheques flying across the tables on a Sunday than Money Mart sees in a month.”

9

Terminal illness is a big hassle and mostly viewed by those of us not affected as something you should be able to walk off if you just got off your butt, washed your hair and did a few laps around the block. 'Get over it!' you want to scream. It's not something we can experience firsthand and then later give any advice on. And it's scary as hell. You immediately must grow up and become an adult when one of your parents faces something like this and then you know you're next in line. Like playing a waiting game with the Bogeyman. I'm hoping to coax my mother out of her illness through positive reinforcement and threats. The only thing I can't do myself is accept and live with the inevitable. This strength isn't something I possess enough of for myself let alone, having enough left over to dole out to others. So, I come across brusque. It's a defense mechanism, and you shouldn't hate me for it.

10

Kate slips off her high heels, unbuttons her blouse and drops it on the floor, unzips her skirt and lets that drop to her feet. She steps out of the pool of clothing, and I undo my own, as she moves towards me in the light cast from the streetlamps outside. She comes to me, and gently pulls me backwards towards the wall. I take her in my arms, [redacted] another. My hands [redacted]. We drop onto the leather ottoman against the wall and [redacted]. My face against her [redacted] my own.

11

Her skin is soft, and her hands and feet cool against mine as we move, the sheets sliding beneath us in a sea of cotton and silk. When I look into her eyes there is incredible volume, but there is no understanding on my part, there is only a deafening silence. When I look into her eyes it's like watching a foreign film without subtitles; words I do not comprehend like a melody accompanying the performance – my desire is tempered by fear - of wanting her and the fear that desire brings… [redacted] and [redacted] shoulders. [redacted] instead and [redacted] all the sadness and all the happiness, all the desire of many months. Then her [redacted] catch the [redacted] Holding each other among the sheets when we have both stilled, I realise I haven't [redacted]. I hold Marta tighter against me.

12

Rodd's chatting up the coffee shop staff as I enter. I clap him on the butt which breaks his stride with the cute brunette barista. "How's it going Stud?" Rodd bows to the girl and I place my order.
"Jess – I heard about your place. Wicked. Know who it was?"
"That was a month ago. Why the sudden interest from everyone?" I take my coffee and bun and smile at the girl in thanks. I motion Rodd over to a table by the window. "We've got an idea it was one of our waiters." I sit down and sip from my coffee – double cappuccino – a bit strong but tasty.
Rodd nods. "Uppity staff. Most white-collar crime is committed by one's own staff."
I laugh. "Well, yeah, it would be … I wouldn't exactly lump tossing a brick through my front window in with stealing office supplies, but I get your point."

As we talk, a trio of redheads walk past the window – not an everyday occurrence. I have a thing for redheads, and for, shall we say, larger women. No, really. I've only ever been on one date with a redhead and she was a complete Nutter, and I've dated a few large women – though I've admired many more from afar. You might think my tastes rather odd, but odder still is that I never really get to indulge them; it's like the things I really like I distance myself from. You know the temptation you get to touch bubbles that form in sugar when it's boiling? You don't get this temptation? Oh. Well, Alex thought this some sort of deranged martyrdom I have but I think if you get what you want you won't want it anymore. Sort of keeps you interested.

I explain this to Rodd. He nods sagely, hoovering the bottom of his latte glass with a straw and signaling for another.

"Jess, I have this theory. I think we have it all wrong about our tastes in the opposite sex. At least in my experience, the way my girlfriends tell it you'd think that men have this ideal in their mind of the sort of woman they want and only target women fitting this ideal, tossing aside all others."
I nod. "I can relate to that."
Rodd nods again, "Mmm, but I can't think of anyone I've known who only dated a certain type of woman. It doesn't work like that. You can't help who you fall in love with; you don't plan to end up with a blonde or a brunette or redhead and then seek the perfect one out. You're sitting on the bus or walking across the street and there they are! Bang! It just happens. It's not like ordering them out of a catalogue you know. Maybe it's a genetic code or a biological factor, like tall people date other tall people and rich people date other rich people. Maybe you only go out with people with boring shoulder length brown hair because everyone in your family had boring shoulder length brown hair and you've always gone out with other people with boring shoulder length brown hair and you wouldn't know what to do with someone who suddenly appeared with short blonde hair – it would be like meeting someone from another planet. See?"
"Mmhm. I'm following you." I nod as I gorge myself on the still warm cinnamon bun dripping with butter.
"Personally, every woman I've ever gone out with has had blonde hair and has been a head shorter than I, and a bit on the chunky side. But the thing is, the thing

women have all wrong about men, is that if this theory of theirs was correct, if men really did target a specific type of woman then we would only be going out with her for her looks. And we don't do that. Not real men anyway. We are, many men that is, together with women who we are comfortable with. Who we like being with? For being who they are. Maybe they're a bit dumpy or their legs aren't perfect or their breasts are a funny shape or their taste in clothes is horrendous or they have babies far too easily or they can't cook, but all in all we stick with them because we, the men, aren't all that shit hot ourselves. I think that's pretty good."

Rodd sits back and admires the two empty latte glasses in front of him, attaching the straws to create a bridge between the two glasses.

"You should publish this theory of yours. I think it's great."

Rodd raises his left eyebrow and smiles. "Yeh. I think we men should get a bit of a pat on the shoulder. It's like potato chips. You think you can eat them every night, if given the chance, but after eating a few bags you get sick of them and are happy to go back to your regular diet of Cheezies. Of course, later the potato chips look tempting all over again but that isn't the point… See, even if we did get this goddess, we had always imagined we wanted we would be dead bored in a week and pack her in for the girl next door anyway."

"Great theory."

I leave Rodd after making him swear to come by with his girlfriend for dinner and then head off to the restaurant.

13

Kate closes the door to the room after I have entered, removes a stack of clothes from the daybed, and places them on a dresser of dark oak. Free of our clothes, my lips trembling against hers, our caresses lengthen, then become more demanding, barely contained within our frantic motion. I [redacted].

Pushing against each other, biting, [redacted] in the darkness of that room. The sheet that has found itself around us tightening, [redacted].

With the passage of our hands, [redacted] me.

The [redacted]. Then the weight of her drops onto me and I take her into my arms.

14

We gave everyone three days holidays and shut Monday, Tuesday and Wednesday – but they really did an exemplary job over the four days I was gone and I'm still trying to refrain from showing them how proud I am of their work. Kate, generous as always, of course sent two club caterings our way as soon as I left. These went off without a hitch thanks to Judith, but there was something obviously mean spirited in their timing. I turned the kitchen over to Frank and Chris in a flash of benevolent brilliance. Of course, I made it very clear that I wouldn't be checking up on them and that they shouldn't call either myself or Barb. It was the baptism by fire of their apprenticeship. This put the fear of God into them while at the same time showing how much I trusted them – a good combination if you're trying to motivate the young and impressionable. This technique worked with me when I was an apprentice as well.

One summer the dining room manager asked Barb and I to organise the place and get it ready for a dinner banquet – even during a chef's apprenticeship you have to do your time as waiter, dishwasher, stores – as well as all the kitchen posts – you're not going to be a very good chef if you have no idea what the waiters are going through – and vice versa. Well, we spent hours getting the place up to speed and then reported back that the job was done, and he could inspect it. He coolly stated that if we said it was perfect then he would take our word for it. This amazed us so completely that we went back and spent another two hours double checking every plate and piece of cutlery for the slightest smudge so as not to let him down.

15

Dark Chocolate Truffles with Bacon (12 pieces)

sprig of fresh rosemary
150 grams dark couverture
100 grams sugar
100 ml white wine
250 ml whipping cream
50 grams rendered bacon fat (this replaces butter and adds a lovely flavour)
1 tablespoon balsamic cream

bring sugar, sprig of rosemary and wine to light boil.
add room temperature cream and return to light boil.
add grated chocolate, and reduce slightly.
remove from heat, remove rosemary, stir in balsamic vinegar and bacon fat.
let cool, and spoon into balls.
toss in cocoa, sprinkle with gold leaf, or eat them naked.

16

If you like eggplant, then you really need to go to Portugal. Or at the very least Italy. Try Portugal first. The tomatoe salads in most any of the coastal restaurants are always amazing in the summer. They are almost exclusively a sort of greenish red beefsteak, very large and thickly cut with onions and balsamic vinegar and then there is a lot of garlic. The fish you can get cheaper anywhere but in Portugal on the other hand, which is funny because they're scooping them out of the ocean at the edge of your table and whacking them over the heads before your eyes but there you go right? Supply and demand. Be careful of the plates of prawns and other delicacies they place on the table while you are ordering because these are not free. Imagine you're in Paris and you eat the dinner roll and then see a few bucks at the end of your bill. Right well just pump that up a notch and you have Portugal. If you're not sure don't eat it okay? So, you've been warned. When I was there last, the fish was really good, and I had the sun setting behind the guy working the grill and there were kids tootling by on their mopeds which added extra charm. If you aren't sure what to order, then get the King Fish with the huge eyes. Start with some prawns sautéed in garlic and don't forget the tomatoe salad – which you might have because now you're thinking about this huge fish, am I right? Wine? Forget about it! You know what you heard about the scary Algarve wines fondly known to the locals as 'Dog Throttler'? Not true. No matter how hard I tried I only found wine from the north of Portugal on offer and they were all excellent. The whites especially from around Porto where light and tasty.

17

Marta, from what I remember, is out with the girls tonight. I'm left to weep for myself. Which is pretty easy. I mean, you just need focus. And, I can clean to distract myself. I get rid of all the stuff that tend to pile up over time; papers, empty coffee cups, those plastic container things from contact lens solution and absolutely anything that's on the computer desk. I solved some of the computer desk space problem by getting one of those arms that floats the monitor two feet off the desk which I think is real cool and I spend the night imagining I´m trading currencies at Smith Barney. 'Who´s got ten million September Francs?!' I yell into the night. The whole idea of sorrow it lends itself to being freed from being an adult. Allowing a more adolescent stupor. I should not bother wearing anything but an old t shirt and sweatpants, sit in front of the TV while dirty laundry overflows from the hamper, takeaway food containers pile up in the kitchen, the dog takes to sitting on the leather couch, and drink beer. Or scotch. And I don't have a dog.

18

I was in Lourdes once. Accidentally. I was on a train, and it stopped in Lourdes. I noticed the name on the station, and I thought, oh, I wonder if this is the *real* Lourdes. For a Catholic, it never really seemed like a real place – it was never really within reach. So, I was sitting in this train stopped in Lourdes. And, I got out. Oh Lord … what a carnival. I wanted to leave with a holy medal and a postcard but there was something, possibly … decidedly touristy about the town that made it impossible to leave without a miniature statue of Our Lady Perhaps as I had one with a magnet on her feet that stuck to the metal dashboard of my first car, a 1963 Ford Valiant. They don't make cars with metal dashboards anymore, and I know why, because they don't make Mary statues with magnets on their feet anymore either. I thought, as this was the time of my immersion into the Faith, that this must be the reason, the need for this statue. This was when I was truly religious, this point in my life when I had religion. Well, I wasn't crawling on my knees down the church aisle, nor was I filling up empty cola bottles with water from the grotto, I wasn't being photographed in front of the shrine of our Lady, nor was I carrying a big assed candle that required a second person on the other end … I wasn't doing any of those things. didn't even feel comfortable taking any pictures. It just seemed too wrong. Even when I picked up a figure of Bernadette carved in wood, and only after I placed it on the counter and discovered it cost 50 euro for this tiny item, even then, I felt it would be irreverent to put it back in favour of a cheaper one. So, I splashed some water on my mouth from the grotto – people were drinking it! Filling up empty coke bottles for the ride home – I mean … do they have no self-respect? - I crossed myself, lit an inconspicuous candle and asked our Lady to make everyone feel better. And I cried a little bit too, nothing ostentatious about it, no wailing. But I bought a figure of Mary anyway.

What's the most horrible sacrilege to the image of our Lady in Lourdes? Is it the Mary soap on a rope? The glow in the dark Mary statue ringed with sparkly lights? The plastic bottle shaped in the form of our Lady with a screw top cap on her head. Or is it the equally practical pen, in which Mary ascends or descends into the grotto as you move the pen up and down? I think it's none of these things. I think, really and I could be wrong, the number one curio that no pilgrim should go home without must be the image of our Lady and St Bernadette in the grotto plastic place mats. These will come in handy for placing over the TV table on which you slop down your Swanson microwave hungry man dinner while watching Wheel of Fortune. Sacramentals. Not just for worship anymore.

19

Katrin Lawson, Food & Wine …

I made a new friend over breakfast on my last morning in Nice and I'm wondering if they're reading today - and whether they found a solution to their problem. I'd also like to recommend their restaurant, Marlies – but I forgot to ask where it was. If the food there is as interesting as the chef owner, Jessie Watkins, then it should be a treat. Marlies isn't in Europe, that much I know – if that narrows it down and anyone comes across Marlies in their travels, please let me know where it is. I'd love to eat there one day and see what became of my breakfast companion.

It has been too long, and probably never was, that I took a vacation and wrote nothing at all. Actually writing nothing for two weeks! My instagram account does not count. Fingers must be kept lubricated other than by covering squirming children with sunscreen or, accidentally, with bbq sauce. So after two years and with no children to entertain this trip, I went to the south of France revisited some of my past lovers – wine, sun, palm trees – made a new lover – buttery olives – and felt utterly relaxed and happy to be be away but in familiar waters. Jet lag means I am still awake and I hear through the stillness of my house the movement of children also awake in the middle of the night. I went for groceries this evening – after a few hours of stolen sleep as the washing machine ran and the kitchen became an obstacle course due to my half empty suitcase, open and still there. I walked through the store dying to speak French again … I gave into buying olives that were a poor substitute for those I found in Nice.

When I returned to my kitchen, I held a heavy bottle of golden chardonnay, covered in condensation, in my hand. I poured a glass and thought of the hot sunshine of a very few days previous, of old friends and new, of laughing and enjoying so many flavours of a December summer – of the tang of new wines on my tongue, of the smell of the asparagus and chocolate I had in Cannes, the rich peppery steaks and grilled peppers I enjoyed in Monaco, and the sea salt tinge of my morning coffees in Nice - all lingering in the back of my mouth.

This all happened a few days ago - but it feels like I might have imagined the entire thing.

Printed in Poland
by Amazon Fulfillment
Poland Sp. z o.o., Wrocław

58017962R00226